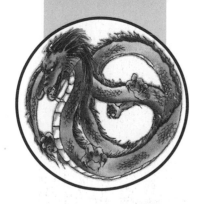

"One of the best manga ever, it can be enjoyed by female and male readers alike."

—Protoculture Addicts

"Watase has a gift for involving characterization. Though she sometimes uses Miaka for laughs, she also lets us see her heroine's compassion and courage. The Emperor Hotohori is not quite as noble as he seems, nor is the wily Tamahome as self-centered as he would have others believe him to be. Even treacherous empress-candidate Nuriko has many levels. Watase's storytelling is an engaging one. She paces her story well and knows when to pump up the energy."

—Tony Isabella

"There are two points in Fushigi Yugi's favor. The first is Watase herself, who has written margin notes for the compilation. Unlike many creators who rabbit on about trivia, she wants to talk about her craft, and has interesting points to make about research and the creative points to make about research and the creative process. The second is that the strip succeeds in being quite charming; in spite of its derivative storyline—at one point a character admits the similarities to an RPG! But any comic that leaves me wanting to know what happens next definitely delivers value for money."

—Manga Max

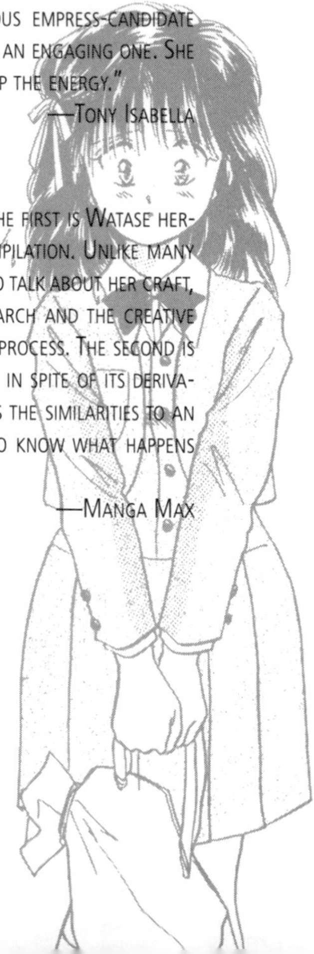

ANIMERICA EXTRA GRAPHIC NOVEL

fushigi yûgi™

The Mysterious Play
VOL. 3: DISCIPLE

This volume contains the FUSHIGI YÛGI installments from ANIMERICA EXTRA Vol. 2, No. 11 through Vol. 3, No. 4 in their entirety.

STORY & ART BY YÛ WATASE

English Adaptation/Yuji Oniki
Touch-Up Art & Lettering/Bill Spicer
Cover Design/Hidemi Sahara
Layout & Graphics/Carolina Ugalde
Editor/William Flanagan
Managing Editor/Annette Roman

Editor-in-Chief/Hyoe Narita
Publisher/Seiji Horibuchi
V.P. of Sales & Marketing/Rick Bauer

Printed in Canada

Published by Viz Communications, Inc.
P.O. Box 77010, San Francisco, CA 94107

10 9 8 7 6
First printing, August 2000
Fourth printing, January 2002
Fifth printing, March 2002
Sixth printing, June 2002

ANIMERICA EXTRA GRAPHIC NOVEL

fushigi yûgi™

The Mysterious Play
VOL. 3: DISCIPLE

Story & Art By
YÛ WATASE

CONTENTS

STORY THUS FAR

Chipper junior high-school girl Miaka is trying to study as hard as she can to get into Jonan High School like her mother wants her to. During a study session in the City Central Library, Miaka and her best friend Yui are physically drawn into the world of a strange book—*The Universe of the Four Gods*. The dashing-but-greedy Tamahome rescues them both before they are returned to the real world.

After an argument with her Mother, Miaka returns alone to the world of the book, and is offered the role of the lead character, the Priestess of Suzaku. After a few months of adventures, Miaka returns to her modern world again aided by Yui, but this time it is Yui who has disappeared! During her short time back home, Miaka realizes how much she has come to love Tamahome.

Returning a third time to ancient China, this time to find Yui, Miaka is told that in order to avert a war between Hong-Nan and its neighboring country of Qu-Dong, she must gather all seven celestial warriors of Suzaku. She knows about the handsome Tamahome, regal Hotohori, and super-strong, crossdressing Nuriko, but four of her warriors still remain undiscovered. Miaka sets out with Nuriko to find Tamahome again, but as soon as she is reunited with him, Miaka is abducted by a mysterious man in the shadows!!

THE UNIVERSE OF THE FOUR GODS is based on ancient China, but Japanese pronunciation of Chinese names differs slightly from their Chinese equivalents. Here is a short glossary of the Japanese pronunciation of the Chinese names in this graphic novel:

CHINESE	JAPANESE	PERSON OR PLACE	MEANING
Hong-Nan	Konan	Southern Kingdom	Crimson South
Qu-Dong	Kutô	Eastern Kingdom	Gathered East
Zhong-Rong	Chûei	Second son	Loyalty & Honor
Chun-Jing	Shunkei	Third son	Spring & Respect
Yu-Lun	Gyokuran	Eldest daughter	Jewel & Orchid
Jie-Lian	Yuiren	Youngest daughter	Connection & Lotus
Tai Yi-Jun	Tai Itsukun	An oracle	Preeminent Person
Daichi-San	Daikyokuzan	A mountain	Greatest Mountain
Lai Lai	Nyan Nyan	A servant	Nanny

No da: An emphatic. A verbal exclamation point placed at the end of a sentence or phrase.

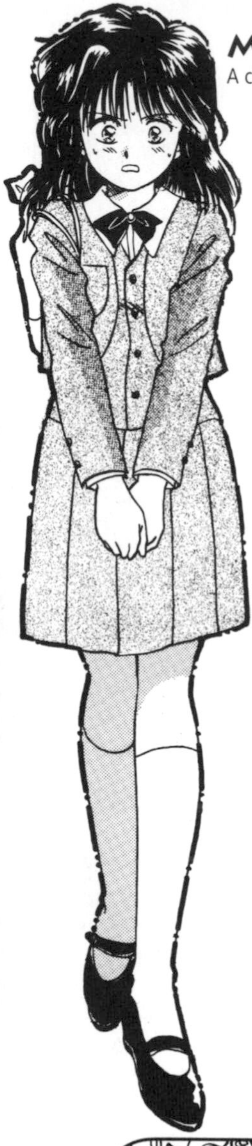

MIAKA
A chipper junior-high-school glutton.

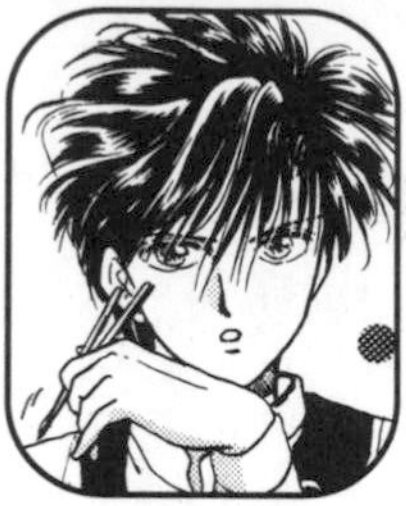

TAMAHOME
A dashing miser and a Celestial Warrior of Suzaku.

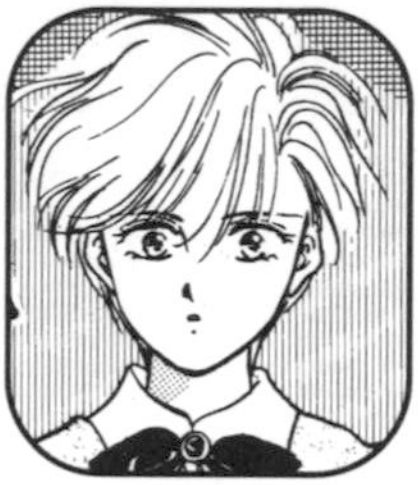

YUI
Miaka's intelligent best friend.

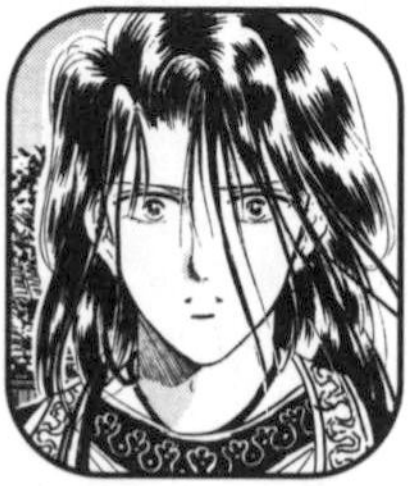

HOTOHORI
The beautiful emperor of Hong-Nan, and a Celestial Warrior of Suzaku.

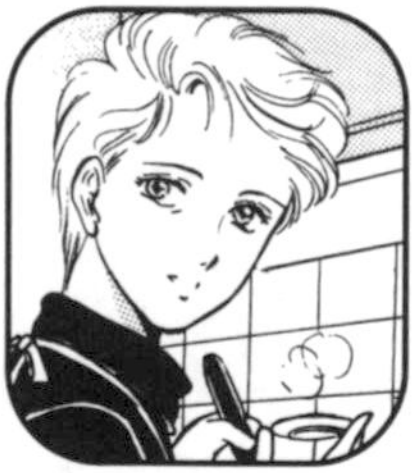

MIAKA'S MOTHER
A divorced single mother.

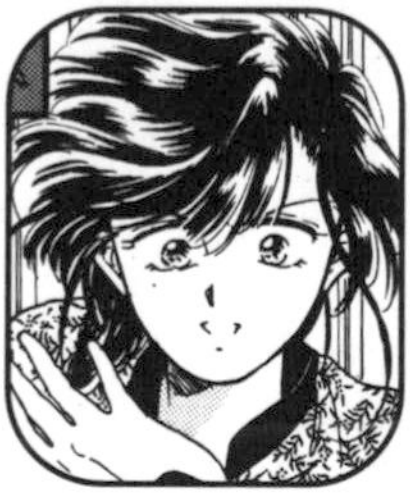

NURIKO
An amazingly strong prospective bride for Hotohori, and a Celestial Warrior of Suzaku.

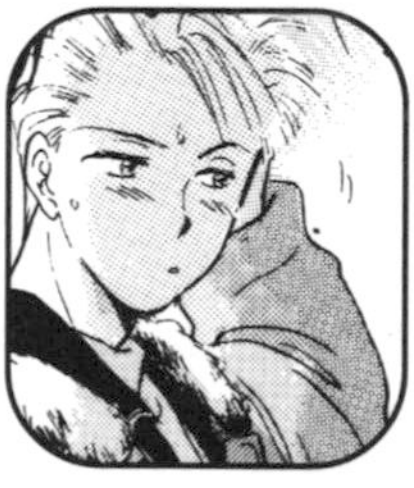

KEISUKE
Miaka's kind, college-student brother.

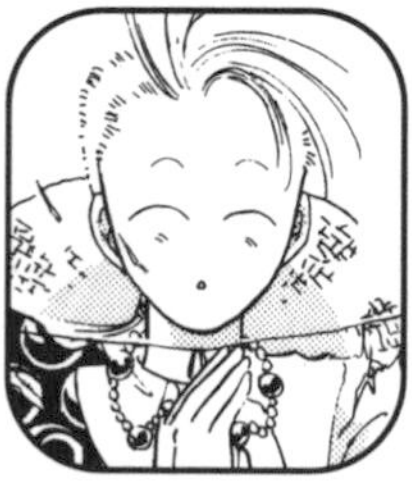

CHICHIRI
A mysterious monk, seemingly with magical powers.

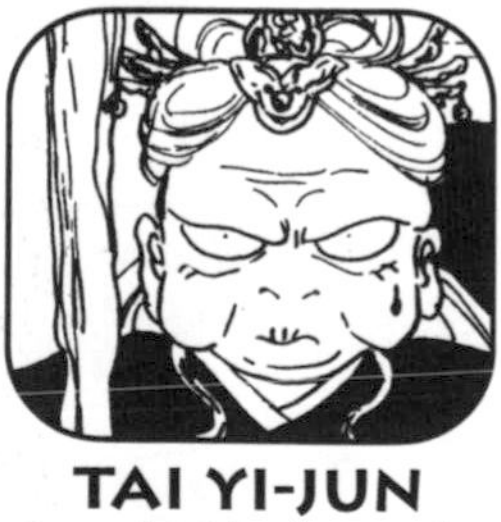

TAI YI-JUN
An aged oracle who gave the scroll *The Universe of the Four Gods* to Hotohori's ancestors.

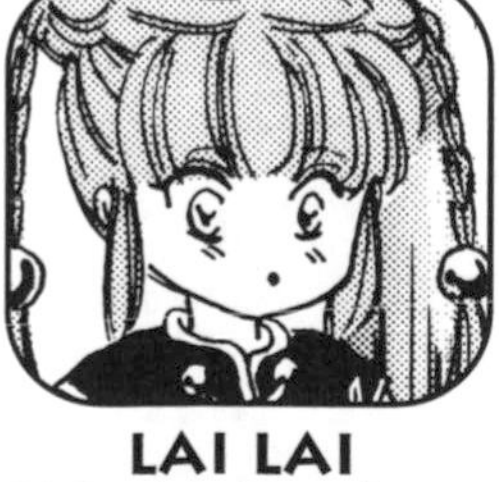

LAI LAI
Tai Yi-Jun's assistant who can seemingly multiply herself.

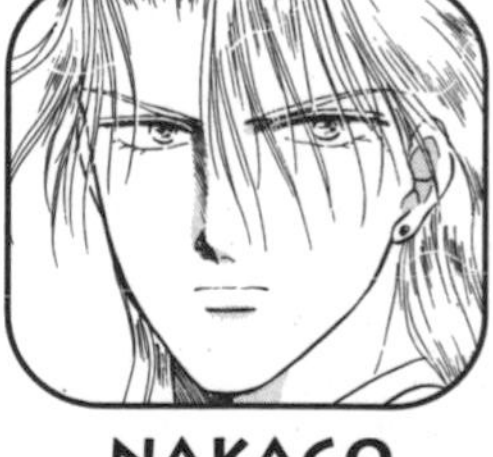

NAKAGO
A handsome Celestial Warrior of Seiryu.

CHAPTER THIRTEEN
THE INVISIBLE ENEMY

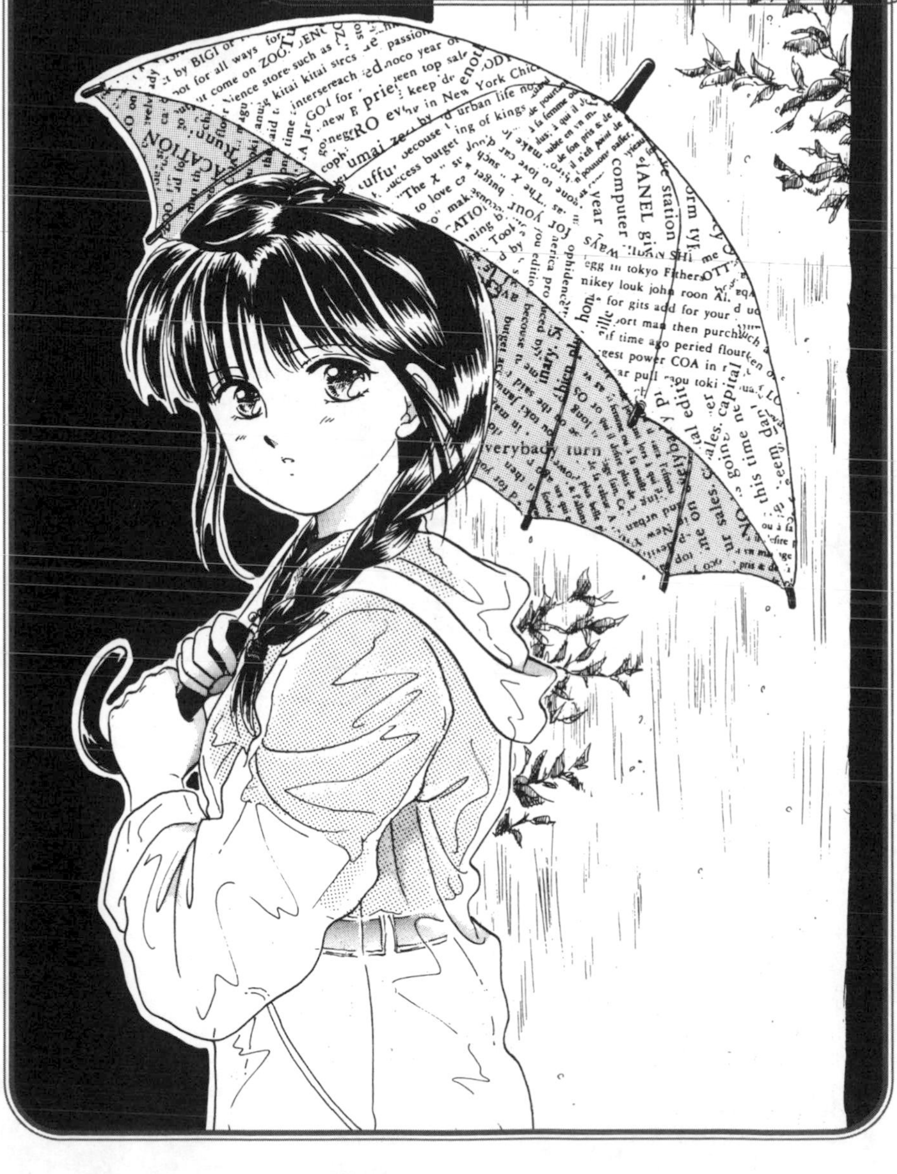

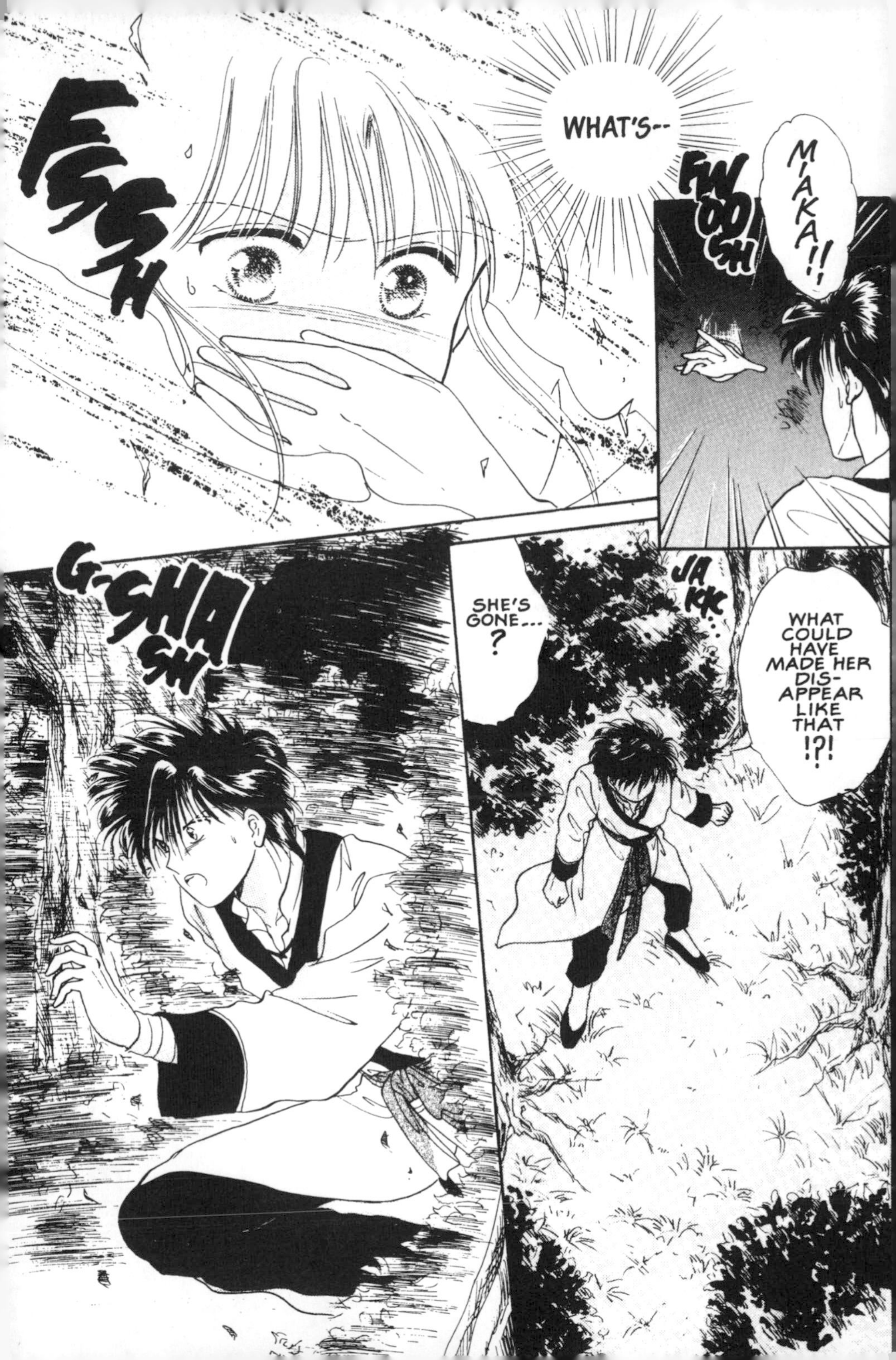
FSSSH
WHAT'S--
FWOOSH
MIAKA!!
G-SHASH
SHE'S GONE...?
JAKK...
WHAT COULD HAVE MADE HER DIS-APPEAR LIKE THAT!?!

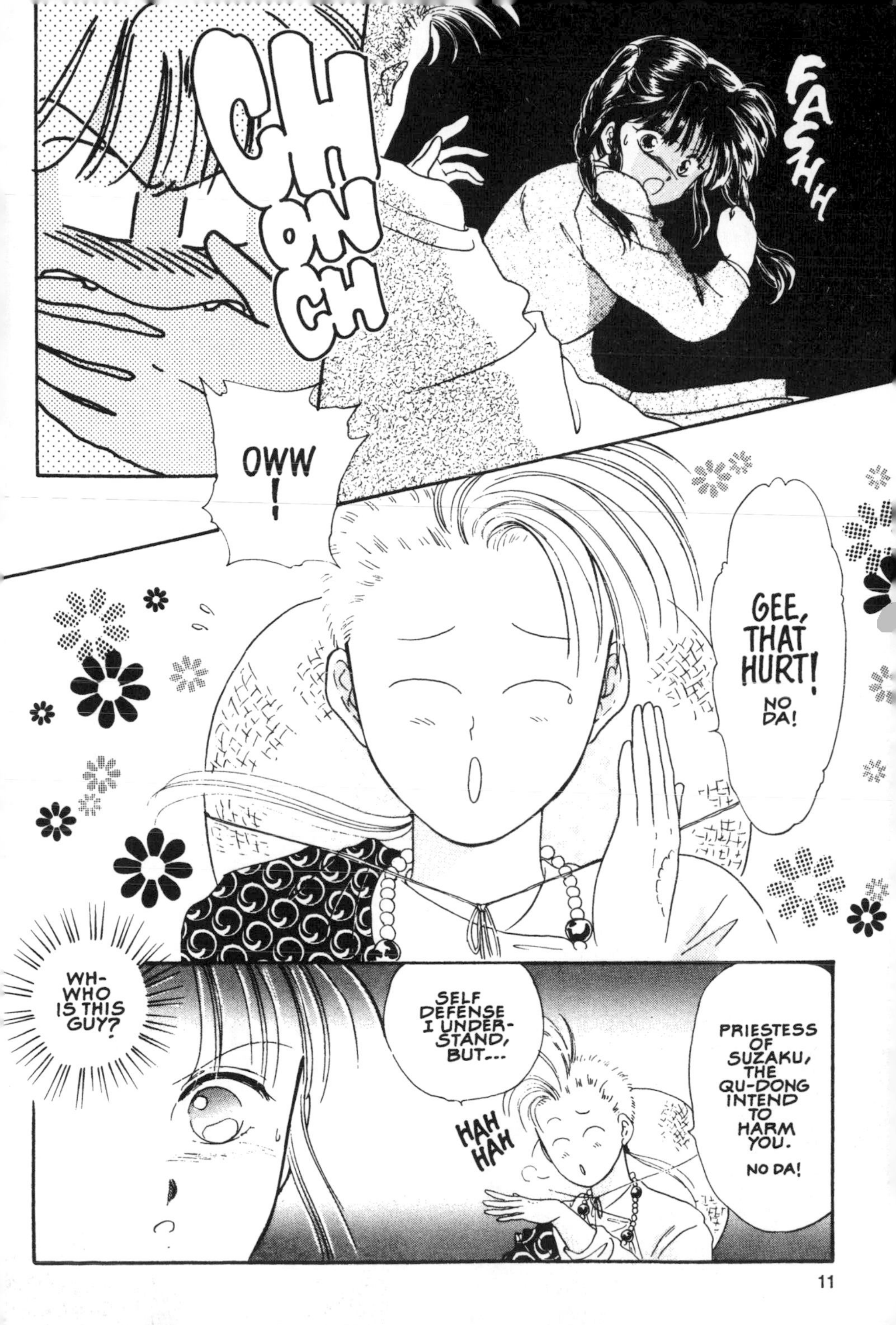

CHONCH
FASHH
OWW!
GEE, THAT HURT! NO DA!
WH-WHO IS THIS GUY?
SELF DEFENSE I UNDERSTAND, BUT...
HAH HAH
PRIESTESS OF SUZAKU, THE QU-DONG INTEND TO HARM YOU. NO DA!

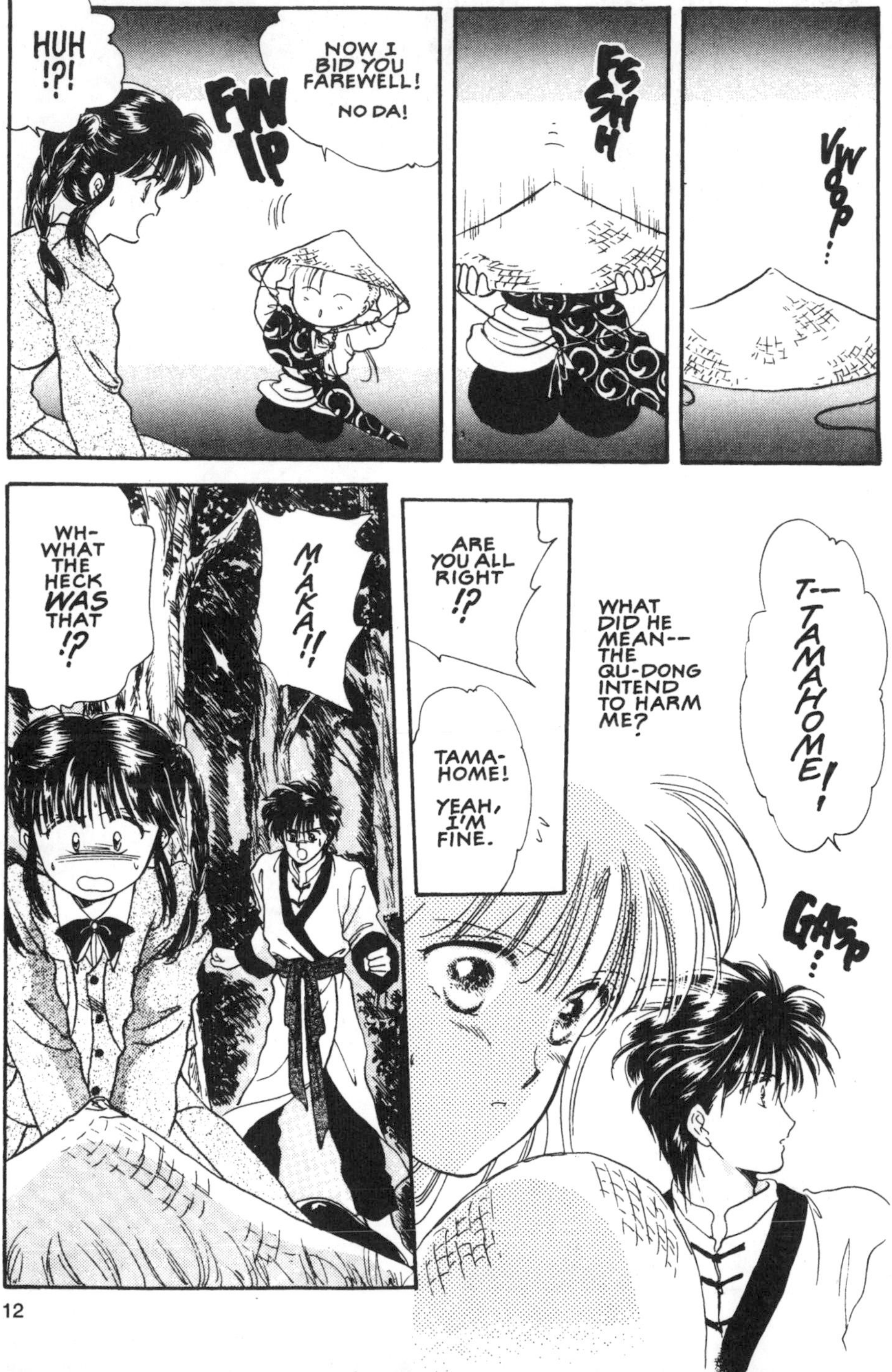
HUH !?!
NOW I BID YOU FAREWELL! NO DA!
FWIP
FSSHH
VWOOP...
WH-WHAT THE HECK WAS THAT !?
MIAKA!!
ARE YOU ALL RIGHT !?
TAMA-HOME! YEAH, I'M FINE.
WHAT DID HE MEAN-- THE QU-DONG INTEND TO HARM ME?
T-- TAMAHOME!
GASP...

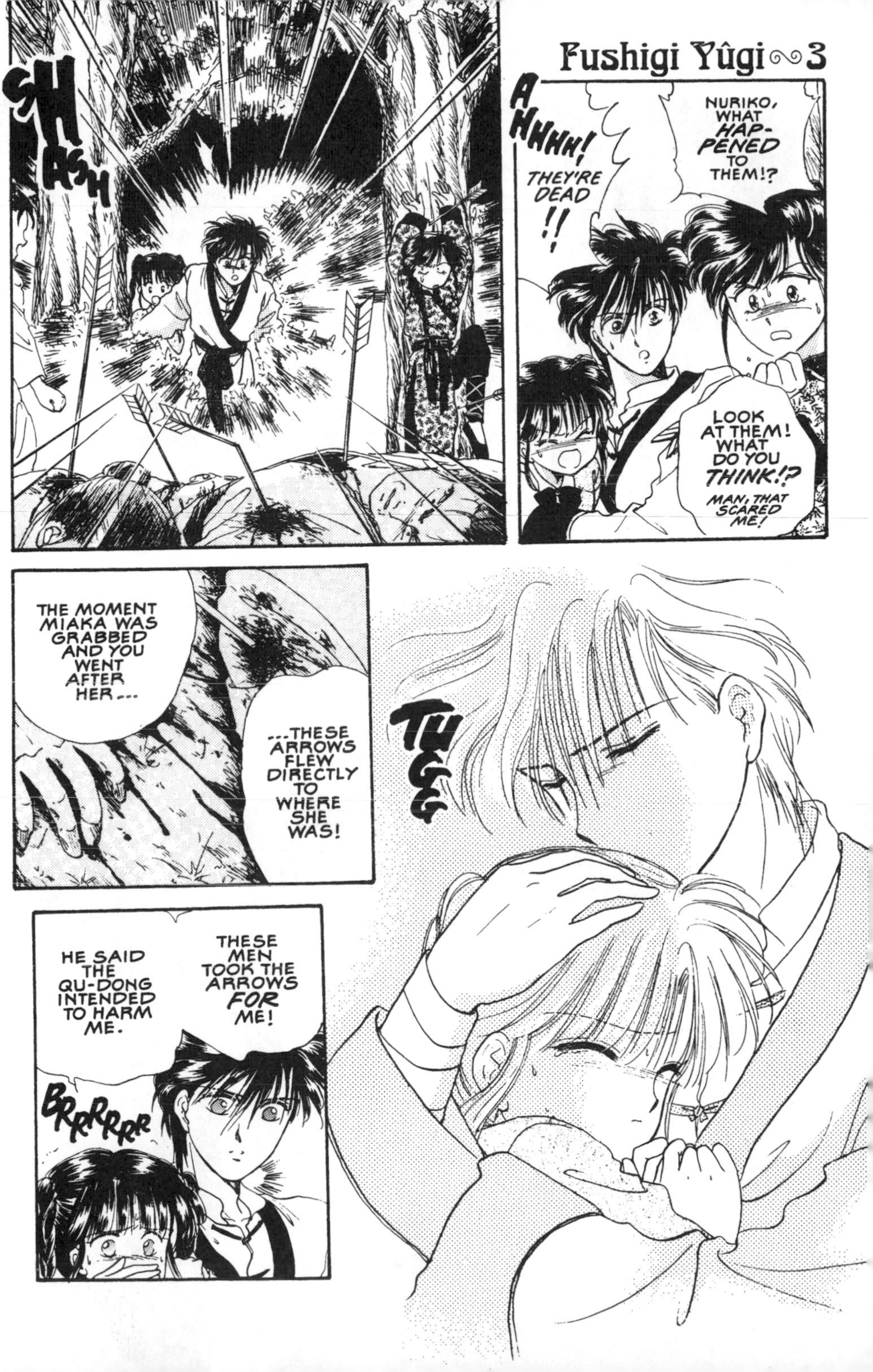
SHHASH
AHHHHH!
THEY'RE DEAD!!
NURIKO, WHAT HAPPENED TO THEM!?
LOOK AT THEM! WHAT DO YOU THINK!?
MAN, THAT SCARED ME!
THE MOMENT MIAKA WAS GRABBED AND YOU WENT AFTER HER...
...THESE ARROWS FLEW DIRECTLY TO WHERE SHE WAS!
HE SAID THE QU-DONG INTENDED TO HARM ME.
THESE MEN TOOK THE ARROWS FOR ME!
BRRRRRR
TUGG

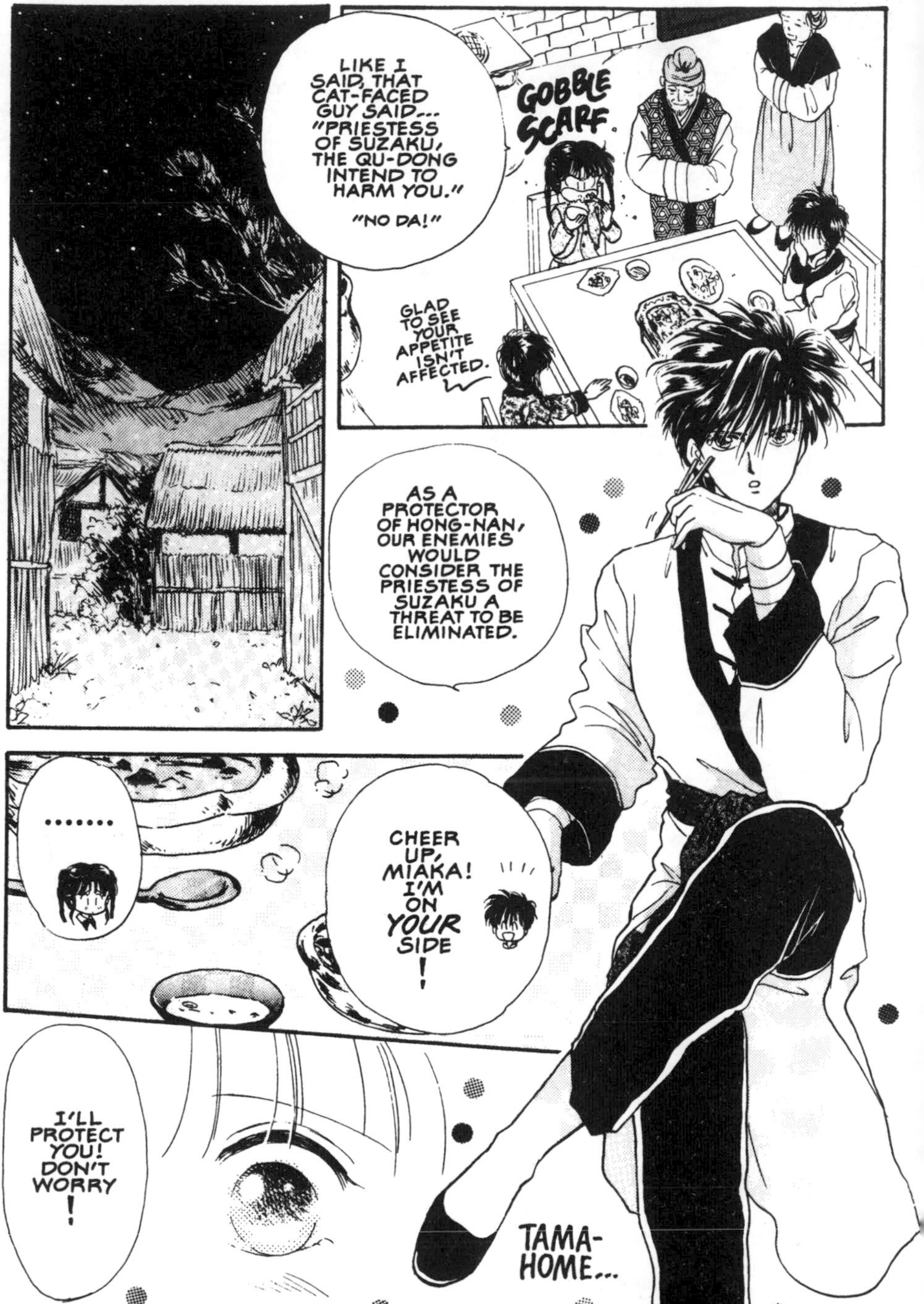
LIKE I SAID, THAT CAT-FACED GUY SAID... "PRIESTESS OF SUZAKU, THE QU-DONG INTEND TO HARM YOU."
"NO DA!"
GOBBLE SCARF
GLAD TO SEE YOUR APPETITE ISN'T AFFECTED.
AS A PROTECTOR OF HONG-NAN, OUR ENEMIES WOULD CONSIDER THE PRIESTESS OF SUZAKU A THREAT TO BE ELIMINATED.
....
CHEER UP, MIAKA! I'M ON YOUR SIDE!
I'LL PROTECT YOU! DON'T WORRY!
TAMA-HOME...

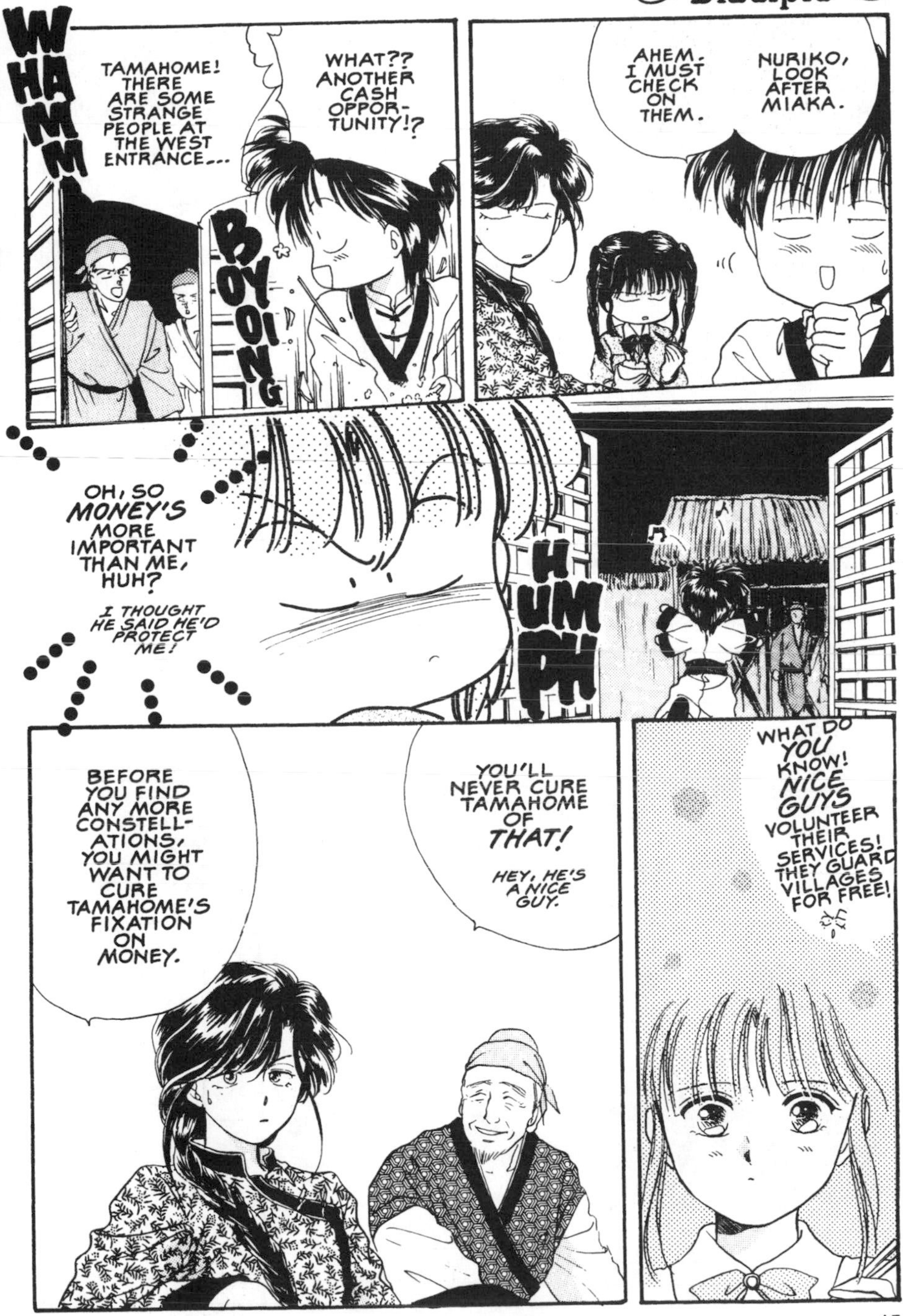
WHAMM
TAMAHOME! THERE ARE SOME STRANGE PEOPLE AT THE WEST ENTRANCE...
WHAT?? ANOTHER CASH OPPOR-TUNITY!?
BOYOING
AHEM. I MUST CHECK ON THEM.
NURIKO, LOOK AFTER MIAKA.
OH, SO MONEY'S MORE IMPORTANT THAN ME, HUH?
I THOUGHT HE SAID HE'D PROTECT ME!
HUMPH
BEFORE YOU FIND ANY MORE CONSTELL-ATIONS, YOU MIGHT WANT TO CURE TAMAHOME'S FIXATION ON MONEY.
YOU'LL NEVER CURE TAMAHOME OF THAT!
HEY, HE'S A NICE GUY.
WHAT DO YOU KNOW! NICE GUYS VOLUNTEER THEIR SERVICES! THEY GUARD VILLAGES FOR FREE!

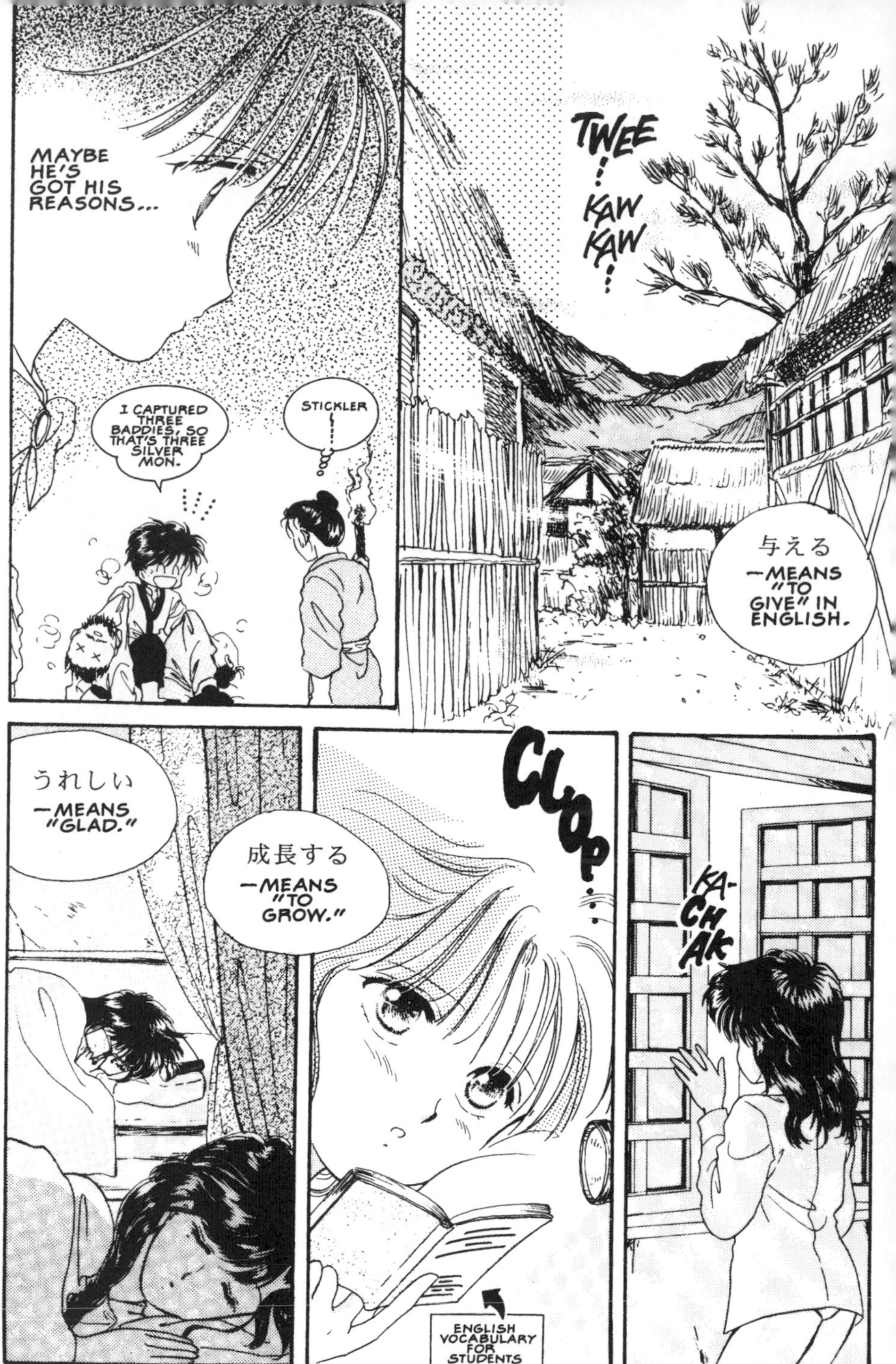
MAYBE HE'S GOT HIS REASONS...
I CAPTURED THREE BADDIES, SO THAT'S THREE SILVER MON.
STICKLER
TWEE! KAW KAW!
与える —MEANS "TO GIVE" IN ENGLISH.
うれしい —MEANS "GLAD."
成長する —MEANS "TO GROW."
CLOP...
ENGLISH VOCABULARY FOR STUDENTS
KA-CHAK

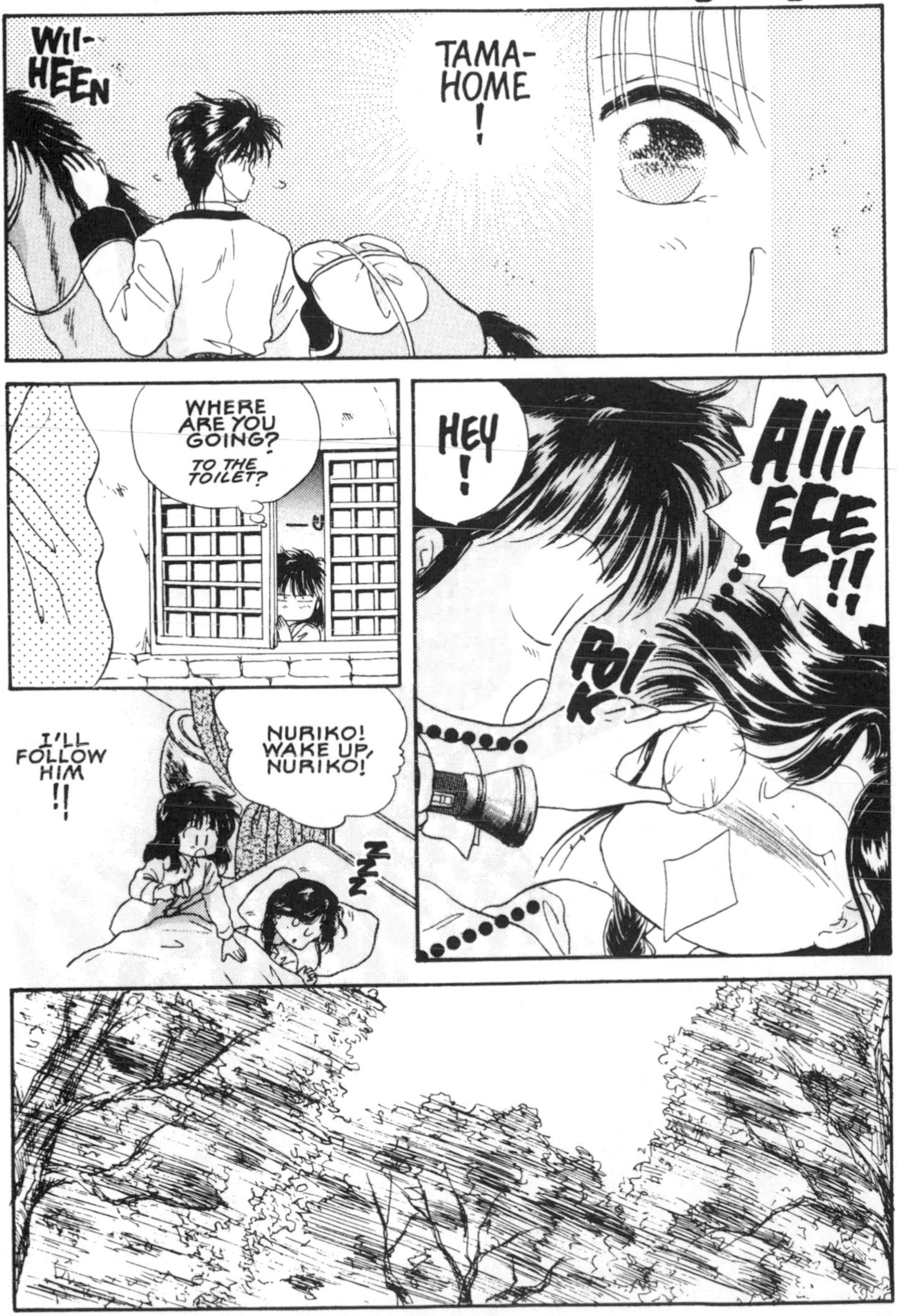
WII-
HEEN
TAMA-
HOME
!
WHERE ARE YOU GOING?
TO THE TOILET?
I'LL FOLLOW HIM !!
NURIKO! WAKE UP, NURIKO!
HEY
!
AIIIEEE!!
POIK

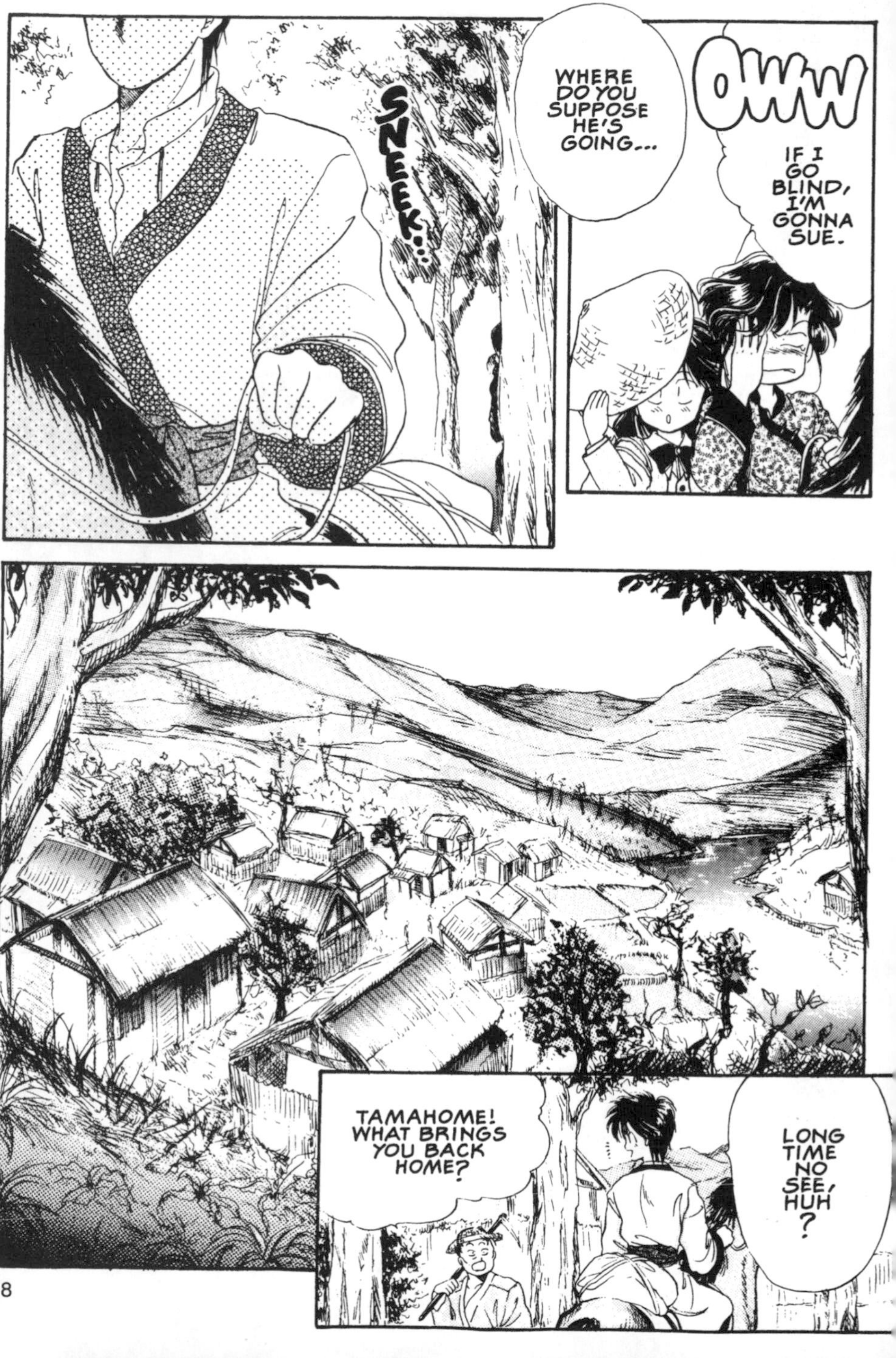
SNEEK...
WHERE DO YOU SUPPOSE HE'S GOING...
OWW
IF I GO BLIND, I'M GONNA SUE.
TAMAHOME! WHAT BRINGS YOU BACK HOME?
LONG TIME NO SEE, HUH?

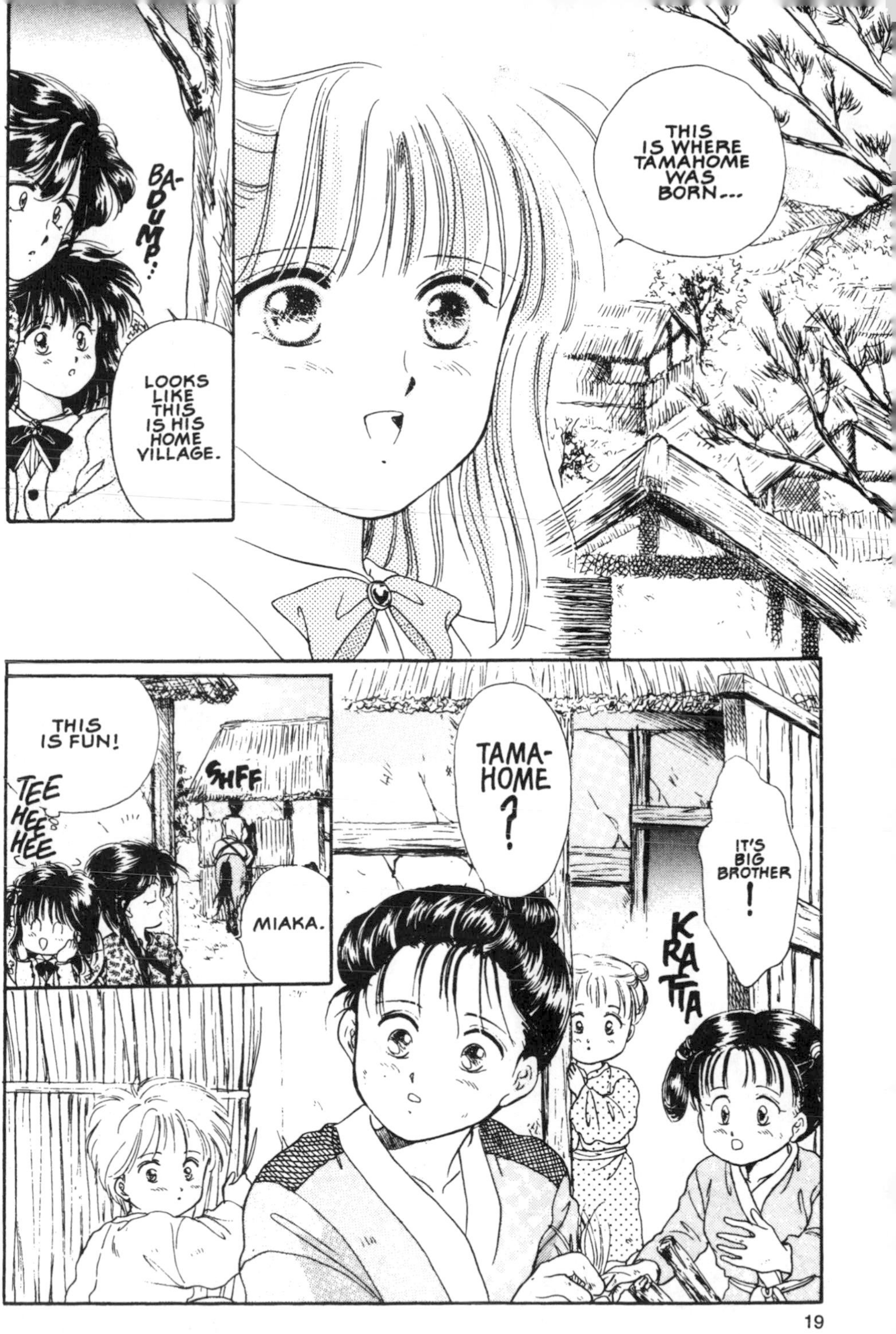
BA-DUMP...
LOOKS LIKE THIS IS HIS HOME VILLAGE.
THIS IS WHERE TAMAHOME WAS BORN...
THIS IS FUN!
TEE HEE HEE
SHFF
MIAKA.
TAMA-HOME?
IT'S BIG BROTHER!
KRATTA

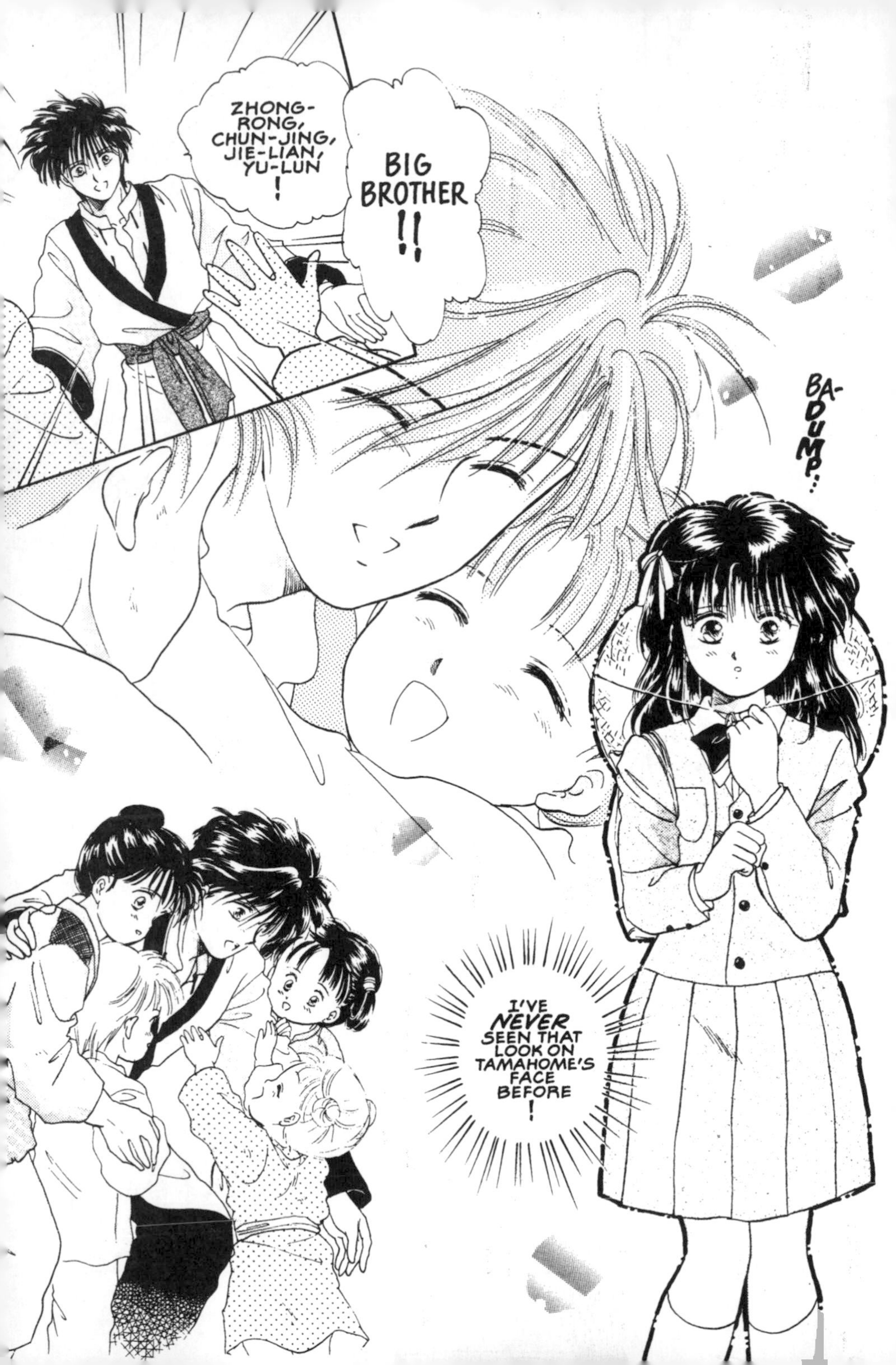
ZHONG-RONG, CHUN-JING, JIE-LIAN, YU-LUN!
BIG BROTHER!!
BA-DUMP!!
I'VE NEVER SEEN THAT LOOK ON TAMAHOME'S FACE BEFORE!

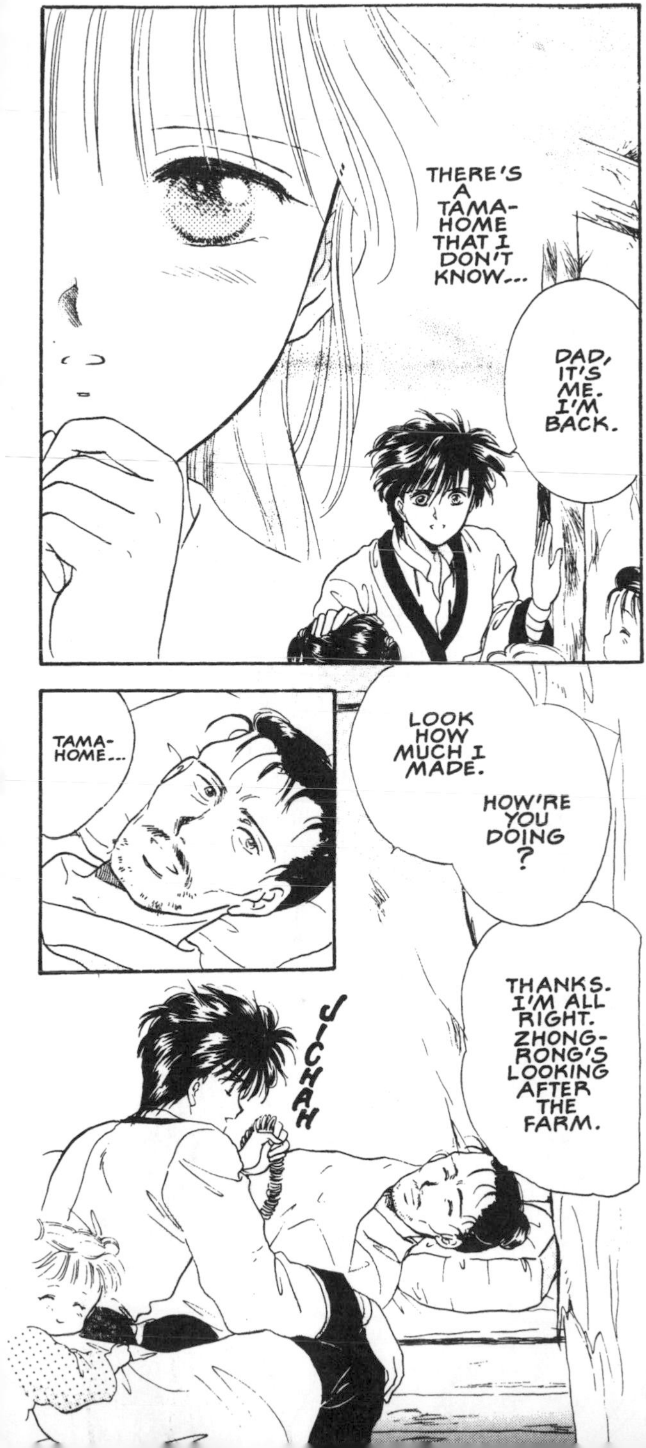

THERE'S A TAMA-HOME THAT I DON'T KNOW...
DAD, IT'S ME. I'M BACK.
TAMA-HOME...
LOOK HOW MUCH I MADE.
HOW'RE YOU DOING?
THANKS. I'M ALL RIGHT. ZHONG-RONG'S LOOKING AFTER THE FARM.
JICHAH

Disciple

How are you all doing? This'll be the start of the third volume!! Time passes quickly. Right now, I'm drawing the last issue of the volume. I thought at first, given this rapid pace, the story might be completed soon, but that ain't-a gonna happen. (Where'd the old-west sheriff come from?) If I don't watch myself, it could easily go into 10 volumes. *That might not even be enough.* Enjoy the ride! I received many letters of encouragement after my whining in volume 2. I really wasn't begging for letters. Sorry to have worried you. I'm all right. I usually don't get depressed at all. Nobody could be depressed and still be a successful manga artist. Usually I draw with a grin on my face. *But sometimes I frown when I concentrate.*

I like my manga and my drawings! (You can't draw if you hate your own drawings!) When I said I couldn't face my own art, I was just exaggerating. When I see the first printing of my manga, I'm really happy, and I'm always asking for my editor to send me more copies. I was just complaining because my art hasn't fully matured. I'll keep on improving, waiting for that day when I'm perfect. *Will it ever really come?* One thing I know for sure: more than anything else, I love drawing manga. Nobody could like drawing manga more than I do! *But I'll bet other manga artists say the same thing.* Maybe my readership has gotten wider because I only hear, "I can't stand your manga," once in a very blue moon. They can say it if they want. They're just criticizing my entire existence, that's all. *I'm crushed!!*

→ I said I like them--not that I'm any good at them! ☺

Recently several other manga-artist friends and I have come up with the proper response. "Then why don't you try drawing manga, huh!? You can't even draw, you loser!!" Actually this thought occurs to many a manga artist when his or her work is rejected by an editor. (Yeah!) And I've decided to say that to anyone with harsh criticism of my work!
Like I ever could! I'm just acting strong.

Sniff

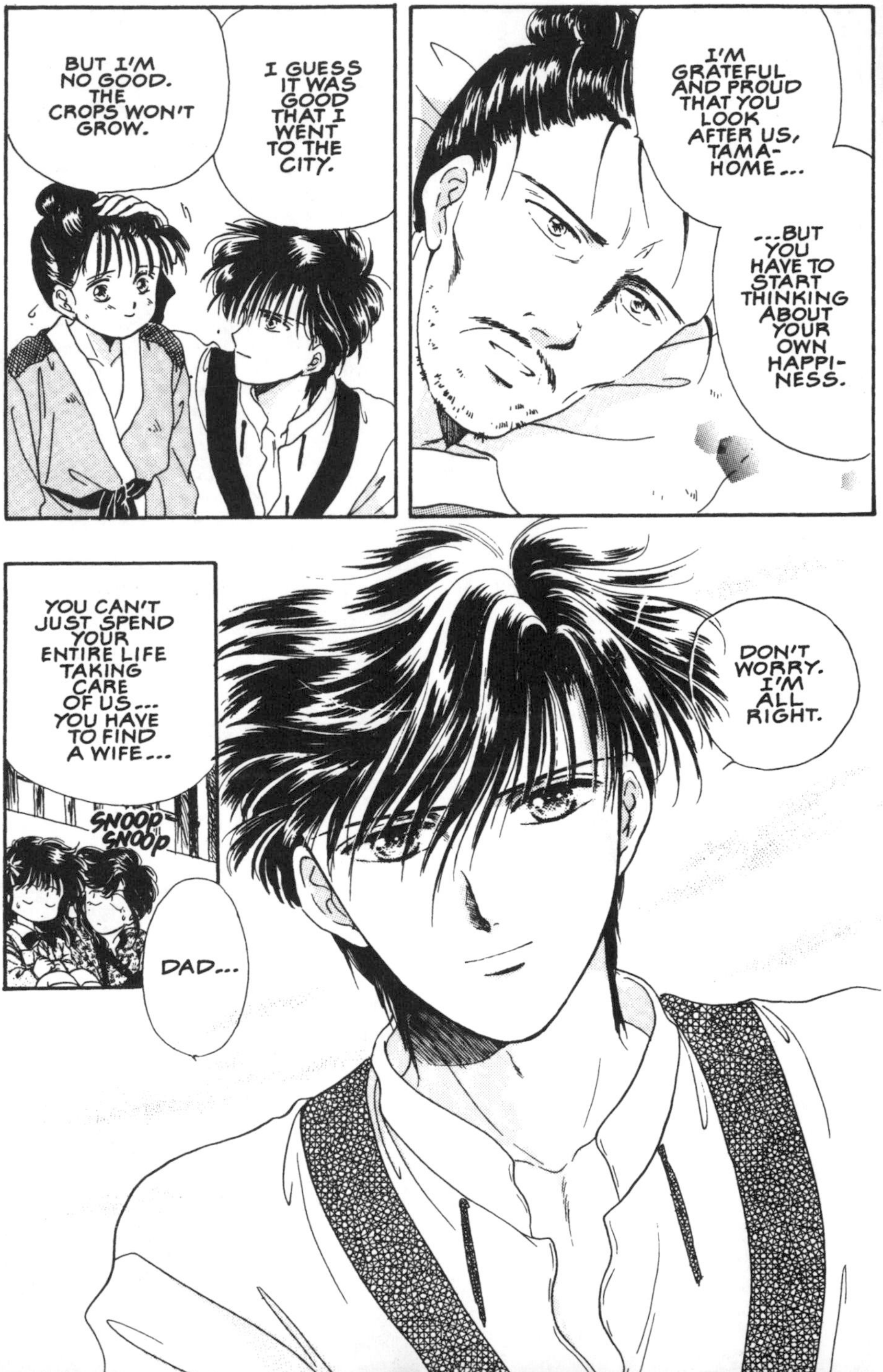
BUT I'M NO GOOD. THE CROPS WON'T GROW.
I GUESS IT WAS GOOD THAT I WENT TO THE CITY.
I'M GRATEFUL AND PROUD THAT YOU LOOK AFTER US, TAMA-HOME...
...BUT YOU HAVE TO START THINKING ABOUT YOUR OWN HAPPINESS.
YOU CAN'T JUST SPEND YOUR ENTIRE LIFE TAKING CARE OF US... YOU HAVE TO FIND A WIFE...
SNOOP SNOOP
DON'T WORRY. I'M ALL RIGHT.
DAD...

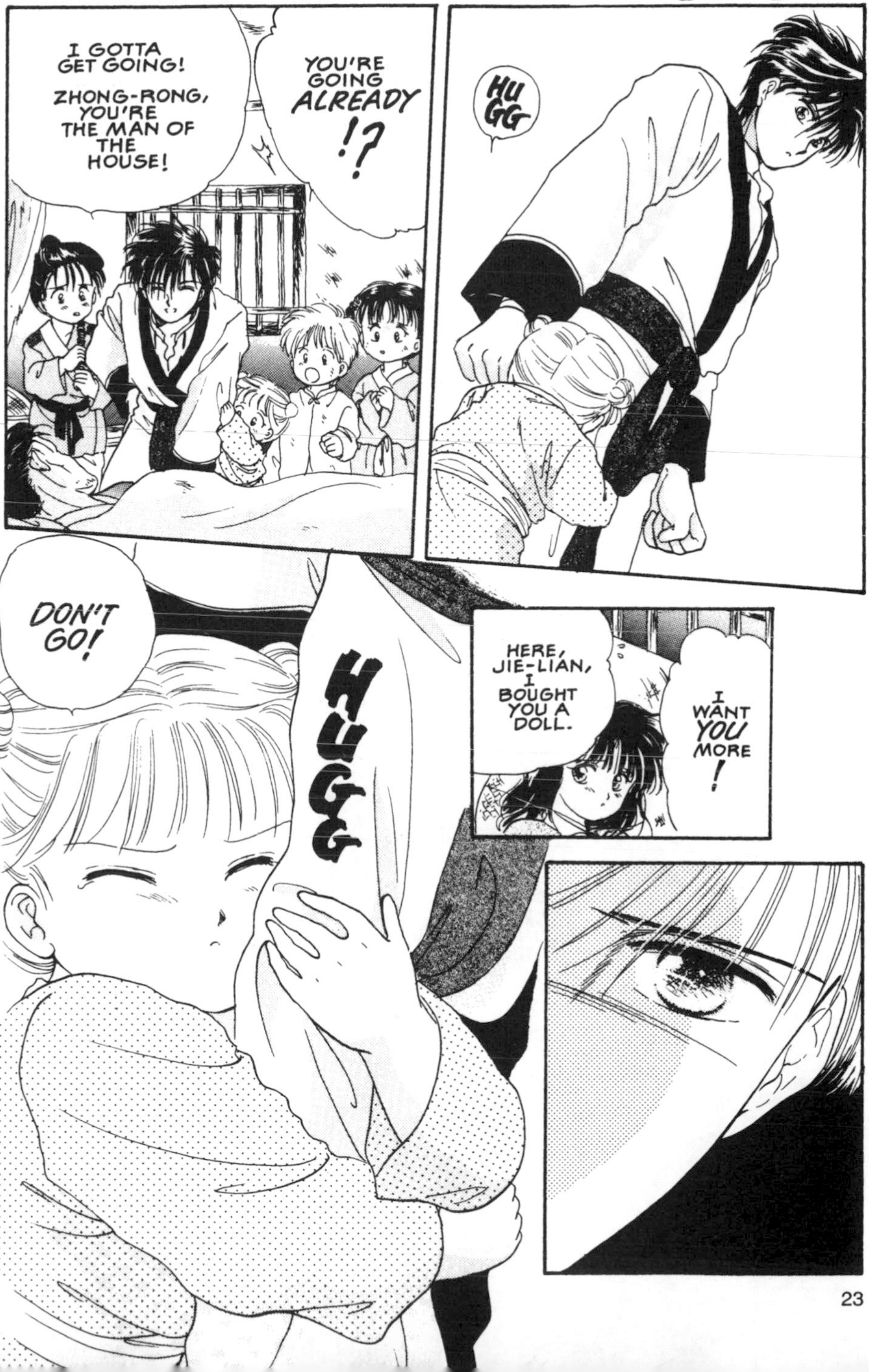
I GOTTA GET GOING!
ZHONG-RONG, YOU'RE THE MAN OF THE HOUSE!
YOU'RE GOING ALREADY !?
HUGG
DON'T GO!
HUGG
HERE, JIE-LIAN, I BOUGHT YOU A DOLL.
I WANT YOU MORE!

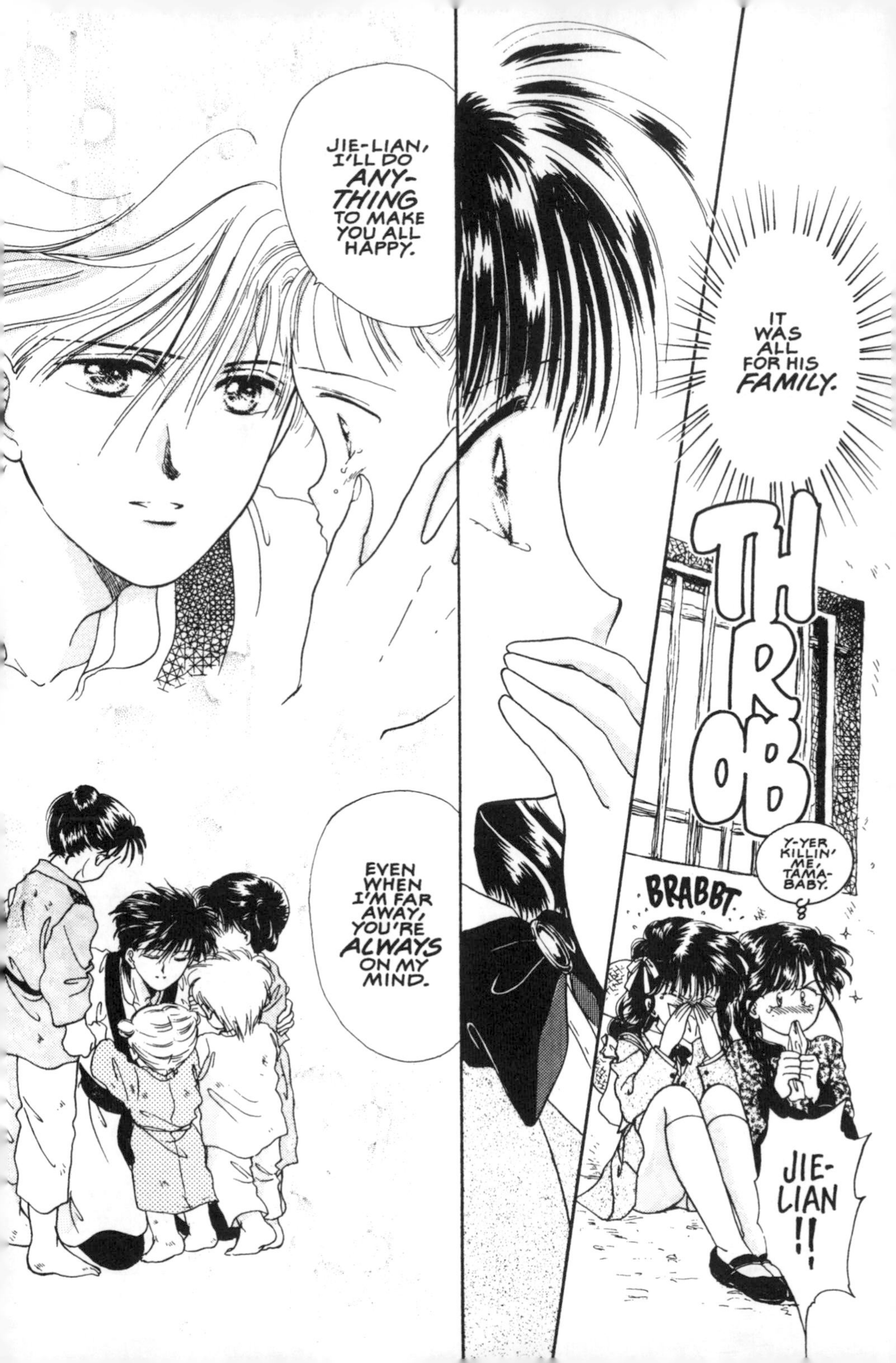
JIE-LIAN, I'LL DO ANYTHING TO MAKE YOU ALL HAPPY.
EVEN WHEN I'M FAR AWAY, YOU'RE ALWAYS ON MY MIND.
IT WAS ALL FOR HIS FAMILY.
THROB
Y-YER KILLIN' ME, TAMA-BABY.
BRABBT
JIE-LIAN!!

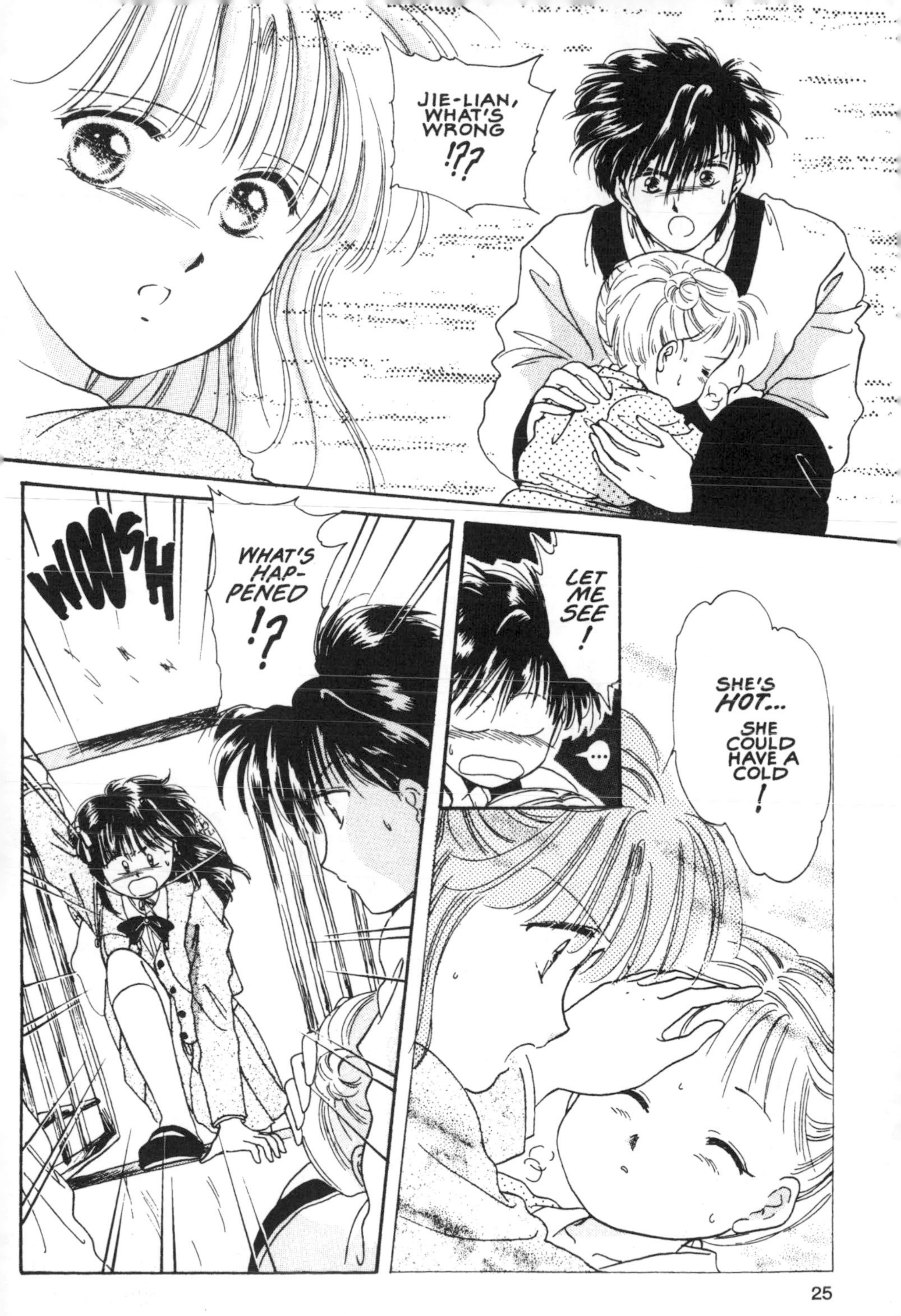
JIE-LIAN, WHAT'S WRONG !??
WOOSH
WHAT'S HAP-PENED !?
LET ME SEE !
...
SHE'S HOT... SHE COULD HAVE A COLD !

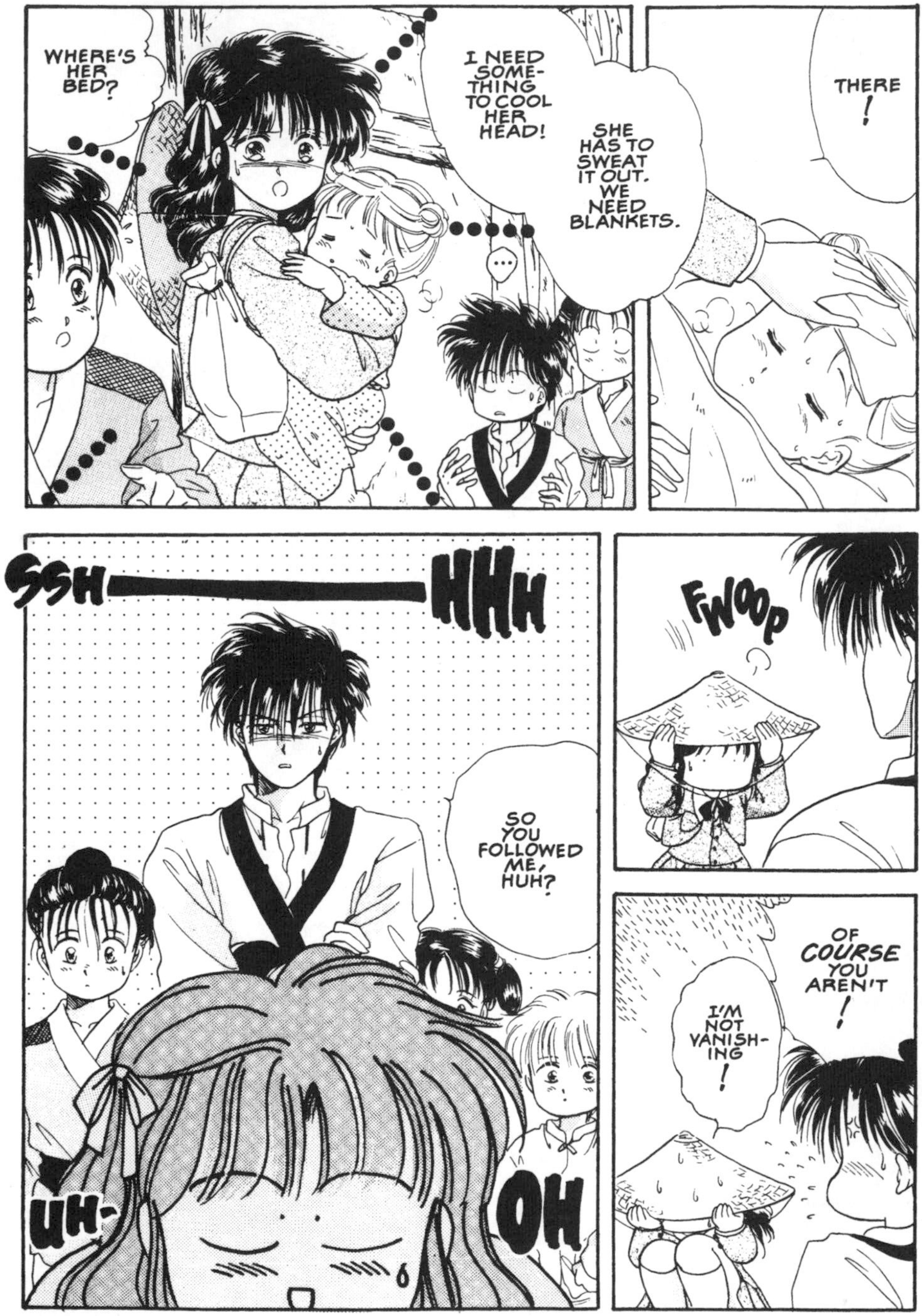
WHERE'S HER BED?
I NEED SOMETHING TO COOL HER HEAD!
SHE HAS TO SWEAT IT OUT. WE NEED BLANKETS.
...
THERE!
SSH——HHH
SO YOU FOLLOWED ME, HUH?
UH-OH
FWOOP
I'M NOT VANISHING!
OF COURSE YOU AREN'T!

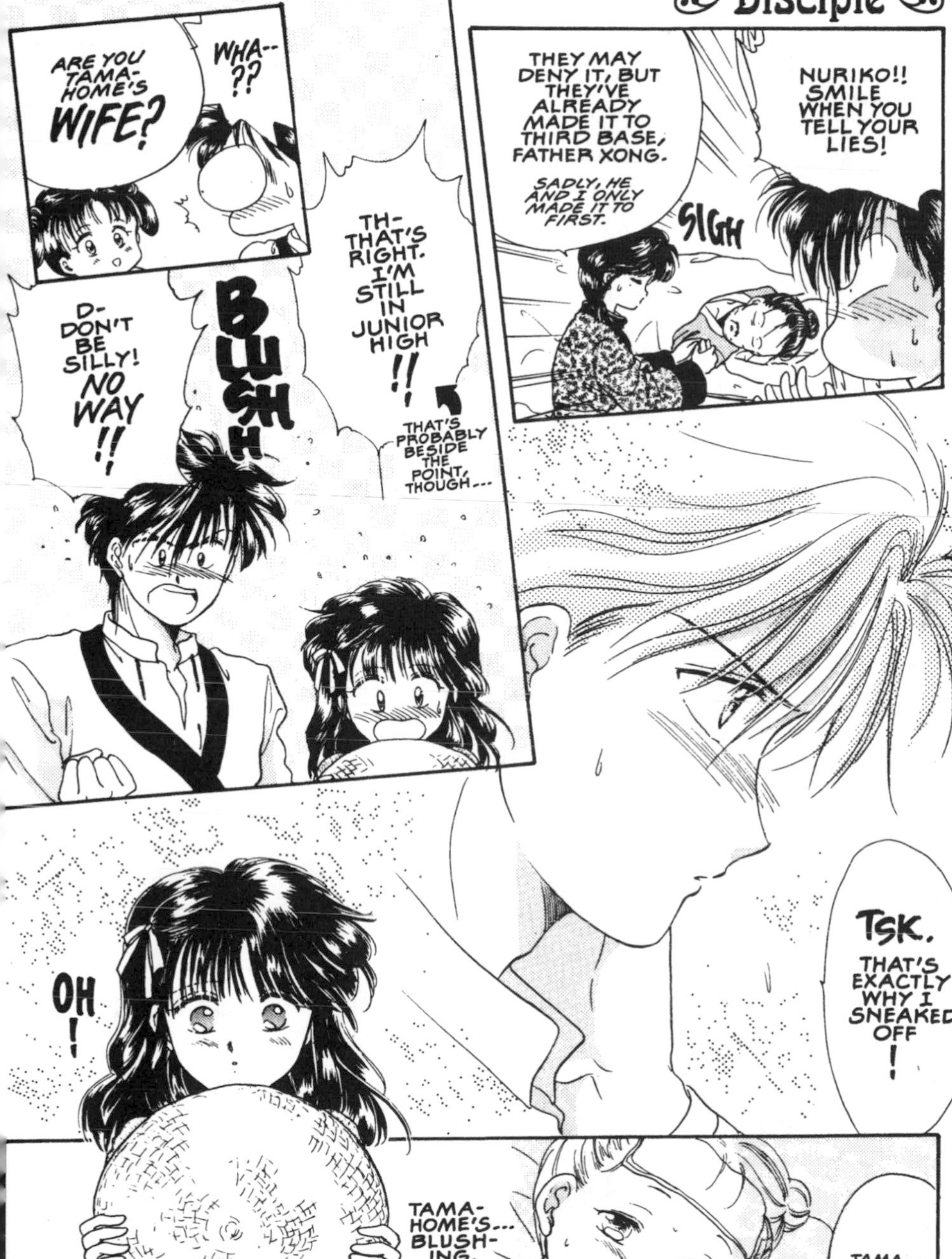
ARE YOU TAMA-HOME'S WIFE?
WHA-- ??
D-DON'T BE SILLY! NO WAY !!
BLUSHH
TH-THAT'S RIGHT. I'M STILL IN JUNIOR HIGH !!
THAT'S PROBABLY BESIDE THE POINT, THOUGH...
THEY MAY DENY IT, BUT THEY'VE ALREADY MADE IT TO THIRD BASE, FATHER XONG.
SADLY, HE AND I ONLY MADE IT TO FIRST.
SIGH
NURIKO!! SMILE WHEN YOU TELL YOUR LIES!
OH !
TSK. THAT'S EXACTLY WHY I SNEAKED OFF !
TAMA-HOME'S... BLUSH-ING.
TAMA... HOME.

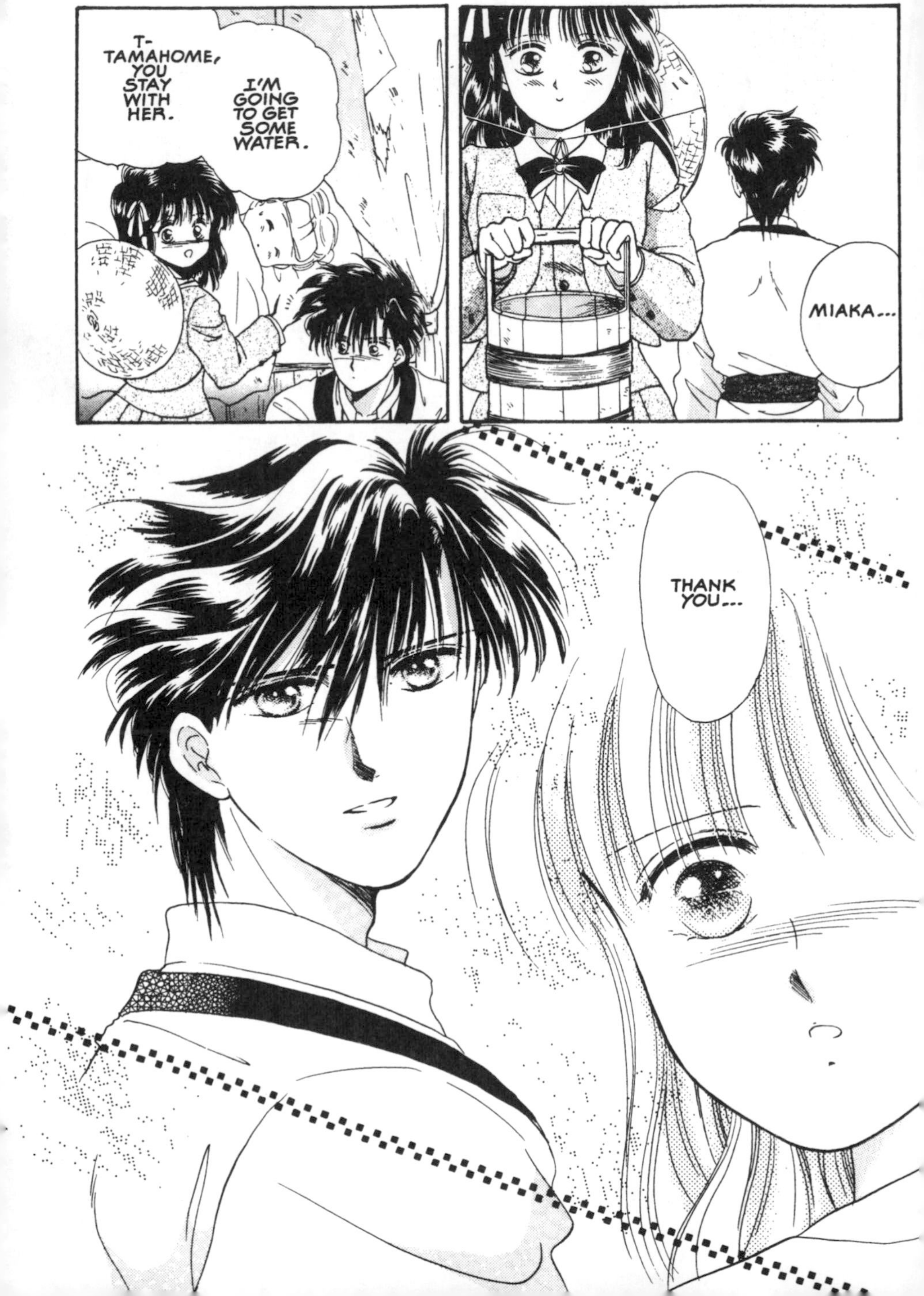
T-
TAMAHOME, YOU STAY WITH HER.
I'M GOING TO GET SOME WATER.
MIAKA...
THANK YOU...

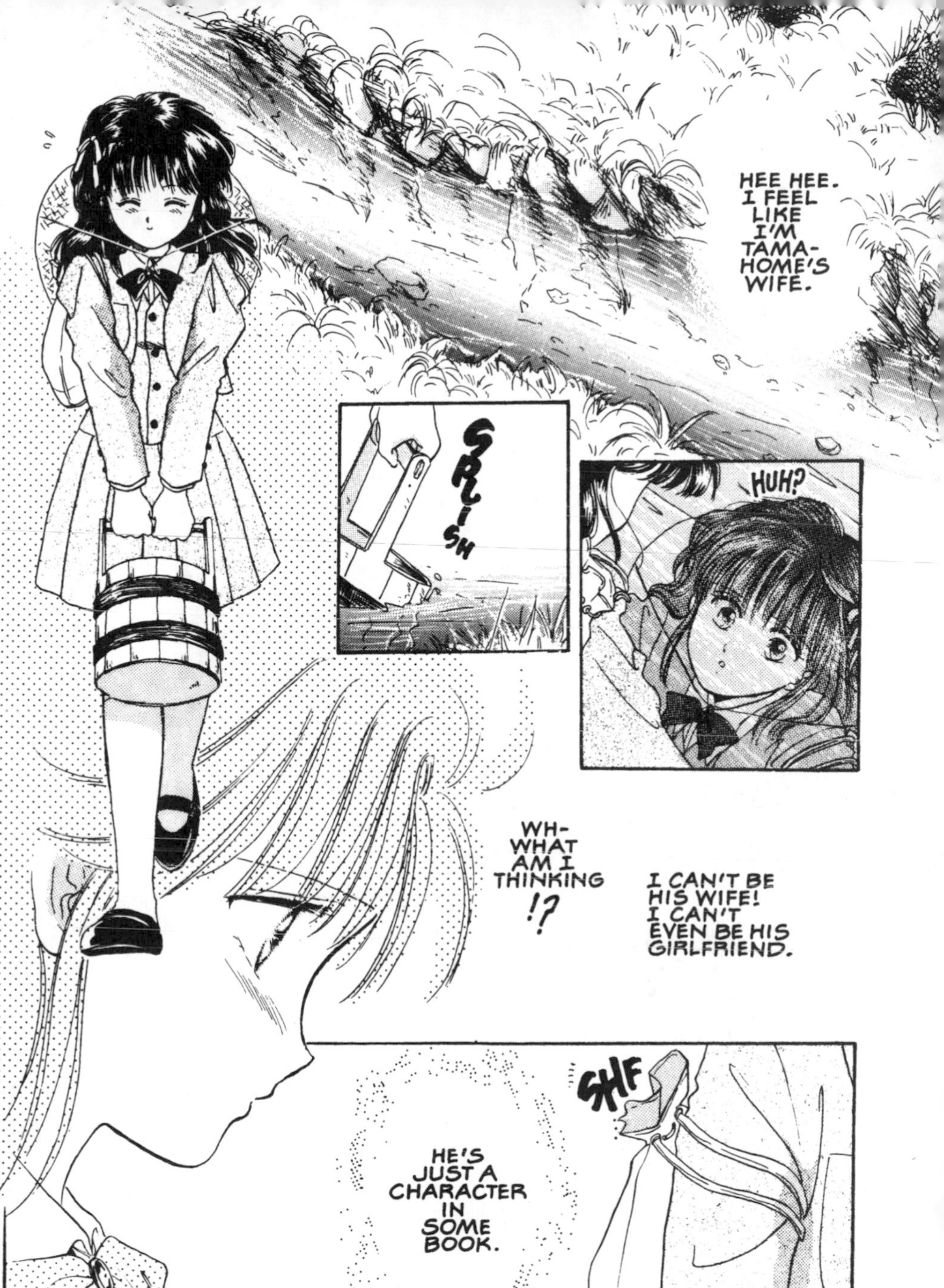
HEE HEE. I FEEL LIKE I'M TAMA-HOME'S WIFE.
SRISH
HUH?
WH-WHAT AM I THINKING !?
I CAN'T BE HIS WIFE! I CAN'T EVEN BE HIS GIRLFRIEND.
HE'S JUST A CHARACTER IN SOME BOOK.
SHF

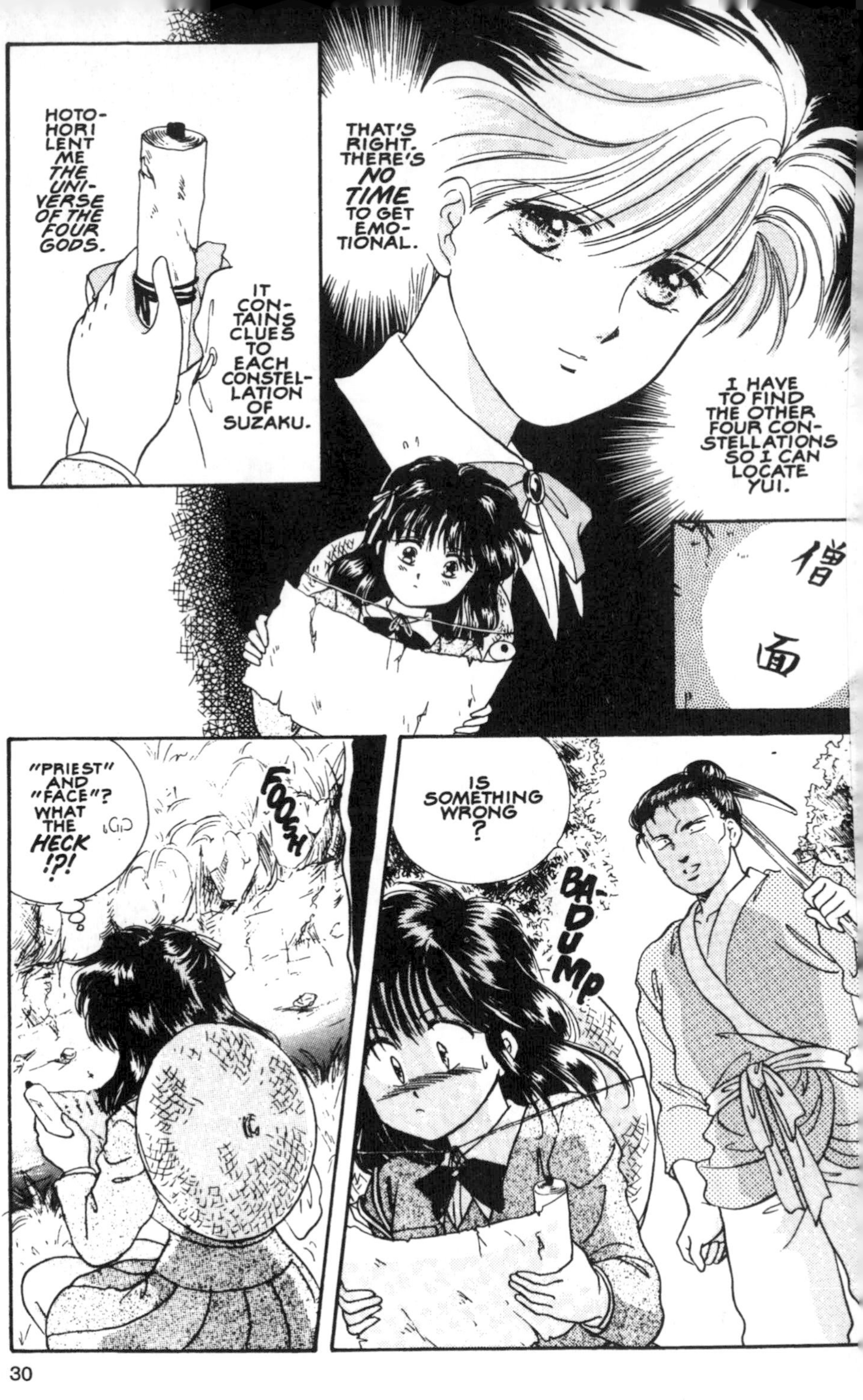

HOTOHORI LENT ME THE UNIVERSE OF THE FOUR GODS.
IT CONTAINS CLUES TO EACH CONSTELLATION OF SUZAKU.
THAT'S RIGHT. THERE'S NO TIME TO GET EMOTIONAL.
I HAVE TO FIND THE OTHER FOUR CONSTELLATIONS SO I CAN LOCATE YUI.
僧面
"PRIEST" AND "FACE"? WHAT THE HECK !?!
FOOSH
IS SOMETHING WRONG?
BA-DUMP

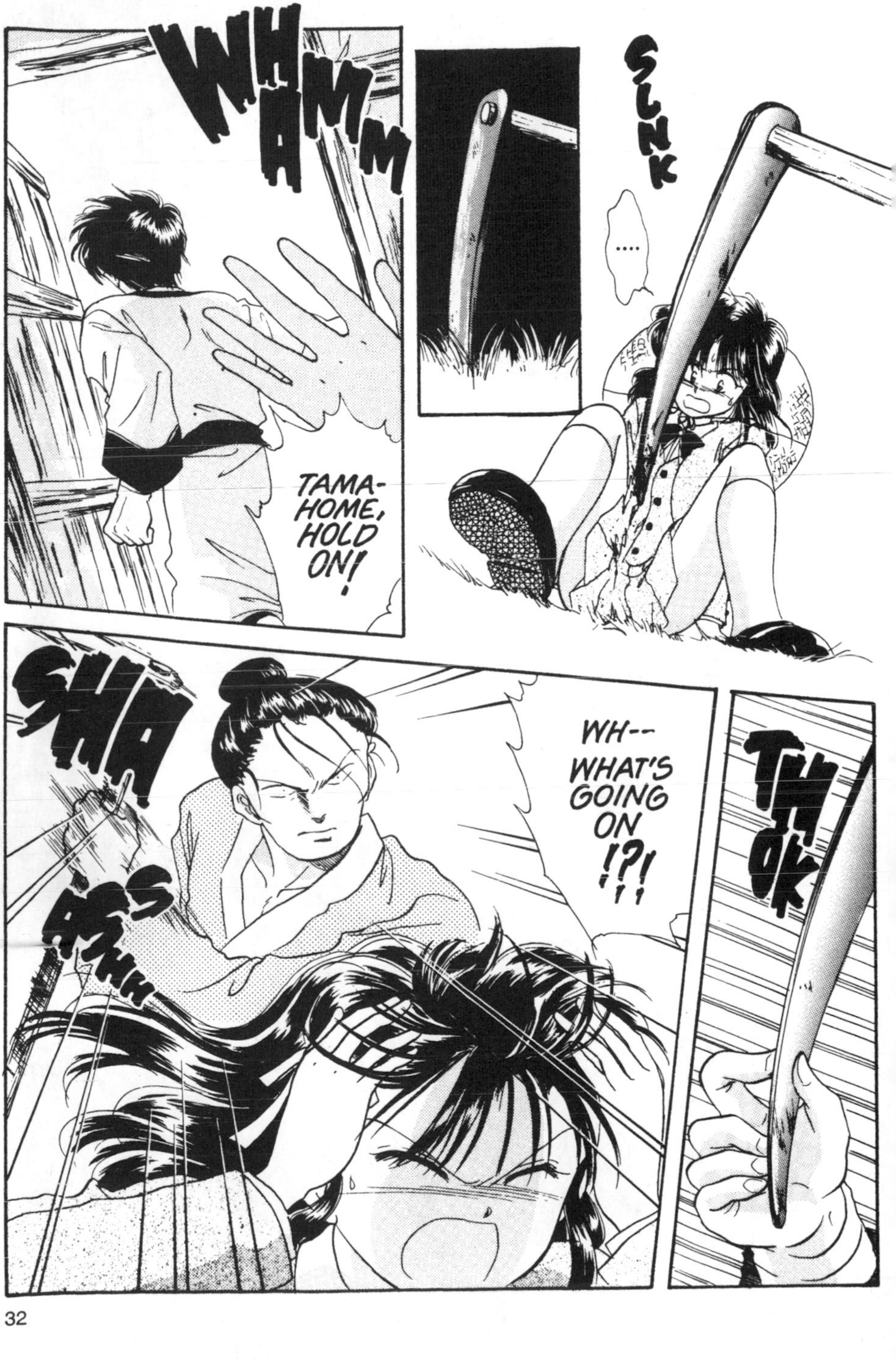
TAMA-HOME, HOLD ON!
SLNK
....
WH-- WHAT'S GOING ON !?!
THOK

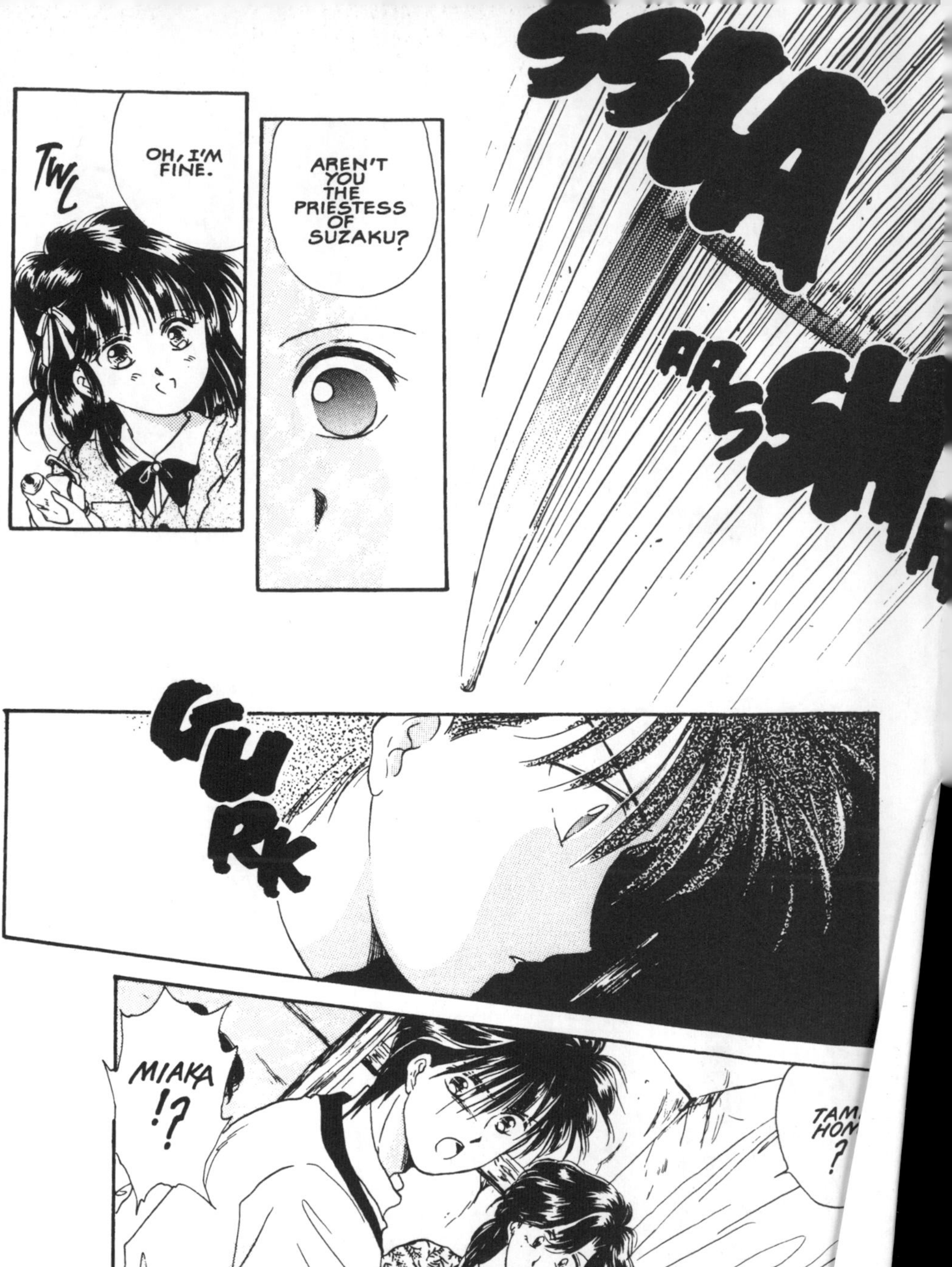
TWL
OH, I'M FINE.
AREN'T YOU THE PRIESTESS OF SUZAKU?
SSHA
GURK
MIAKA !?
TAM HOM ?

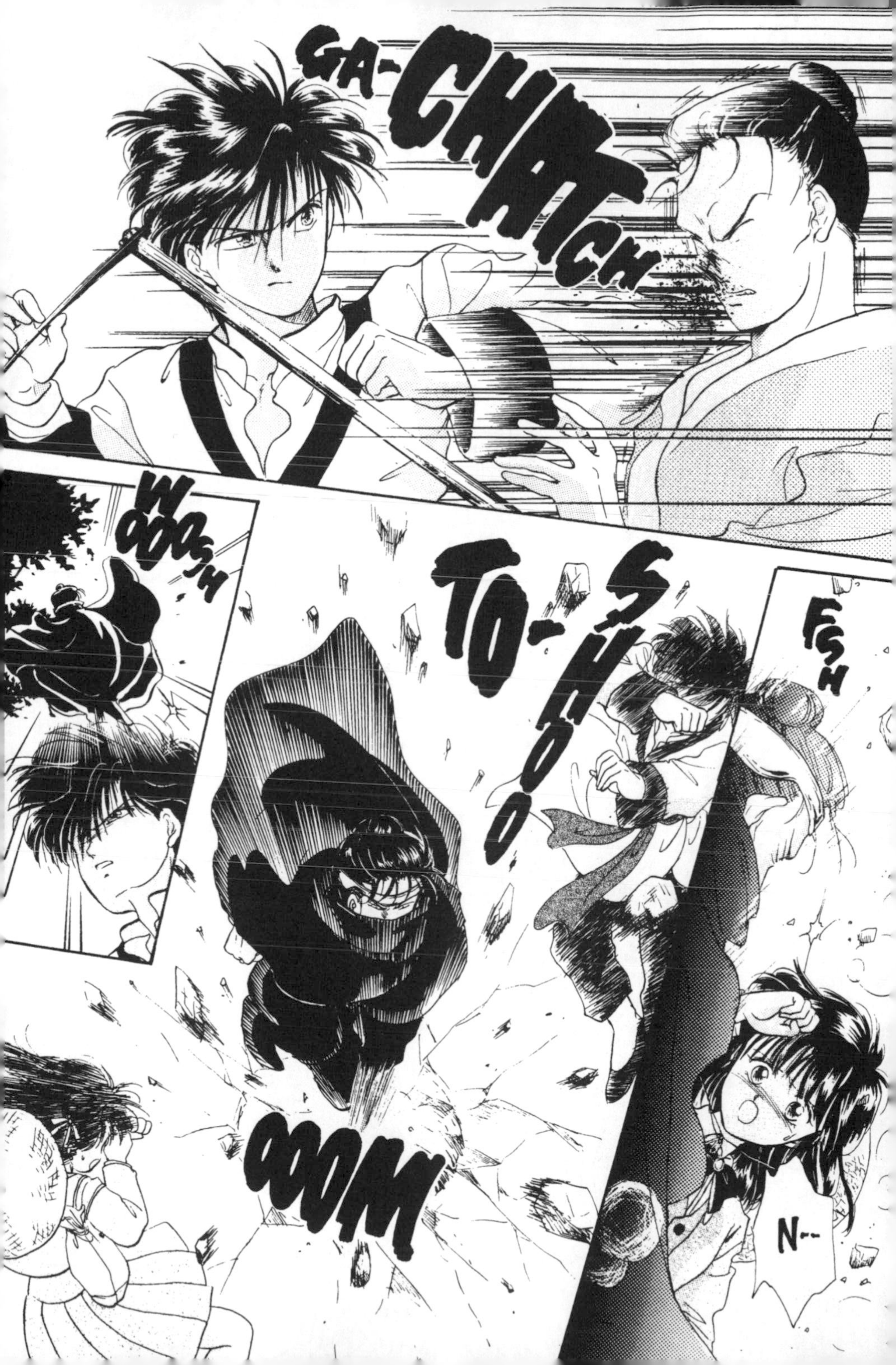
GA-CHATCH
WOOOSH
TO-
SHOOOO
OOOM
FSH
N--

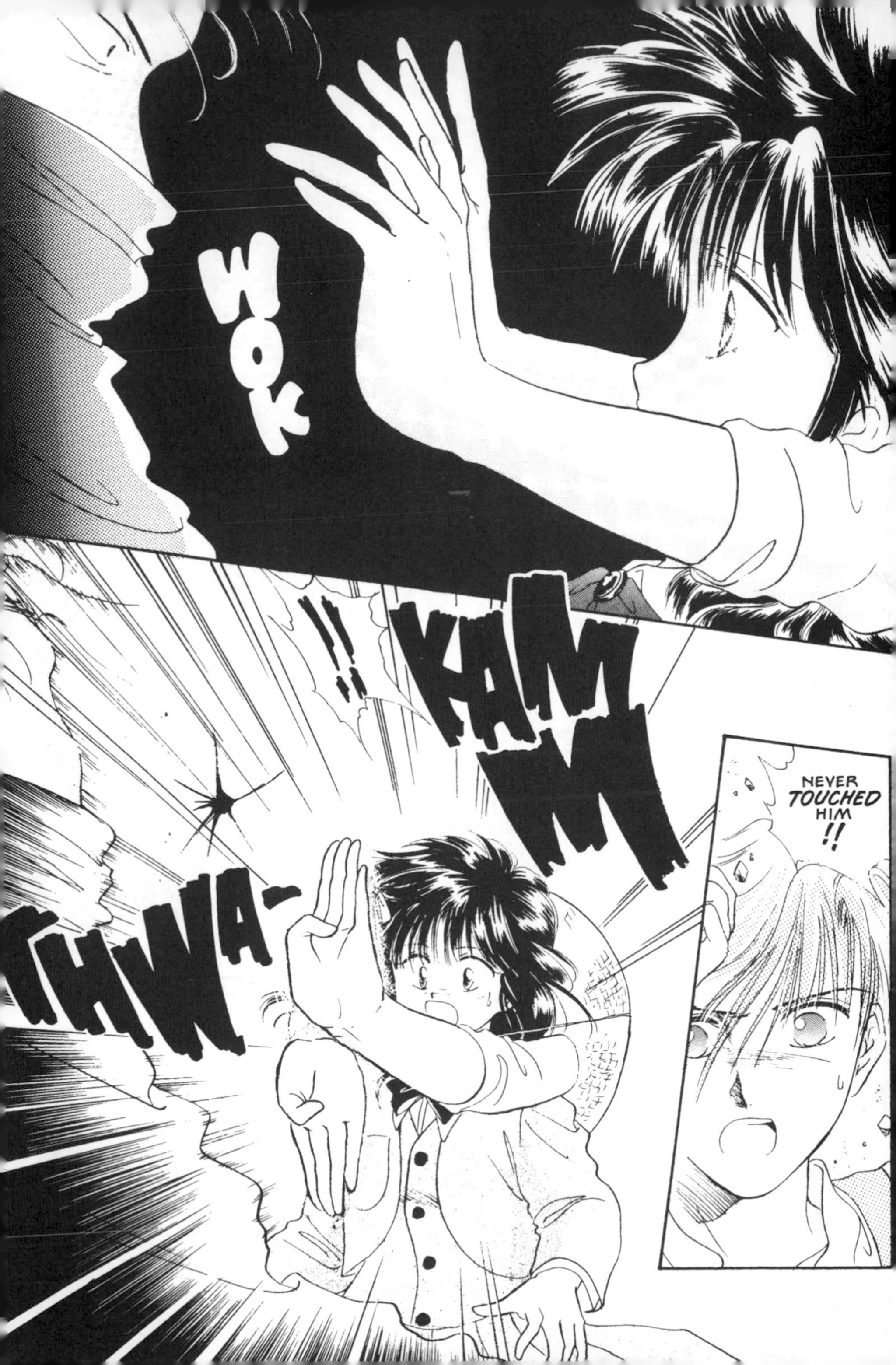
WOK
!!
KAMM
THWA-
NEVER TOUCHED HIM !!

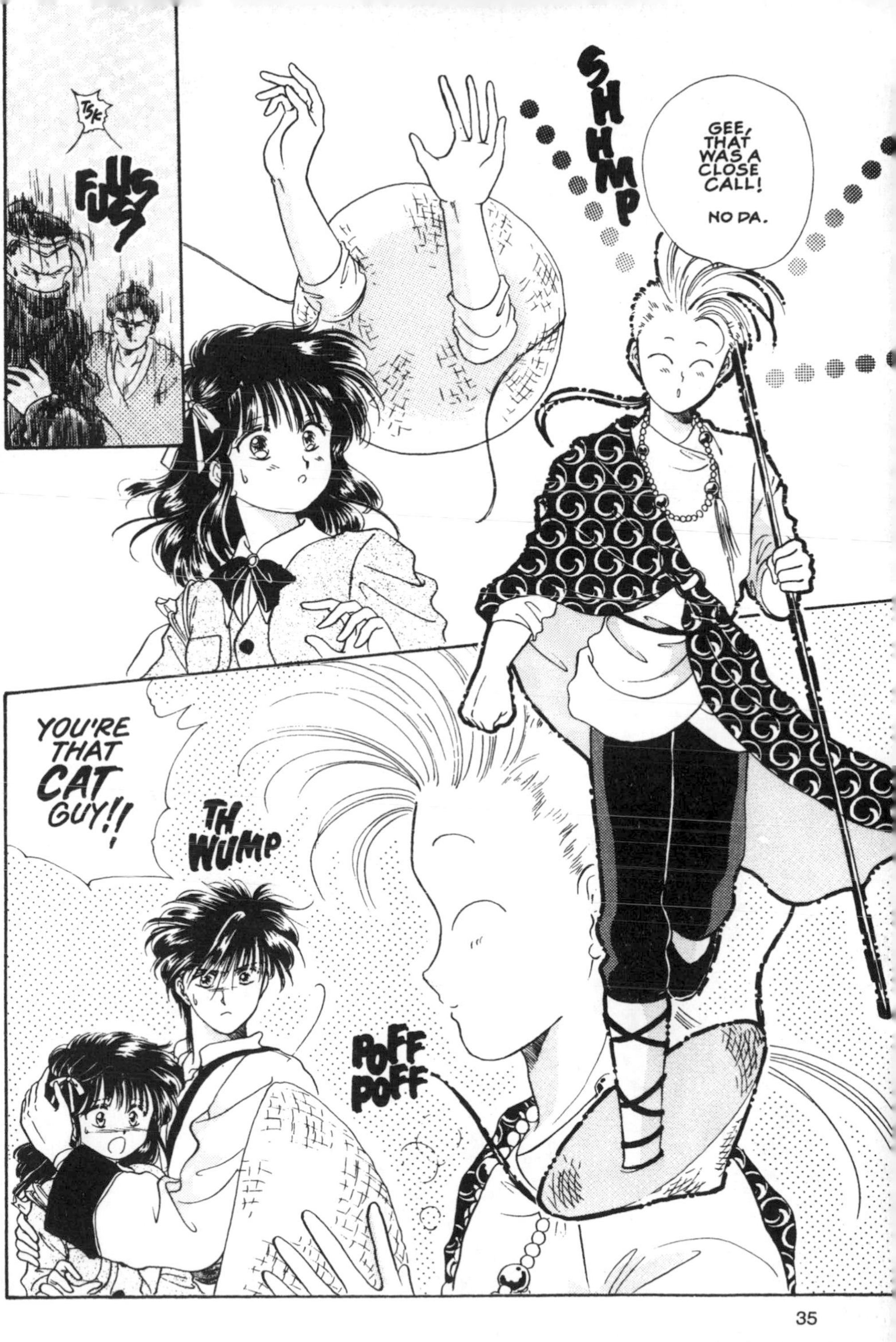
TSK
FUSS
SHHMP
GEE, THAT WAS A CLOSE CALL!
NO DA.
YOU'RE THAT CAT GUY!!
THWUMP
POFF POFF

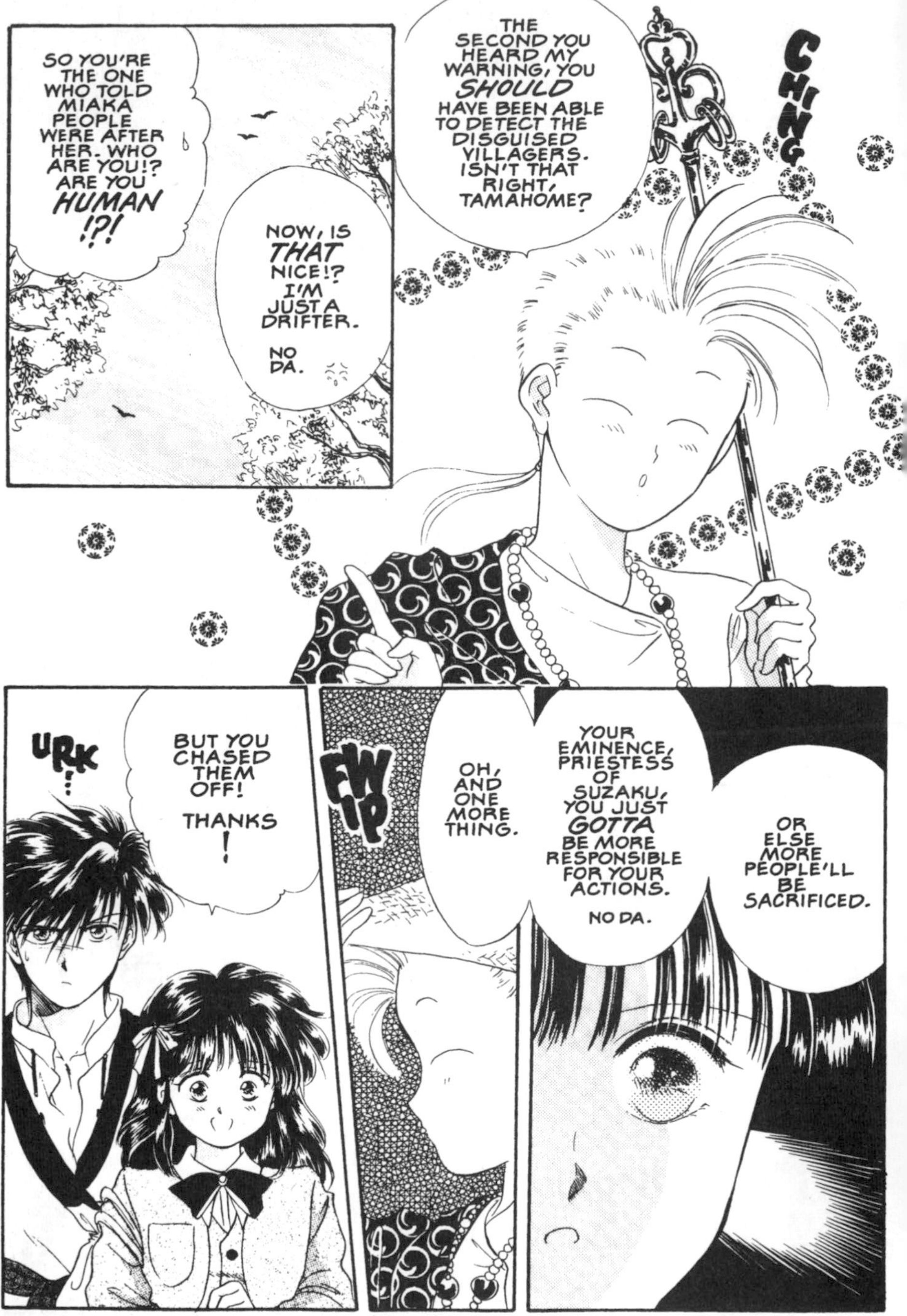
SO YOU'RE THE ONE WHO TOLD MIAKA PEOPLE WERE AFTER HER. WHO ARE YOU!? ARE YOU HUMAN !?!
NOW, IS THAT NICE!? I'M JUST A DRIFTER.
NO DA.
THE SECOND YOU HEARD MY WARNING, YOU SHOULD HAVE BEEN ABLE TO DETECT THE DISGUISED VILLAGERS. ISN'T THAT RIGHT, TAMAHOME?
CHING
URK
BUT YOU CHASED THEM OFF!
THANKS!
FWIP
OH, AND ONE MORE THING.
YOUR EMINENCE, PRIESTESS OF SUZAKU, YOU JUST GOTTA BE MORE RESPONSIBLE FOR YOUR ACTIONS.
NO DA.
OR ELSE MORE PEOPLE'LL BE SACRIFICED.

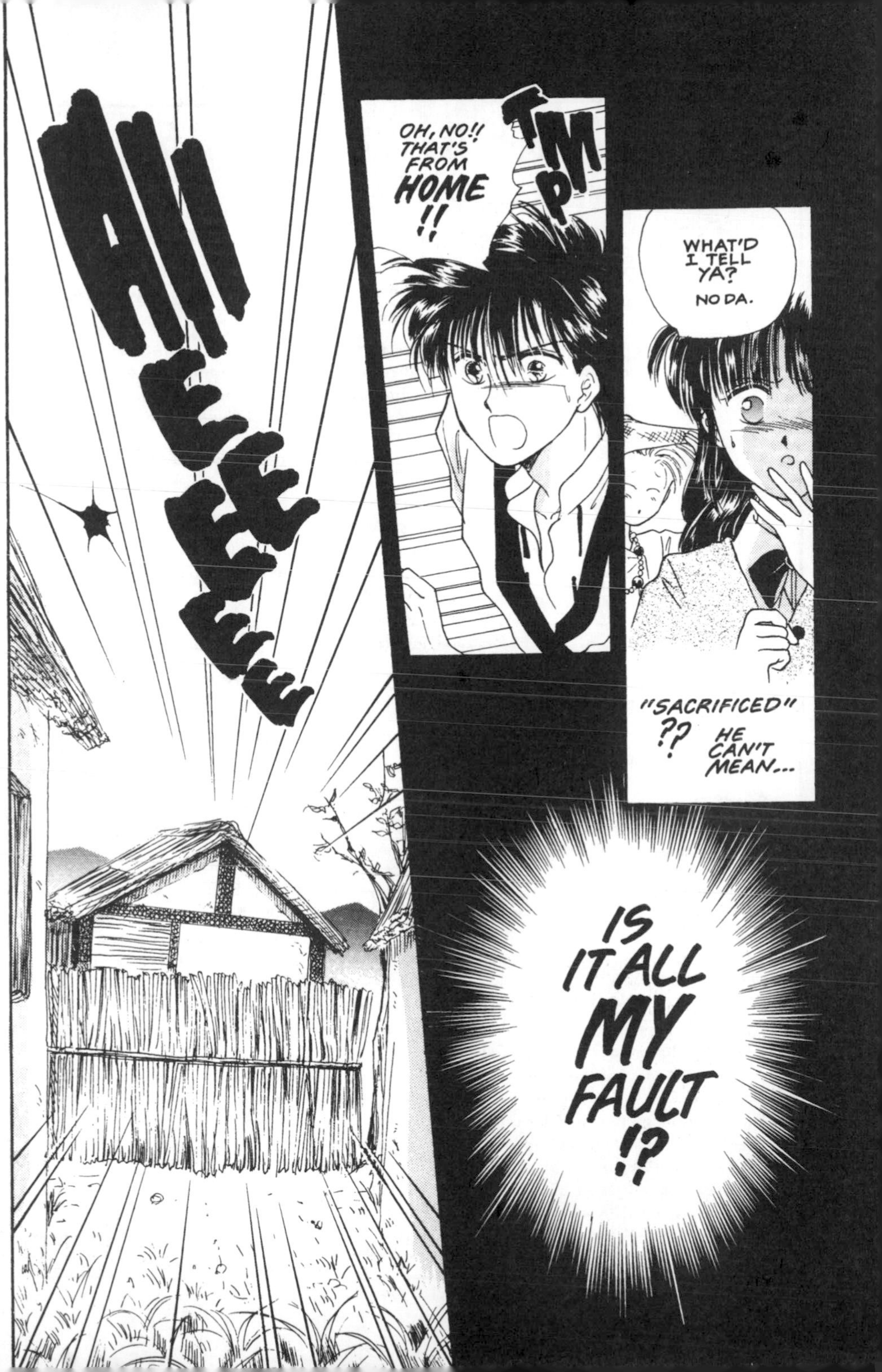
AIIEEEEE
OH, NO!! THAT'S FROM HOME!!
TMP
WHAT'D I TELL YA? NO DA.
"SACRIFICED"?? HE CAN'T MEAN...
IS IT ALL MY FAULT!?

Tell me more about "The Universe of the Four Gods"

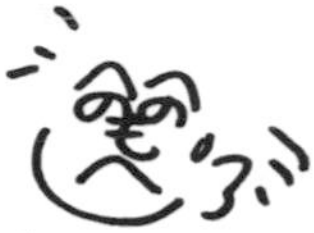

This is one of the questions I hear frequently. If you keep reading the story, you'll find out all about it. But for the impatient fans who still INSIST! I've decided to expose a few details.

I've never seen constellations attributed to the four gods, so I might be the first. (Usually they've been used as compass directions or for the identities of monsters. Other than that, their names have been used for invocations.)
The anime OAV Maryū Senki used them as monsters. I think Suzaku was female, but this anime gets pretty heavily into erotic-grotesque so I can't recommend it...
I'll describe the gods and their constellations. (That way you can find them in the night sky.)

We'll list the Four Gods according to ancient Chinese astrological names rather than geographical areas (which might appear later in the story) or compass directions.

EASTERN SEIRYU SEVEN CONSTELLATIONS (MAY-JULY) Suboshi (Virgo), Amiboshi (Virgo), Tomo (Libra), Soi (Scorpio), Nakago (Scorpio), Ashitare (Scorpio), Mi (Sagittarius)

WESTERN BYAKKO SEVEN CONSTELLATIONS (NOVEMBER-JANUARY) Tokaki (Andromeda), Tatara (Aries), Kokie (Aries), Subaru (Taurus), Amefuri (Taurus), Toroki (Orion), Karasuki (Orion)

SOUTHERN SUZAKU SEVEN CONSTELLATIONS (FEBRUARY-MAY) Chichiri (Gemini), Tamahome (Cancer), Nuriko (Hydra), Hotohori (Hydra), Chiriko (Hydra), Tasuki (Crater), Mitsukake (Corvus)

NORTHERN GENBU SEVEN CONSTELLATIONS (AUGUST-NOVEMBER) Hikitsu (Sagittarius), Inami (Capricorn), Uruki (Aquarius), Tomite (Aquarius), Urumiya (Aquarius), Hatsui (Pegasus), Namame (Pegasus)

Usually, when you see the character for Chichiri's name, you read it as "i," and when you see the character for Tamahome's name, you see it as "ki," etc. So most of the tables list the constellation names with the Chinese pronunciations for each of the characters. There are very few which list the Japanese phonetic reading such as "Tamahome," but in the Buddhist Philosophy Encyclopedia I have, the character was listed as "Tamahome." *(You'll only find this book at a large book store. It costs a whopping ¥80,000!)*
The rest I looked up in the constellation tables in the appendices of a Japanese/Chinese dictionary I used in high school. A star in "Hotohori" is second magnitude, and the brightest star in Suzaku *(Alpha Hadrae, also known as Alphard or the Solitary One.—Ed.)*
The names for the four gods were taken from these constellation listings. The Southern Seven Star Constellations look like they have short tails so the ancients called them a bird, the Western Seven Star Constellations resemble a tiger, and so on.
Between February and May you can see the Suzaku constellations appear in the night sky. The brightest star in Cancer is Tamahome.
I love the cosmos, so I get a kick out of naming my characters after constellations.
I've also been told that "Nuriko" is "Meriko" but I think it can be named both ways (most of the time it's called Nuriko). Also Mitsukake can be read as both Mitsukake and Mitsuuchi. Some said that Tamahome and crew were a part of Byakko, but they're mistaken.

Genbu is pretty sad. Dragons like Seiryu are kind of cool, but the idea of a turtle and snake copulating!! Bleagh! I am not into that!!

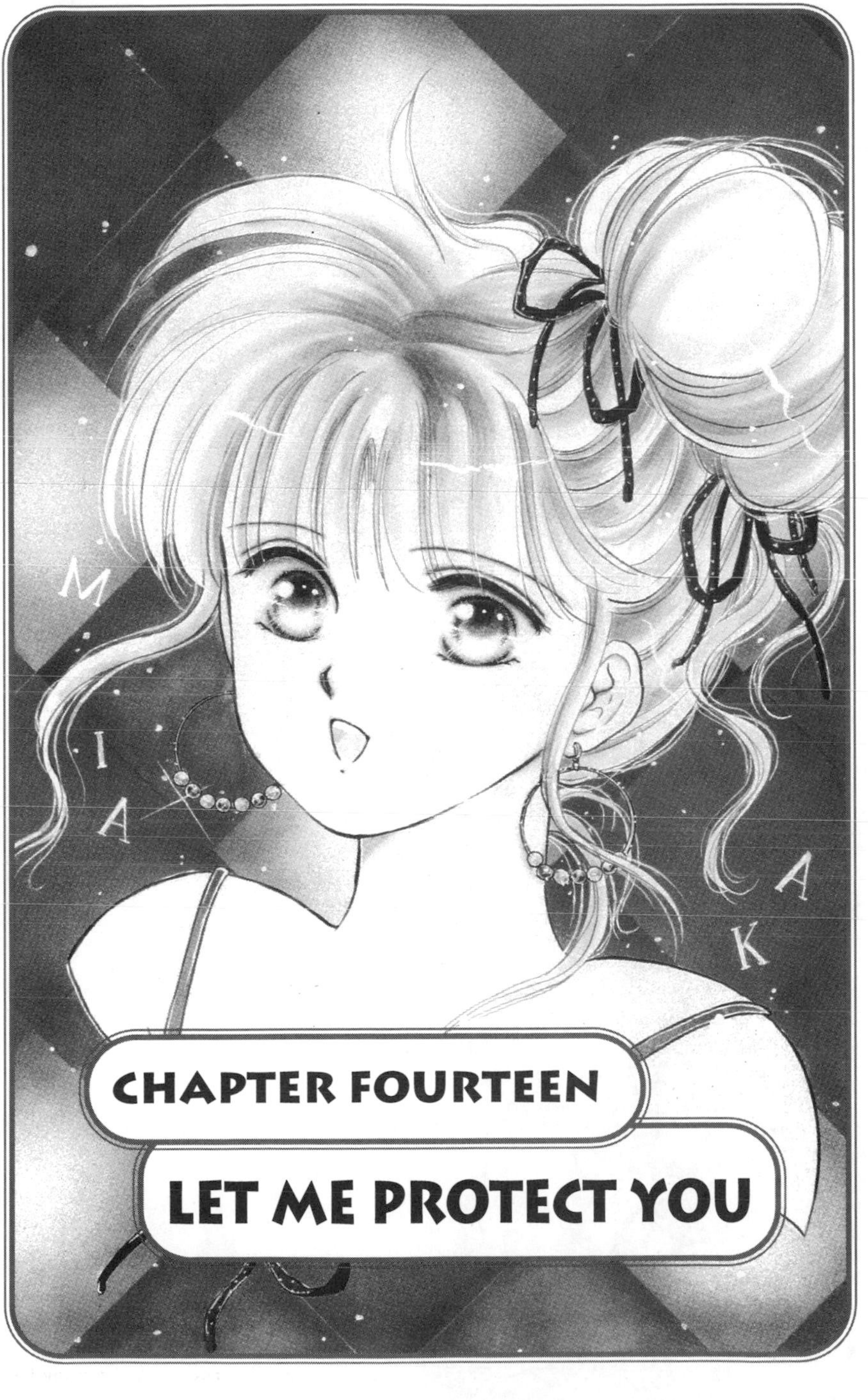
MIAKA

CHAPTER FOURTEEN

LET ME PROTECT YOU

LAI LAI

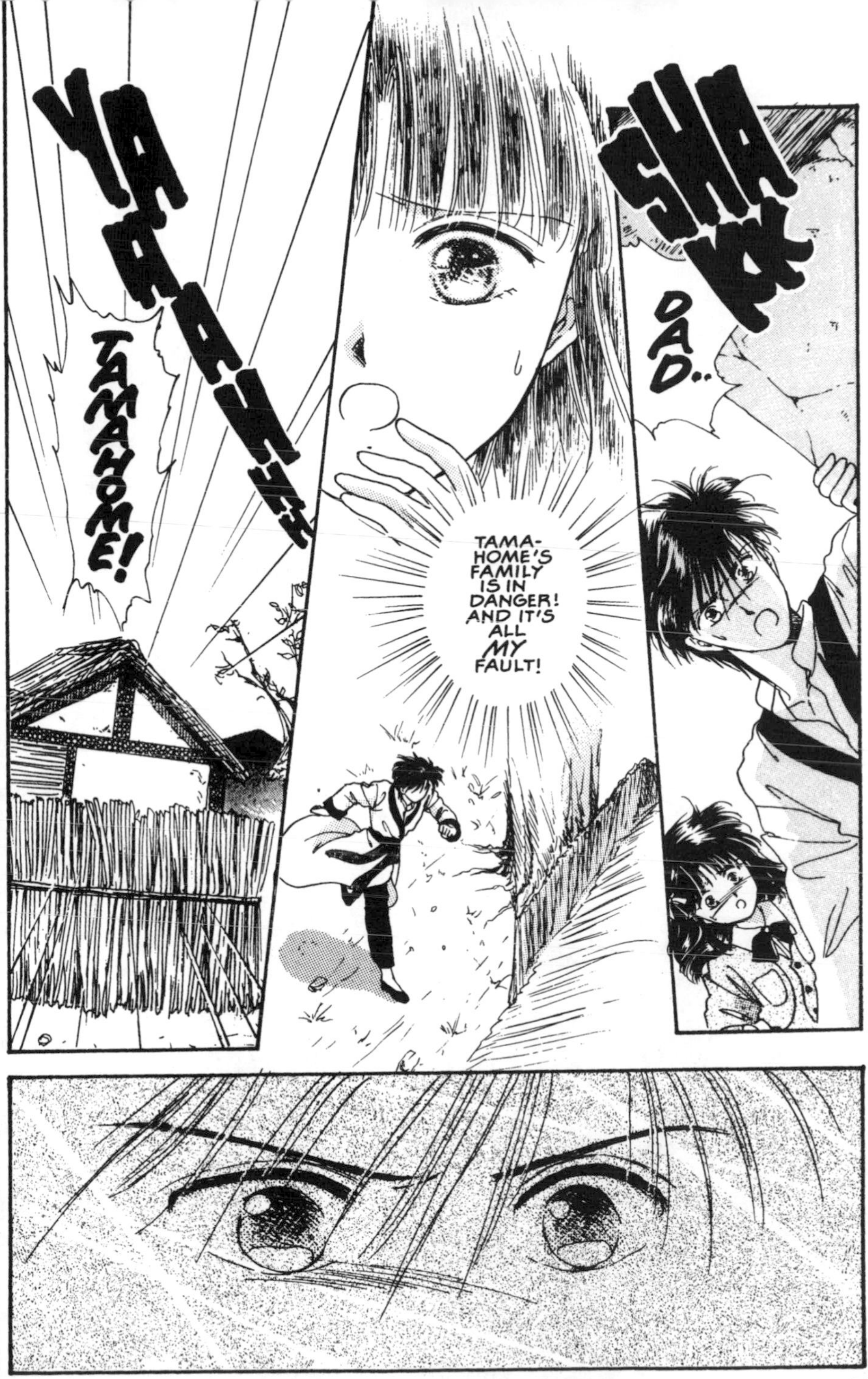
SHAKK
DAD..
TAMA-HOME'S FAMILY IS IN DANGER! AND IT'S ALL MY FAULT!
YAAAHHHH
TAMAHOME!

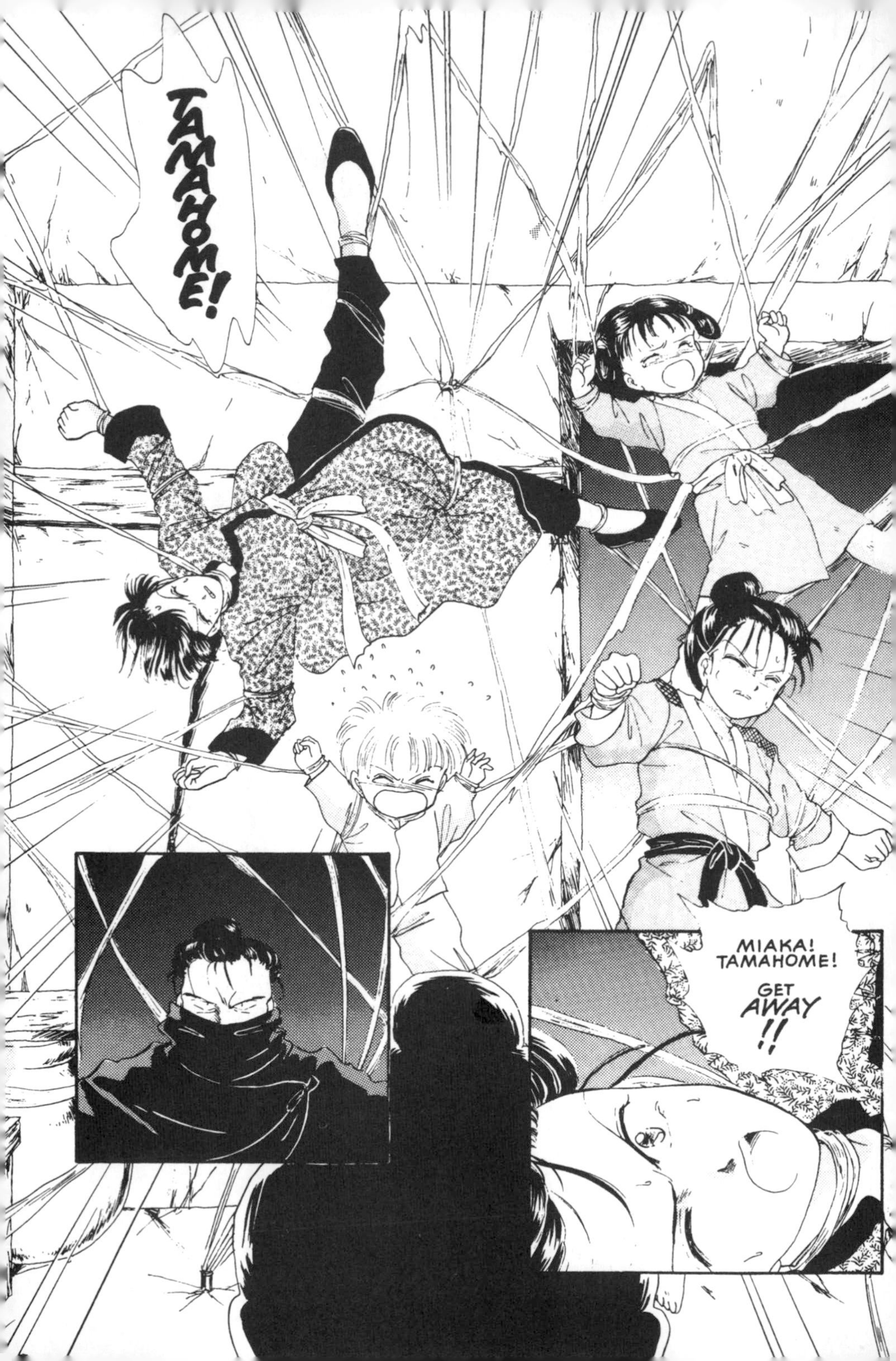
TAMAHOME!
MIAKA! TAMAHOME!
GET AWAY!!

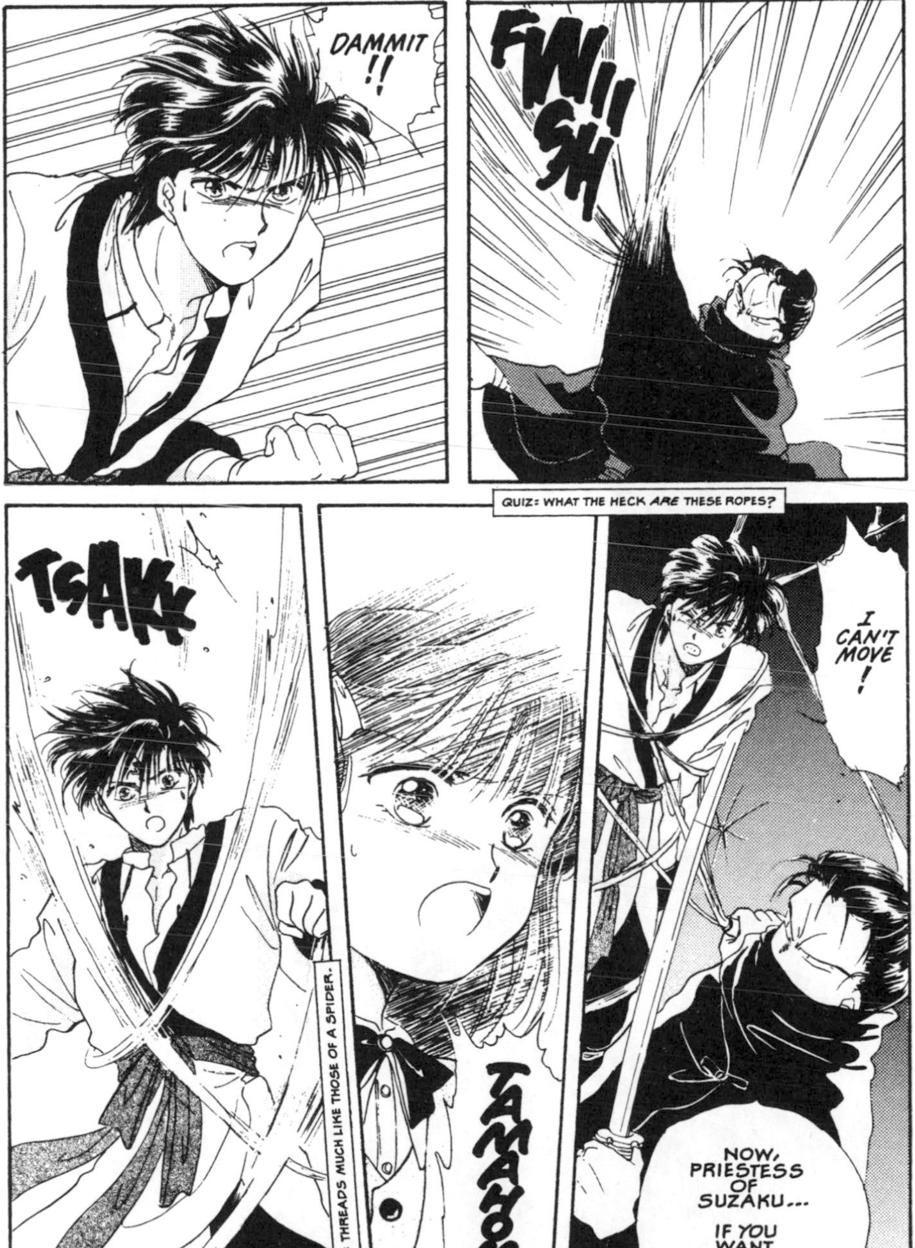
DAMMIT!!
FWIISH
QUIZ: WHAT THE HECK ARE THESE ROPES?
TSAKK
ANSWER: THREADS MUCH LIKE THOSE OF A SPIDER.
TAMAHOME!
I CAN'T MOVE!
NOW, PRIESTESS OF SUZAKU...
IF YOU WANT THESE PEOPLE TO LIVE...

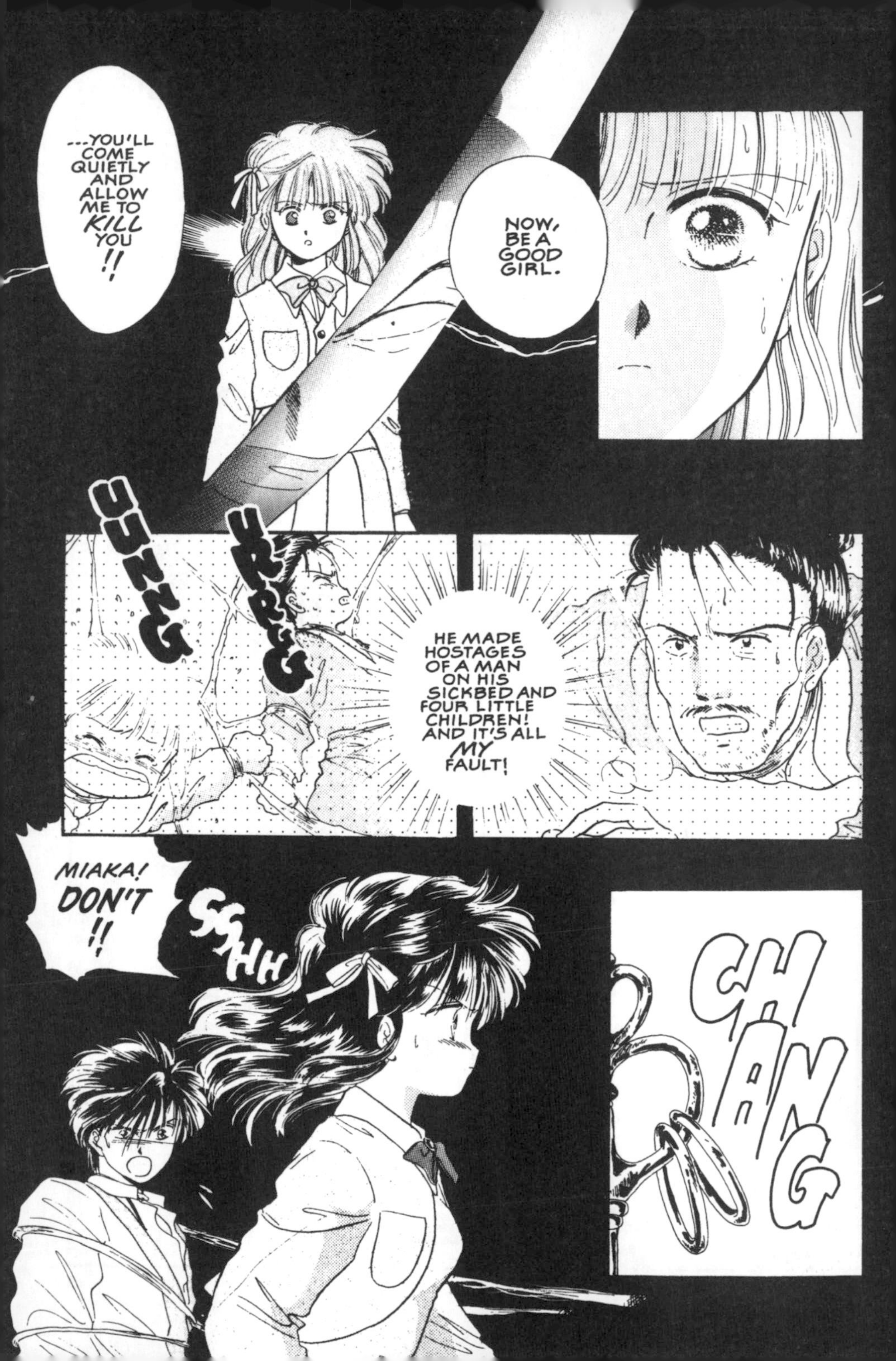
NOW, BE A GOOD GIRL.
...YOU'LL COME QUIETLY AND ALLOW ME TO KILL YOU!!
UUNNG
URRRG
HE MADE HOSTAGES OF A MAN ON HIS SICKBED AND FOUR LITTLE CHILDREN! AND IT'S ALL MY FAULT!
MIAKA! DON'T!!
SSHHH
CHANG

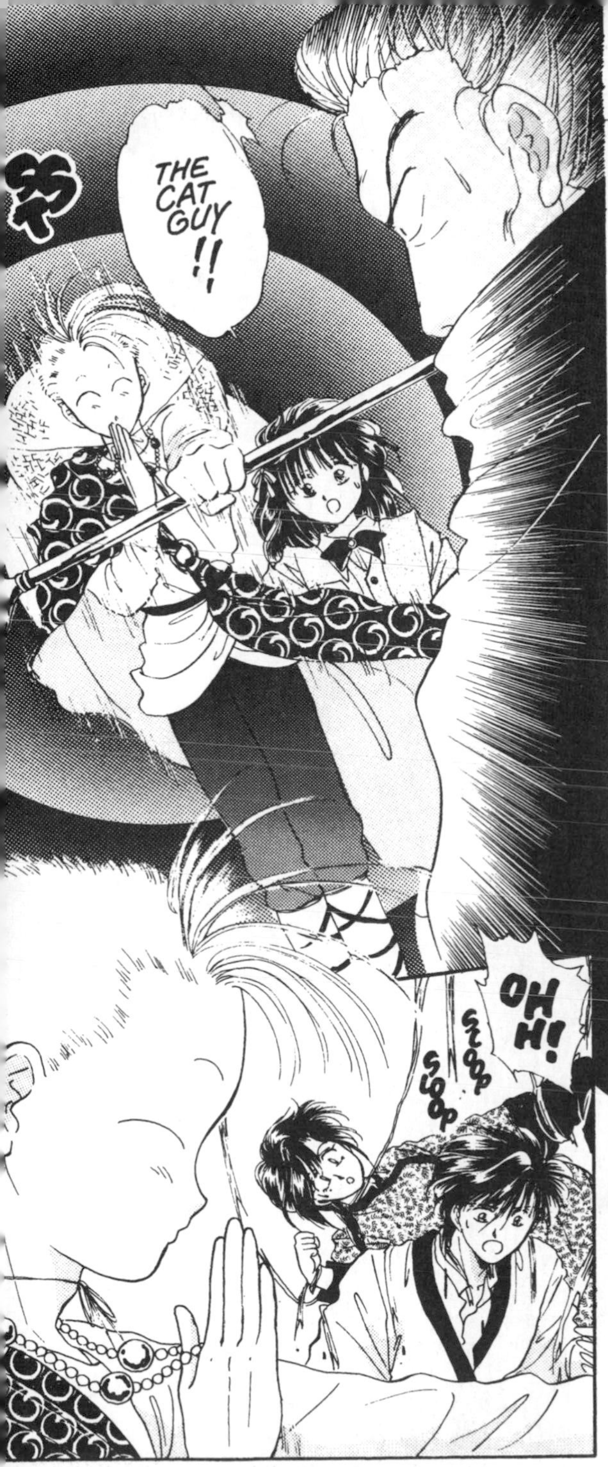
THE CAT GUY !!
OH H!
SLOOP
SLOOP

Disciple

I mentioned before how I've been reading your fan mail, and I'm surprised at the huge number of questions. You're all so concerned about the remaining warriors in the constellations of Suzaku. Some of you have even sent me illustrations and suggestions for the rest of the warriors. But to tell the truth, I decided on all seven characters before I even started drawing the comic. So I'll introduce them one by one the same way I envisioned them. I find it fascinating how all the characters get their own fans. The Tamahome fans don't like Hotohori, and the Hotohori fans look down on Tamahome. (There are really very few who like both!) Nuriko's been gaining popularity. Keisuke, Miaka's brother, has a set of fans, too. Well they're all cute so I don't mind. All of my assistants rate their favorites differently. Sometimes they play "Who'd be the best voice actor for each character?" and everyone gets all worked up. Fans have suggested some in their letters, but most of them don't seem right to me. (Sorry!) That's not to say my ideas are any better. We had a dramatic section in "Toy Box '93" so I was allowed to choose the actors for Miaka and Tamahome (but only them). I talked it over with my assistants then made my decision. Give it a listen and see what you think. I like voices that are mature and masculine (and a little erotic).

What else? Oh, yes, I heard that all the merchandise at the Animate store sold out! ♡♡ And we got a lot of complaints! I never got any myself!! The least they could do is save a sample for me!! Did you hear there was a bonus poster with every ¥2,000 purchase!? Gimme!! Calendars are posted in bookstores without my knowledge. (Supposedly, they only display July and August!) *And I never knew it had been printed!!* Speaking of calendars, I think you should know that I had to fight to get an original drawing into that calendar. It also took a lot of work to convince my editor that I should draw for the CD book, too.

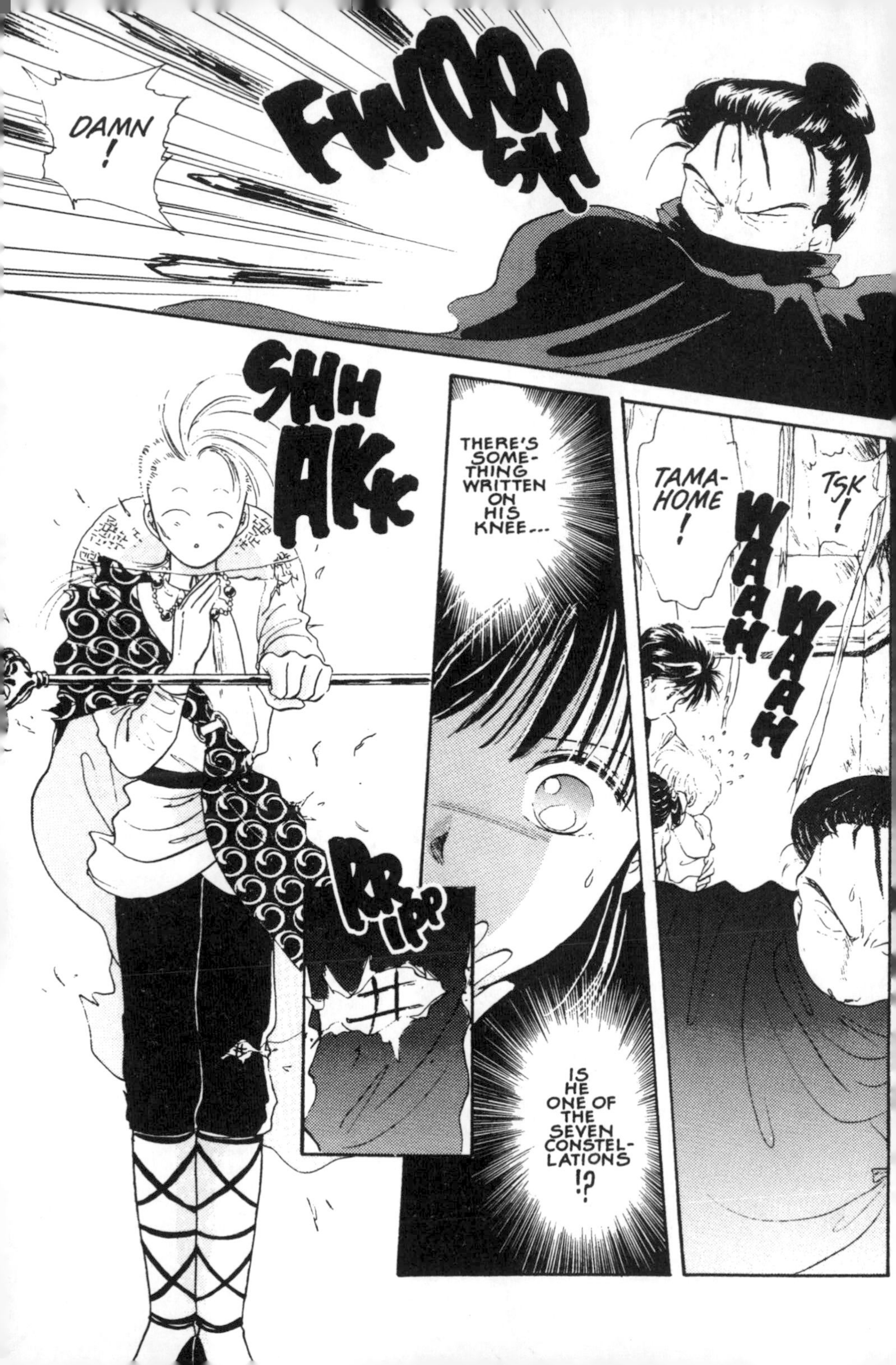
DAMN!
FWOOOSH
SHHAKK
RRIPP
THERE'S SOMETHING WRITTEN ON HIS KNEE...
IS HE ONE OF THE SEVEN CONSTELLATIONS!?
TAMAHOME!
WAAH
WAAAH
TSK!

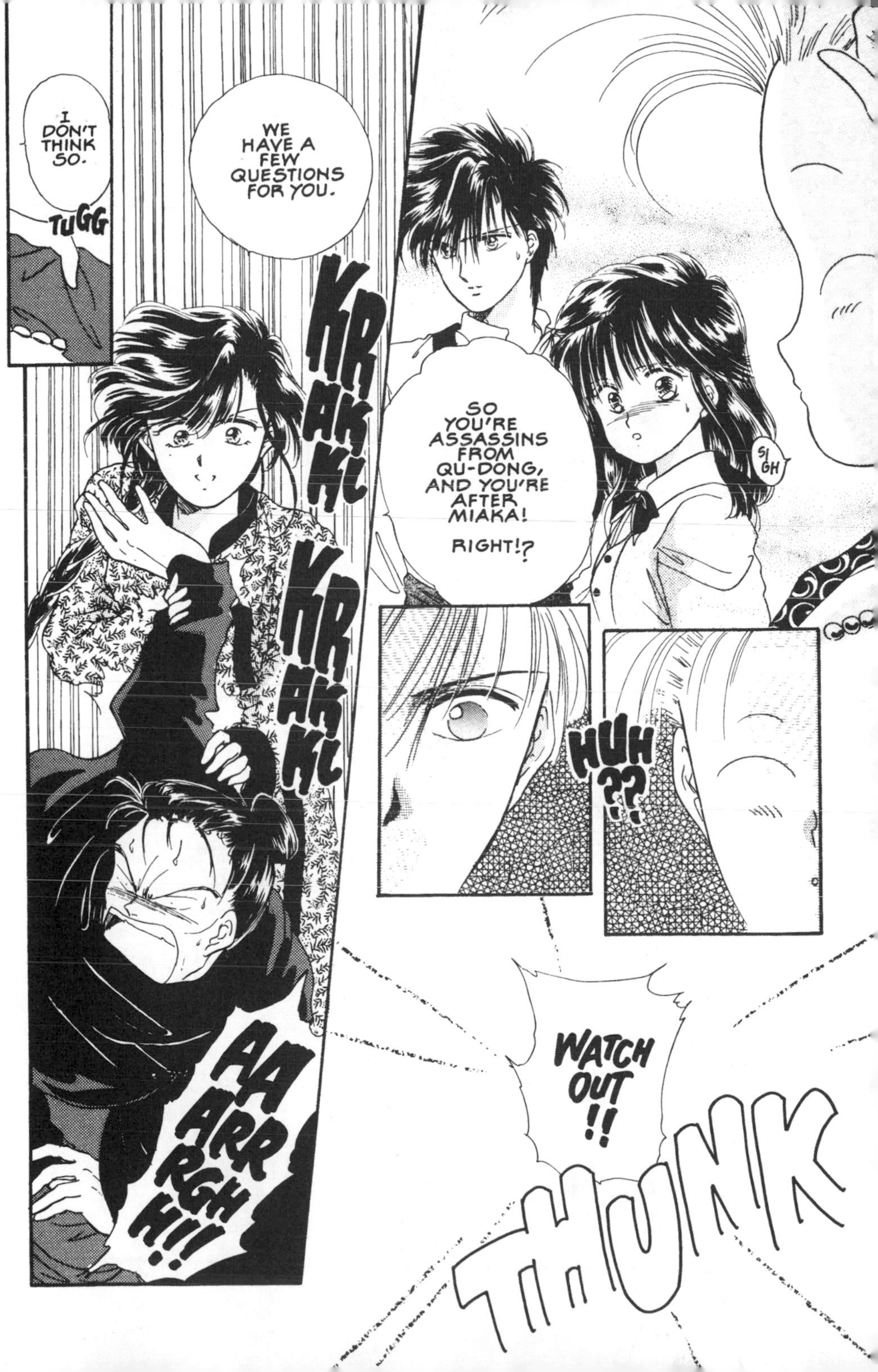
SO YOU'RE ASSASSINS FROM QU-DONG, AND YOU'RE AFTER MIAKA! RIGHT!?
SIGH
HUH ??
WATCH OUT !!
THUNK
WE HAVE A FEW QUESTIONS FOR YOU.
I DON'T THINK SO.
TUGG
KRAKKL
KRAKKL
AAARRRGHH!!

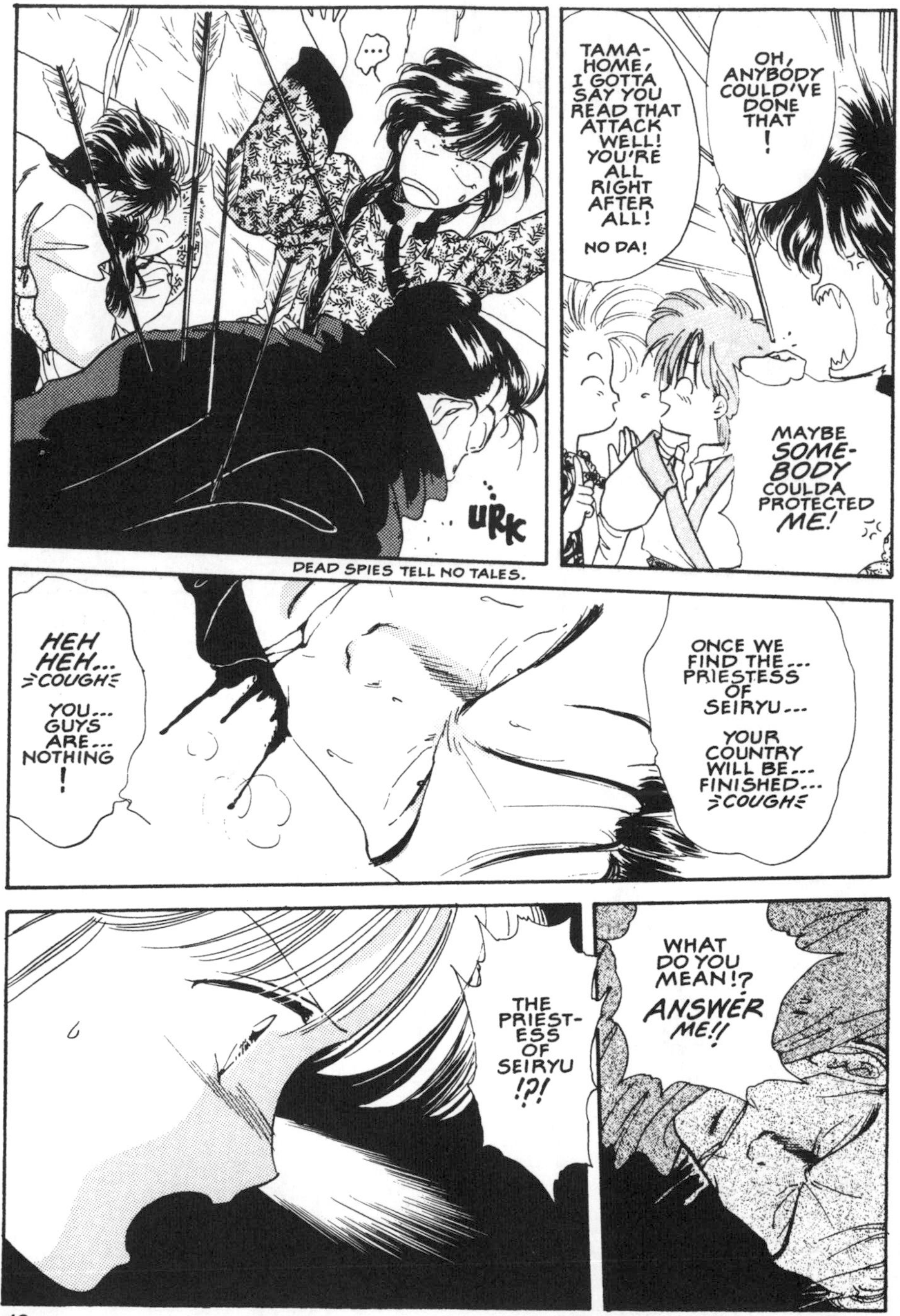
...
URK
DEAD SPIES TELL NO TALES.
TAMA-HOME, I GOTTA SAY YOU READ THAT ATTACK WELL! YOU'RE ALL RIGHT AFTER ALL!
NO DA!
OH, ANYBODY COULD'VE DONE THAT!
MAYBE SOMEBODY COULDA PROTECTED ME!
HEH HEH... *COUGH*
YOU... GUYS ARE... NOTHING!
ONCE WE FIND THE... PRIESTESS OF SEIRYU...
YOUR COUNTRY WILL BE... FINISHED... *COUGH*
THE PRIESTESS OF SEIRYU!?!
WHAT DO YOU MEAN!? ANSWER ME!!

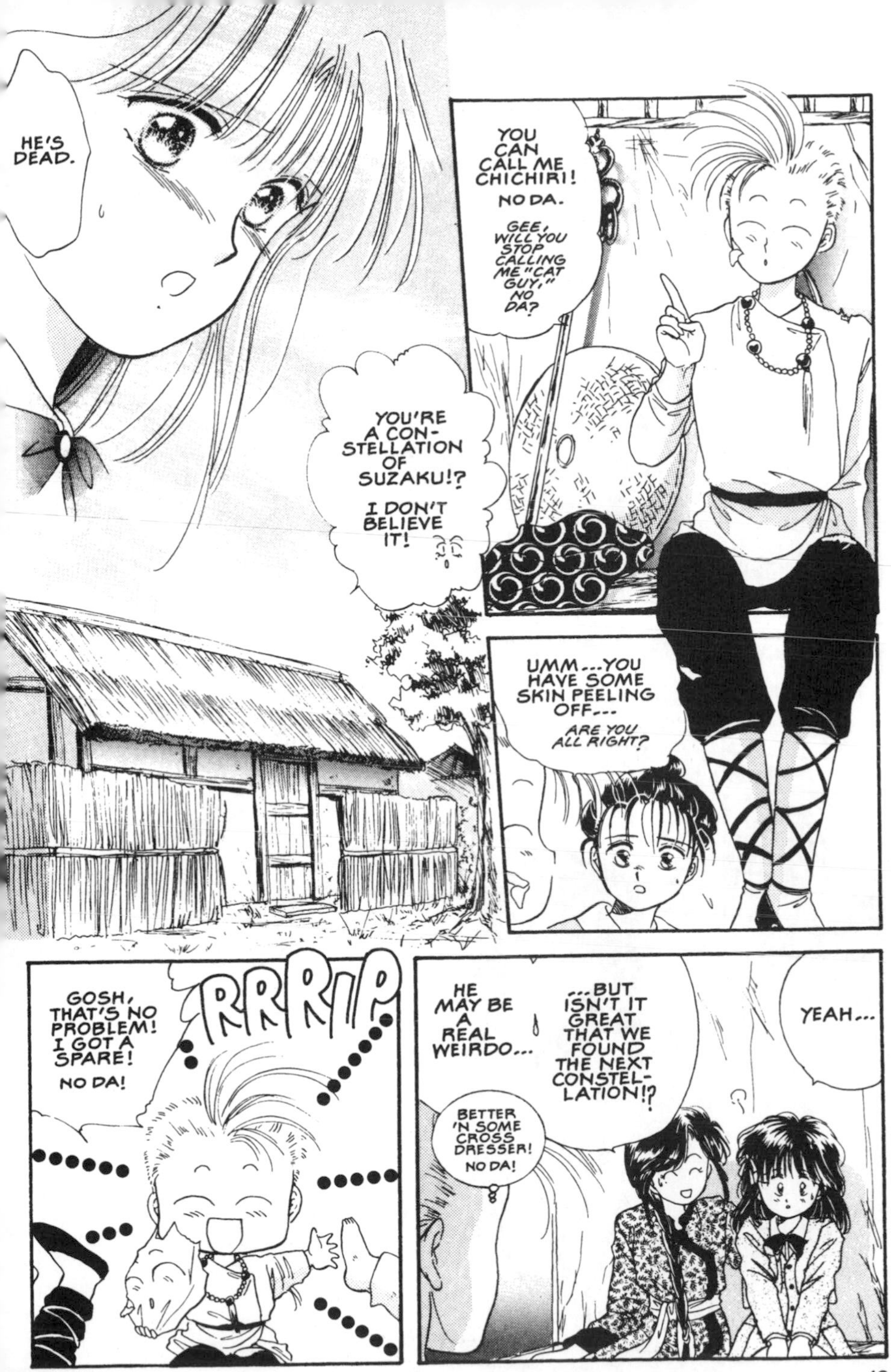
HE'S DEAD.
YOU CAN CALL ME CHICHIRI! NO DA.
GEE, WILL YOU STOP CALLING ME "CAT GUY," NO DA?
YOU'RE A CON-STELLATION OF SUZAKU!? I DON'T BELIEVE IT!
UMM...YOU HAVE SOME SKIN PEELING OFF...
ARE YOU ALL RIGHT?
GOSH, THAT'S NO PROBLEM! I GOT A SPARE! NO DA!
RRRIP
HE MAY BE A REAL WEIRDO...
...BUT ISN'T IT GREAT THAT WE FOUND THE NEXT CONSTEL-LATION!?
BETTER 'N SOME CROSS DRESSER! NO DA!
YEAH...

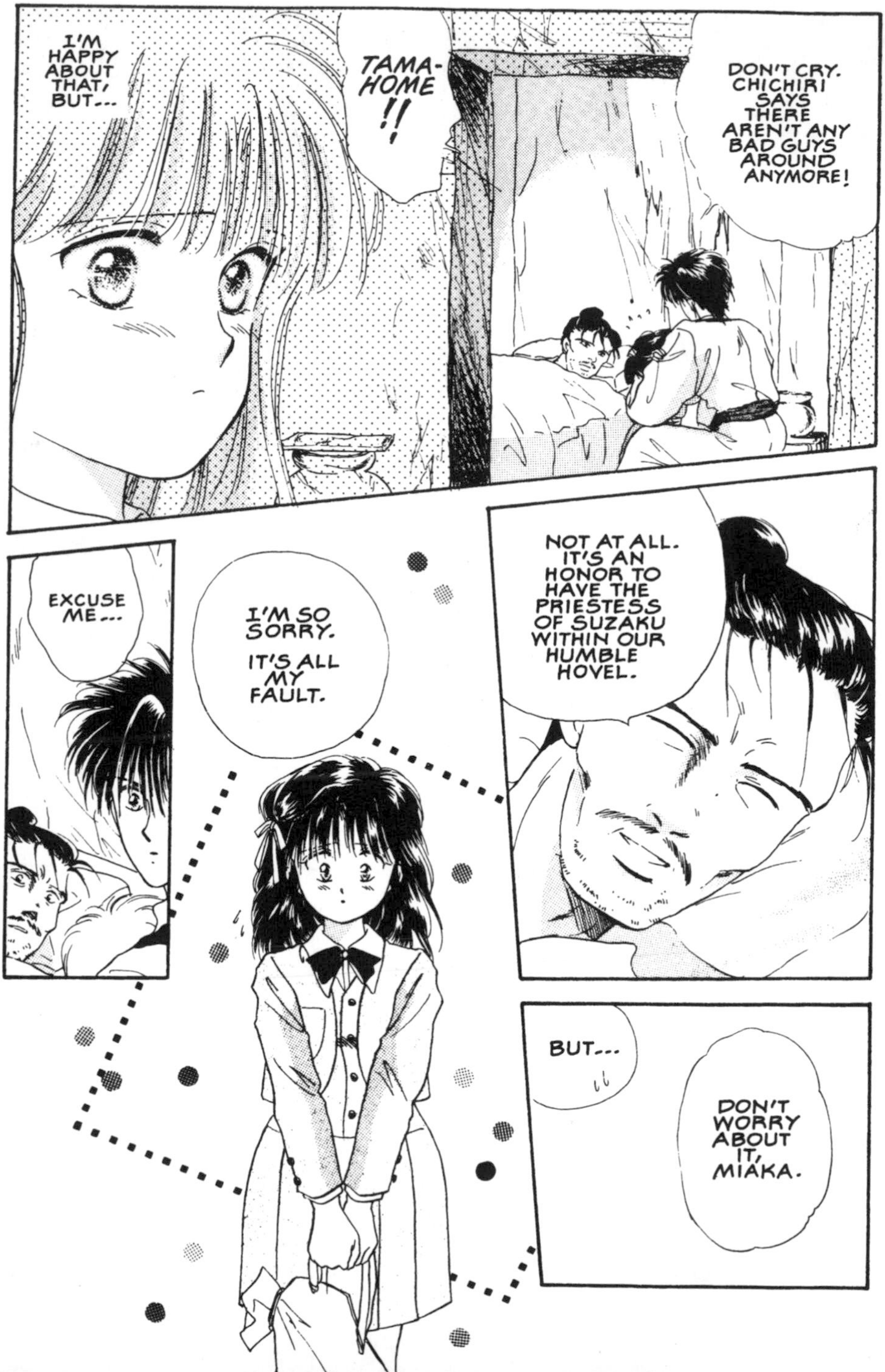
I'M HAPPY ABOUT THAT, BUT...
TAMA-HOME !!
DON'T CRY. CHICHIRI SAYS THERE AREN'T ANY BAD GUYS AROUND ANYMORE!
EXCUSE ME...
I'M SO SORRY.
IT'S ALL MY FAULT.
NOT AT ALL. IT'S AN HONOR TO HAVE THE PRIESTESS OF SUZAKU WITHIN OUR HUMBLE HOVEL.
BUT...
DON'T WORRY ABOUT IT, MIAKA.

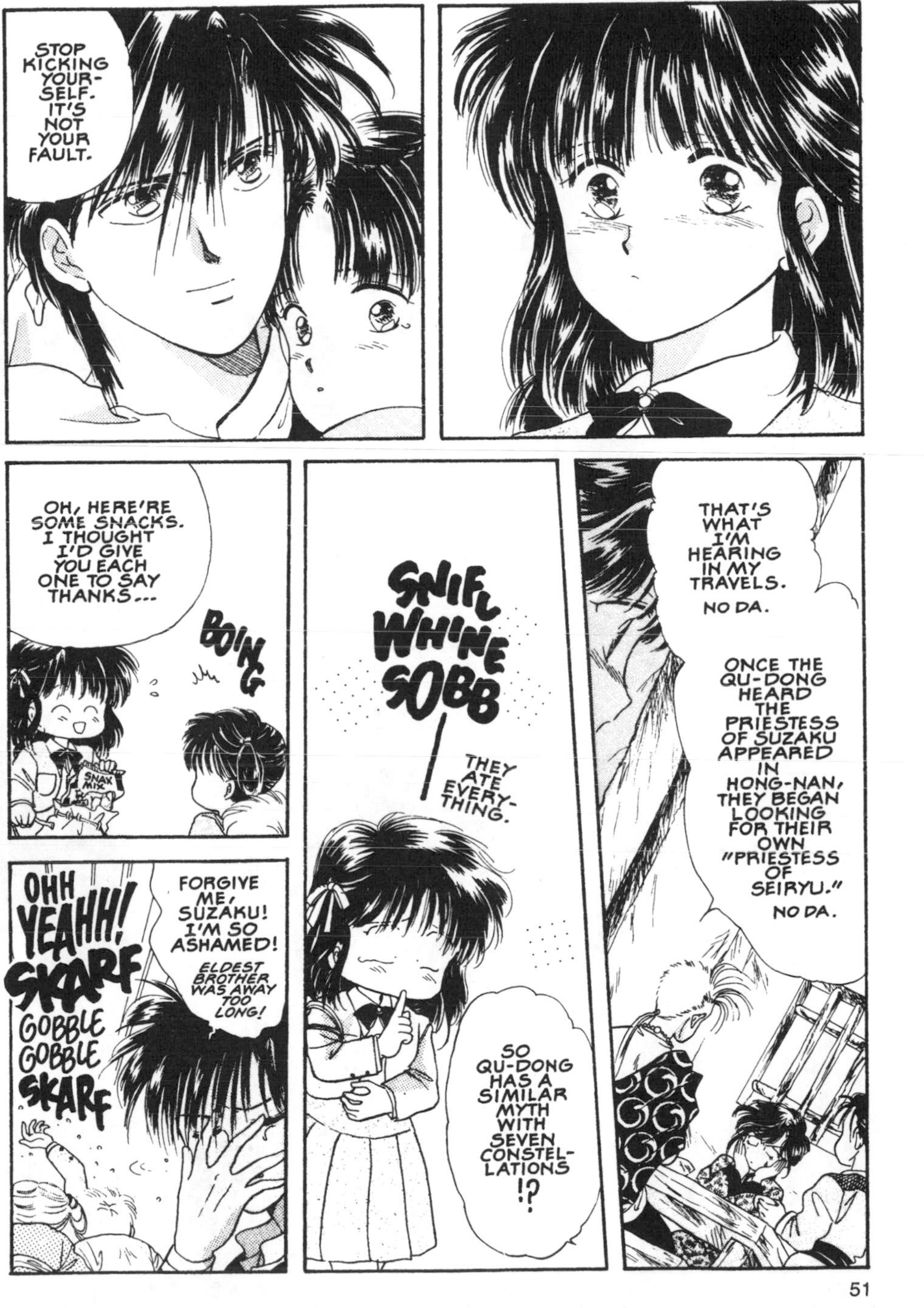
STOP KICKING YOURSELF. IT'S NOT YOUR FAULT.
OH, HERE'RE SOME SNACKS. I THOUGHT I'D GIVE YOU EACH ONE TO SAY THANKS...
BOING
SNAX MIX
OHH YEAHH!
SKARF
GOBBLE GOBBLE
SKARF
FORGIVE ME, SUZAKU! I'M SO ASHAMED!
ELDEST BROTHER WAS AWAY TOO LONG!
SNIFL WHINE SOBB
THEY ATE EVERYTHING.
SO QU-DONG HAS A SIMILAR MYTH WITH SEVEN CONSTELLATIONS !?
THAT'S WHAT I'M HEARING IN MY TRAVELS. NO DA.
ONCE THE QU-DONG HEARD THE PRIESTESS OF SUZAKU APPEARED IN HONG-NAN, THEY BEGAN LOOKING FOR THEIR OWN "PRIESTESS OF SEIRYU." NO DA.

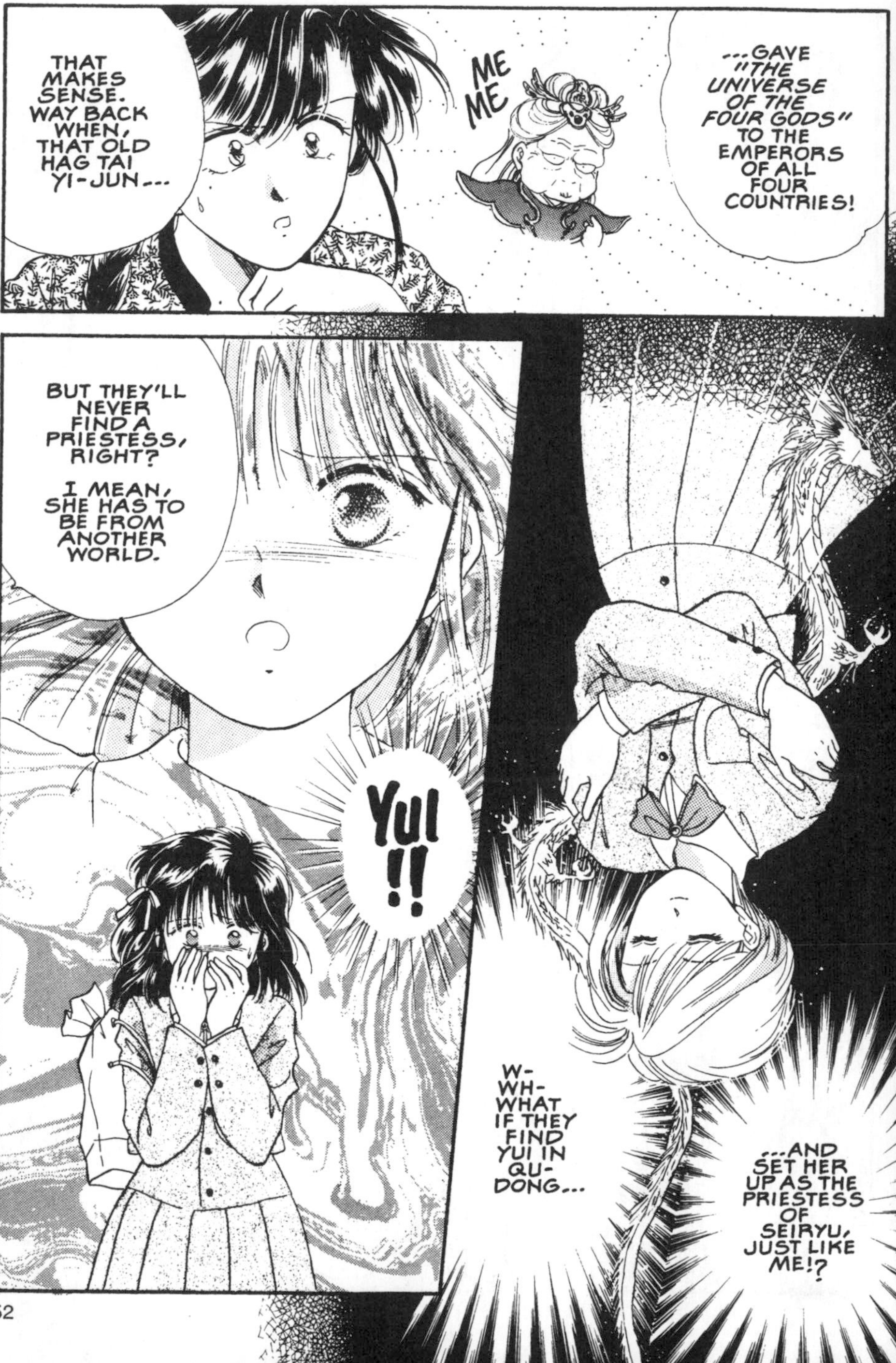
THAT MAKES SENSE. WAY BACK WHEN, THAT OLD HAG TAI YI-JUN...
ME ME
...GAVE "THE UNIVERSE OF THE FOUR GODS" TO THE EMPERORS OF ALL FOUR COUNTRIES!
BUT THEY'LL NEVER FIND A PRIESTESS, RIGHT?
I MEAN, SHE HAS TO BE FROM ANOTHER WORLD.
YUI!!
W-WH-WHAT IF THEY FIND YUI IN QU-DONG...
...AND SET HER UP AS THE PRIESTESS OF SEIRYU, JUST LIKE ME!?

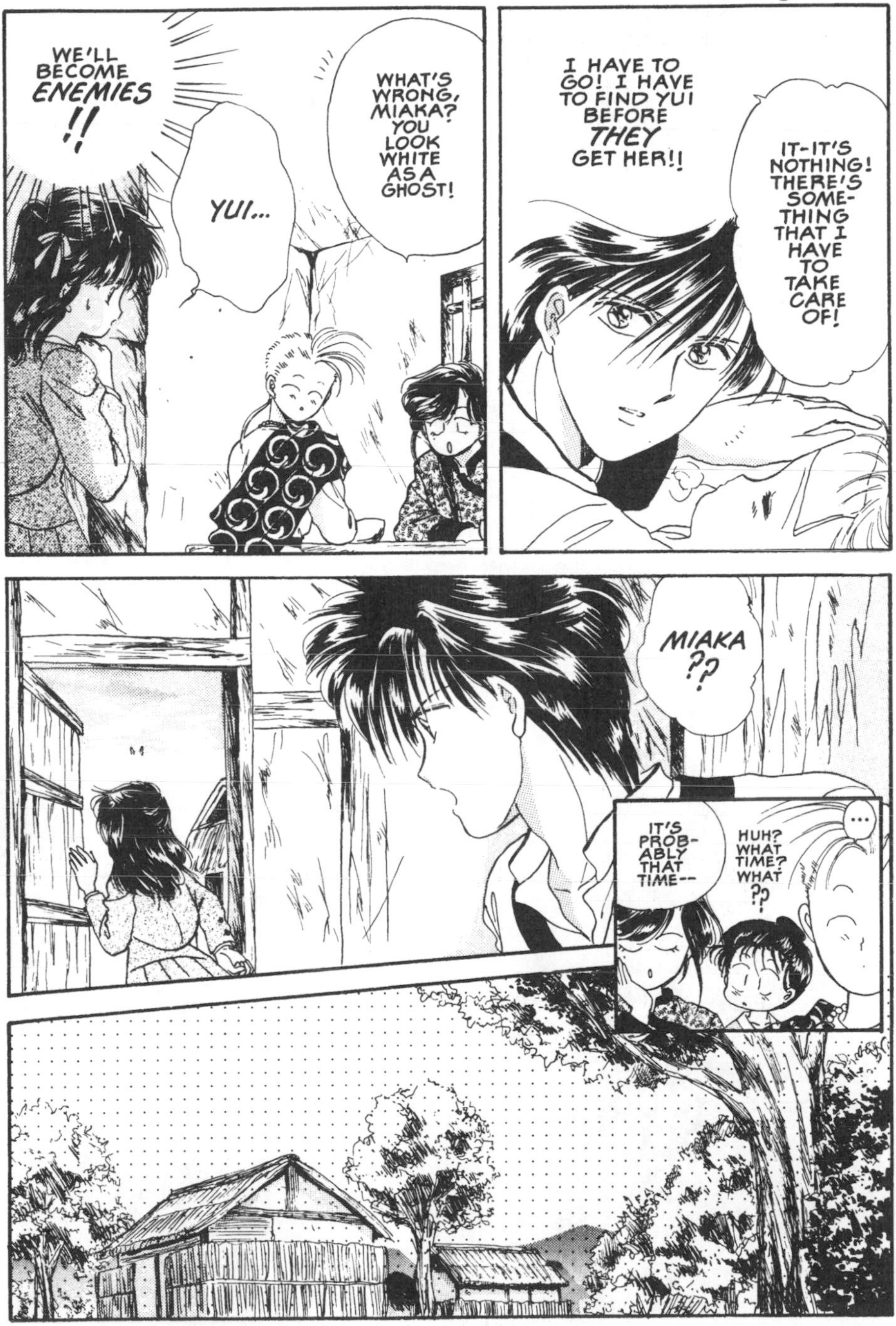
WE'LL BECOME ENEMIES!!
WHAT'S WRONG, MIAKA? YOU LOOK WHITE AS A GHOST!
YUI...
I HAVE TO GO! I HAVE TO FIND YUI BEFORE THEY GET HER!!
IT-IT'S NOTHING! THERE'S SOMETHING THAT I HAVE TO TAKE CARE OF!
MIAKA??
IT'S PROBABLY THAT TIME--
HUH? WHAT TIME? WHAT??
...

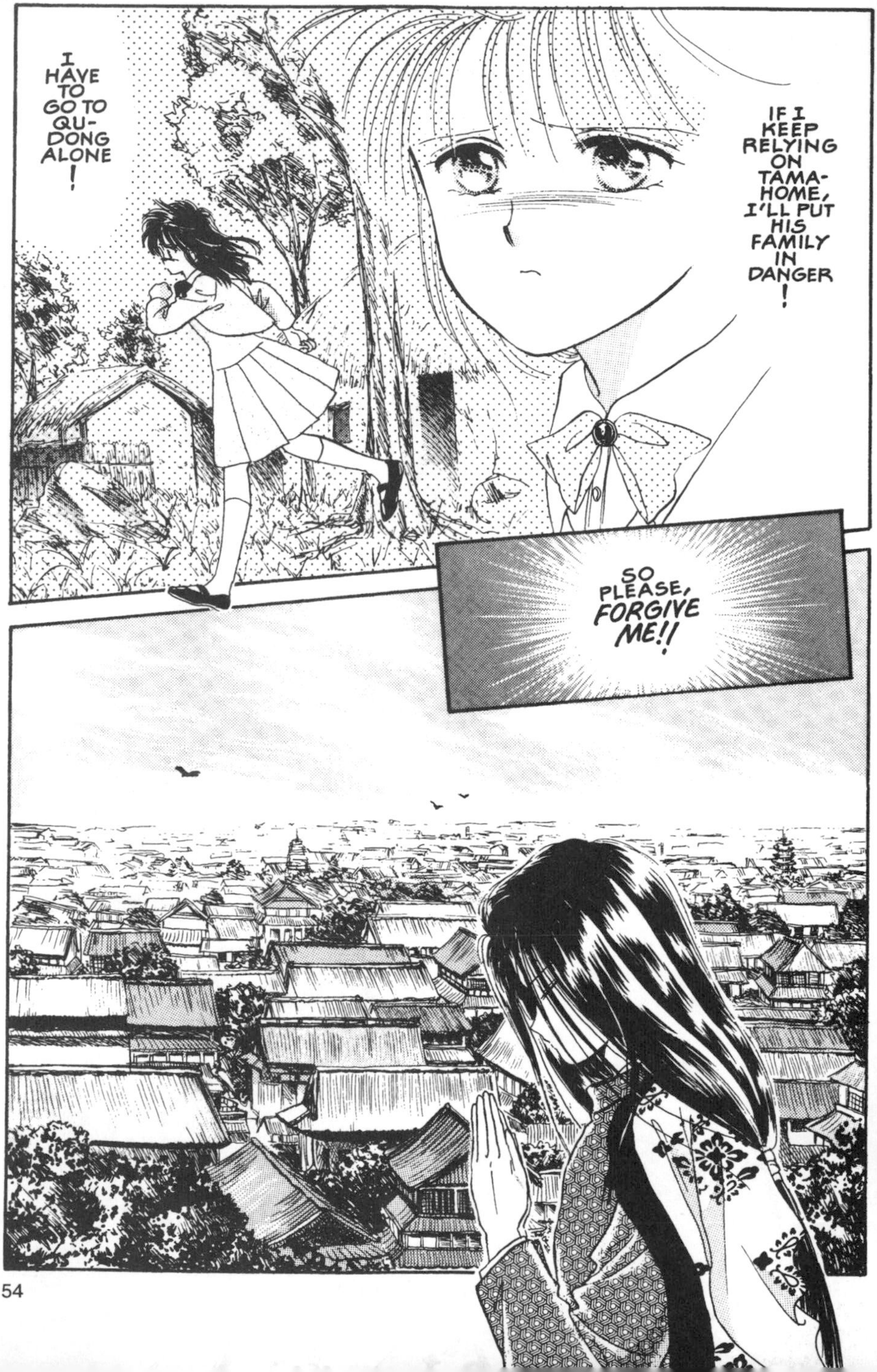
I HAVE TO GO TO QU-DONG ALONE!
IF I KEEP RELYING ON TAMA-HOME, I'LL PUT HIS FAMILY IN DANGER!
SO PLEASE, FORGIVE ME!!

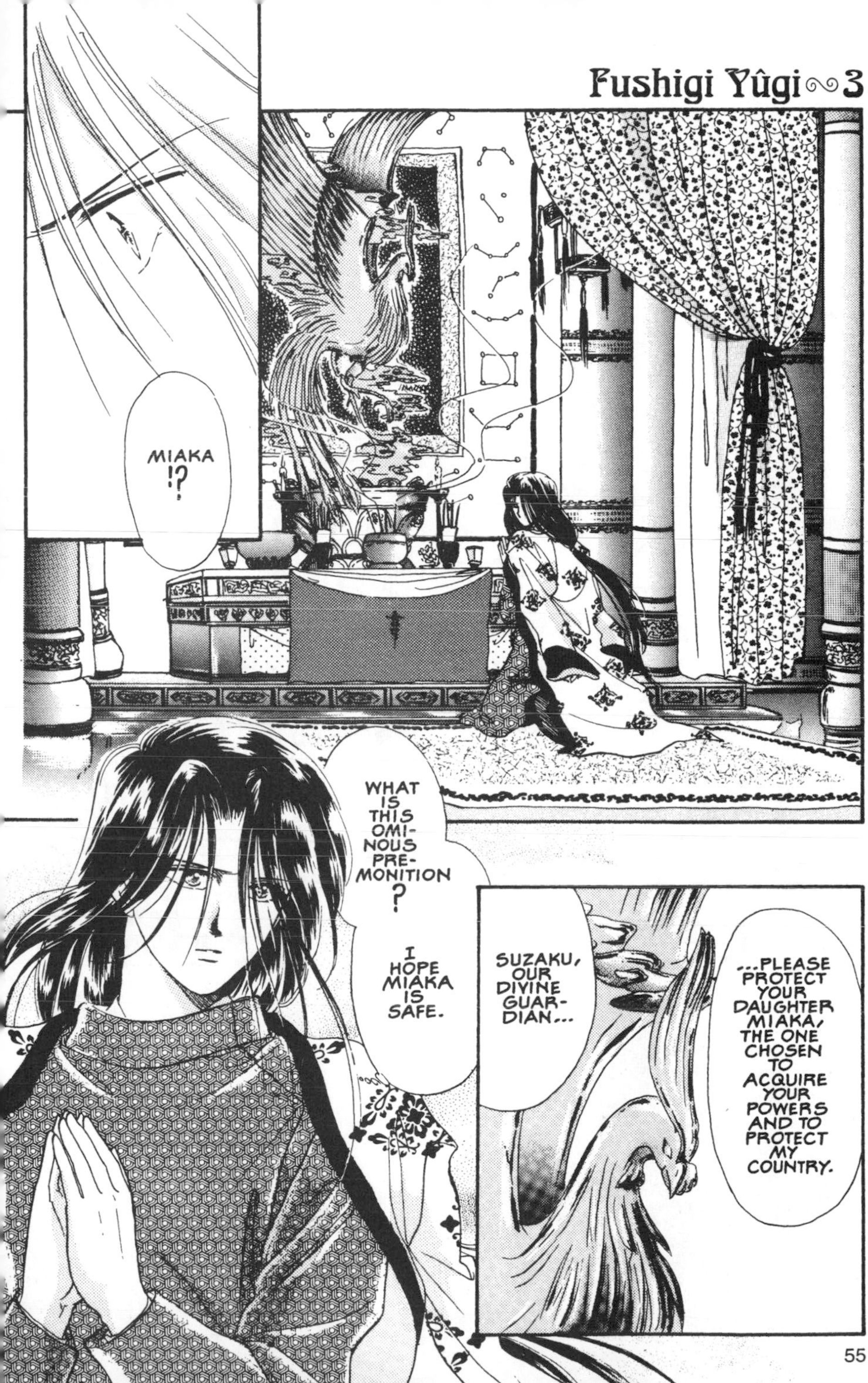
MIAKA !?
WHAT IS THIS OMINOUS PREMONITION?
I HOPE MIAKA IS SAFE.
SUZAKU, OUR DIVINE GUARDIAN...
...PLEASE PROTECT YOUR DAUGHTER MIAKA, THE ONE CHOSEN TO ACQUIRE YOUR POWERS AND TO PROTECT MY COUNTRY.

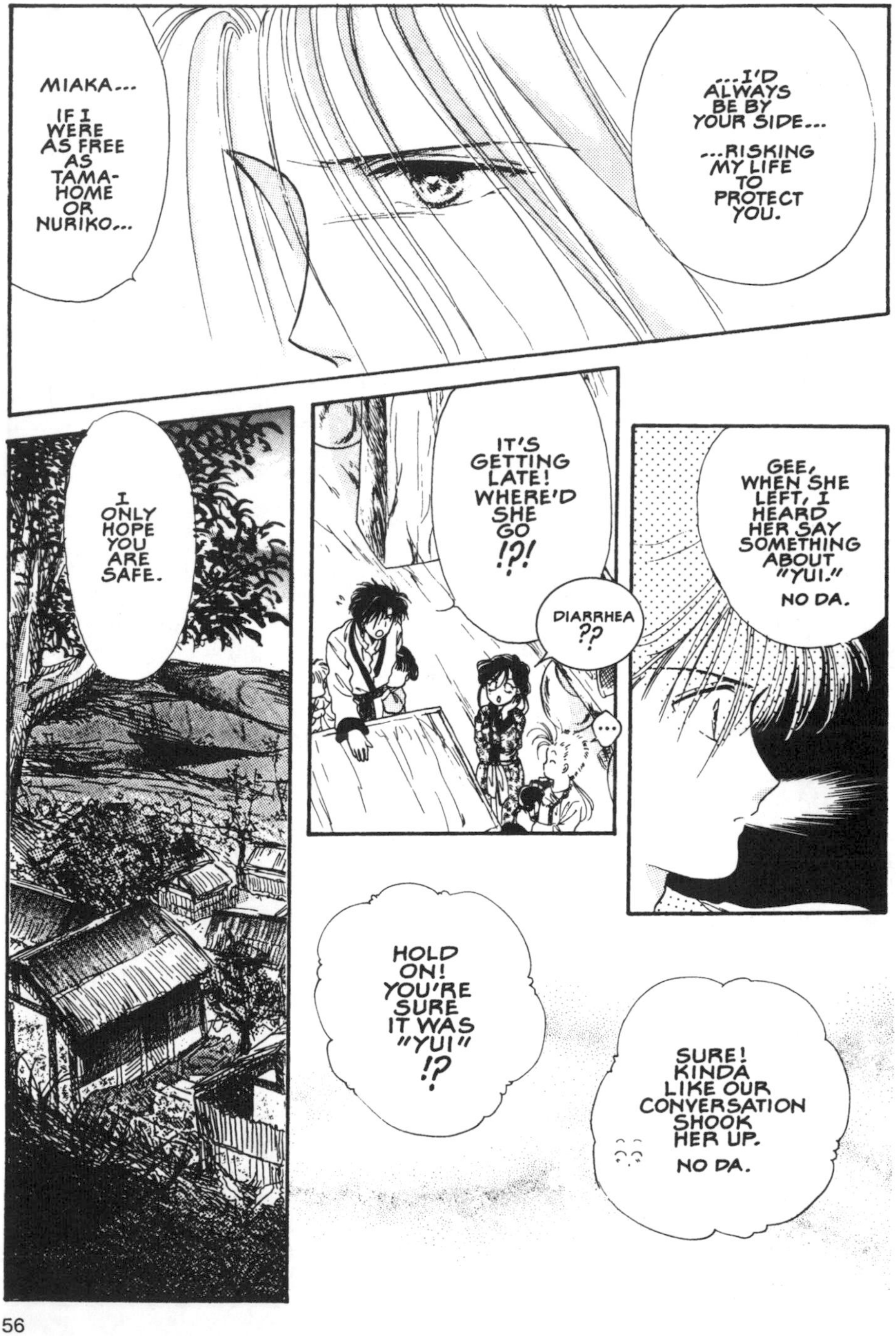
MIAKA...
IF I WERE AS FREE AS TAMA-HOME OR NURIKO...
...I'D ALWAYS BE BY YOUR SIDE...
...RISKING MY LIFE TO PROTECT YOU.
I ONLY HOPE YOU ARE SAFE.
IT'S GETTING LATE! WHERE'D SHE GO !?!
DIARRHEA ??
...
GEE, WHEN SHE LEFT, I HEARD HER SAY SOMETHING ABOUT "YUI." NO DA.
HOLD ON! YOU'RE SURE IT WAS "YUI" !?
SURE! KINDA LIKE OUR CONVERSATION SHOOK HER UP. NO DA.

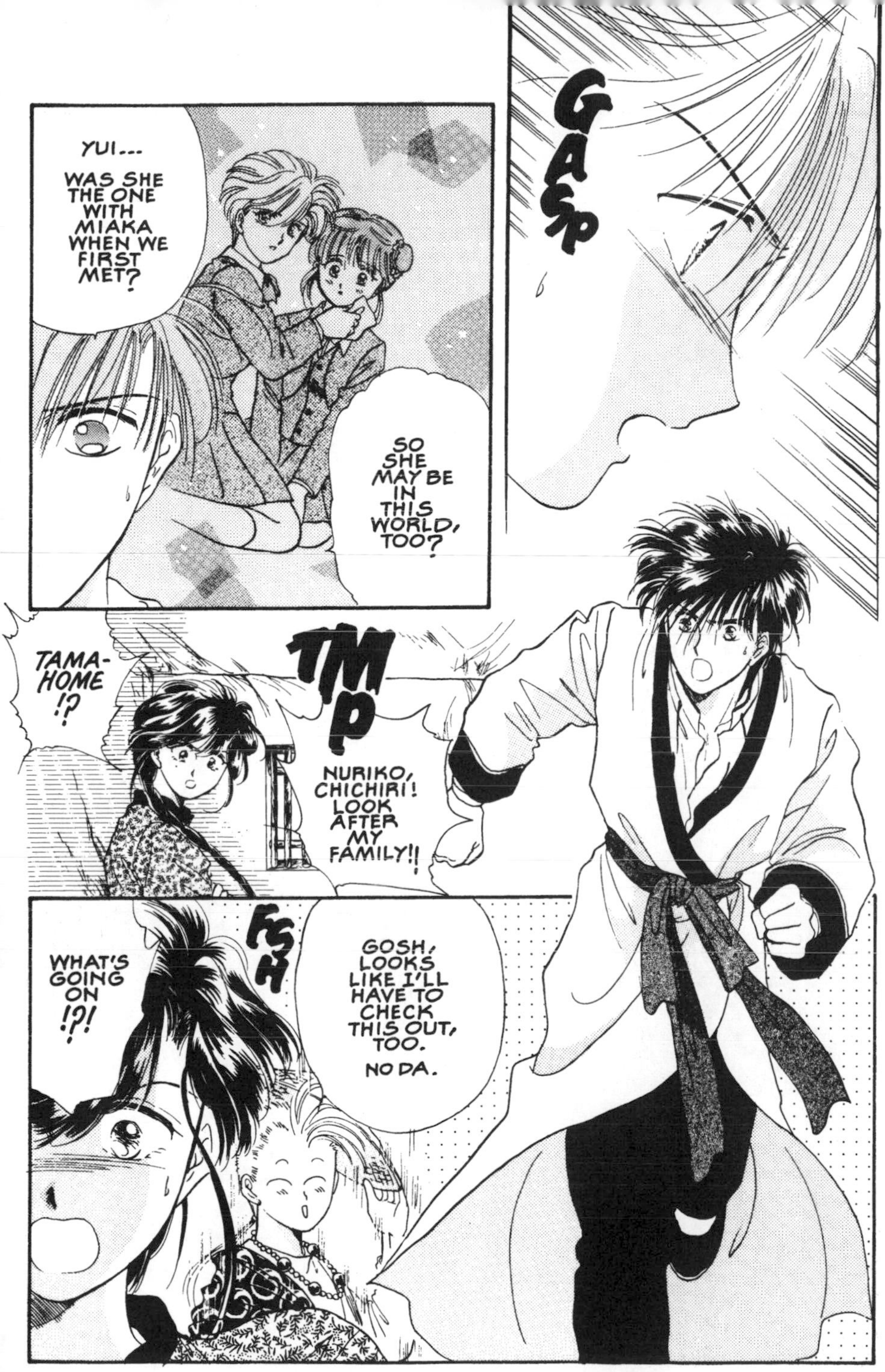
YUI...
WAS SHE THE ONE WITH MIAKA WHEN WE FIRST MET?
SO SHE MAY BE IN THIS WORLD, TOO?
GASP
TAMA-HOME !?
TMP
NURIKO, CHICHIRI! LOOK AFTER MY FAMILY!!
WHAT'S GOING ON !?!
FSH
GOSH, LOOKS LIKE I'LL HAVE TO CHECK THIS OUT, TOO.
NO DA.

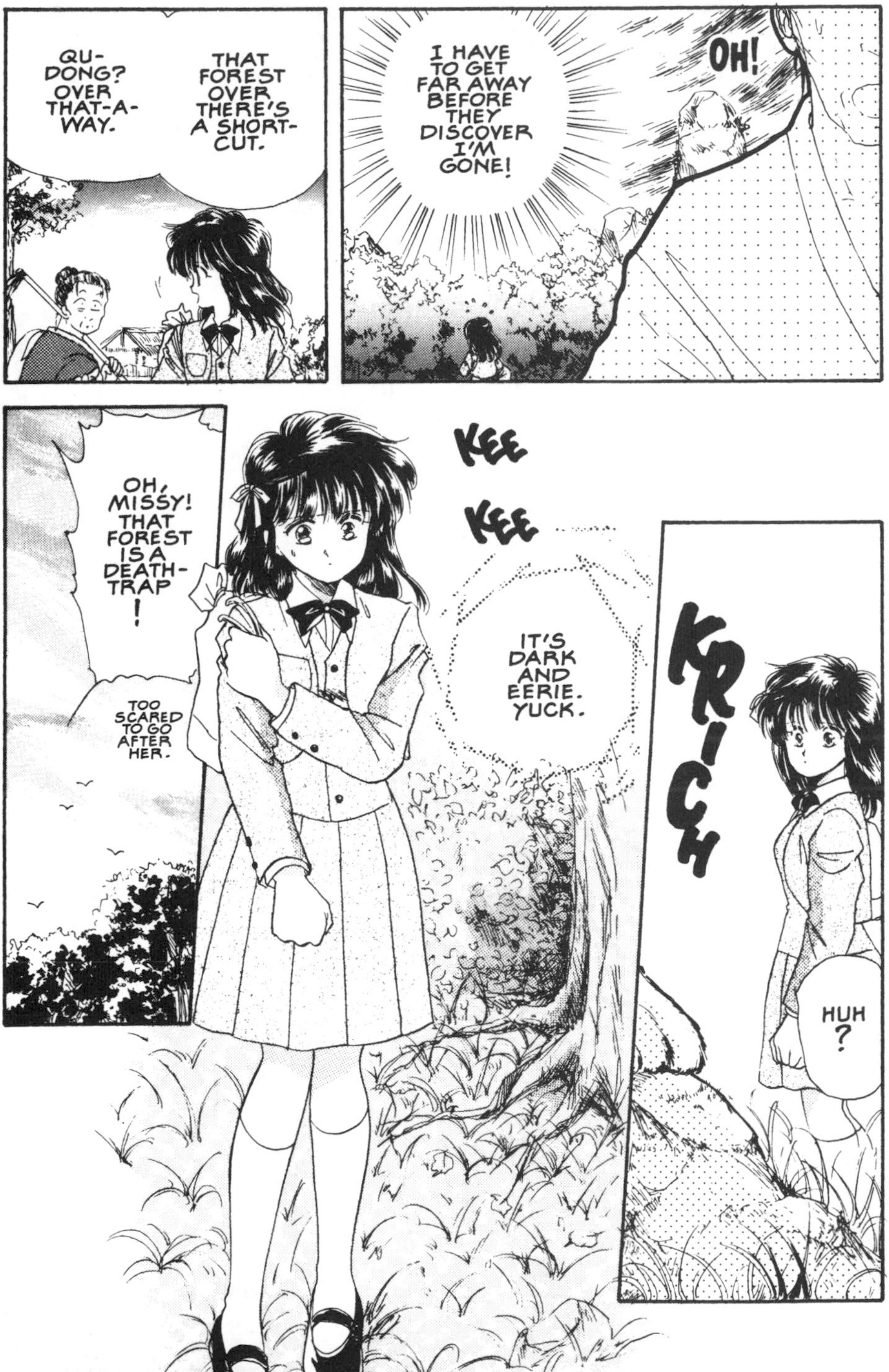
QU-DONG? OVER THAT-A-WAY.
THAT FOREST OVER THERE'S A SHORT-CUT.
I HAVE TO GET FAR AWAY BEFORE THEY DISCOVER I'M GONE!
OH!
OH, MISSY! THAT FOREST IS A DEATH-TRAP!
TOO SCARED TO GO AFTER HER.
KEE
KEE
IT'S DARK AND EERIE. YUCK.
KRICH
HUH?

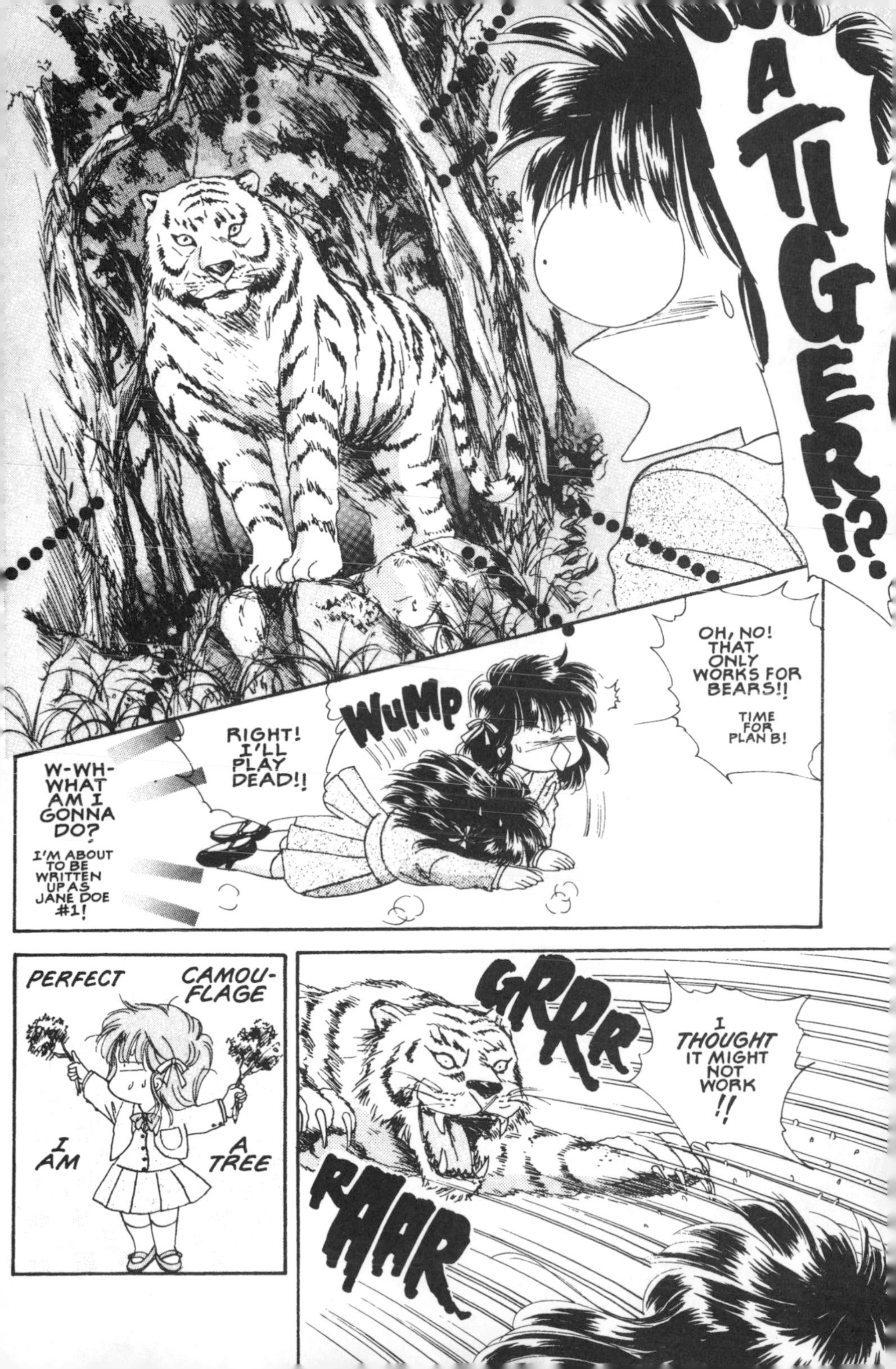

A TIGER!?
W-WH-WHAT AM I GONNA DO?
I'M ABOUT TO BE WRITTEN UP AS JANE DOE #1!
RIGHT! I'LL PLAY DEAD!!
WUMP
OH, NO! THAT ONLY WORKS FOR BEARS!!
TIME FOR PLAN B!
PERFECT
CAMOU-FLAGE
I AM
A TREE
GRRR
RAAR
I THOUGHT IT MIGHT NOT WORK !!

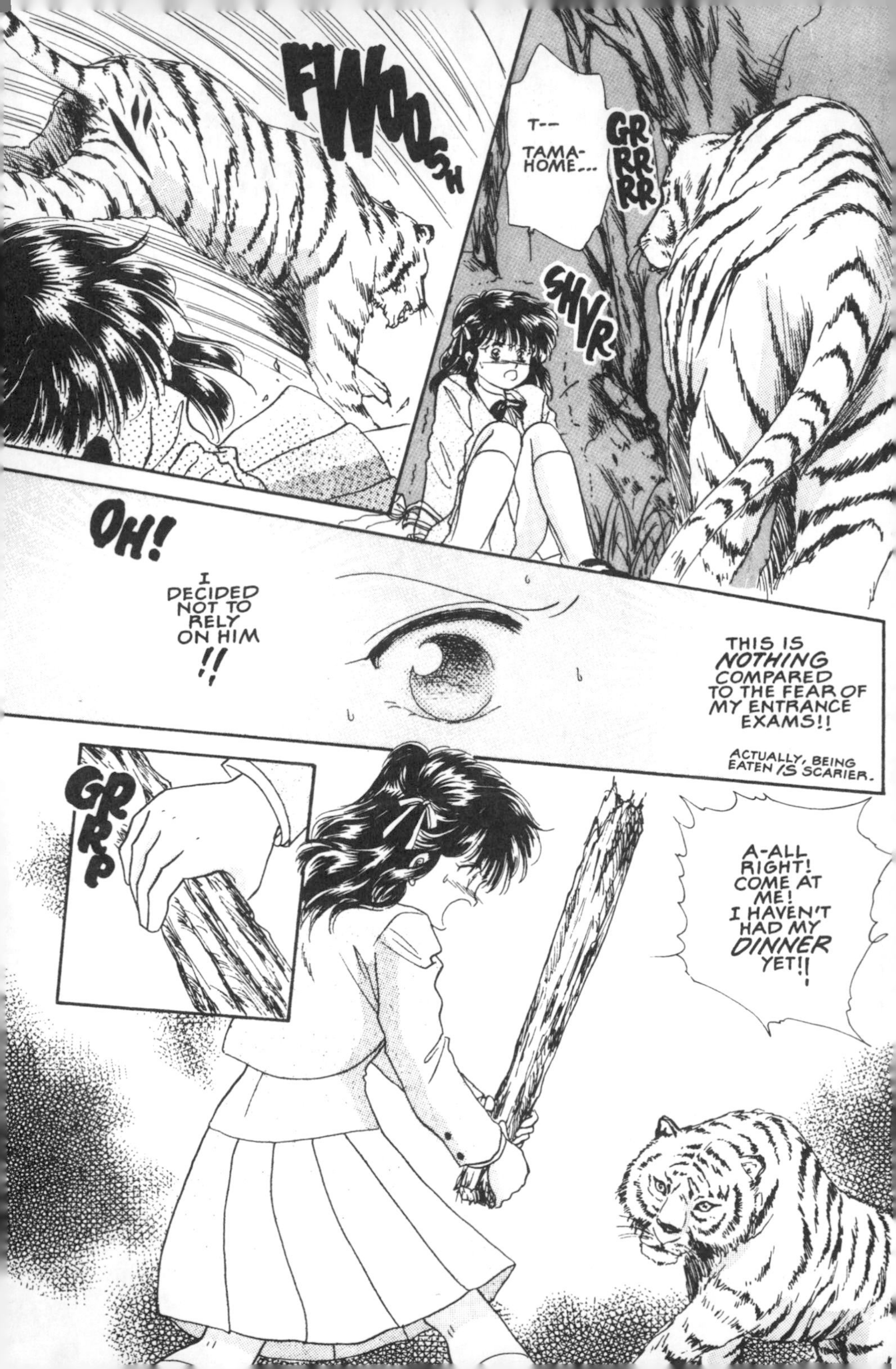
FWOOSH
T--
TAMA-HOME...
GRRRRR
SHVR
OH!
I DECIDED NOT TO RELY ON HIM !!
THIS IS NOTHING COMPARED TO THE FEAR OF MY ENTRANCE EXAMS!!
ACTUALLY, BEING EATEN IS SCARIER.
GRRR
A-ALL RIGHT! COME AT ME! I HAVEN'T HAD MY DINNER YET!!

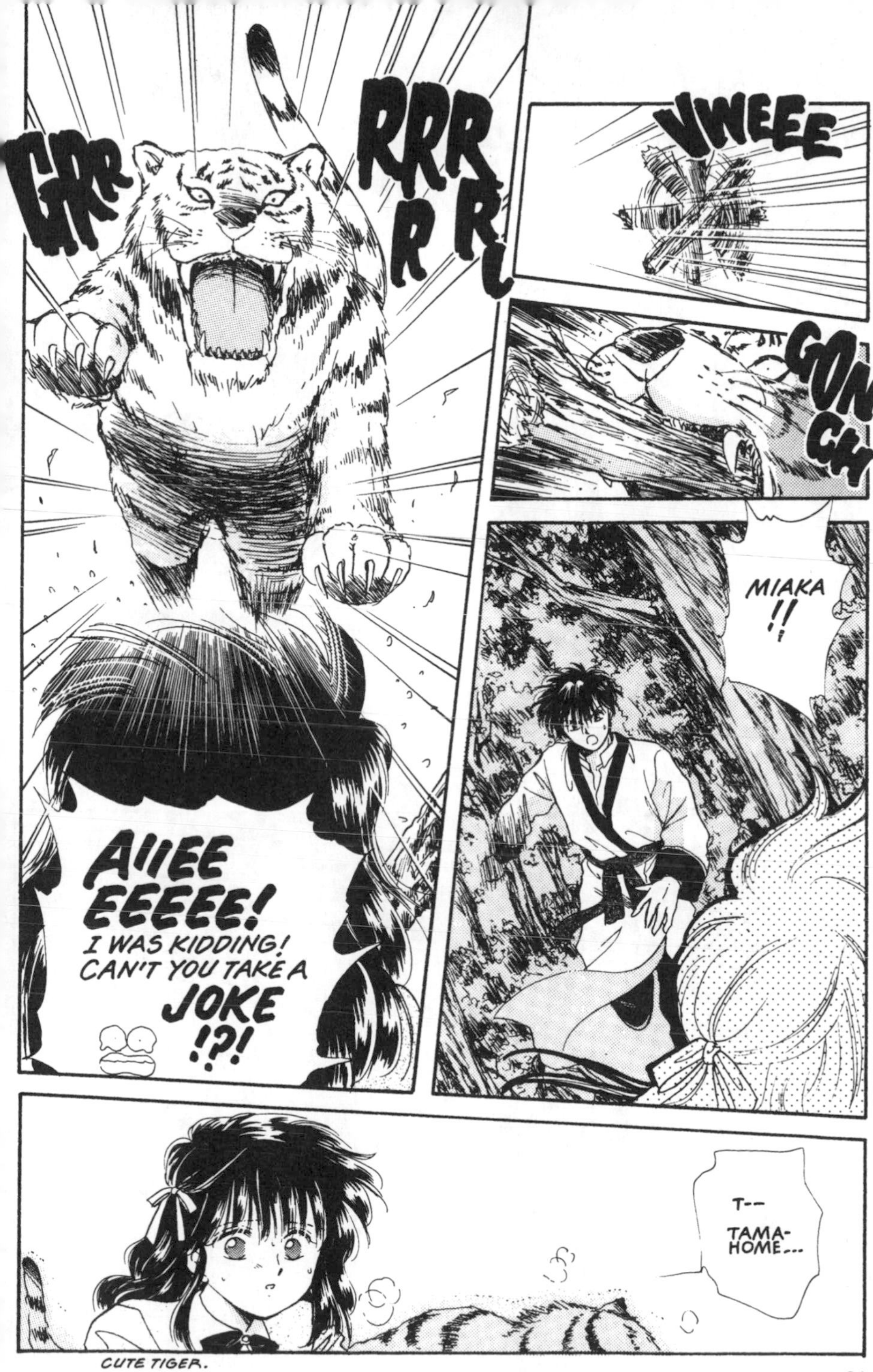
GRR
RRRRRL
AIIEE EEEEEE!
I WAS KIDDING! CAN'T YOU TAKE A JOKE !?!
VWEEE
GONCH
MIAKA !!
T-- TAMA-HOME...

CUTE TIGER.

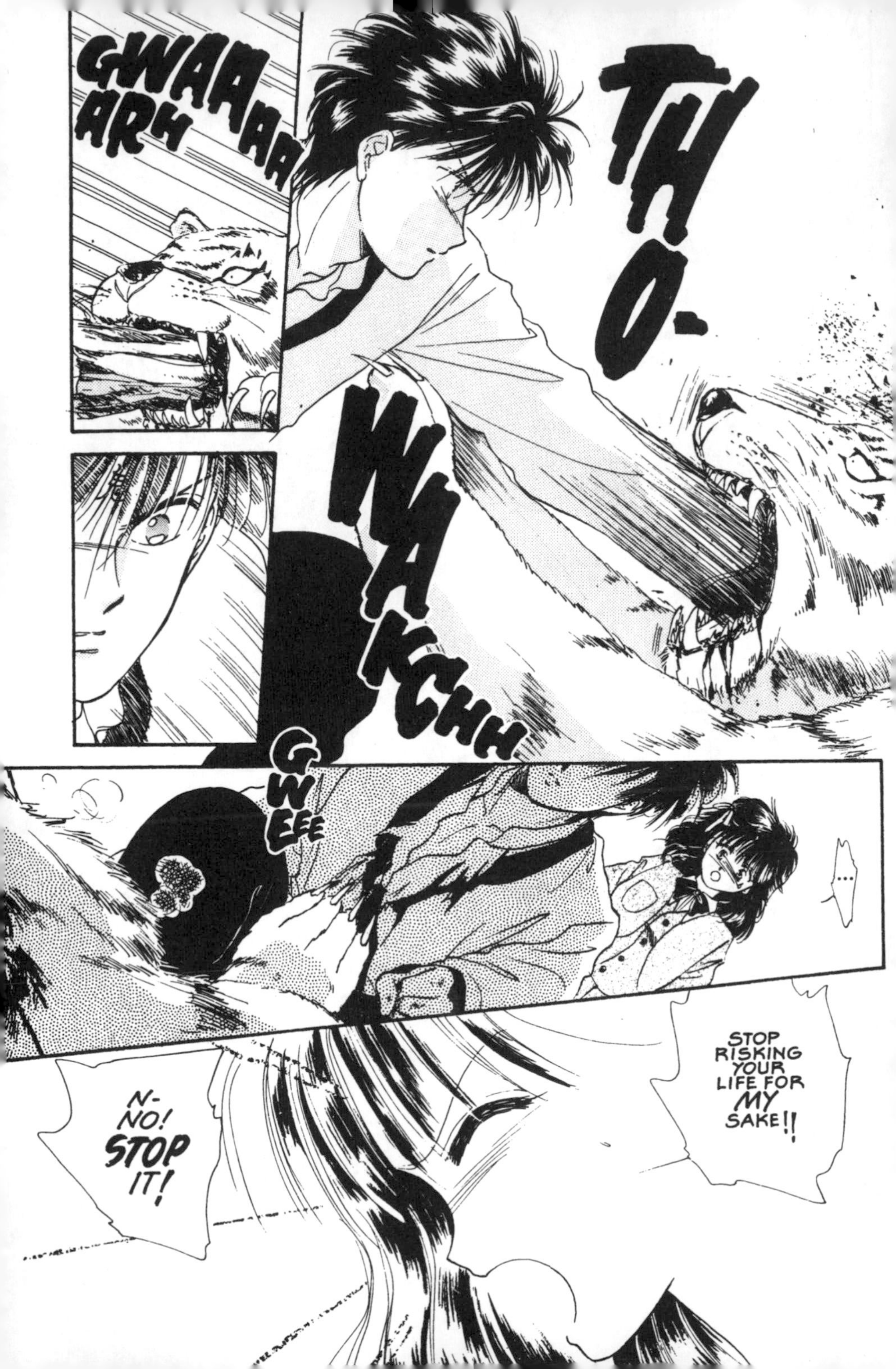
GWAAAAAARH
THO-
WHAKCHH
GWEEE
...
STOP RISKING YOUR LIFE FOR MY SAKE!!
N-NO! STOP IT!

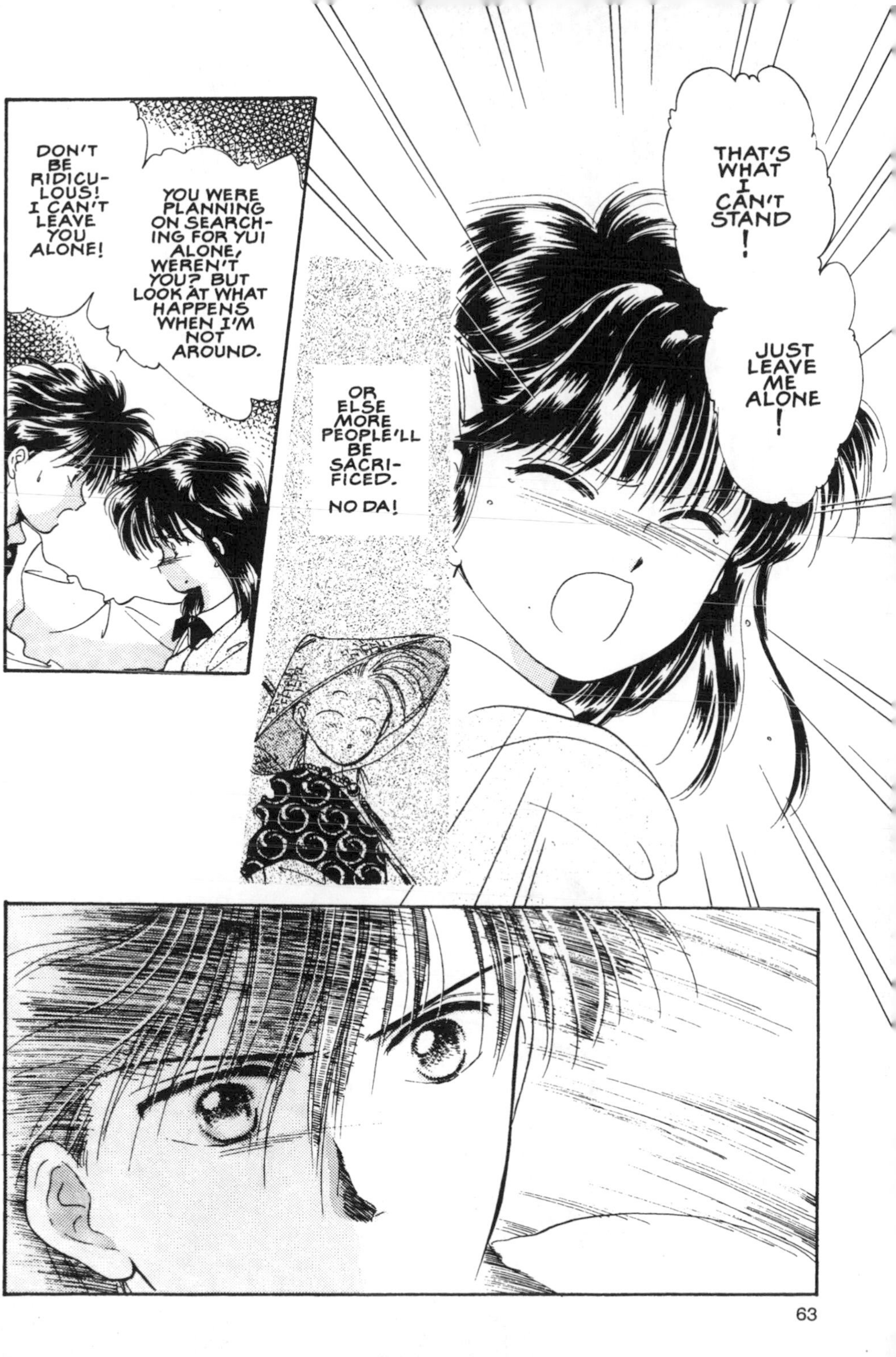
DON'T BE RIDICULOUS! I CAN'T LEAVE YOU ALONE!
YOU WERE PLANNING ON SEARCHING FOR YUI ALONE, WEREN'T YOU? BUT LOOK AT WHAT HAPPENS WHEN I'M NOT AROUND.
OR ELSE MORE PEOPLE'LL BE SACRIFICED.
NO DA!
THAT'S WHAT I CAN'T STAND!
JUST LEAVE ME ALONE!

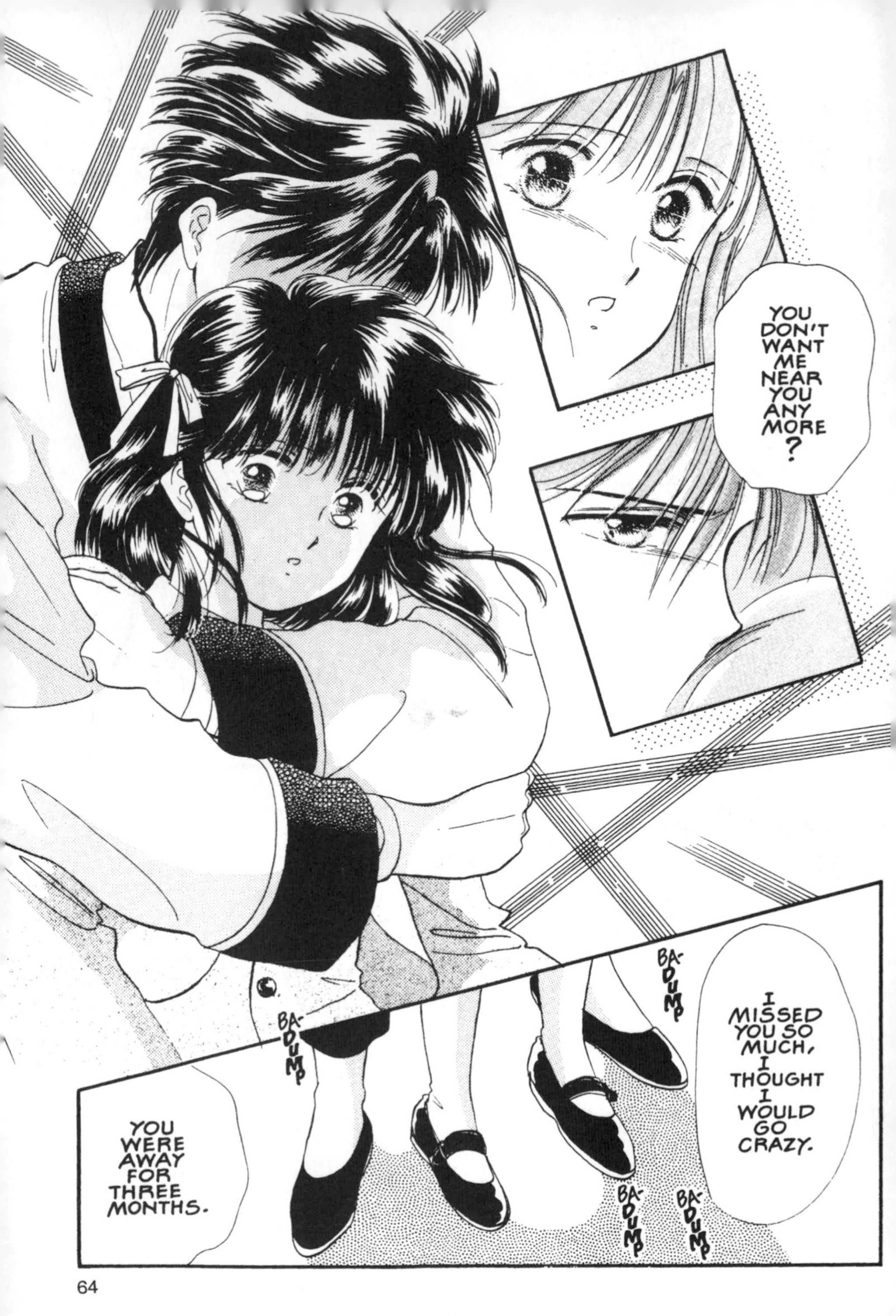
YOU DON'T WANT ME NEAR YOU ANY MORE?
BA-DUMP
BA-DUMP
YOU WERE AWAY FOR THREE MONTHS.
BA-DUMP
BA-DUMP
I MISSED YOU SO MUCH, I THOUGHT I WOULD GO CRAZY.

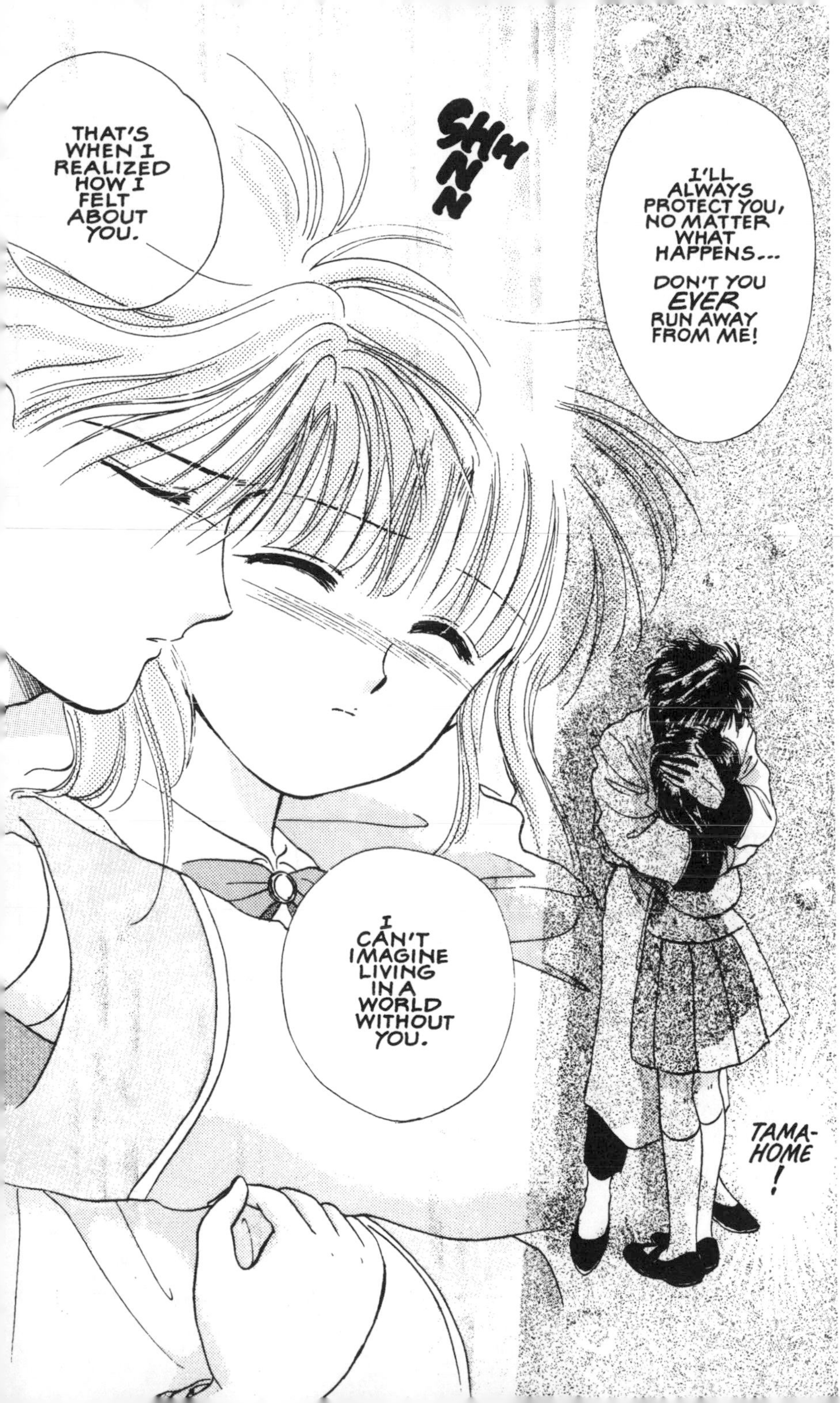
THAT'S WHEN I REALIZED HOW I FELT ABOUT YOU.
SHWNN
I CAN'T IMAGINE LIVING IN A WORLD WITHOUT YOU.
I'LL ALWAYS PROTECT YOU, NO MATTER WHAT HAPPENS...
DON'T YOU EVER RUN AWAY FROM ME!
TAMA-HOME!

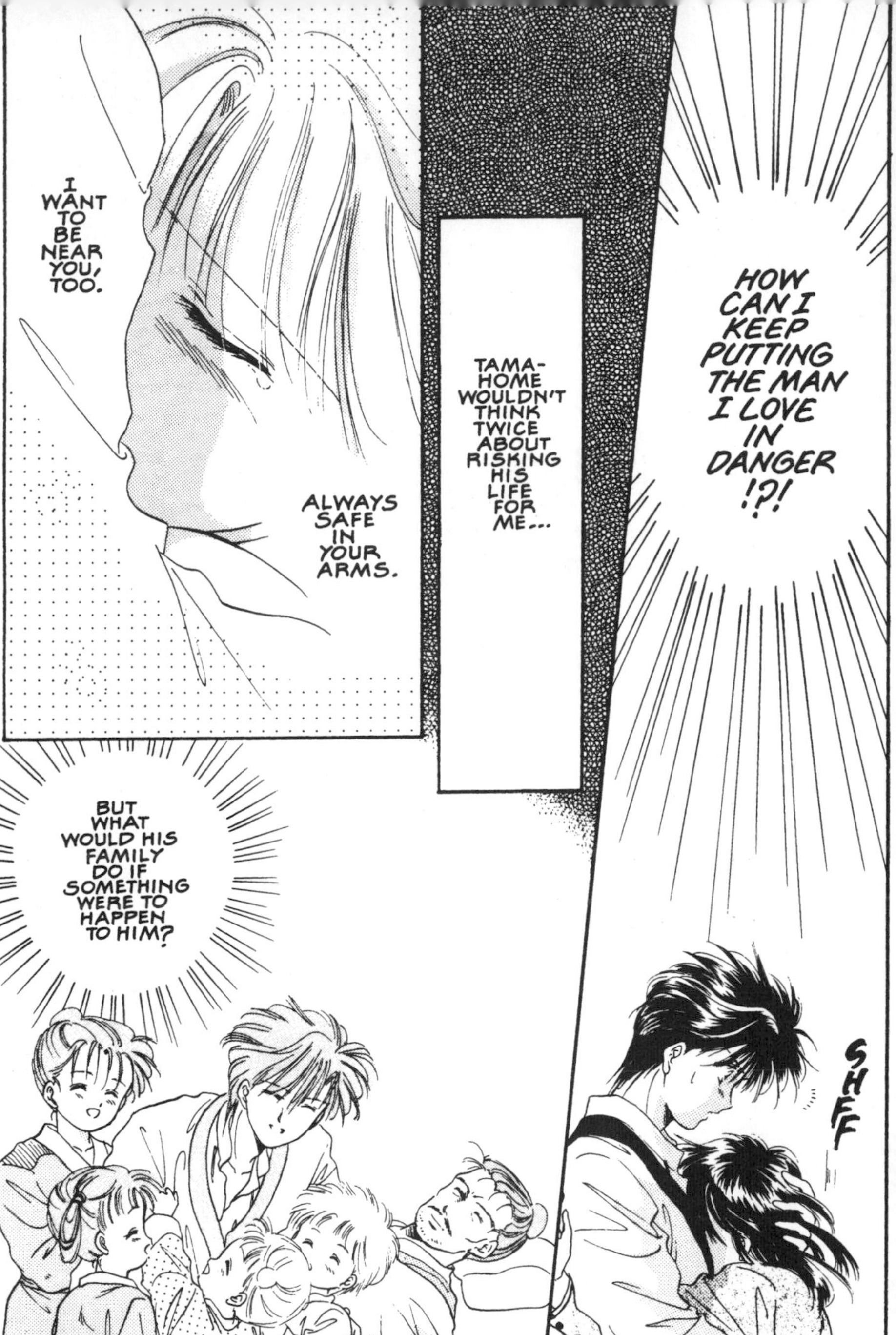
I WANT TO BE NEAR YOU, TOO.
ALWAYS SAFE IN YOUR ARMS.
TAMA-HOME WOULDN'T THINK TWICE ABOUT RISKING HIS LIFE FOR ME...
BUT WHAT WOULD HIS FAMILY DO IF SOMETHING WERE TO HAPPEN TO HIM?
HOW CAN I KEEP PUTTING THE MAN I LOVE IN DANGER!?!
SHFF

WHAT'S WRONG, MIAKA !?!

I-- I CAN'T RUN AWAY... I CAN'T EVEN *MOVE*, I'M SO HUNGRY!

SO HUNGRY I'M MAKING MYSELF SICK!

WA WA WA WA WA WA WA WA WA!

I WON'T GO ANYWHERE. THIS PLACE REALLY IS SCARY.

YOU MEAN IT?

YES! BUT I NEED YOU TO DO ME A FAVOR! THERE'S A BAG OF CANDY IN NURIKO'S SADDLEBAGS! I COULD REALLY USE IT.

ALL RIGHT, I'LL GO GET IT. BUT YOU BETTER BE *RIGHT HERE* WAITING!

BWAAA

I'LL WAIT HERE FOR YOU!

YOU KNOW I'VE GOT A SOFT SPOT FOR FOOD!

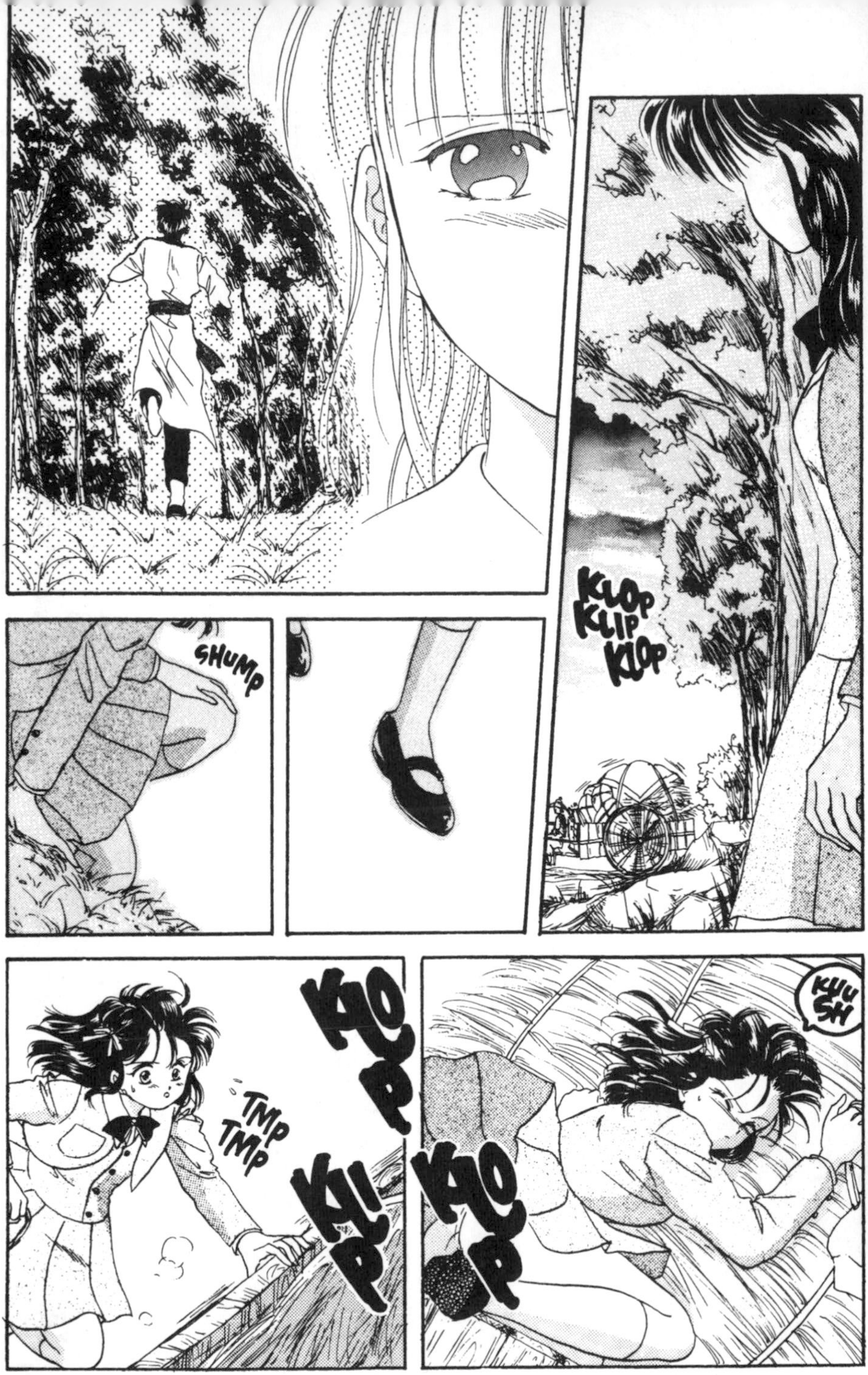
SHUMP
KLOP KLIP KLOP
TMP TMP
KLOP
KLIP
KLOP
KUUSH

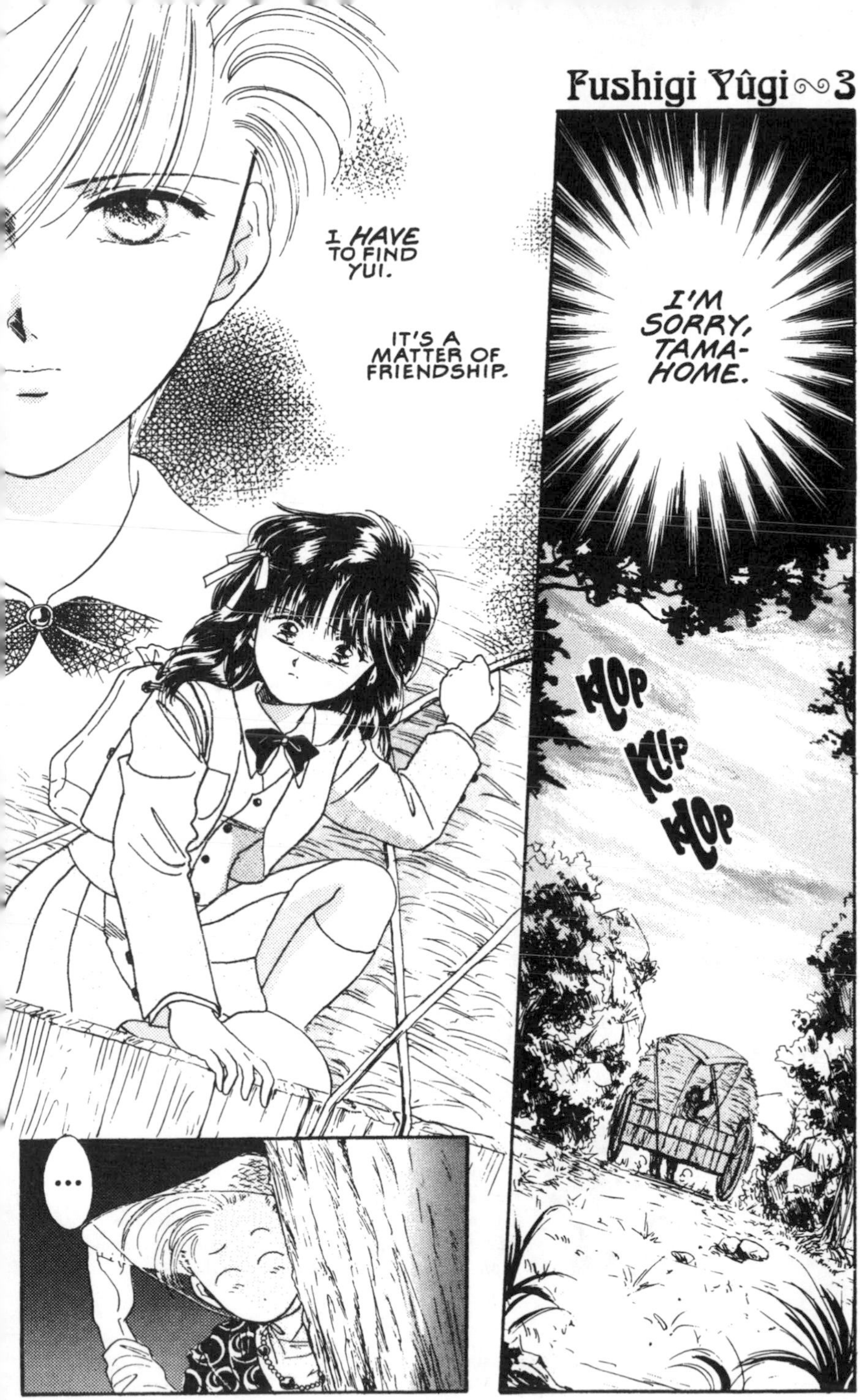
I HAVE TO FIND YUI.
IT'S A MATTER OF FRIENDSHIP.
...
I'M SORRY, TAMA-HOME.
KLOP
KLIP
KLOP

XONG 琮 GUI 鬼 SIU 宿

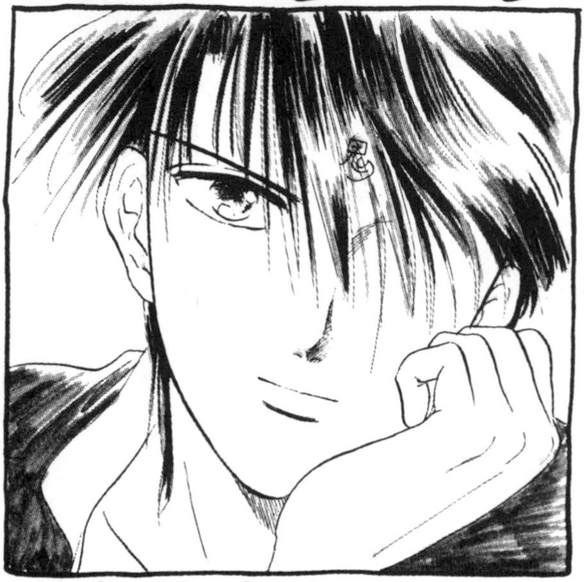

CANCER

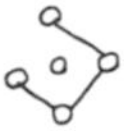

T A M A H O M E

- Born in Bai-Jiang Village, Shou-Shuang Prefecture, Hong-Nan
  Birthday is some time between February and May (because he's a constellation of Suzaku)
  Presently 17 years old
- Relations: father, 2 brothers, 2 sisters Mother: died when he was 12 years old Strengths: martial arts (A natural born talent!)
- Height 5' 9" Blood type O Hobby: Making money
- Eldest son taking the place of his ill father to support his family. *Whatta great big brother!* He's very caring, but at the same time he can cause a lot of trouble for others. *But everyone cuts him a break.* On the outside he is very chipper, and that leads to some comic expressions. But he's tough on the inside (so he thinks). On the other hand, he is very shy. (He had to become stoic for his family's sake.) *That's why he was hard on Miaka in the first issue.* Sacrifices himself for the sake of others, and won't back down against any enemy.

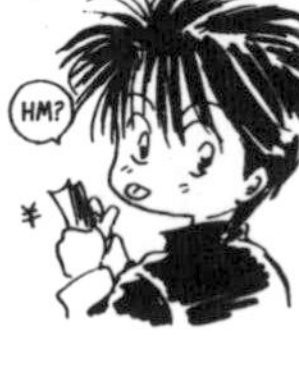
HM?

It looks like you've all become accustomed to the Tamahome with short hair, but have you noticed how his hair's grown since graphic novel #2? My assistants and I complain about how none of the readers wrote in concerning it.

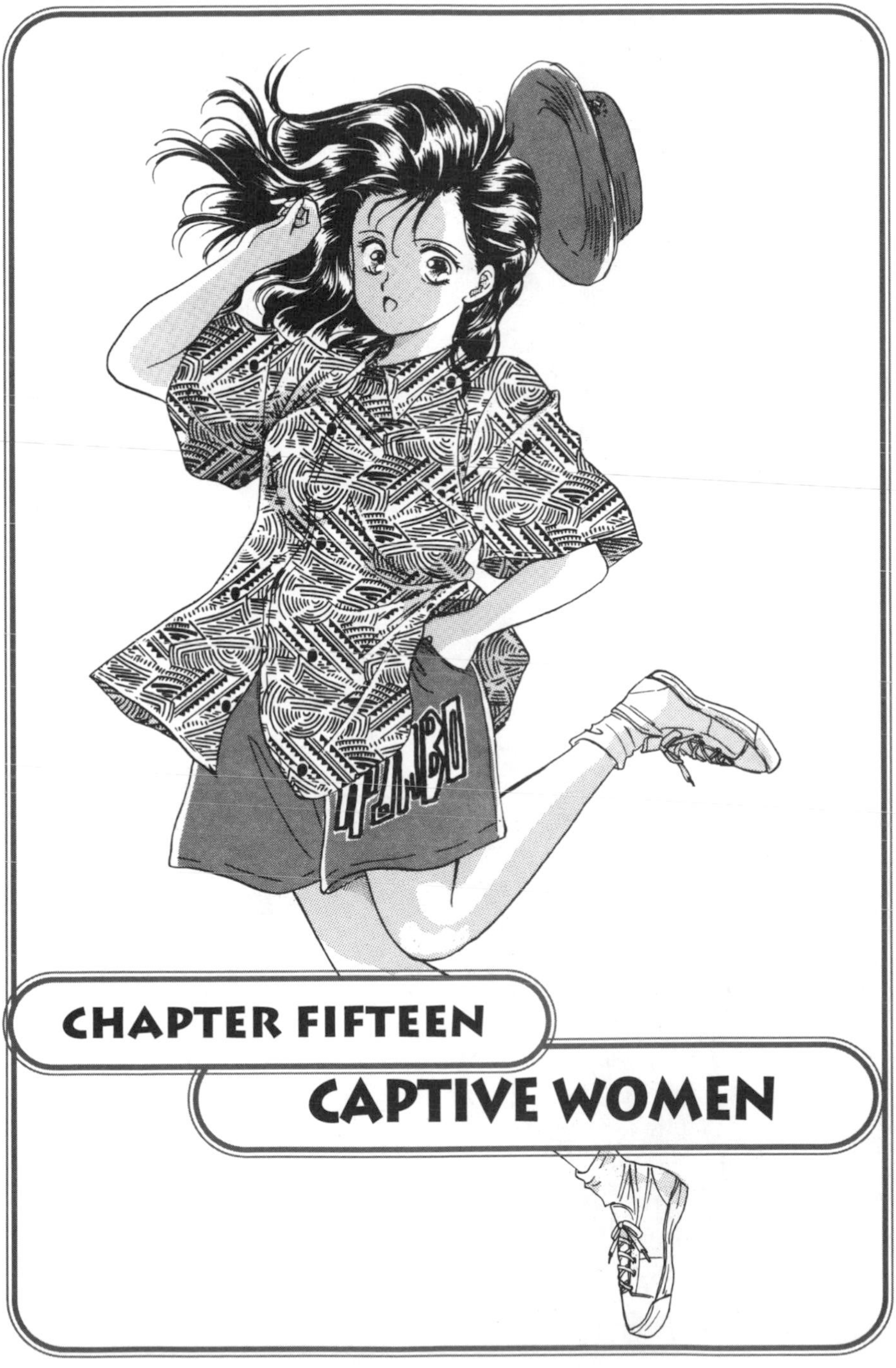

CHAPTER FIFTEEN

CAPTIVE WOMEN

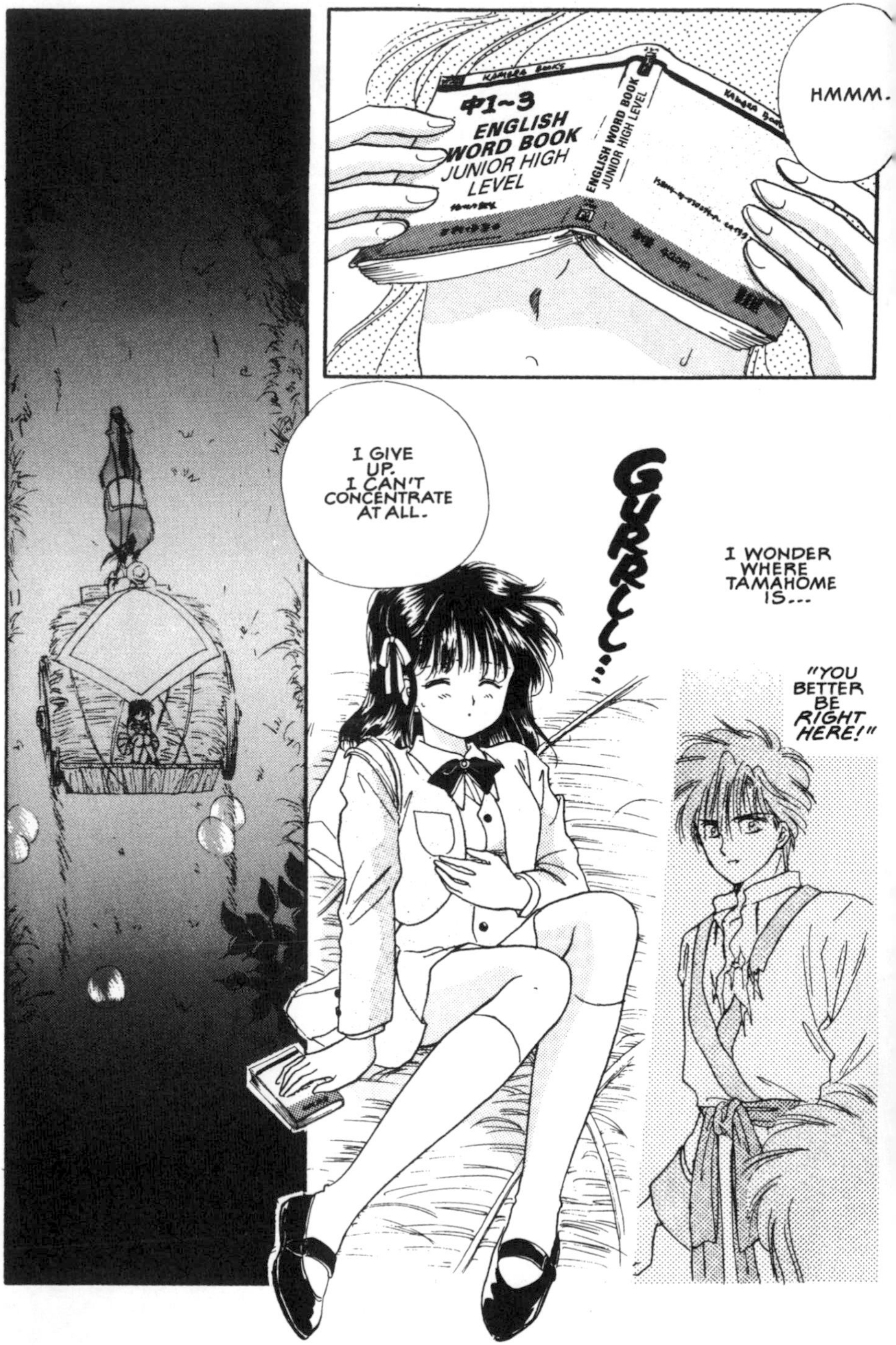
中1~3
ENGLISH WORD BOOK JUNIOR HIGH LEVEL
ENGLISH WORD BOOK JUNIOR HIGH LEVEL
HMMM.
I GIVE UP. I CAN'T CONCENTRATE AT ALL.
GURRLL...
I WONDER WHERE TAMAHOME IS...
"YOU BETTER BE RIGHT HERE!"

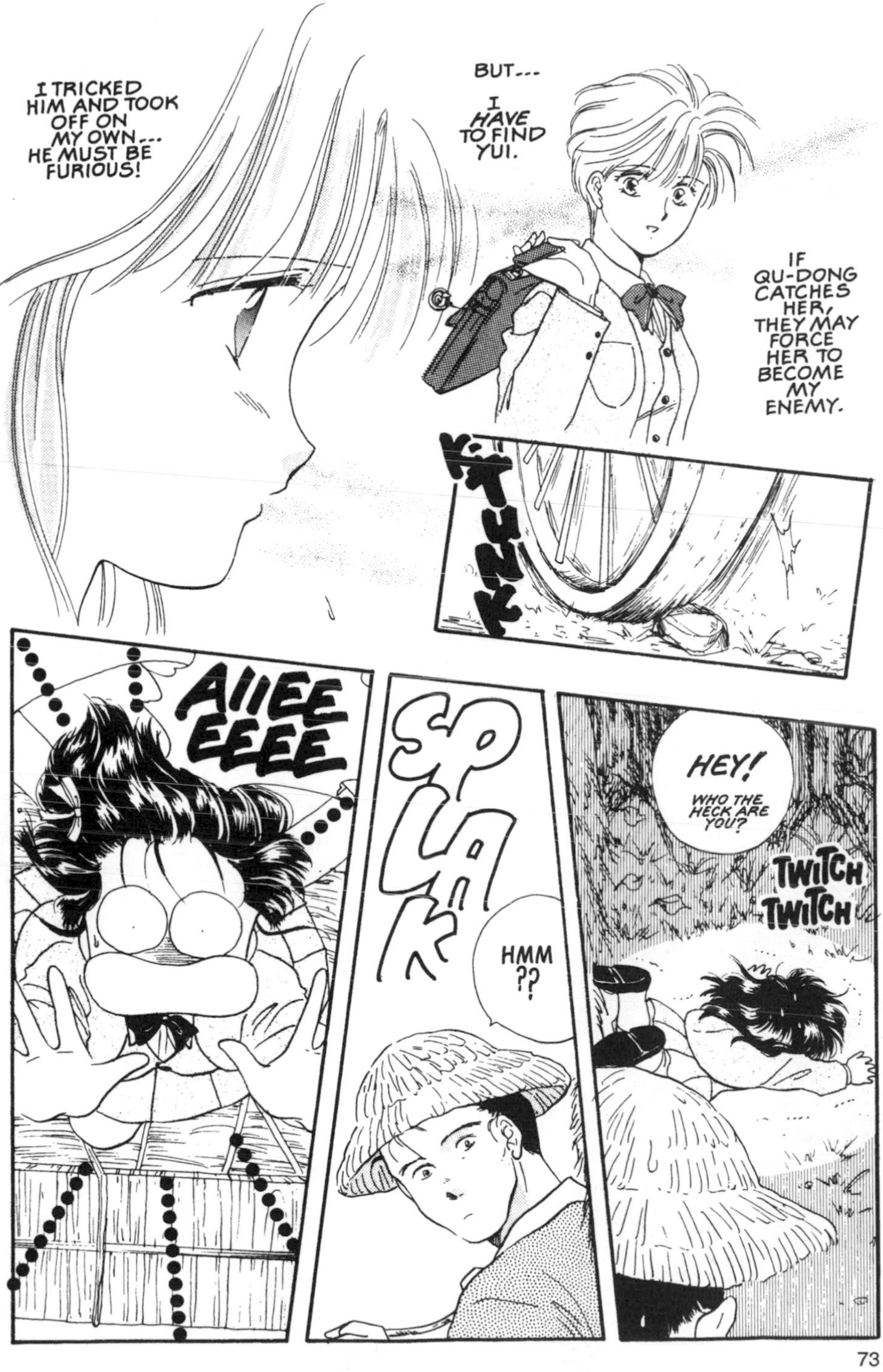
I TRICKED HIM AND TOOK OFF ON MY OWN... HE MUST BE FURIOUS!
BUT...
I HAVE TO FIND YUI.
IF QU-DONG CATCHES HER, THEY MAY FORCE HER TO BECOME MY ENEMY.
K-THUNK
AIIEE EEEE
SPLATK
HMM ??
HEY!
WHO THE HECK ARE YOU?
TWITCH TWITCH

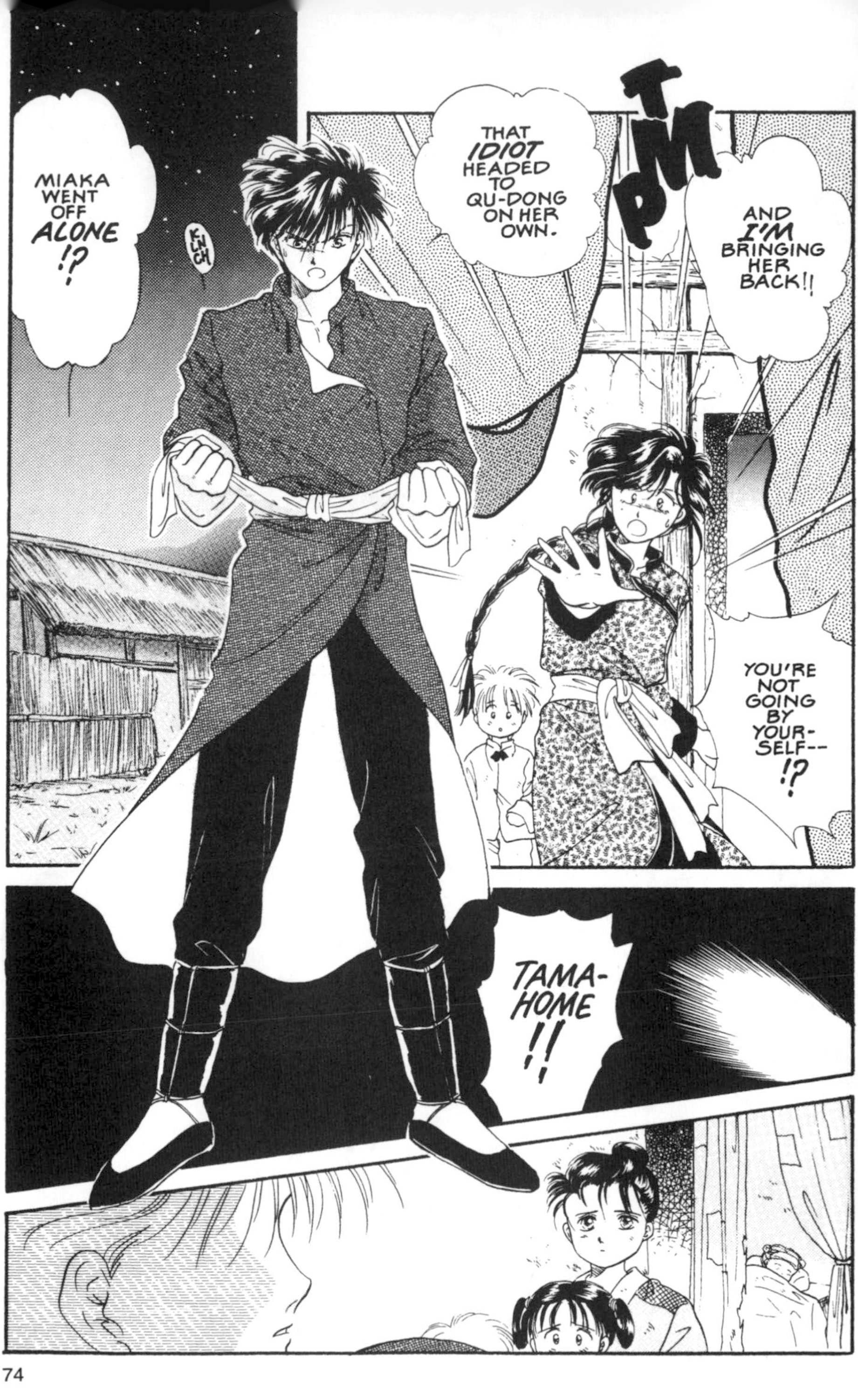

MIAKA WENT OFF ALONE !?
KLINCH
THAT IDIOT HEADED TO QU-DONG ON HER OWN.
TMP
AND I'M BRINGING HER BACK!!
YOU'RE NOT GOING BY YOUR-SELF-- !?
TAMA-HOME !!

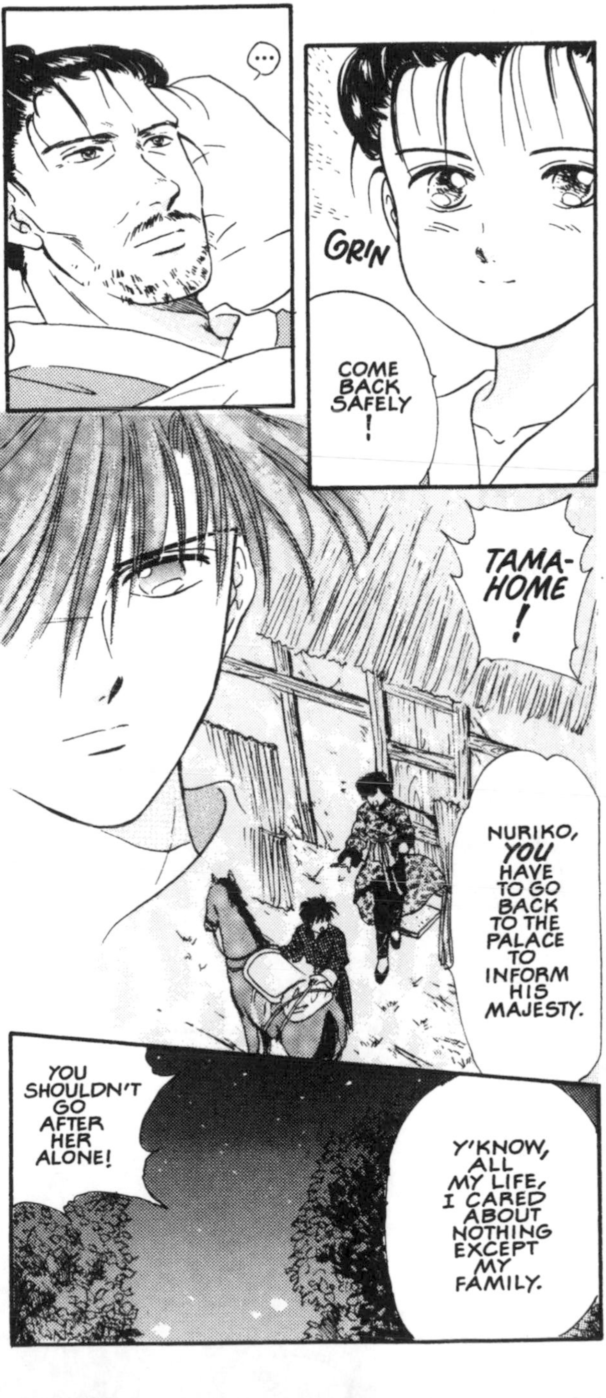
...
GRIN
COME BACK SAFELY!
TAMA-HOME!
NURIKO, YOU HAVE TO GO BACK TO THE PALACE TO INFORM HIS MAJESTY.
YOU SHOULDN'T GO AFTER HER ALONE!
Y'KNOW, ALL MY LIFE, I CARED ABOUT NOTHING EXCEPT MY FAMILY.

Disciple

I was so busy this year, I wasn't able to go home for the annual festival. But much to my amazement, even though I was in Tokyo, the festivals were given a lot of coverage on TV!! I used to think my area was the middle of the boonies, but I guess it's becoming famous. But I couldn't look when one of the ceremonial wagons went crashing into a telephone pole, killing seven people! Things were out of control! What's going on Kishi---da!? *(Must remain anonymous.)* If I'd gone home, I would've been both furious and terrified. But I have no problem watching it on TV.
Hmm. Maybe I should have promoted myself more when I lived there. (Promoted what!?) My little brother really wanted to go back, but my mom isn't too thrilled with the idea. (She's scared.)
My parents were born in Osaka so they're not actually from the town. But the minute I hear the sound of those taiko drums, it starts my blood flowing.
When I was a senior in high school, I always went to the festival wearing a happi coat, but I didn't pull the float. Now guys look pretty good in happi coats. The designs vary from town to town, but our town's design was simple (white lettering on black cloth). The whole town preferred that festival even to New Year's. Town natives who moved away to places over the country take vacations to come home for the festival. (I didn't. Sorry!) They even close down the grade schools for it. Amazing really! The downtown district has its festival in September, and the uptown district has its in October. The uptown kids (like me) had vacation days for both. The year after I moved to Tokyo when I came back for the festival, my cousin (♀) was pulling the float when she fell, but she held onto the rope for a couple dozen meters. Even though she was scraped and bleeding, she caught her feet and still helped out. If you let go of the rope, you get run over by the float, so you can't let go even if you fall. Of course, some of the older guys act as guardians to save you in case of an accident. It can be scary.
Anyway, a lot of famous people are from the area. Kiyohara of the Seibu Lions, the designers, the Koshinos (former neighbors of mine) and a few actors... I'm the first manga artist to come from there (I think).

I'll go back next year!

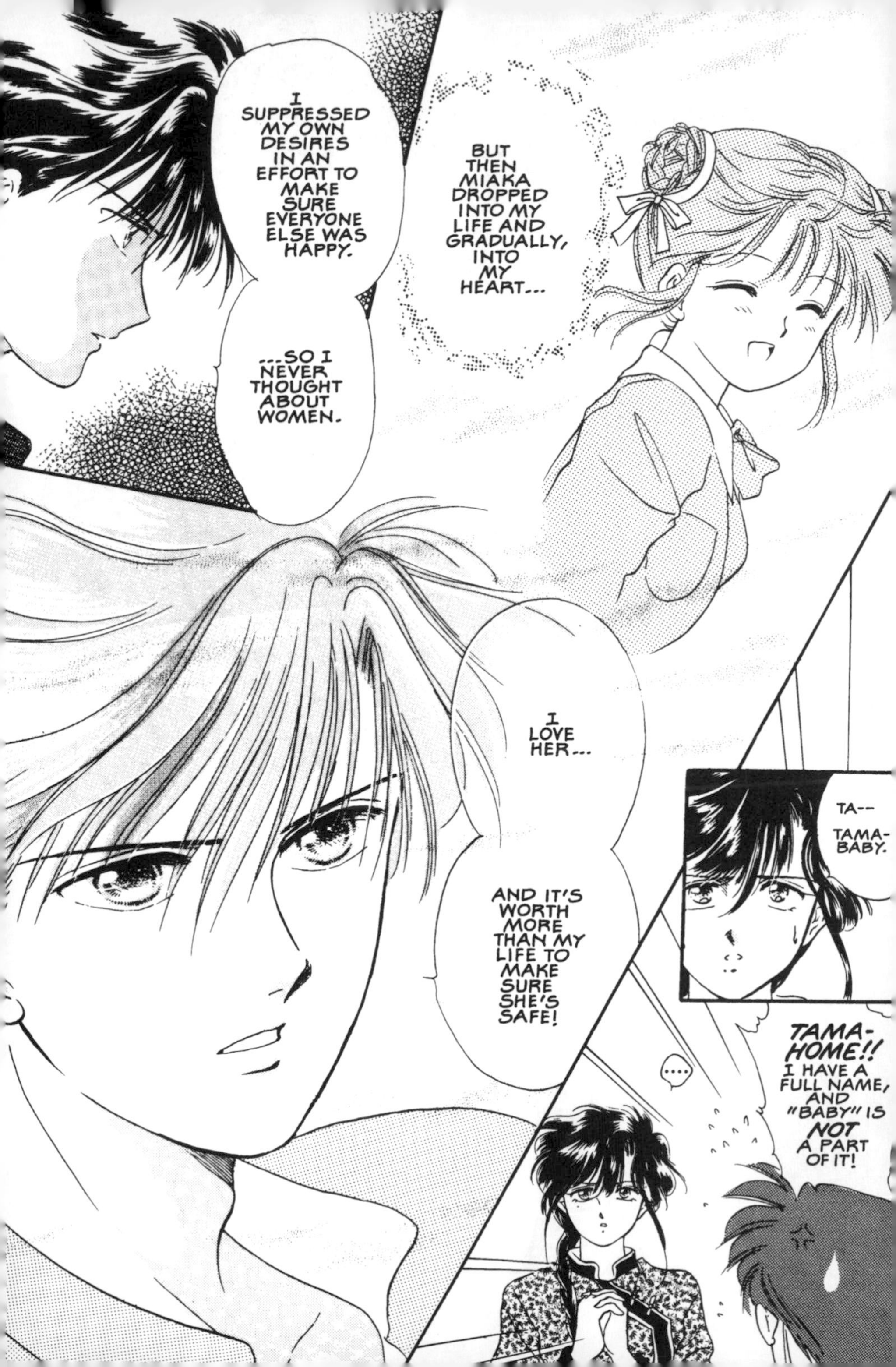
I SUPPRESSED MY OWN DESIRES IN AN EFFORT TO MAKE SURE EVERYONE ELSE WAS HAPPY.
...SO I NEVER THOUGHT ABOUT WOMEN.
BUT THEN MIAKA DROPPED INTO MY LIFE AND GRADUALLY, INTO MY HEART...
I LOVE HER...
AND IT'S WORTH MORE THAN MY LIFE TO MAKE SURE SHE'S SAFE!
TA--
TAMA-BABY.
....
TAMA-HOME!! I HAVE A FULL NAME, AND "BABY" IS NOT A PART OF IT!

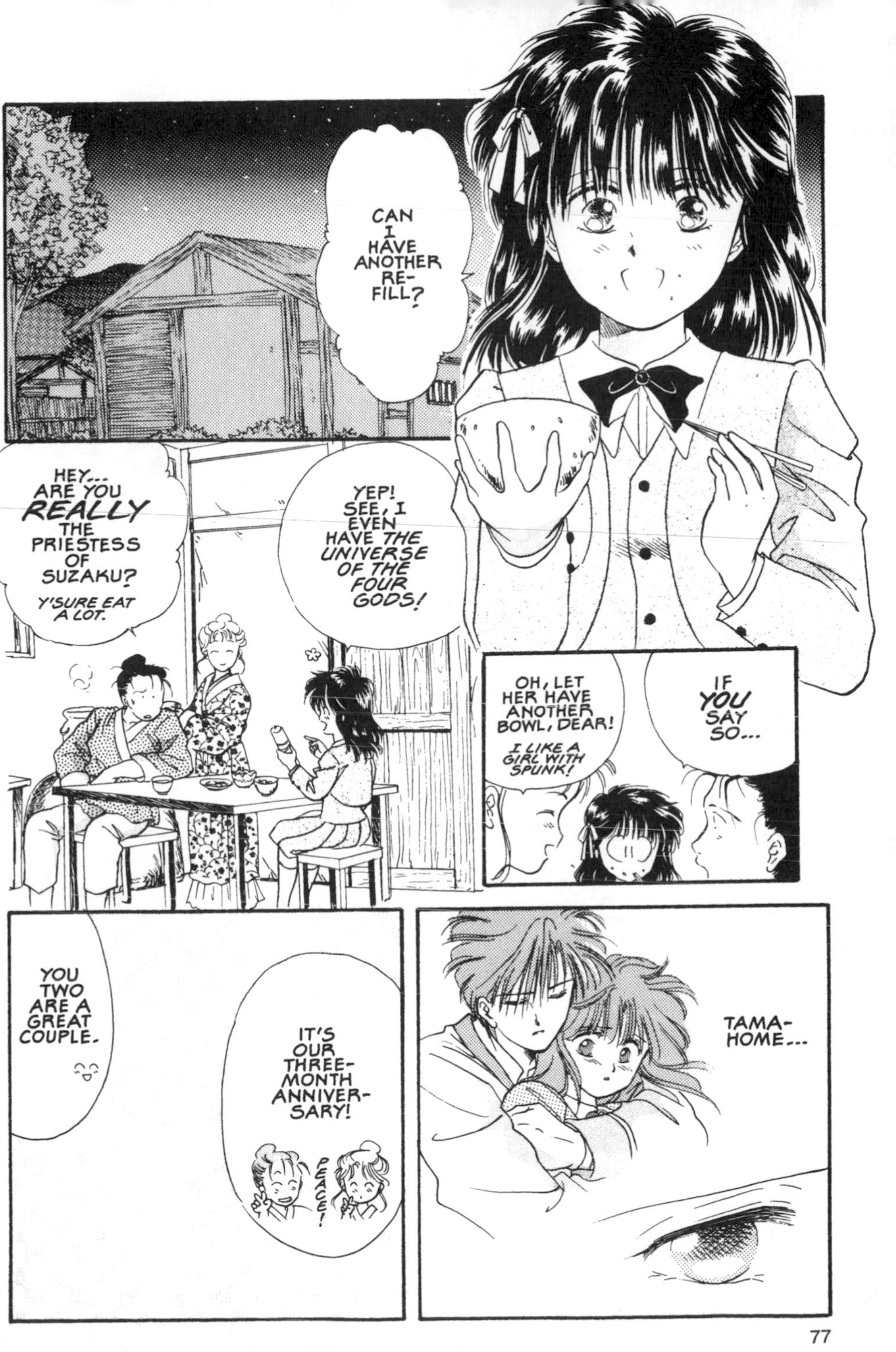
CAN I HAVE ANOTHER RE-FILL?
HEY... ARE YOU *REALLY* THE PRIESTESS OF SUZAKU?
Y'SURE EAT A LOT.
YEP! SEE, I EVEN HAVE *THE UNIVERSE OF THE FOUR GODS!*
OH, LET HER HAVE ANOTHER BOWL, DEAR!
I LIKE A GIRL WITH SPUNK!
IF *YOU* SAY SO...
YOU TWO ARE A GREAT COUPLE.
IT'S OUR THREE-MONTH ANNIVER-SARY!
PEACE!
TAMA-HOME...

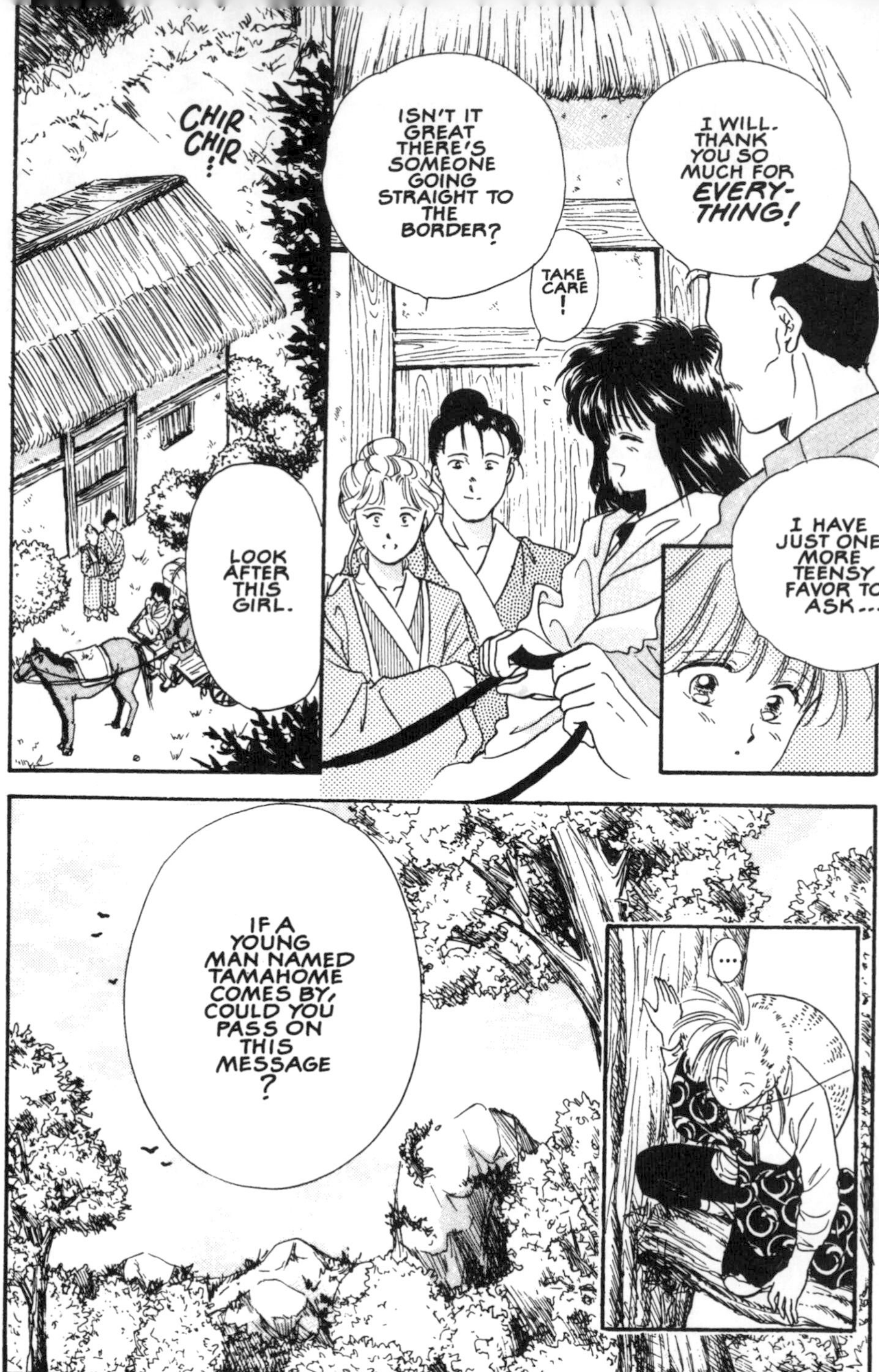
CHIR CHIR!
LOOK AFTER THIS GIRL.
ISN'T IT GREAT THERE'S SOMEONE GOING STRAIGHT TO THE BORDER?
TAKE CARE!
I WILL. THANK YOU SO MUCH FOR EVERYTHING!
I HAVE JUST ONE MORE TEENSY FAVOR TO ASK...
IF A YOUNG MAN NAMED TAMAHOME COMES BY, COULD YOU PASS ON THIS MESSAGE?
...

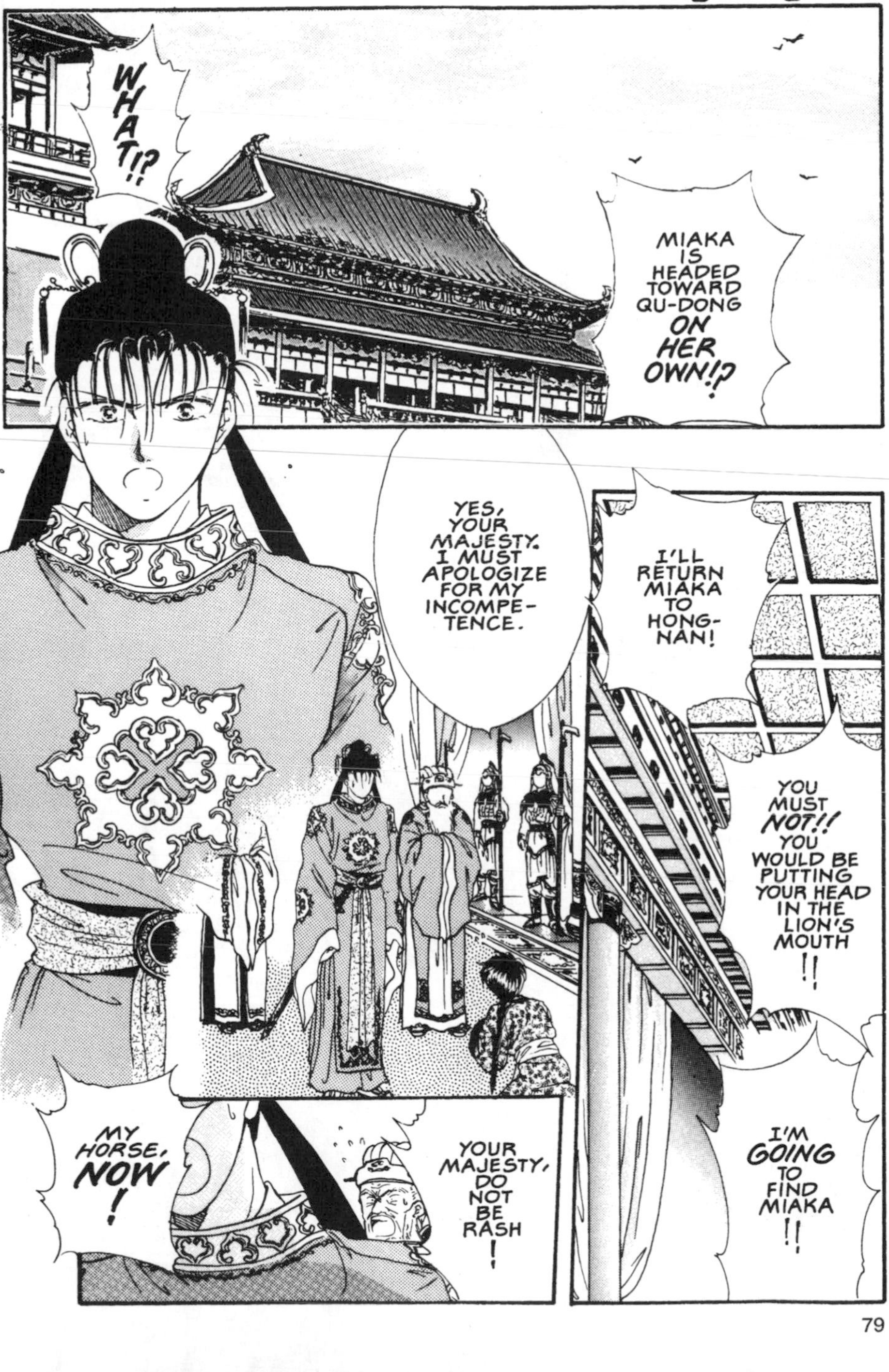
WHAT!?
MIAKA IS HEADED TOWARD QU-DONG ON HER OWN!?
YES, YOUR MAJESTY. I MUST APOLOGIZE FOR MY INCOMPETENCE.
MY HORSE, NOW!
YOUR MAJESTY, DO NOT BE RASH!
I'LL RETURN MIAKA TO HONG-NAN!
YOU MUST NOT!! YOU WOULD BE PUTTING YOUR HEAD IN THE LION'S MOUTH!!
I'M GOING TO FIND MIAKA!!

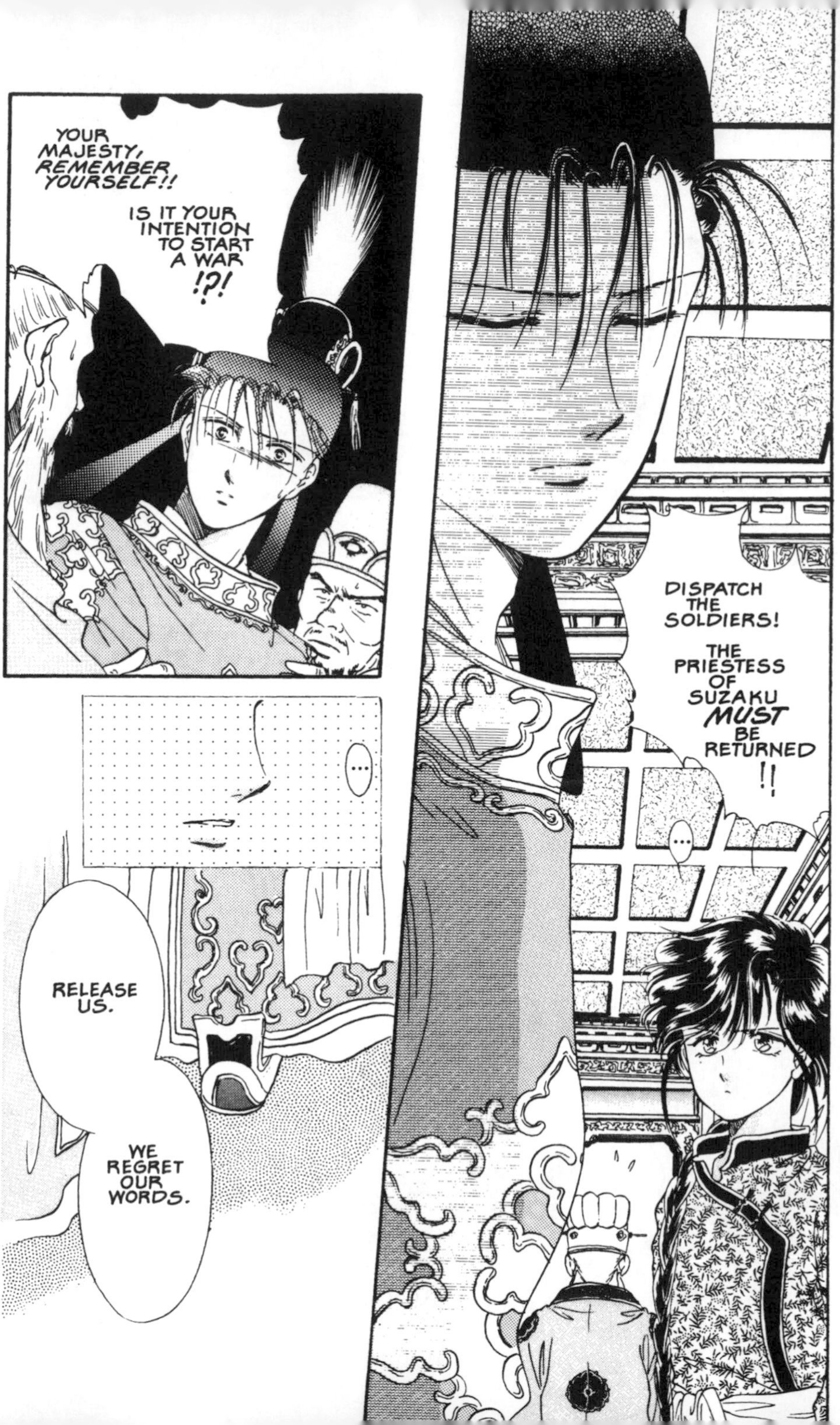
YOUR MAJESTY, REMEMBER YOURSELF!!
IS IT YOUR INTENTION TO START A WAR !?!
...
RELEASE US.
WE REGRET OUR WORDS.
DISPATCH THE SOLDIERS!
THE PRIESTESS OF SUZAKU MUST BE RETURNED !!
...

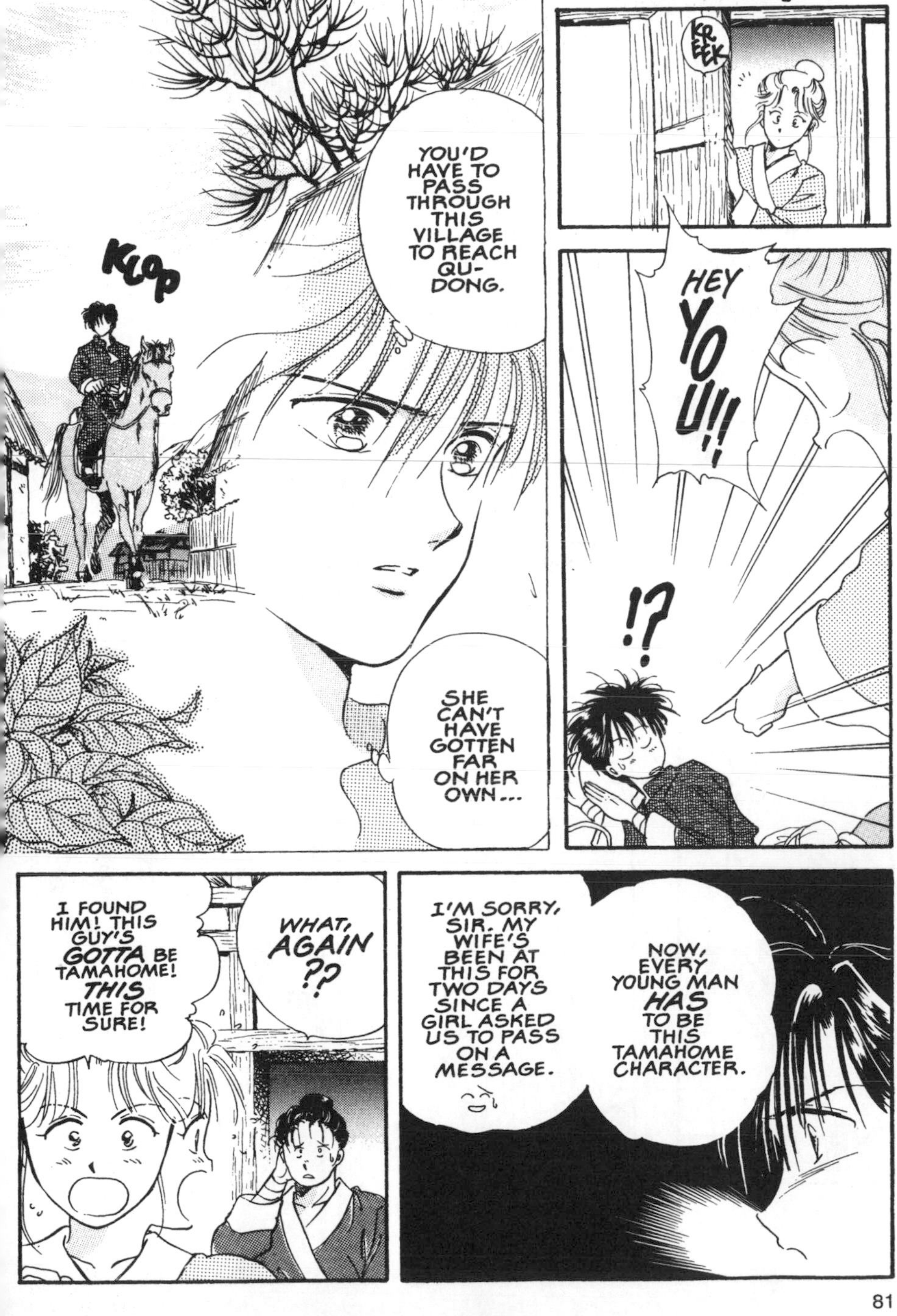
KLOP
YOU'D HAVE TO PASS THROUGH THIS VILLAGE TO REACH QU-DONG.
SHE CAN'T HAVE GOTTEN FAR ON HER OWN...
KREEK
HEY YOU!!
!?
I FOUND HIM! THIS GUY'S GOTTA BE TAMAHOME! THIS TIME FOR SURE!
WHAT, AGAIN??
I'M SORRY, SIR. MY WIFE'S BEEN AT THIS FOR TWO DAYS SINCE A GIRL ASKED US TO PASS ON A MESSAGE.
NOW, EVERY YOUNG MAN HAS TO BE THIS TAMAHOME CHARACTER.

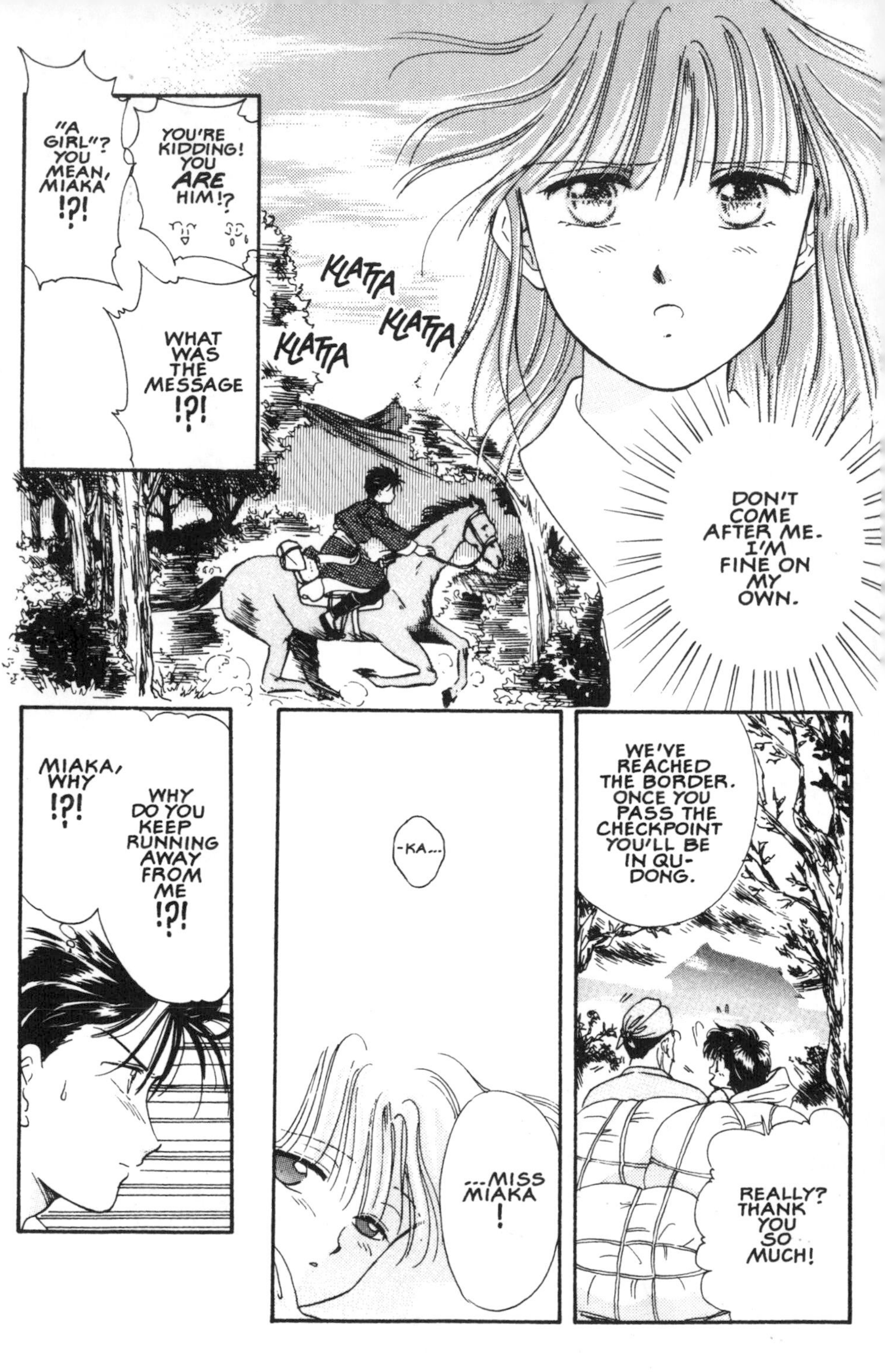
"A GIRL"? YOU MEAN, MIAKA !?!
YOU'RE KIDDING! YOU ARE HIM!?
WHAT WAS THE MESSAGE !?!
KLATTA
KLATTA
KLATTA
DON'T COME AFTER ME. I'M FINE ON MY OWN.
MIAKA, WHY !?!
WHY DO YOU KEEP RUNNING AWAY FROM ME !?!
-KA...
...MISS MIAKA !
WE'VE REACHED THE BORDER. ONCE YOU PASS THE CHECKPOINT YOU'LL BE IN QU-DONG.
REALLY? THANK YOU SO MUCH!

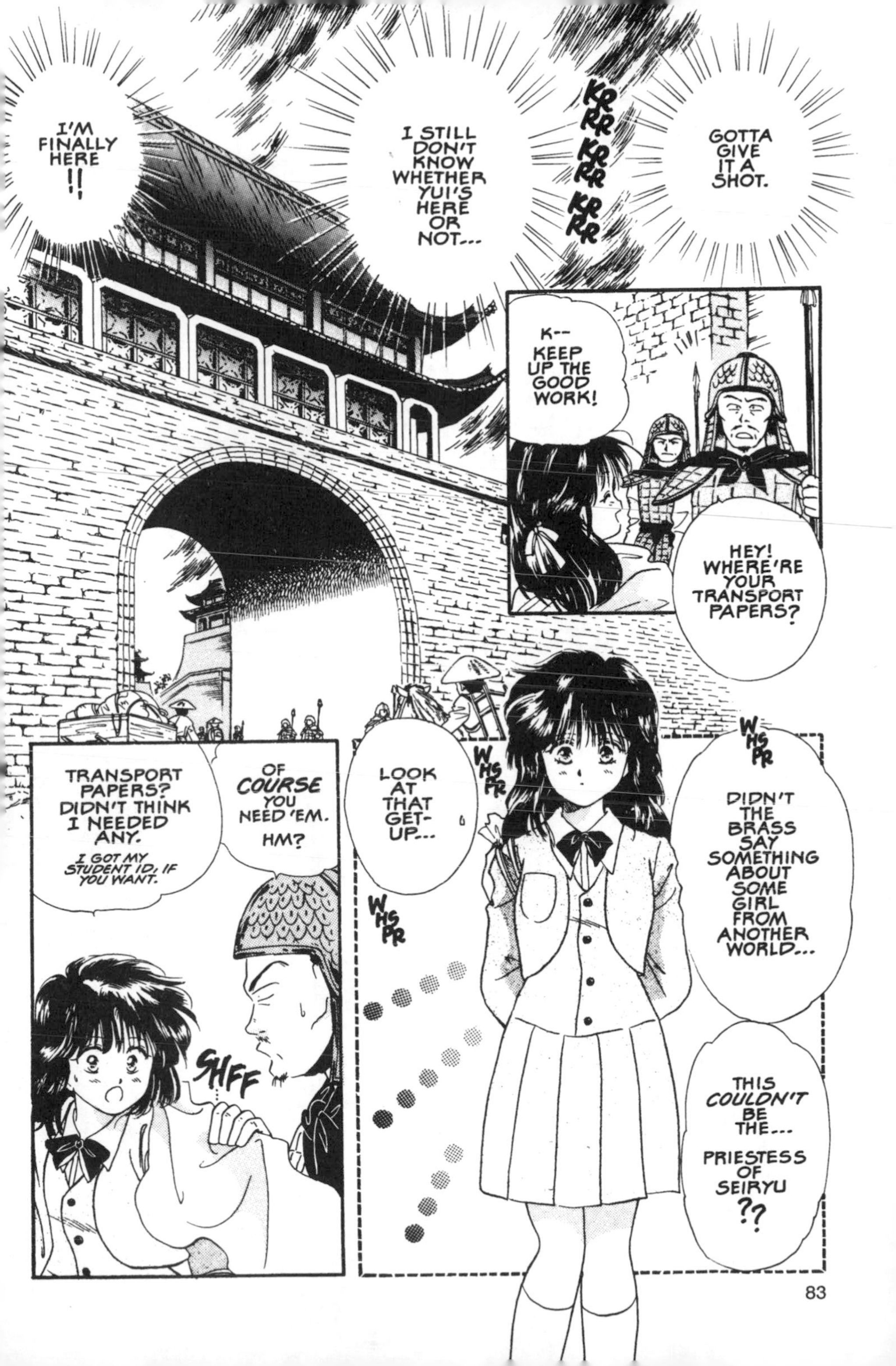
I'M FINALLY HERE!!
I STILL DON'T KNOW WHETHER YUI'S HERE OR NOT...
KRR KRR KRR
GOTTA GIVE IT A SHOT.
K-- KEEP UP THE GOOD WORK!
HEY! WHERE'RE YOUR TRANSPORT PAPERS?
TRANSPORT PAPERS? DIDN'T THINK I NEEDED ANY.
I GOT MY STUDENT ID, IF YOU WANT.
OF *COURSE* YOU NEED 'EM.
HM?
SHFF
LOOK AT THAT GET-UP...
WHSPR
WHSPR
WHSPR
DIDN'T THE BRASS SAY SOMETHING ABOUT SOME GIRL FROM ANOTHER WORLD...
THIS *COULDN'T* BE THE...
PRIESTESS OF SEIRYU??

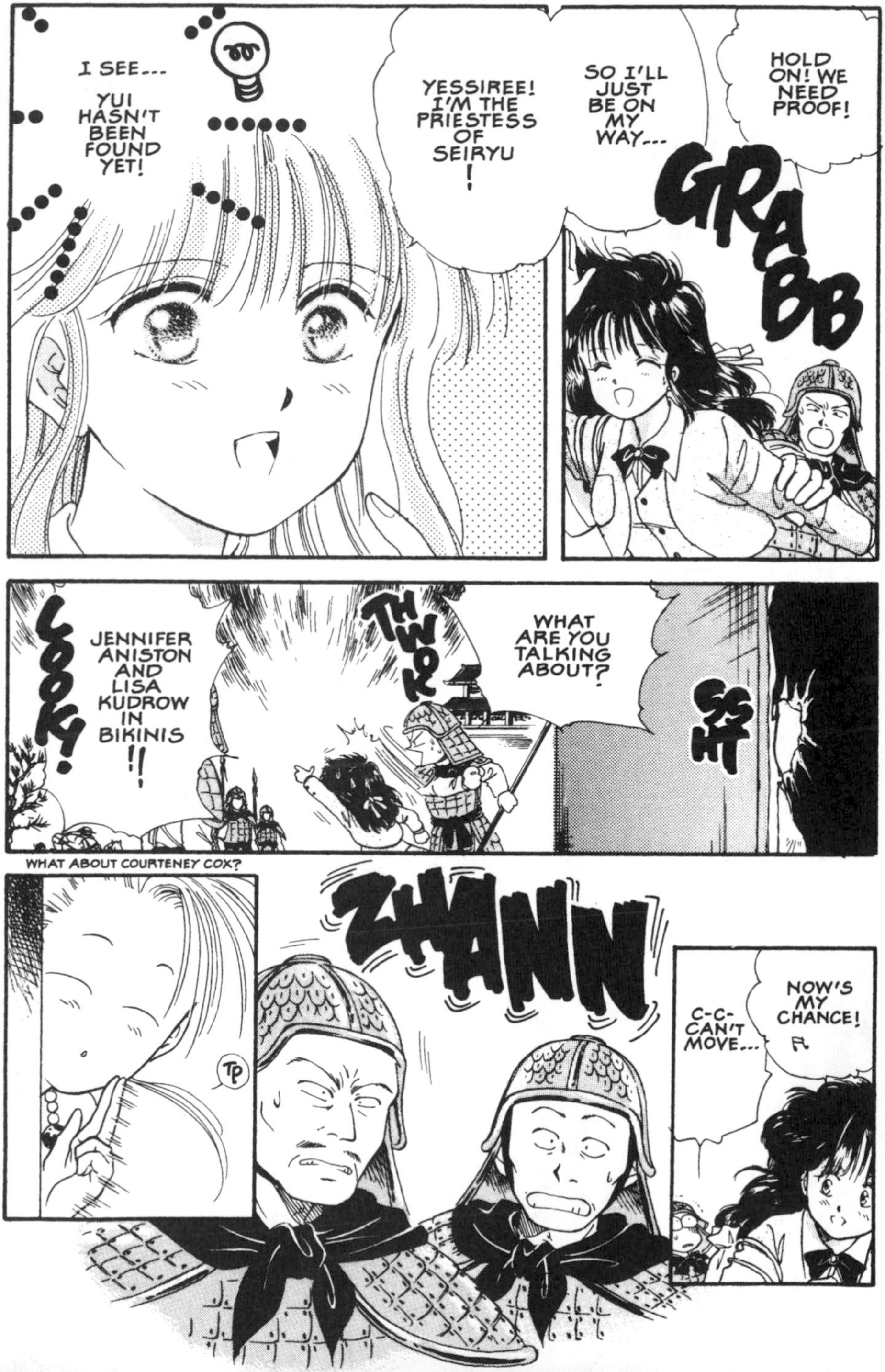
I SEE...
YUI HASN'T BEEN FOUND YET!
YESSIREE! I'M THE PRIESTESS OF SEIRYU!
SO I'LL JUST BE ON MY WAY...
HOLD ON! WE NEED PROOF!
GRABB
LOOK!
JENNIFER ANISTON AND LISA KUDROW IN BIKINIS!!
THWOK
WHAT ARE YOU TALKING ABOUT?
SSHT
WHAT ABOUT COURTENEY COX?
TP
ZHANN
C-C-CAN'T MOVE...
NOW'S MY CHANCE!

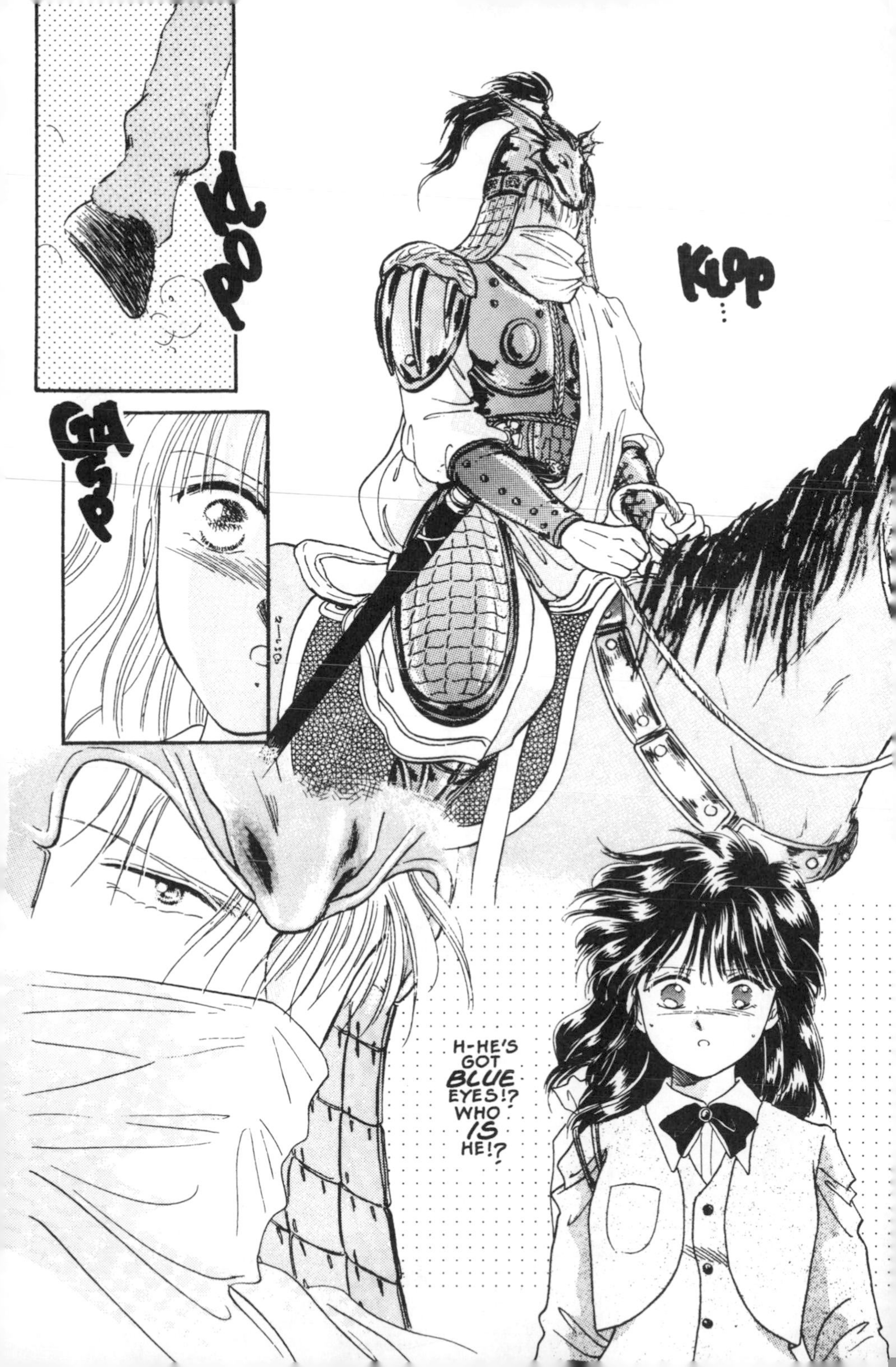
KLOP...
POK
GASP
H-HE'S GOT BLUE EYES!? WHO IS HE!?

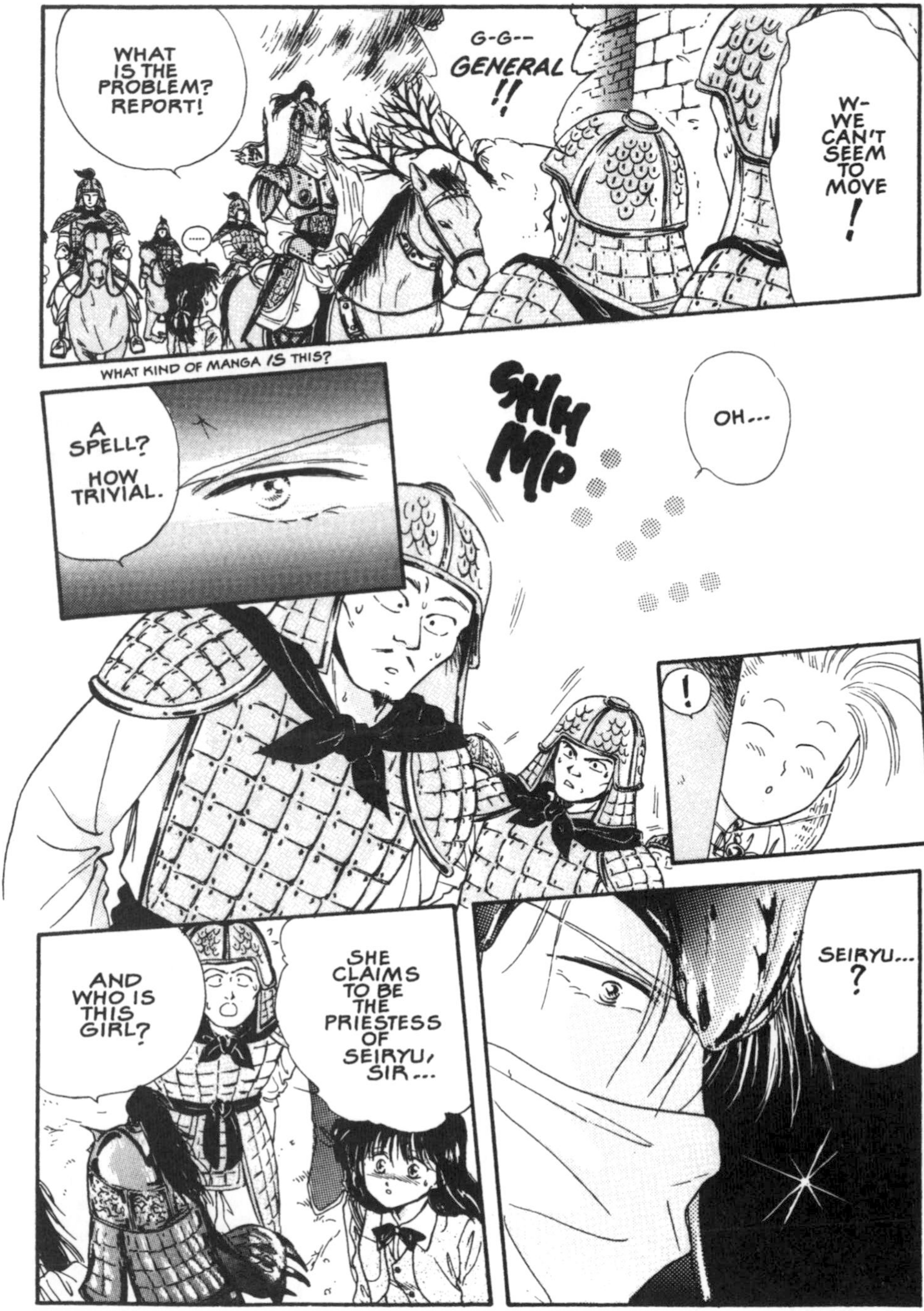

WHAT IS THE PROBLEM? REPORT!
.....
G-G-- GENERAL!!
W-WE CAN'T SEEM TO MOVE!
WHAT KIND OF MANGA IS THIS?
A SPELL? HOW TRIVIAL.
SHHMP
OH...
!
AND WHO IS THIS GIRL?
SHE CLAIMS TO BE THE PRIESTESS OF SEIRYU, SIR...
SEIRYU...?

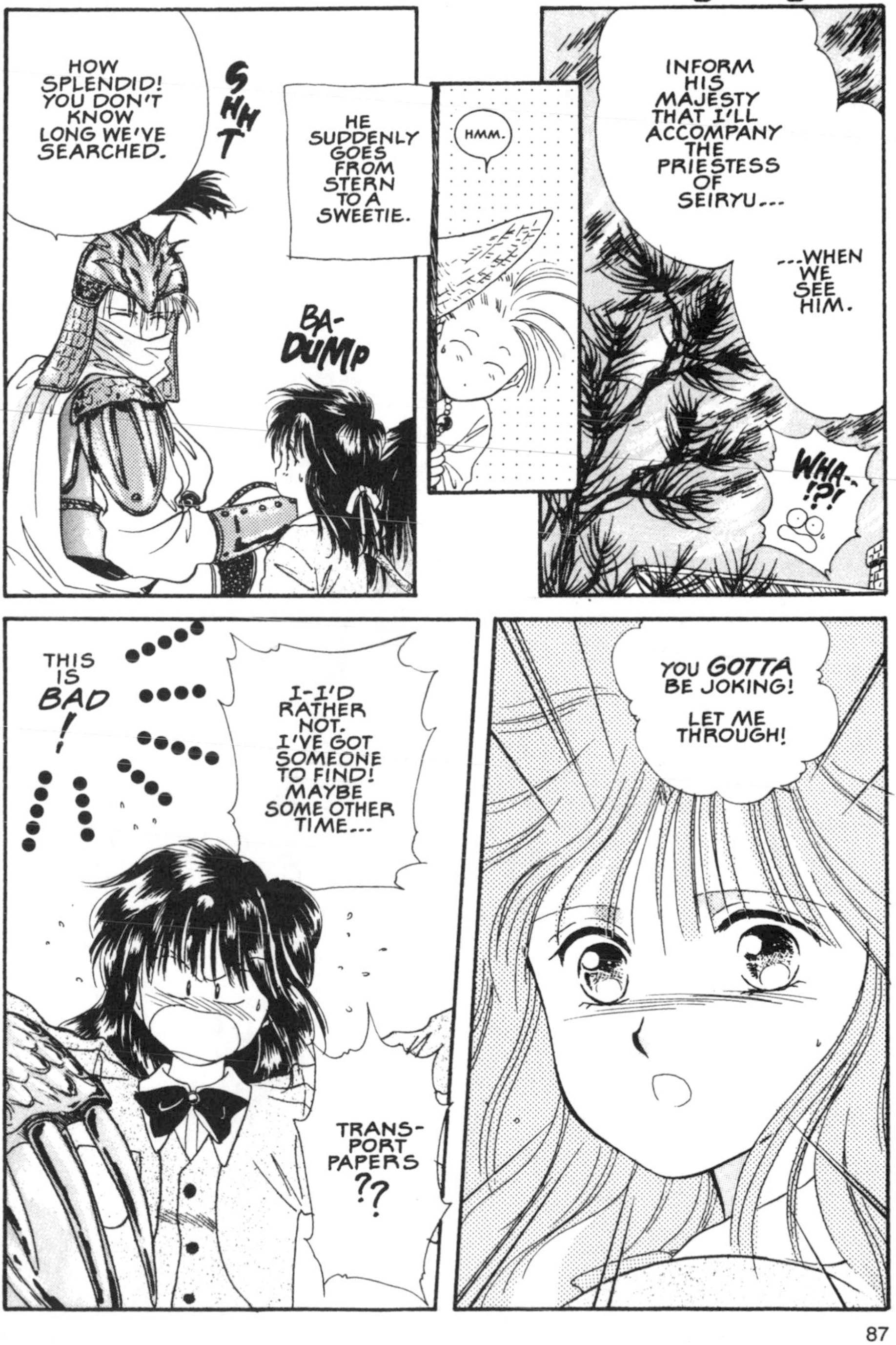
HOW SPLENDID! YOU DON'T KNOW LONG WE'VE SEARCHED.
SHHT
HE SUDDENLY GOES FROM STERN TO A SWEETIE.
BA-DUMP
HMM.
INFORM HIS MAJESTY THAT I'LL ACCOMPANY THE PRIESTESS OF SEIRYU...
...WHEN WE SEE HIM.
WHA-!?!
THIS IS BAD!
I-I'D RATHER NOT. I'VE GOT SOMEONE TO FIND! MAYBE SOME OTHER TIME...
TRANSPORT PAPERS??
YOU GOTTA BE JOKING!
LET ME THROUGH!

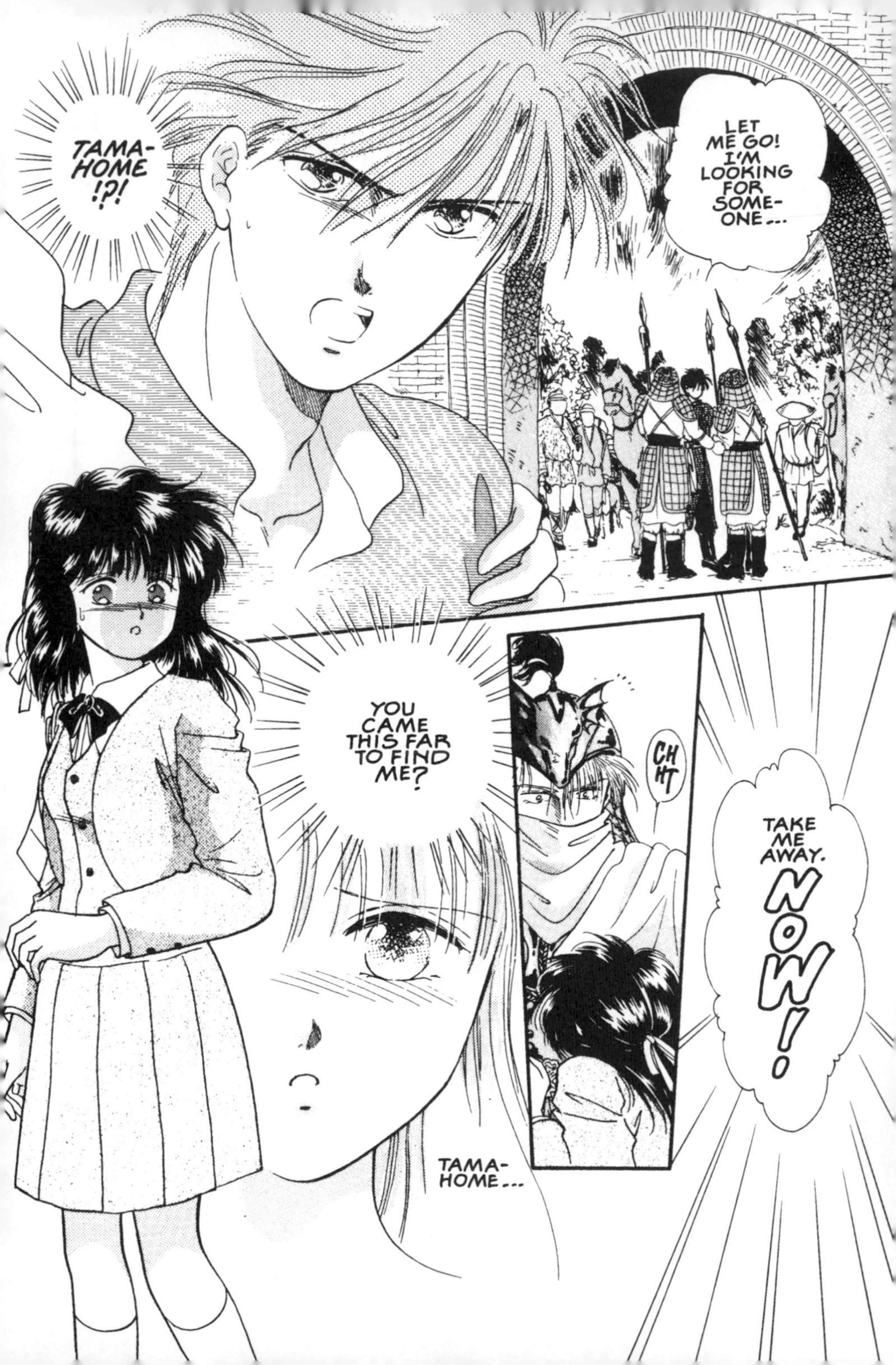
TAMA-HOME!?!
LET ME GO! I'M LOOKING FOR SOME-ONE...
YOU CAME THIS FAR TO FIND ME?
TAMA-HOME...
CH HT
TAKE ME AWAY. NOW!!

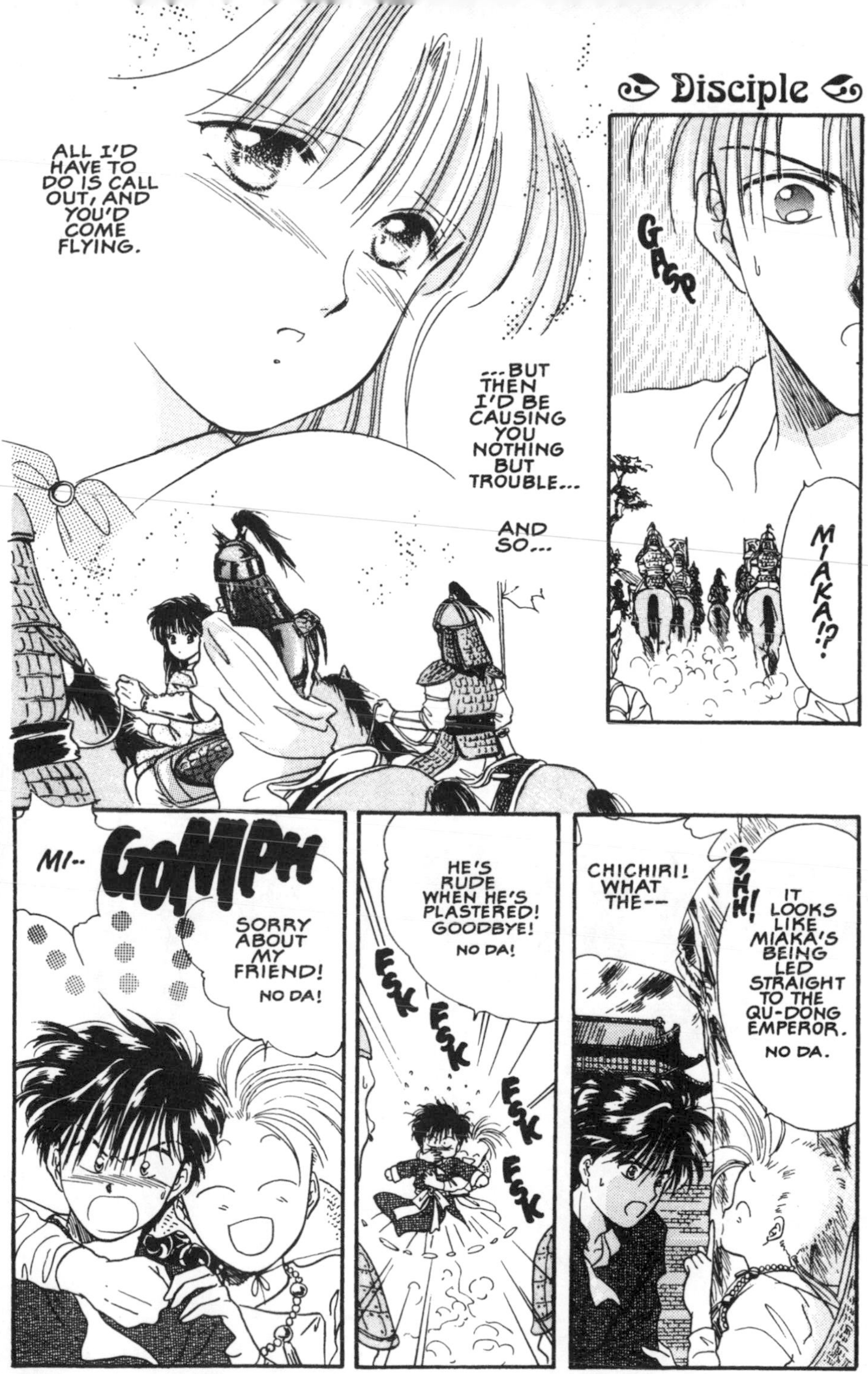
ALL I'D HAVE TO DO IS CALL OUT, AND YOU'D COME FLYING.
...BUT THEN I'D BE CAUSING YOU NOTHING BUT TROUBLE...
AND SO...
GASP
MIAKA!?
MI-- GOMPH
SORRY ABOUT MY FRIEND! NO DA!
HE'S RUDE WHEN HE'S PLASTERED! GOODBYE! NO DA!
ESK ESK ESK ESK
CHICHIRI! WHAT THE--
SHH!
IT LOOKS LIKE MIAKA'S BEING LED STRAIGHT TO THE QU-DONG EMPEROR. NO DA.

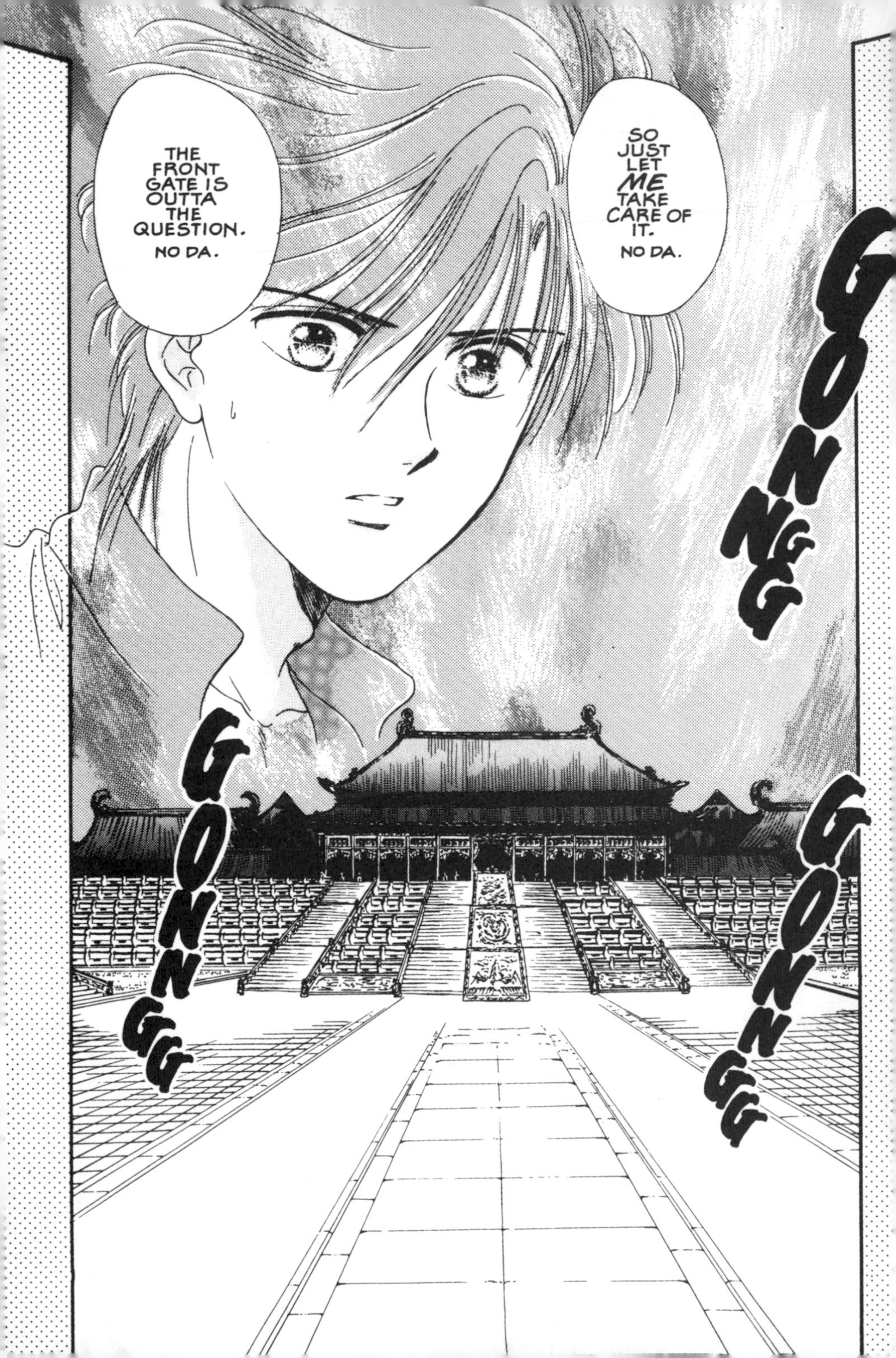
THE FRONT GATE IS OUTTA THE QUESTION. NO DA.
SO JUST LET ME TAKE CARE OF IT. NO DA.
GONNG
GONNGG
GONNGG

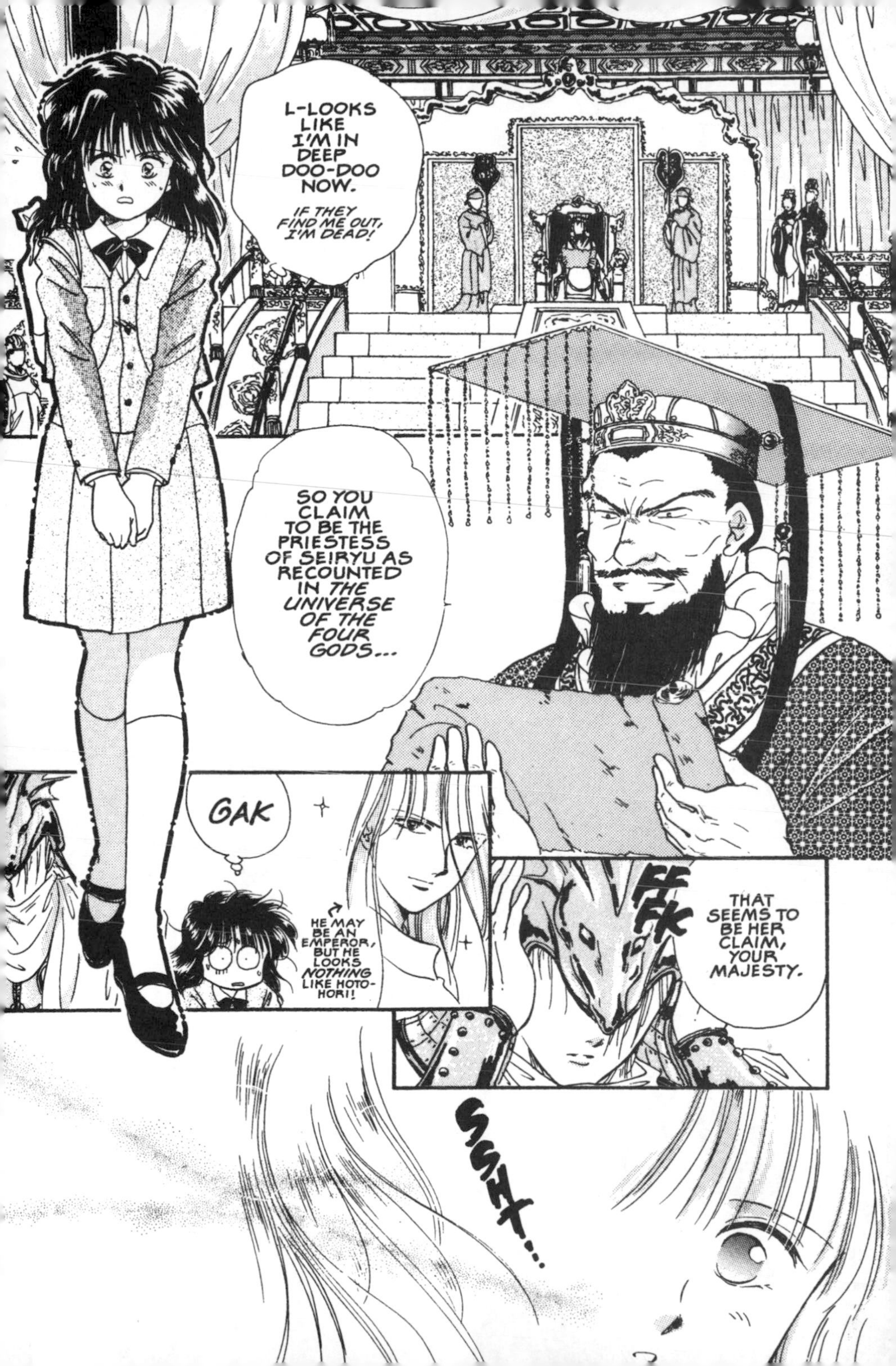
L-LOOKS LIKE I'M IN DEEP DOO-DOO NOW.
IF THEY FIND ME OUT, I'M DEAD!
SO YOU CLAIM TO BE THE PRIESTESS OF SEIRYU AS RECOUNTED IN THE UNIVERSE OF THE FOUR GODS...
GAK
HE MAY BE AN EMPEROR, BUT HE LOOKS NOTHING LIKE HOTO-HORI!
FFFK
THAT SEEMS TO BE HER CLAIM, YOUR MAJESTY.
SSHT...

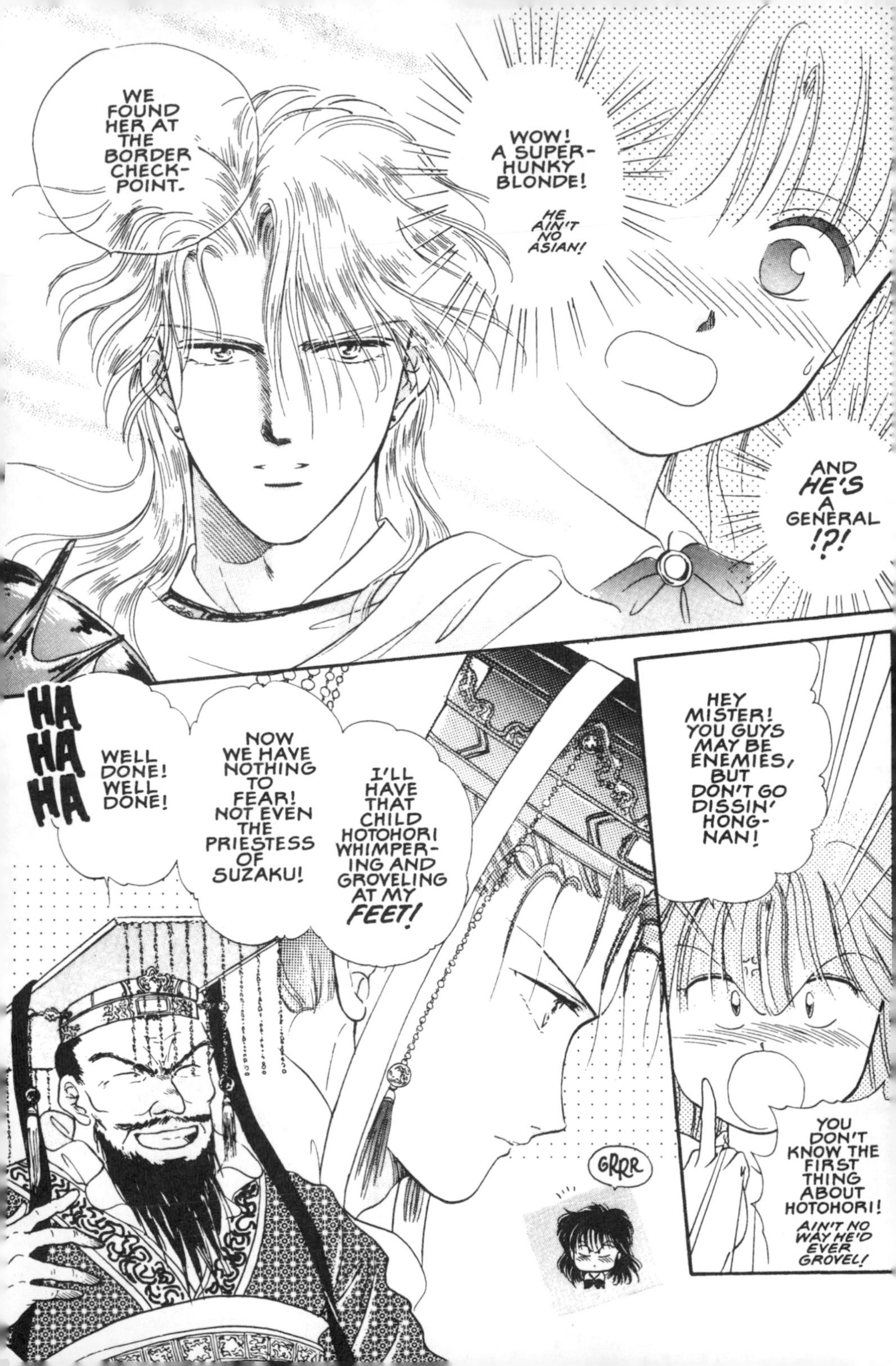
WE FOUND HER AT THE BORDER CHECK-POINT.
WOW! A SUPER-HUNKY BLONDE!
HE AIN'T NO ASIAN!
AND HE'S A GENERAL !?!
HA HA HA
WELL DONE! WELL DONE!
NOW WE HAVE NOTHING TO FEAR! NOT EVEN THE PRIESTESS OF SUZAKU!
I'LL HAVE THAT CHILD HOTOHORI WHIMPER-ING AND GROVELING AT MY FEET!
GRRR
HEY MISTER! YOU GUYS MAY BE ENEMIES, BUT DON'T GO DISSIN' HONG-NAN!
YOU DON'T KNOW THE FIRST THING ABOUT HOTOHORI!
AIN'T NO WAY HE'D EVER GROVEL!

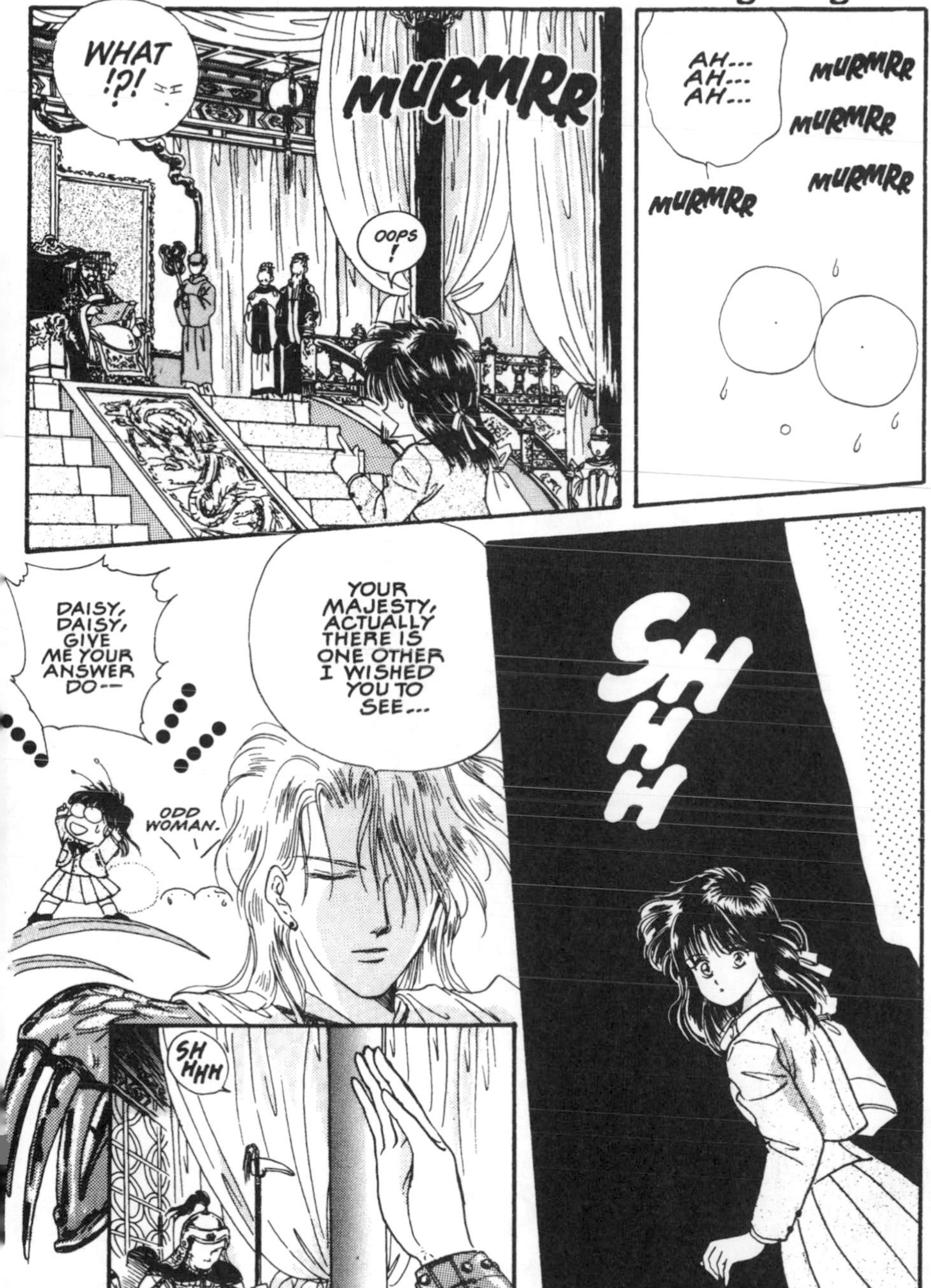
WHAT !?!
MURMRR
OOPS !
AH... AH... AH...
MURMRR
MURMRR
MURMRR
MURMRR
DAISY, DAISY, GIVE ME YOUR ANSWER DO--
YOUR MAJESTY, ACTUALLY THERE IS ONE OTHER I WISHED YOU TO SEE...
ODD WOMAN.
SHHHH
SH HHH

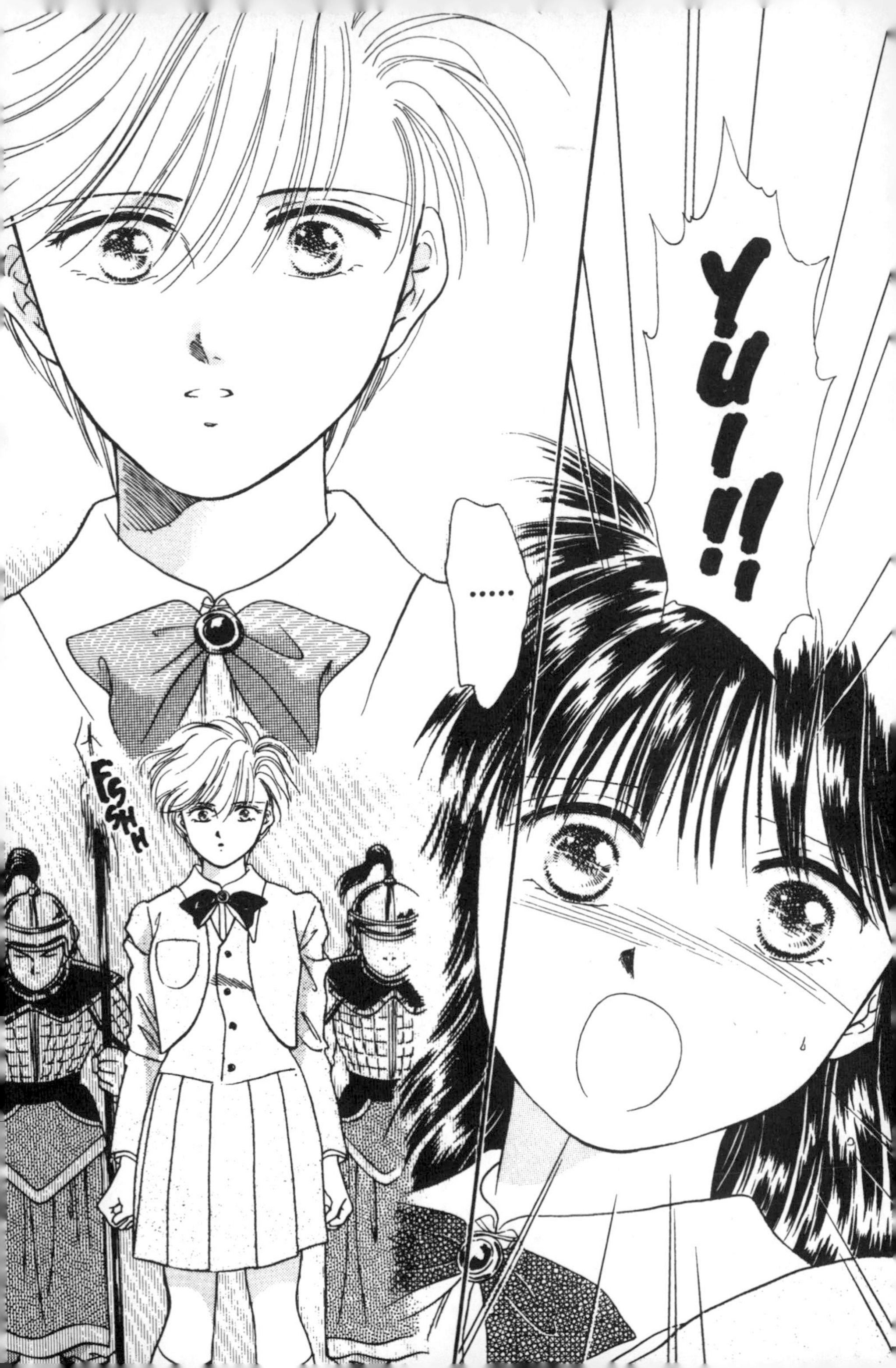
FSSHH
.....
YUI!!

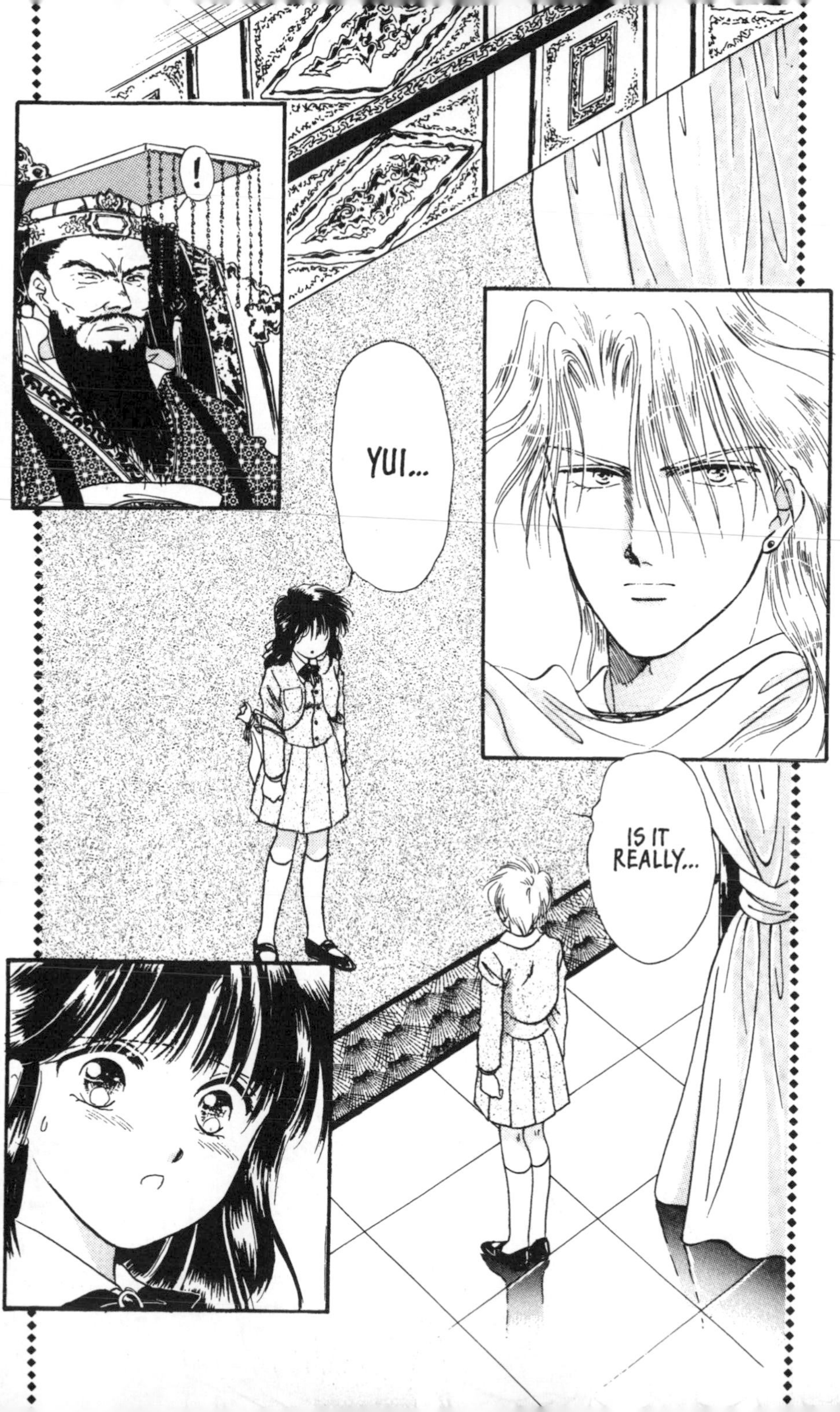
!
YUI...
IS IT REALLY...

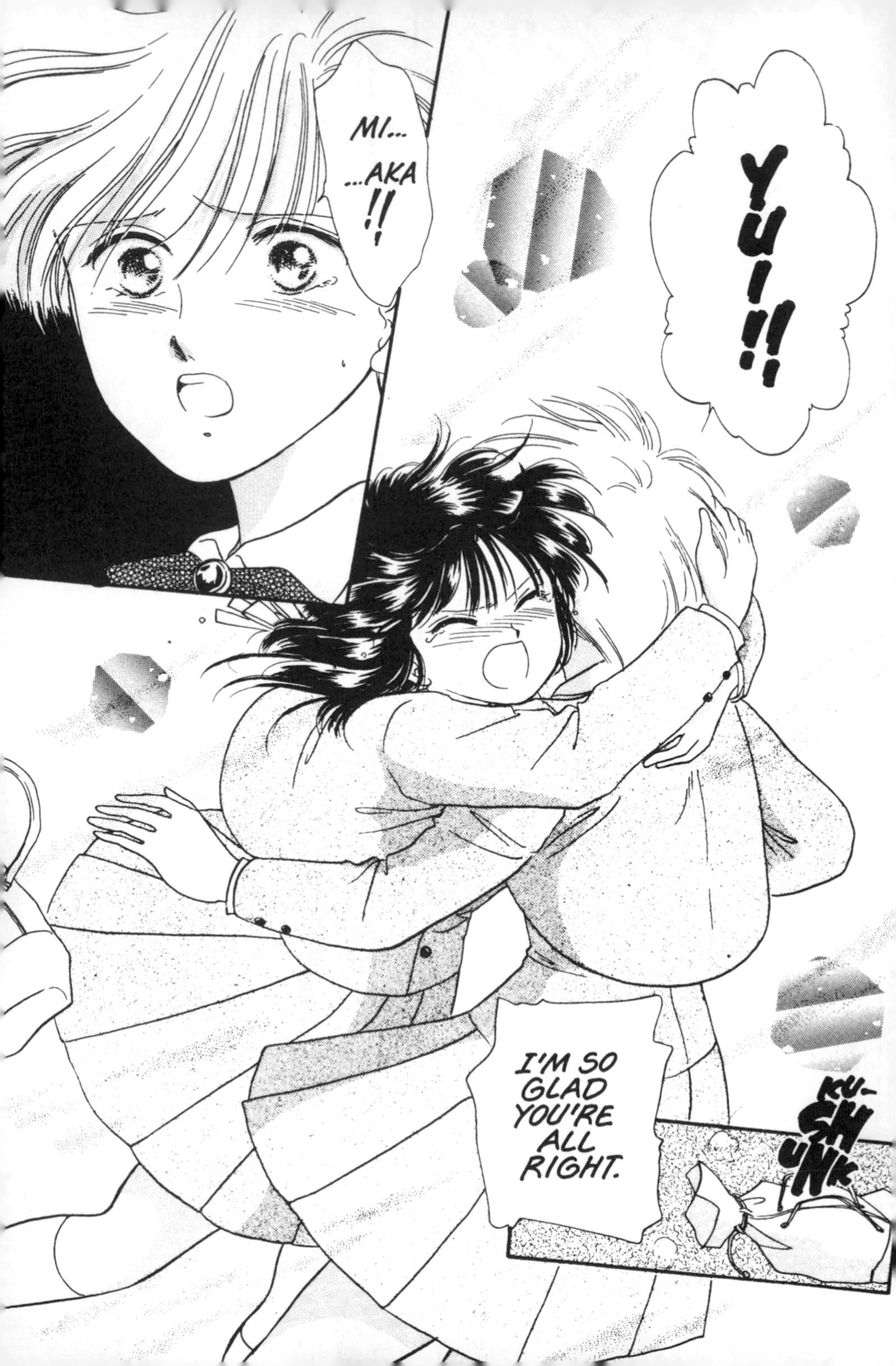
MI... ...AKA !!
YUI-!!
I'M SO GLAD YOU'RE ALL RIGHT.
KU-SHUNK

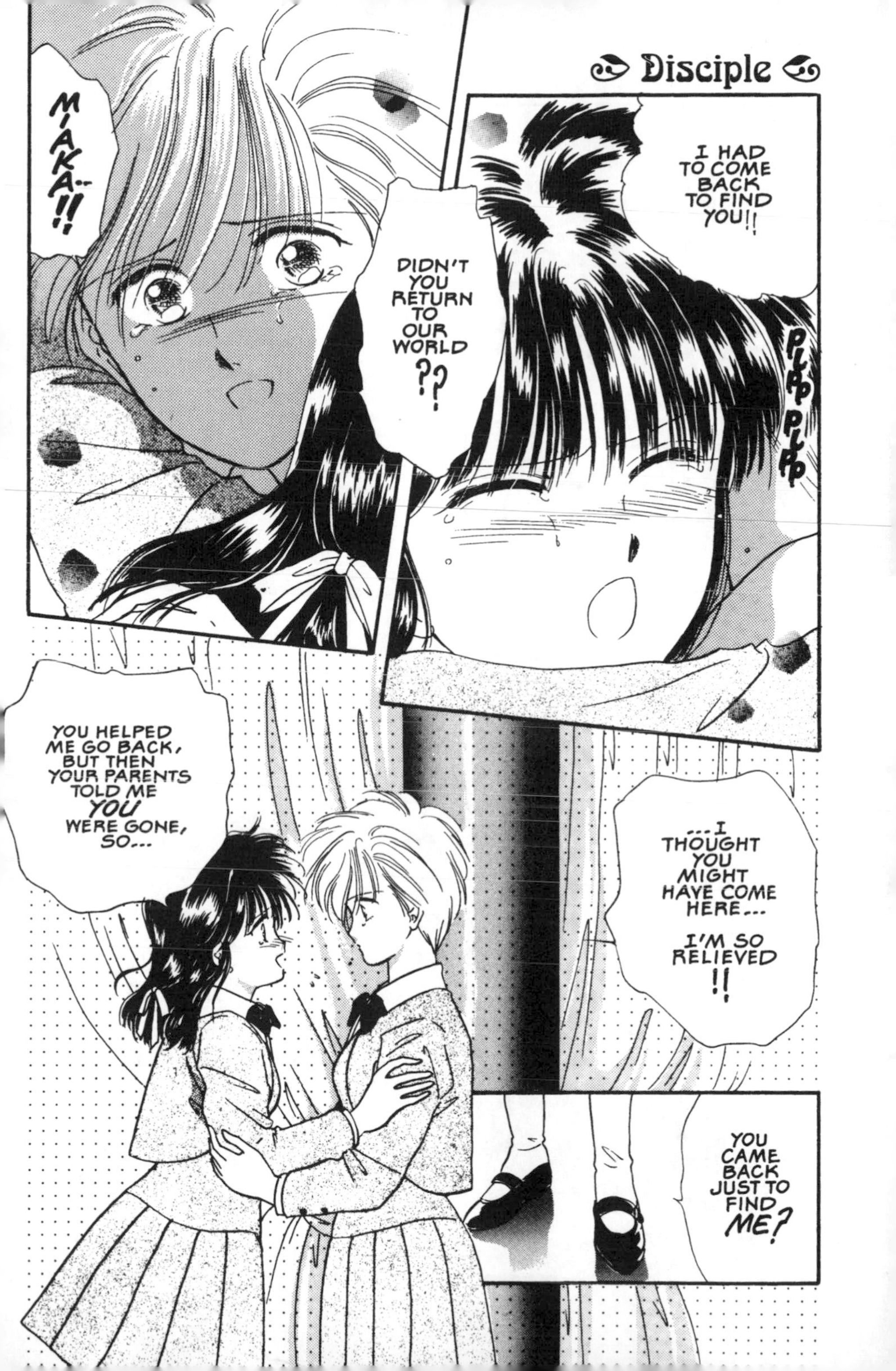
MIAKA...!!
DIDN'T YOU RETURN TO OUR WORLD??
I HAD TO COME BACK TO FIND YOU!!
PLIPP PLIPP
YOU HELPED ME GO BACK, BUT THEN YOUR PARENTS TOLD ME YOU WERE GONE, SO...
...I THOUGHT YOU MIGHT HAVE COME HERE... I'M SO RELIEVED!!
YOU CAME BACK JUST TO FIND ME?

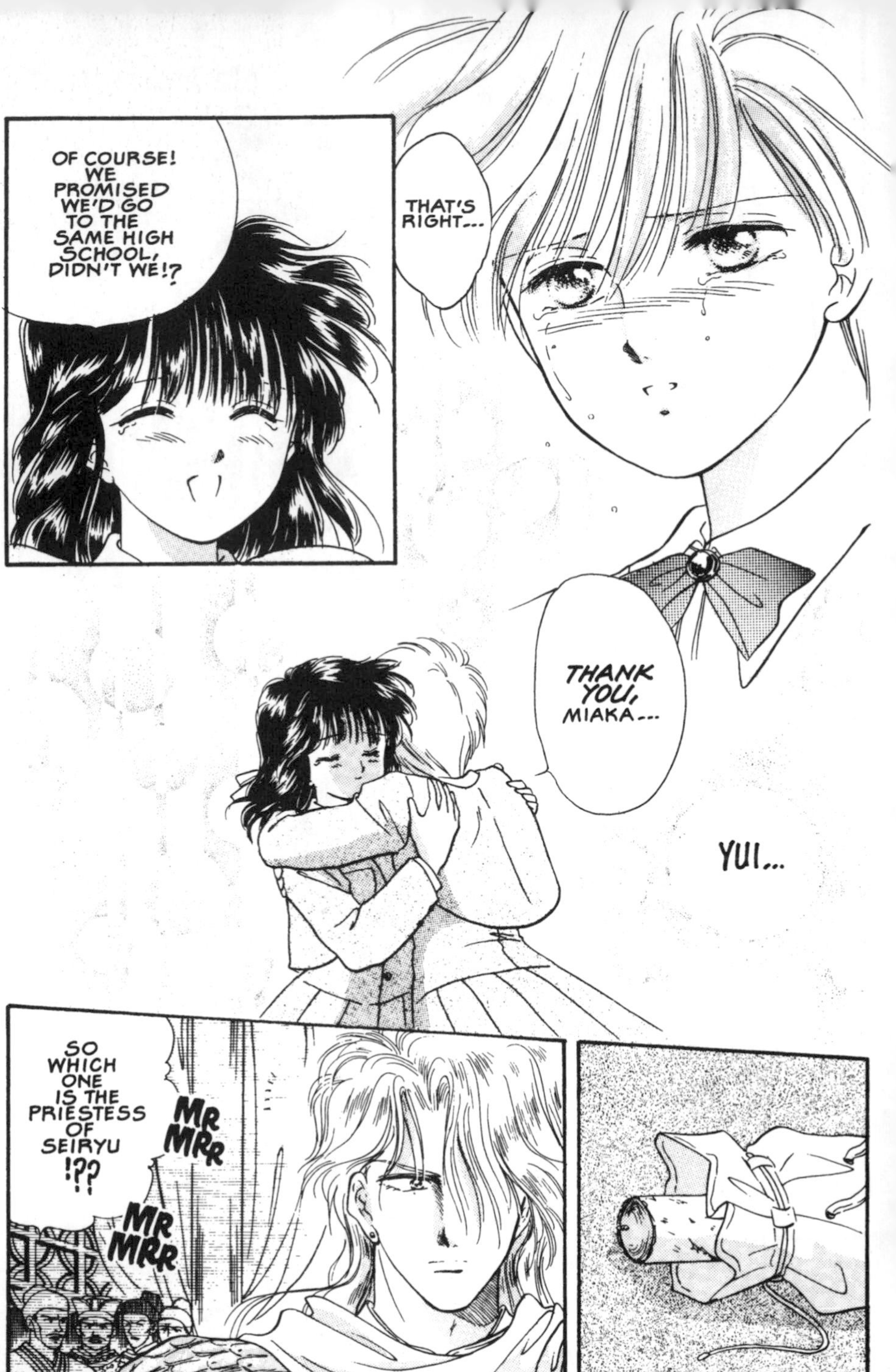
OF COURSE! WE PROMISED WE'D GO TO THE SAME HIGH SCHOOL, DIDN'T WE!?
THAT'S RIGHT...
THANK YOU, MIAKA...
YUI...
SO WHICH ONE IS THE PRIESTESS OF SEIRYU !??
MR MRR
MR MRR

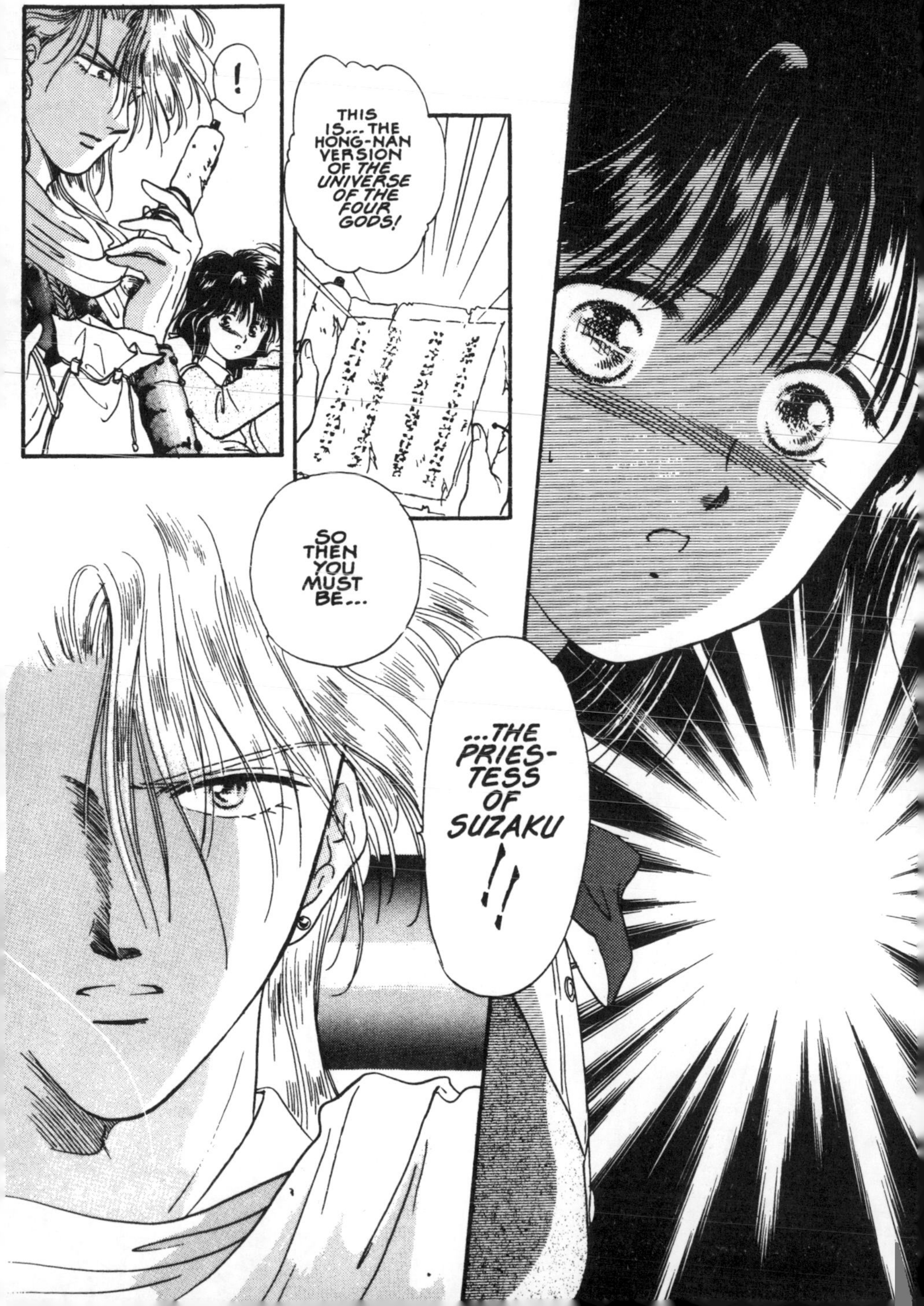
!
THIS IS... THE HONG-NAN VERSION OF *THE UNIVERSE OF THE FOUR GODS!*
SO THEN YOU MUST BE...
...THE PRIESTESS OF SUZAKU !!

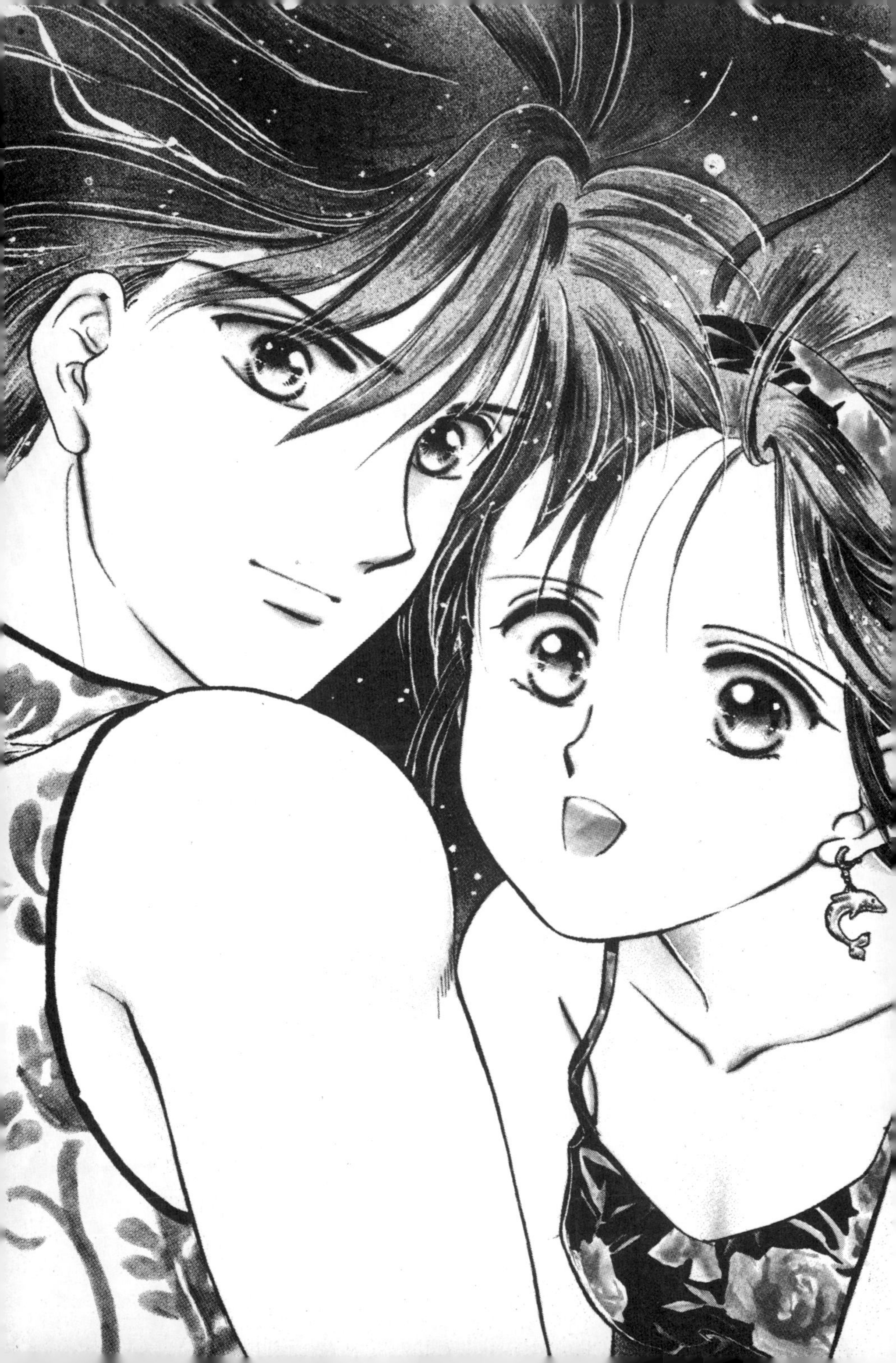

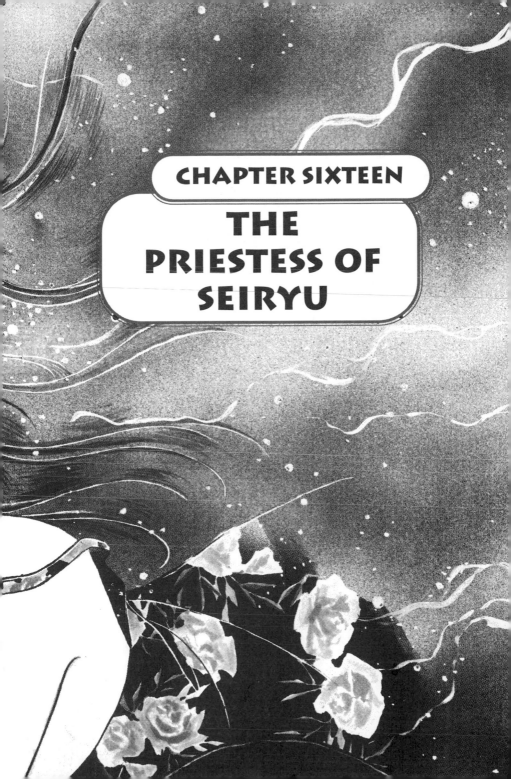

CHAPTER SIXTEEN
THE PRIESTESS OF SEIRYU

NICE

YUI WITH LONG HAIR...
SHE HAD IT LONG UNTIL THE 8th GRADE. SHE
CUT IT SHORT TO AVOID ALL THE ATTENTION
SHE WAS GETTING FROM THE BOYS.

I'M SO
PROUD
SHE'S MY
FRIEND!

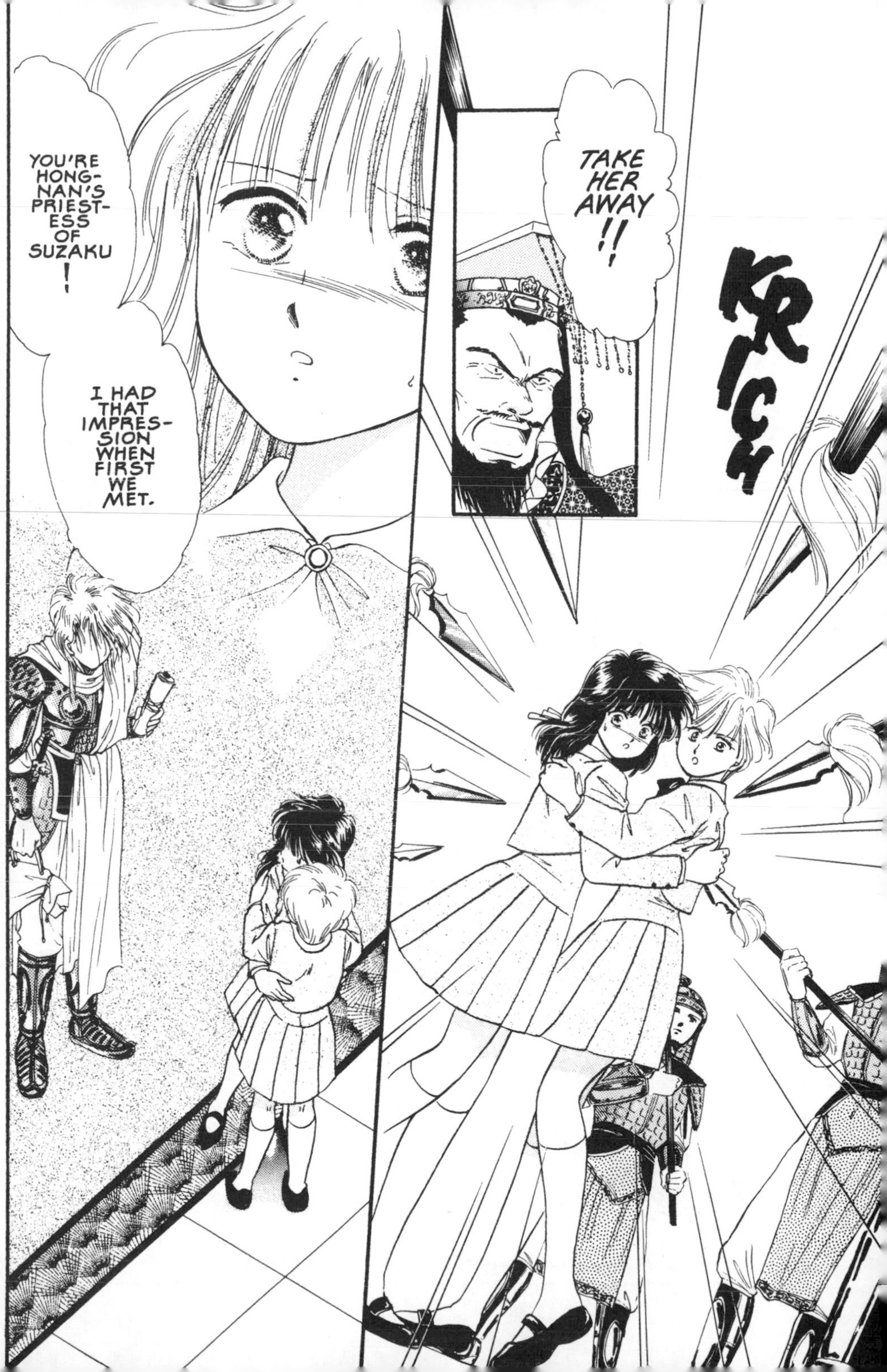
YOU'RE HONG-NAN'S PRIEST-ESS OF SUZAKU !
I HAD THAT IMPRES-SION WHEN FIRST WE MET.
TAKE HER AWAY !!
KRICH

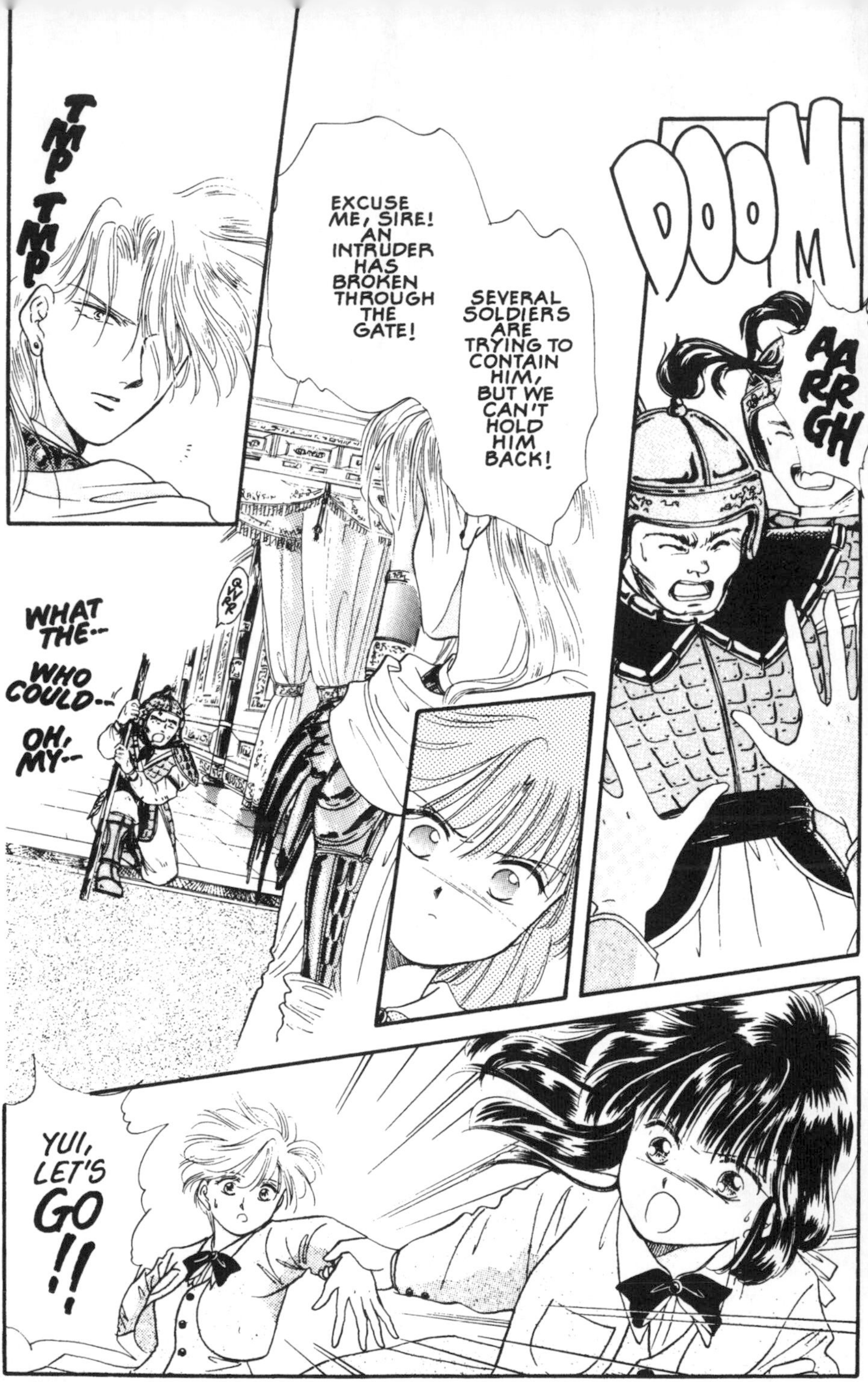
TMP TMP TMP
EXCUSE ME, SIRE! AN INTRUDER HAS BROKEN THROUGH THE GATE!
SEVERAL SOLDIERS ARE TRYING TO CONTAIN HIM, BUT WE CAN'T HOLD HIM BACK!
DOOM
AARRGH
WHAT THE--
WHO COULD--
OH, MY--
YUI, LET'S GO!!

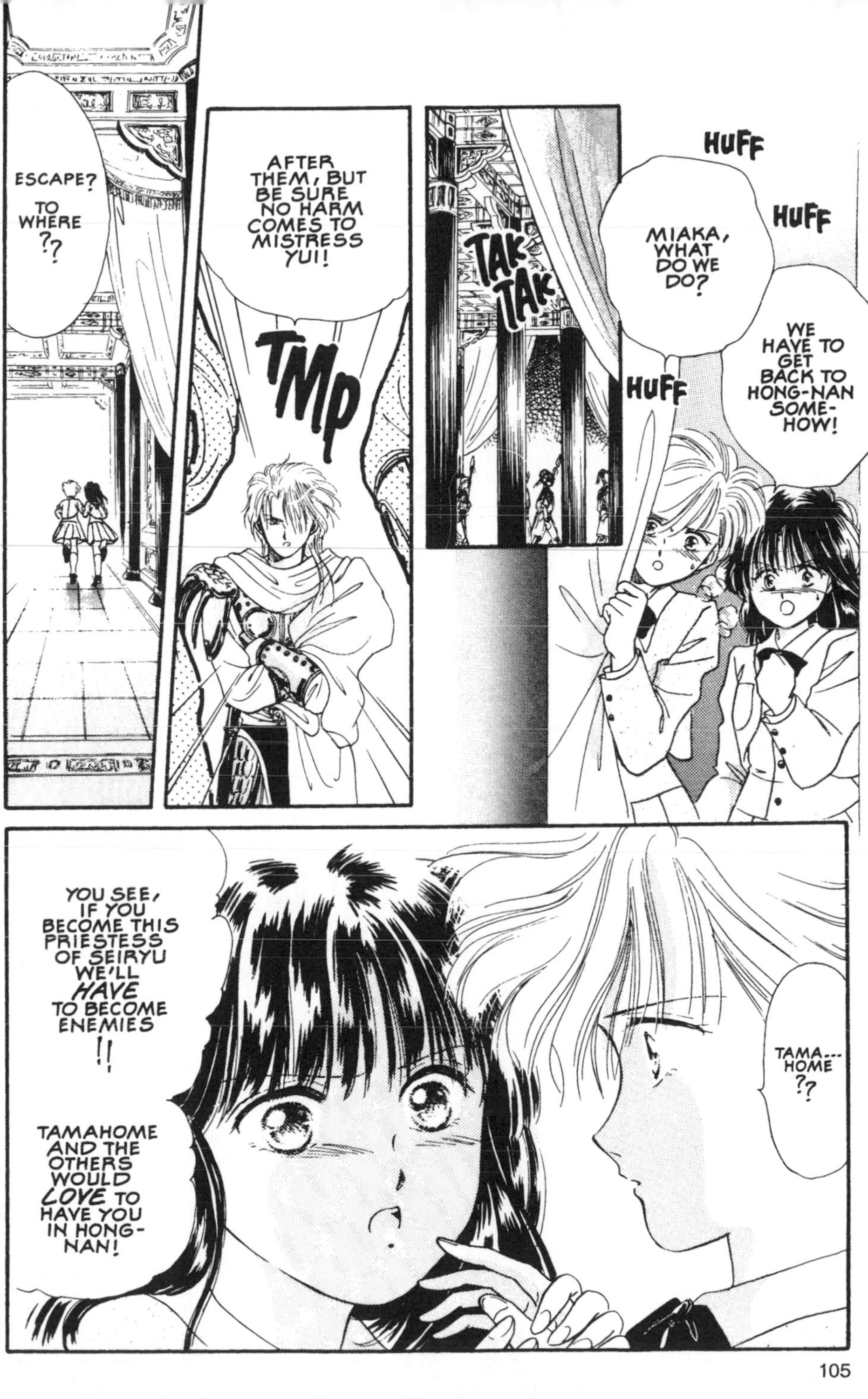
ESCAPE? TO WHERE ??
AFTER THEM, BUT BE SURE NO HARM COMES TO MISTRESS YUI!
TMP
TAK TAK
HUFF
HUFF
MIAKA, WHAT DO WE DO?
WE HAVE TO GET BACK TO HONG-NAN SOME-HOW!
HUFF
YOU SEE, IF YOU BECOME THIS PRIESTESS OF SEIRYU WE'LL HAVE TO BECOME ENEMIES !!
TAMAHOME AND THE OTHERS WOULD LOVE TO HAVE YOU IN HONG-NAN!
TAMA... HOME ??

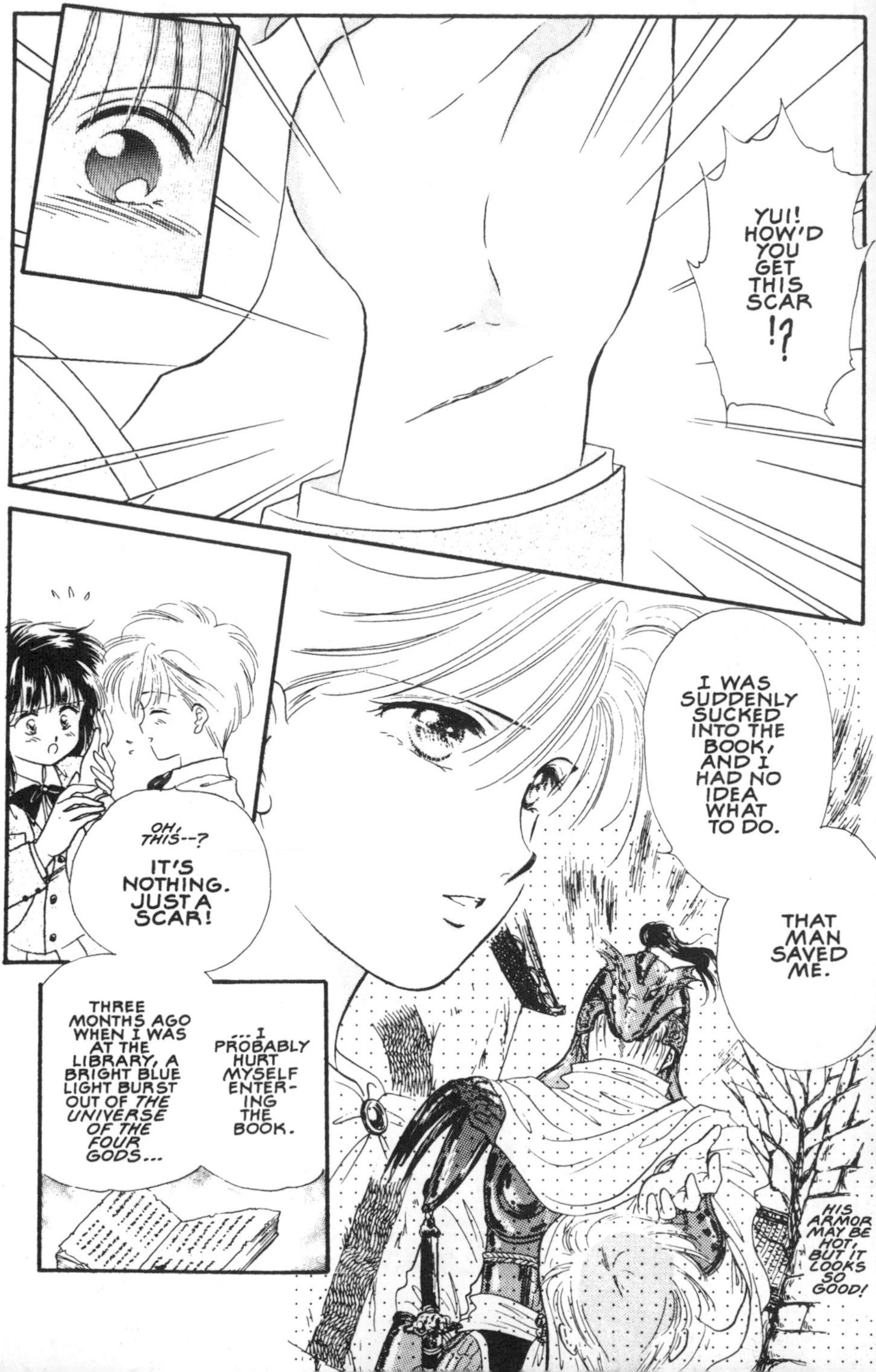
YUI! HOW'D YOU GET THIS SCAR !?
OH, THIS--?
IT'S NOTHING. JUST A SCAR!
THREE MONTHS AGO WHEN I WAS AT THE LIBRARY, A BRIGHT BLUE LIGHT BURST OUT OF *THE UNIVERSE OF THE FOUR GODS*...
...I PROBABLY HURT MYSELF ENTER-ING THE BOOK.
I WAS SUDDENLY SUCKED INTO THE BOOK, AND I HAD NO IDEA WHAT TO DO.
THAT MAN SAVED ME.
HIS ARMOR MAY BE HOT, BUT IT LOOKS SO GOOD!

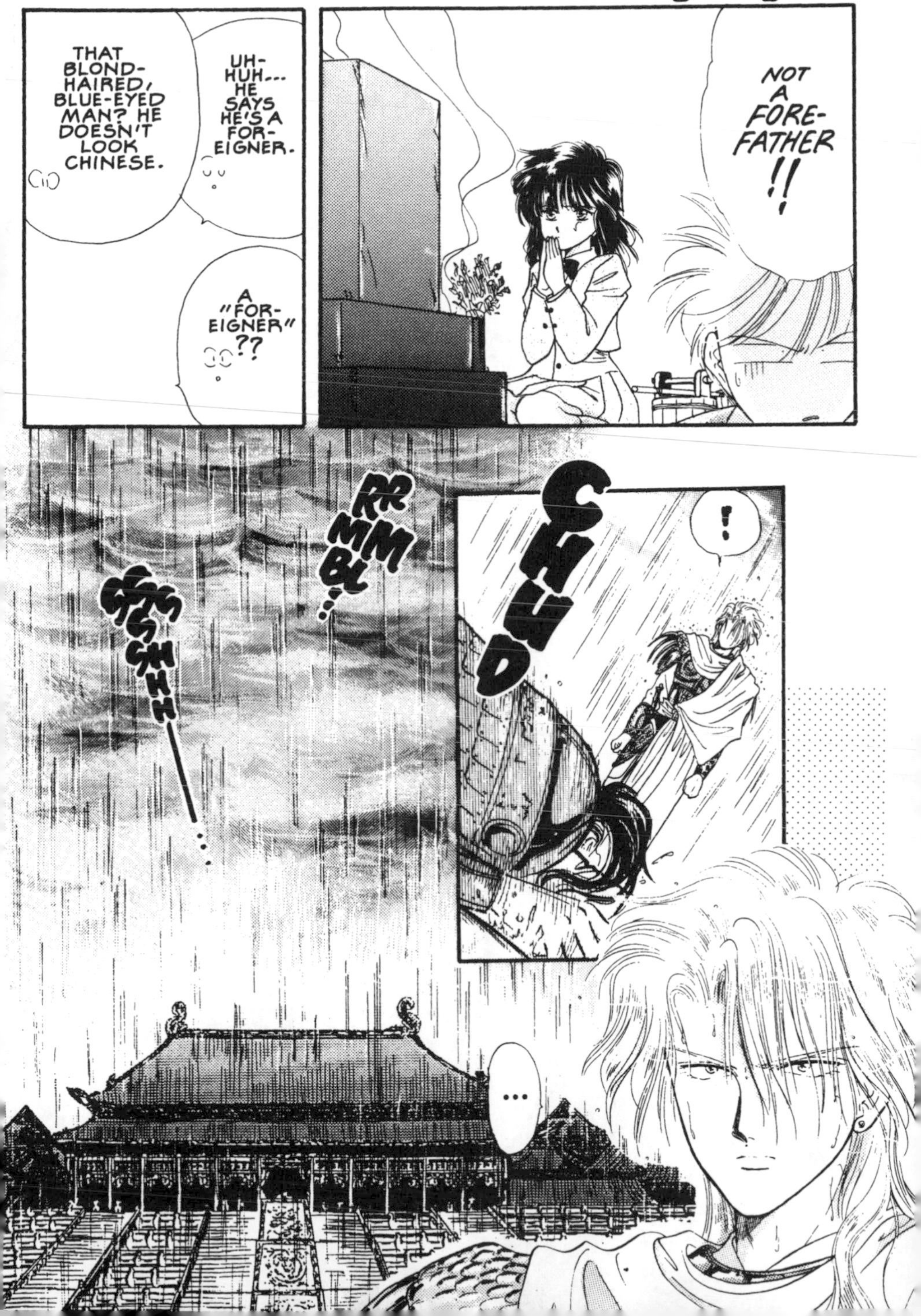
THAT BLOND-HAIRED, BLUE-EYED MAN? HE DOESN'T LOOK CHINESE.
UH-HUH... HE SAYS HE'S A FOREIGNER.
A "FOREIGNER"??
NOT A FOREFATHER!!
GSSSHHH—...
RRMMBL...
CHUD
!
...

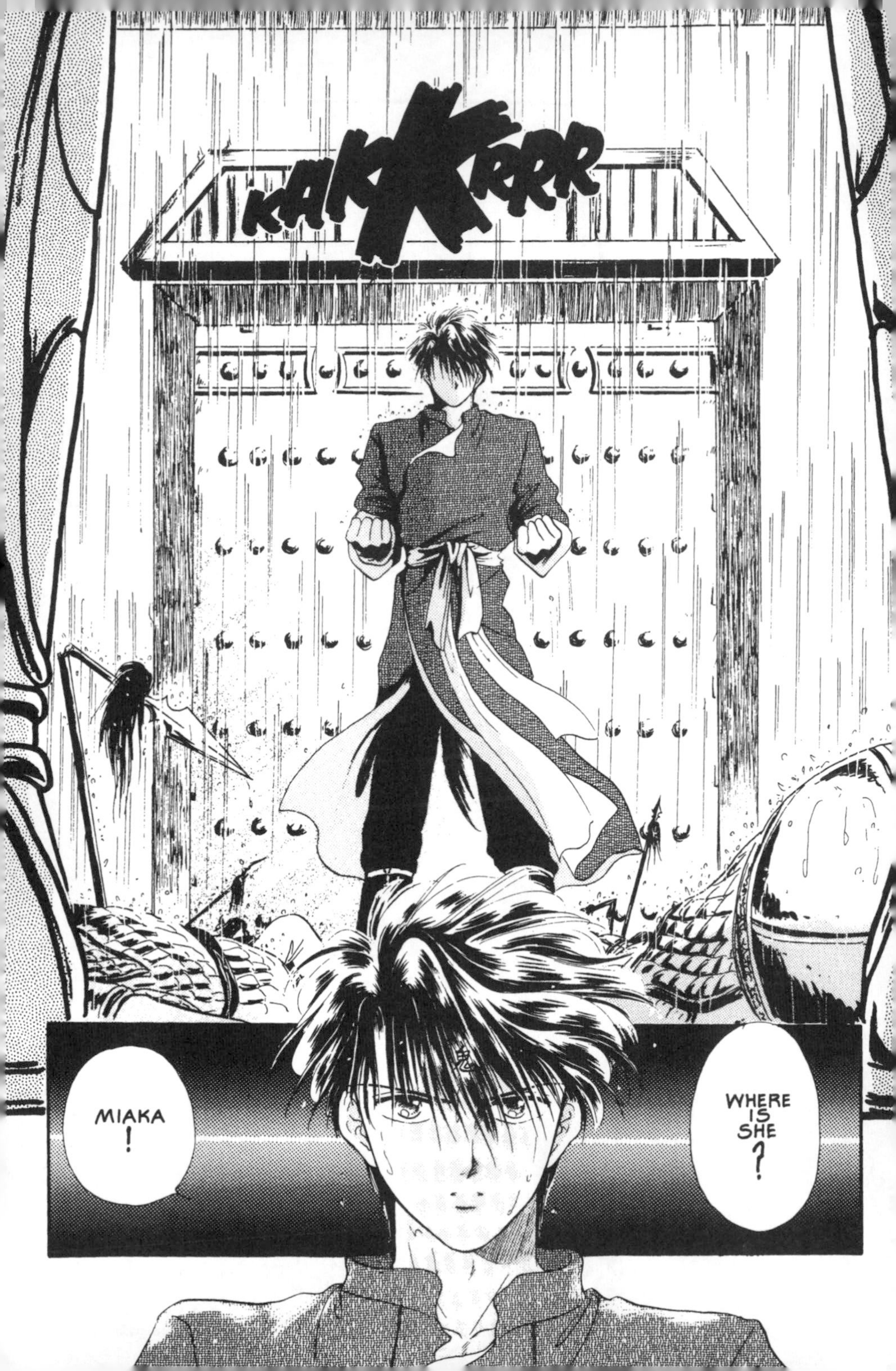
KAKKRRR
MIAKA!
WHERE IS SHE?

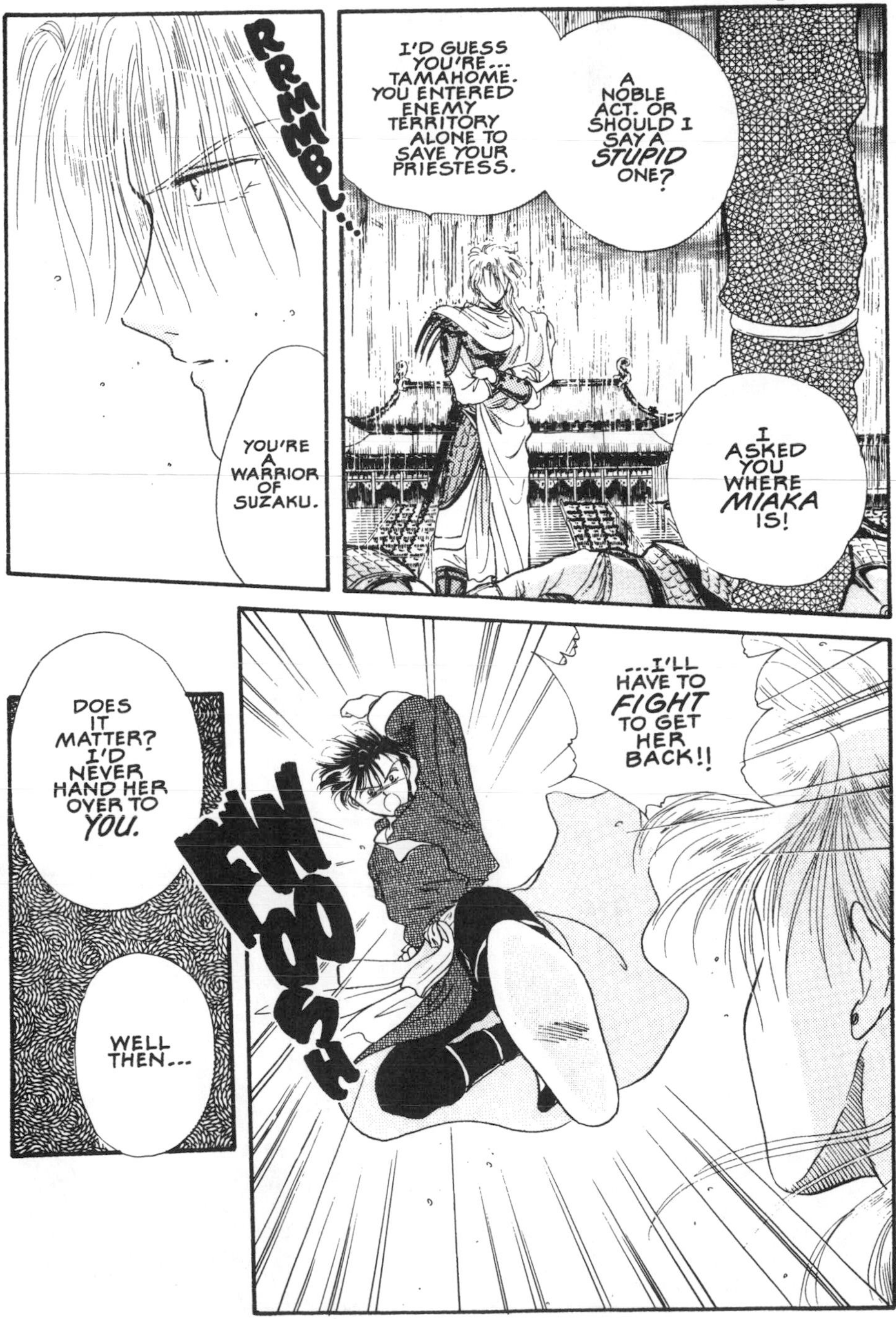
RRMMBL...
YOU'RE A WARRIOR OF SUZAKU.
I'D GUESS YOU'RE... TAMAHOME. YOU ENTERED ENEMY TERRITORY ALONE TO SAVE YOUR PRIESTESS.
A NOBLE ACT. OR SHOULD I SAY A STUPID ONE?
I ASKED YOU WHERE MIAKA IS!
DOES IT MATTER? I'D NEVER HAND HER OVER TO YOU.
WELL THEN...
...I'LL HAVE TO FIGHT TO GET HER BACK!!
FWOOSH

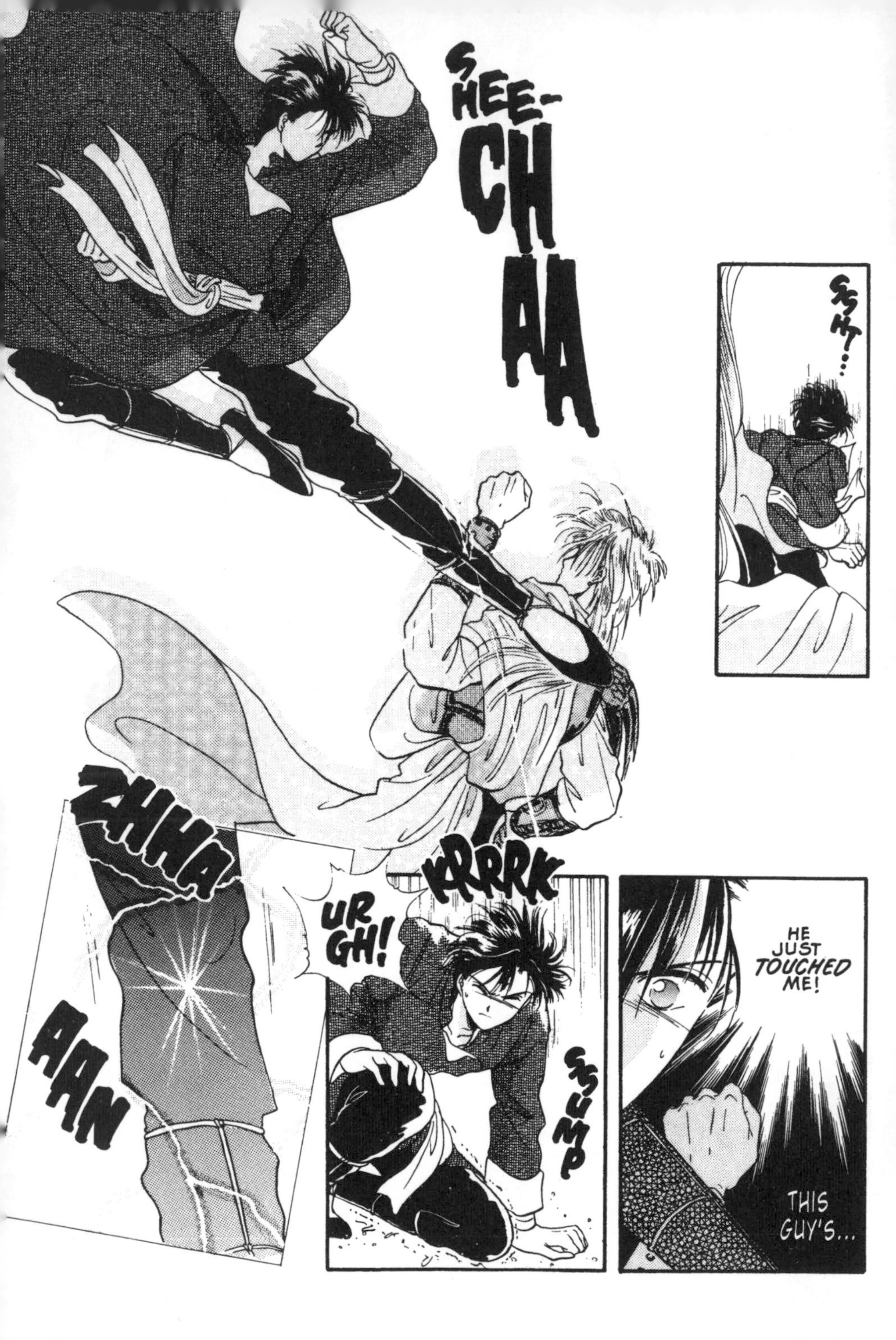
SHEE-CHAAA
SSHT...
ZHHAAAN
URGH!
KRRRK
SSUMP
HE JUST TOUCHED ME!
THIS GUY'S...

...GOOD
!!

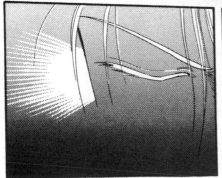

TAMAHOME, GET *AWAY!* NO DA!

PROTECTING TAMAHOME

TP

ZHINN

A SPELL? ANOTHER CON-STELLATION, PERHAPS?

KRr RKK

THANKS, CHICHIRI !!

WAKK

DAA !!

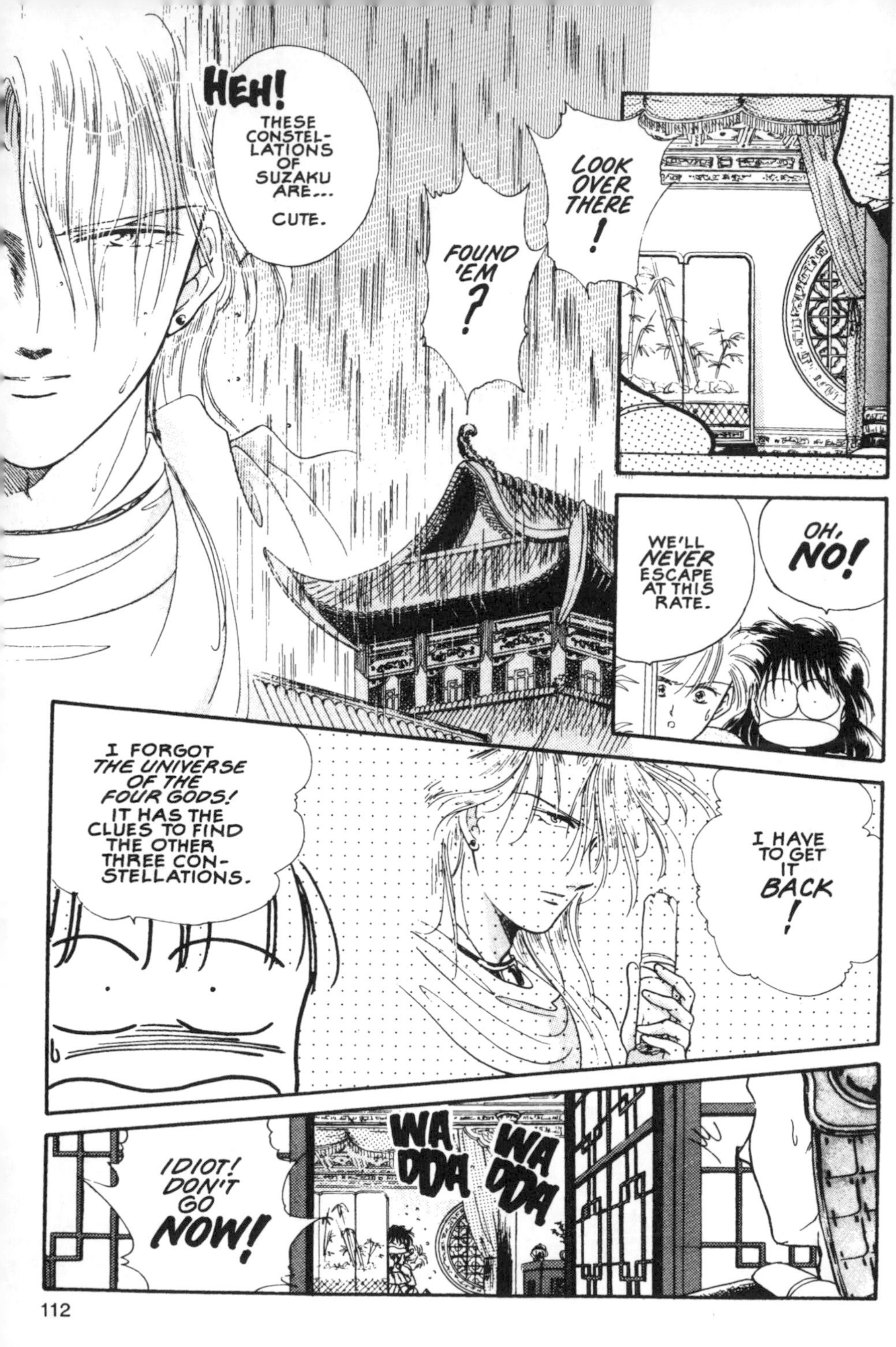
HEH!
THESE CONSTELLATIONS OF SUZAKU ARE... CUTE.
FOUND 'EM?
LOOK OVER THERE!
WE'LL NEVER ESCAPE AT THIS RATE.
OH, NO!
I FORGOT THE UNIVERSE OF THE FOUR GODS! IT HAS THE CLUES TO FIND THE OTHER THREE CONSTELLATIONS.
I HAVE TO GET IT BACK!
IDIOT! DON'T GO NOW!
WADDA WADDA

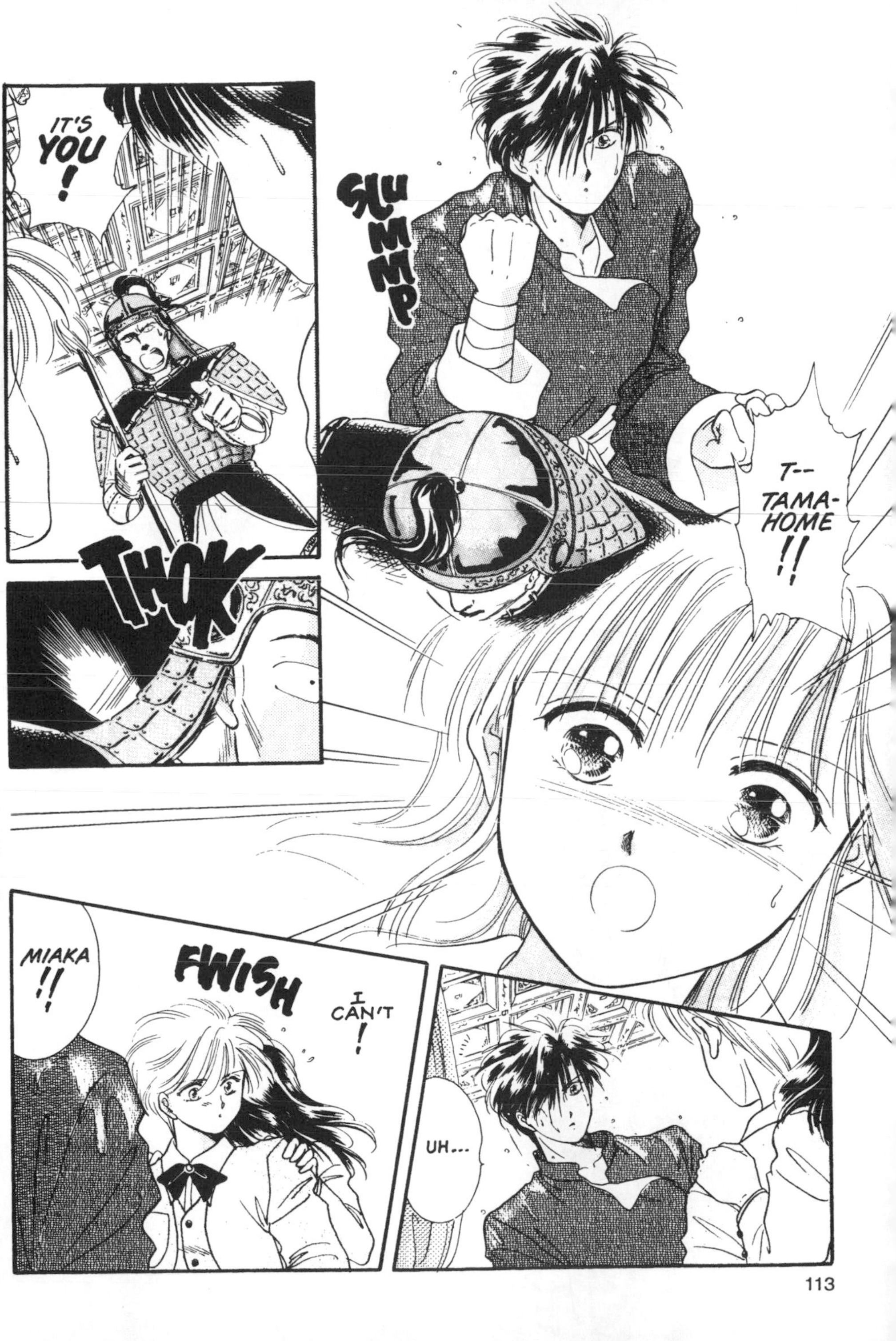
IT'S YOU!
THOK
SLUMMP
T-- TAMA-HOME!!
MIAKA!!
FWISH
I CAN'T!
UH...

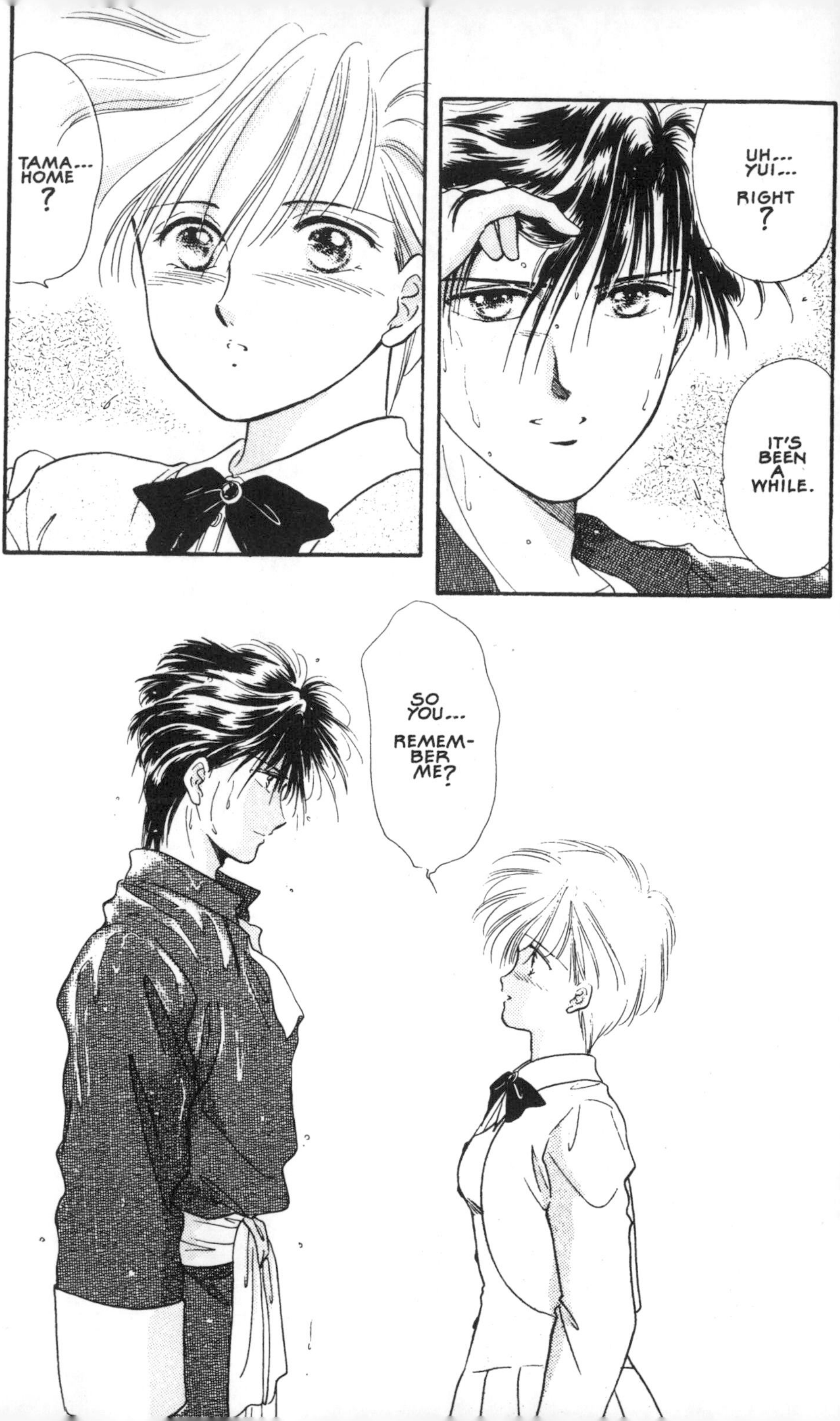
TAMA... HOME?
UH... YUI... RIGHT?
IT'S BEEN A WHILE.
SO YOU... REMEMBER ME?

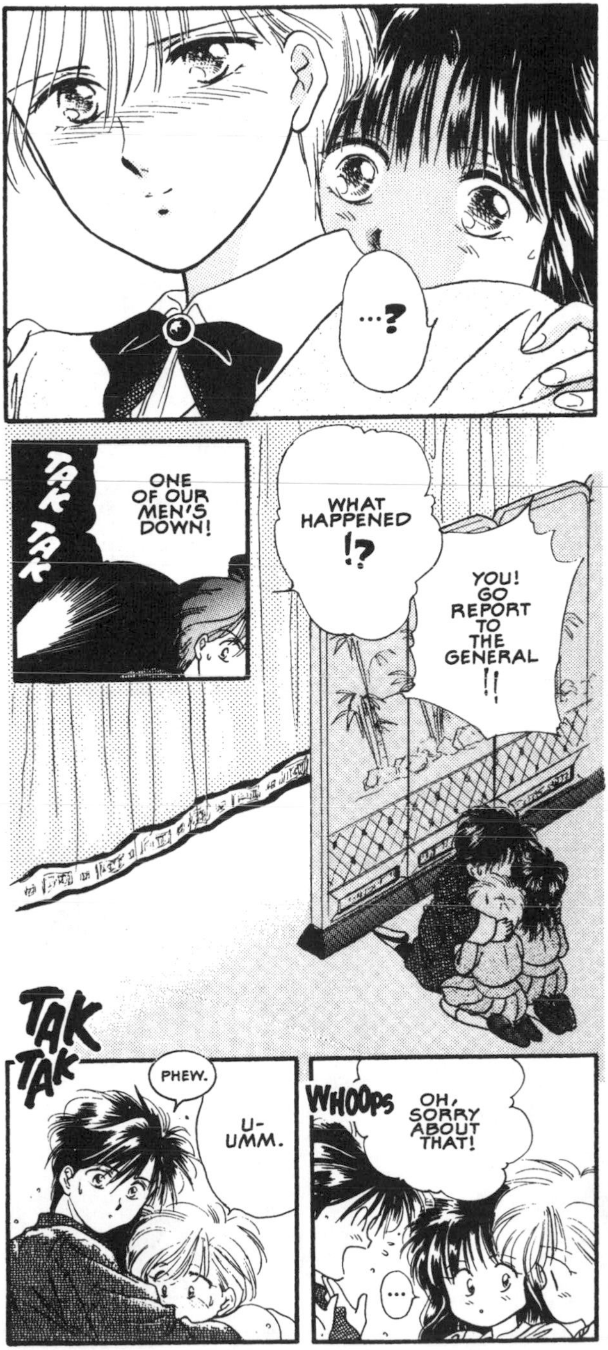
...?
TAK TAK
ONE OF OUR MEN'S DOWN!
WHAT HAPPENED !?
YOU! GO REPORT TO THE GENERAL !!
TAK TAK
PHEW.
U-UMM.
WHOOPS
OH, SORRY ABOUT THAT!
...

Disciple

"Where did the title Fushigi Yûgi come from?" I usually don't have trouble coming up with titles but this one gave me a hard time.
I've been planning this story since I was eighteen, but its tentative title, "Suzaku," just didn't seem right, so I had to work really hard for a title that would fit the right image.
I looked through a whole bunch of magazines to come up with a good rhyming title, and that's how I came up with "Fushigi Yûgi." I actually think it's a pretty nice title. The kanji for "Yûgi" show up a lot in Hong Kong films. There's Bruce Lee's "Shibô Yûgi" (The Game of Death) for example. I didn't intend it to mean "frolic," but a nuance more like "game". I guess it would mean "Mysterious Game."*
I was talking about computer games with my assistant M. who insisted that "Fushigi Yûgi" would be a great computer game. We talked about this endlessly. It's not just because we were talking about my story, but because it seemed really fun. Computer games usually begin by introducing the story with drawings, but this one would start with opening the book *The Universe of the Four Gods*. Then a map would come up and you'd see Qu-Dong, Hotohori's palace, Daichi-san, and Tamahome's village. You could follow the plot the same way as the manga, or you could start from any random location and try to find all seven celestial warriors. It'd be an RPG game, so you'd have random enemies appearing, and everybody has different powers and abilities so the way to fight would always change. When you start losing, you could call on Chichiri who'd suddenly appear and cast a spell. If Tamahome dies (for example), he might be revived at a certain location if he has enough money stored away.
Other ideas: If you go to Qu-Dong immediately without gaining enough experience points, you'd get yourself killed. If Miaka's a player-character, you'd have to have a gauge, not just for power, but for love too.
Of course, she'd have to lose a lot of love points when she's away from Tamahome. When she returns to reality, that's the end of the game. Miaka could get advice from her brother. The ideas go on and on.

To be continued...!

*But something like "Miracle Game" just sounds so corny!

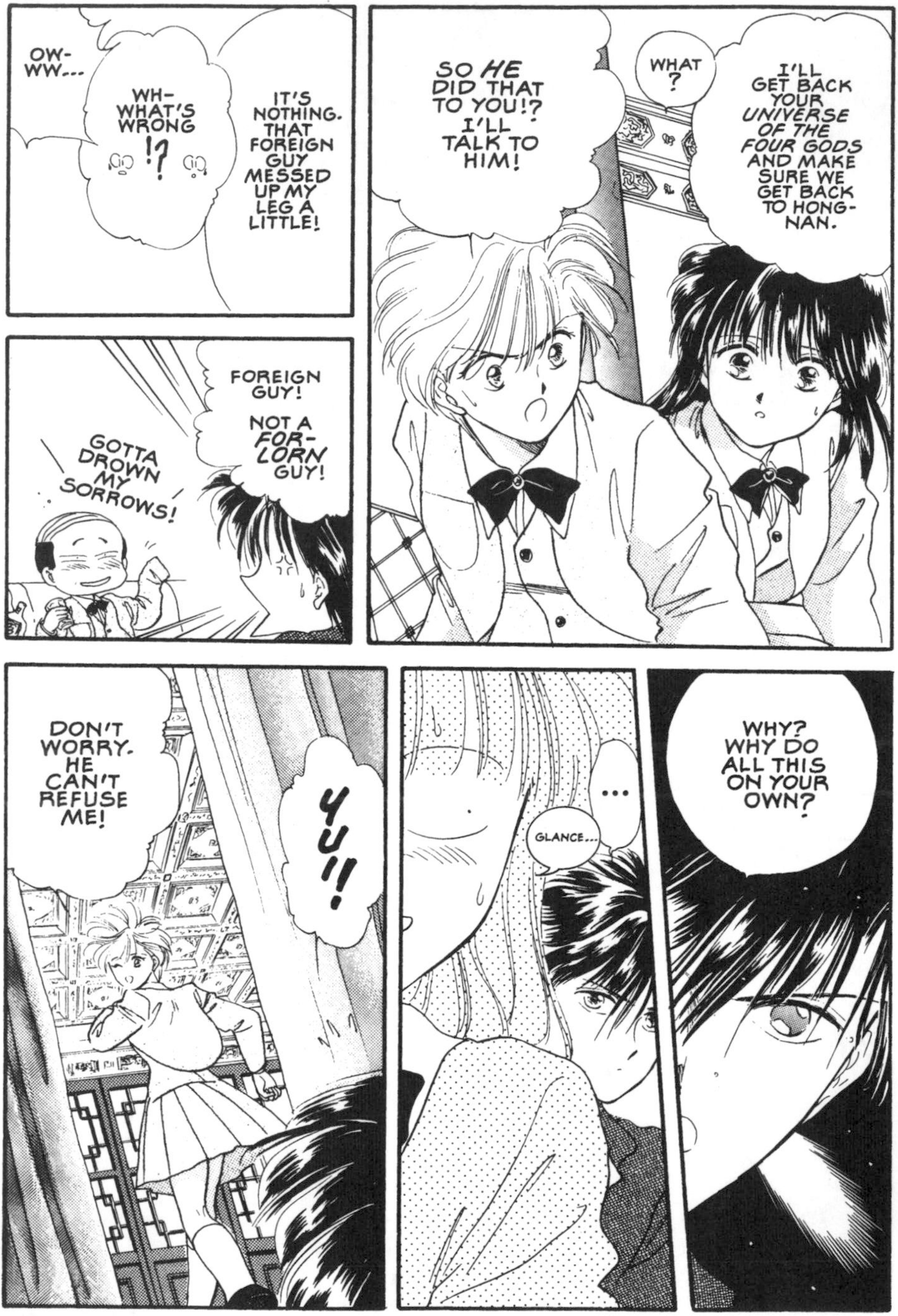
OW-WW...
WH-WHAT'S WRONG !?
IT'S NOTHING. THAT FOREIGN GUY MESSED UP MY LEG A LITTLE!
FOREIGN GUY! NOT A FOR-LORN GUY!
GOTTA DROWN MY SORROWS!
SO HE DID THAT TO YOU!? I'LL TALK TO HIM!
WHAT ?
I'LL GET BACK YOUR UNIVERSE OF THE FOUR GODS AND MAKE SURE WE GET BACK TO HONG-NAN.
DON'T WORRY. HE CAN'T REFUSE ME!
YUI!!
...
GLANCE...
WHY? WHY DO ALL THIS ON YOUR OWN?

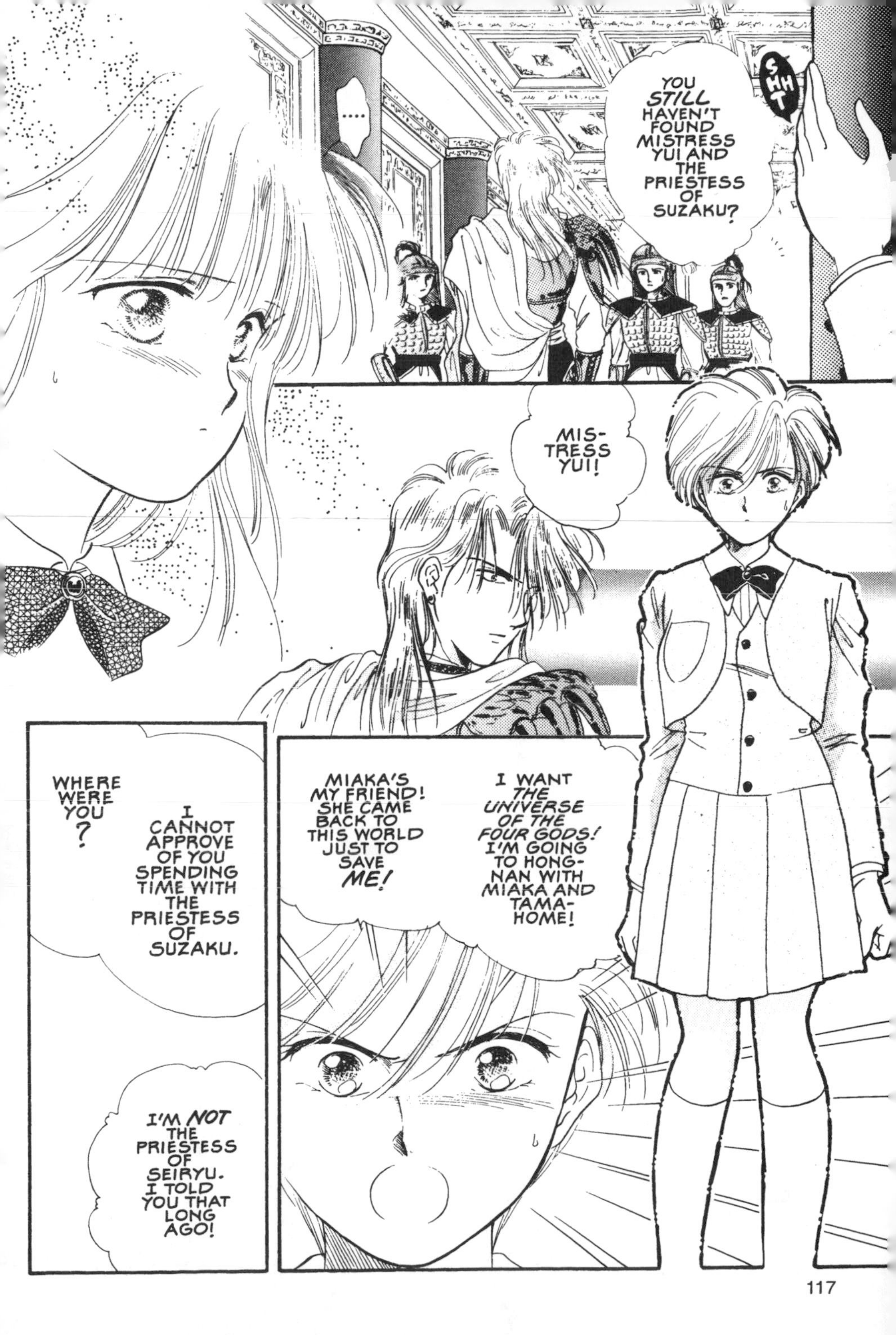
....
YOU STILL HAVEN'T FOUND MISTRESS YUI AND THE PRIESTESS OF SUZAKU?
SHHT
MIS-TRESS YUI!
WHERE WERE YOU?
I CANNOT APPROVE OF YOU SPENDING TIME WITH THE PRIESTESS OF SUZAKU.
I'M NOT THE PRIESTESS OF SEIRYU. I TOLD YOU THAT LONG AGO!
MIAKA'S MY FRIEND! SHE CAME BACK TO THIS WORLD JUST TO SAVE ME!
I WANT THE UNIVERSE OF THE FOUR GODS! I'M GOING TO HONG-NAN WITH MIAKA AND TAMA-HOME!

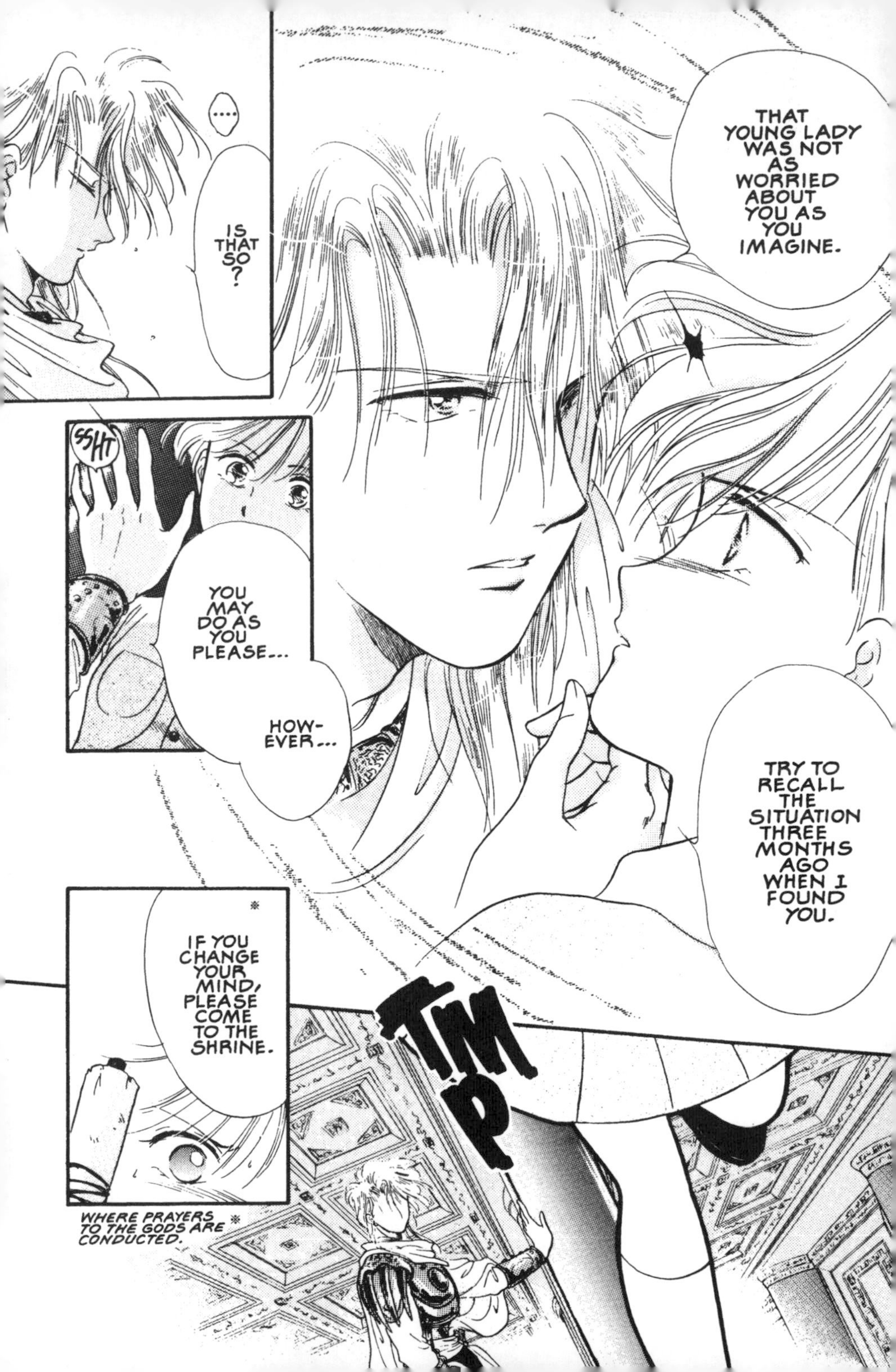
....
IS THAT SO?
THAT YOUNG LADY WAS NOT AS WORRIED ABOUT YOU AS YOU IMAGINE.
SSHT
YOU MAY DO AS YOU PLEASE...
HOW-EVER...
TRY TO RECALL THE SITUATION THREE MONTHS AGO WHEN I FOUND YOU.
IF YOU CHANGE YOUR MIND, PLEASE COME TO THE SHRINE. ※
TMP

※ WHERE PRAYERS TO THE GODS ARE CONDUCTED.

YOU SAID THAT YOU CAN'T ACCEPT MY PROTECTION.

WHY?

I CAN HANDLE IT ON MY OWN.

BESIDES, THIS IS JUST BETWEEN MY FRIEND AND ME, SO...

HU FF HU FF

...IT HAS *NOTHING* TO DO WITH ME?

DO I JUST CAUSE TROUBLE FOR YOU?

!!

MIAKA !

119

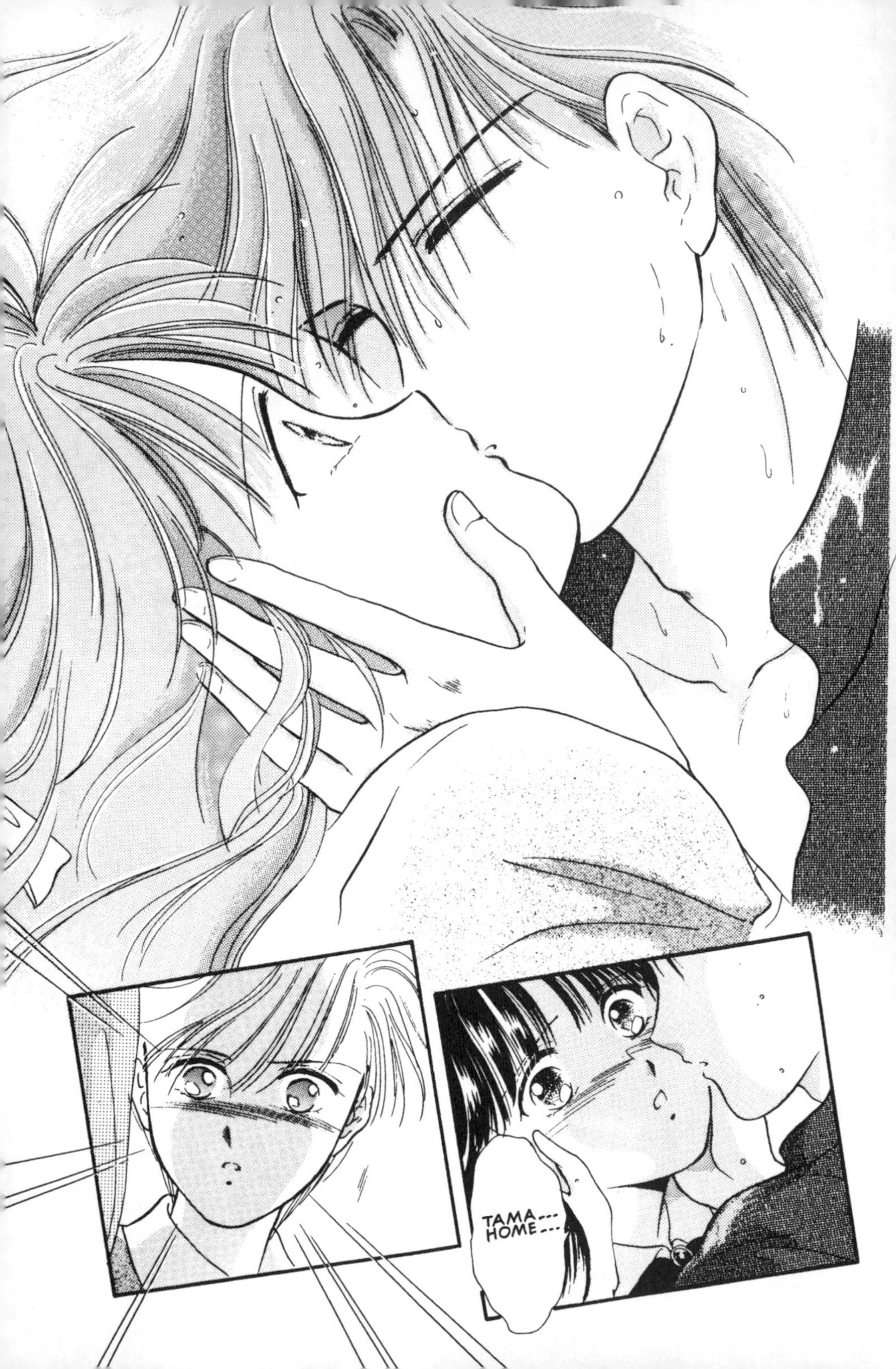
TAMA---
HOME---

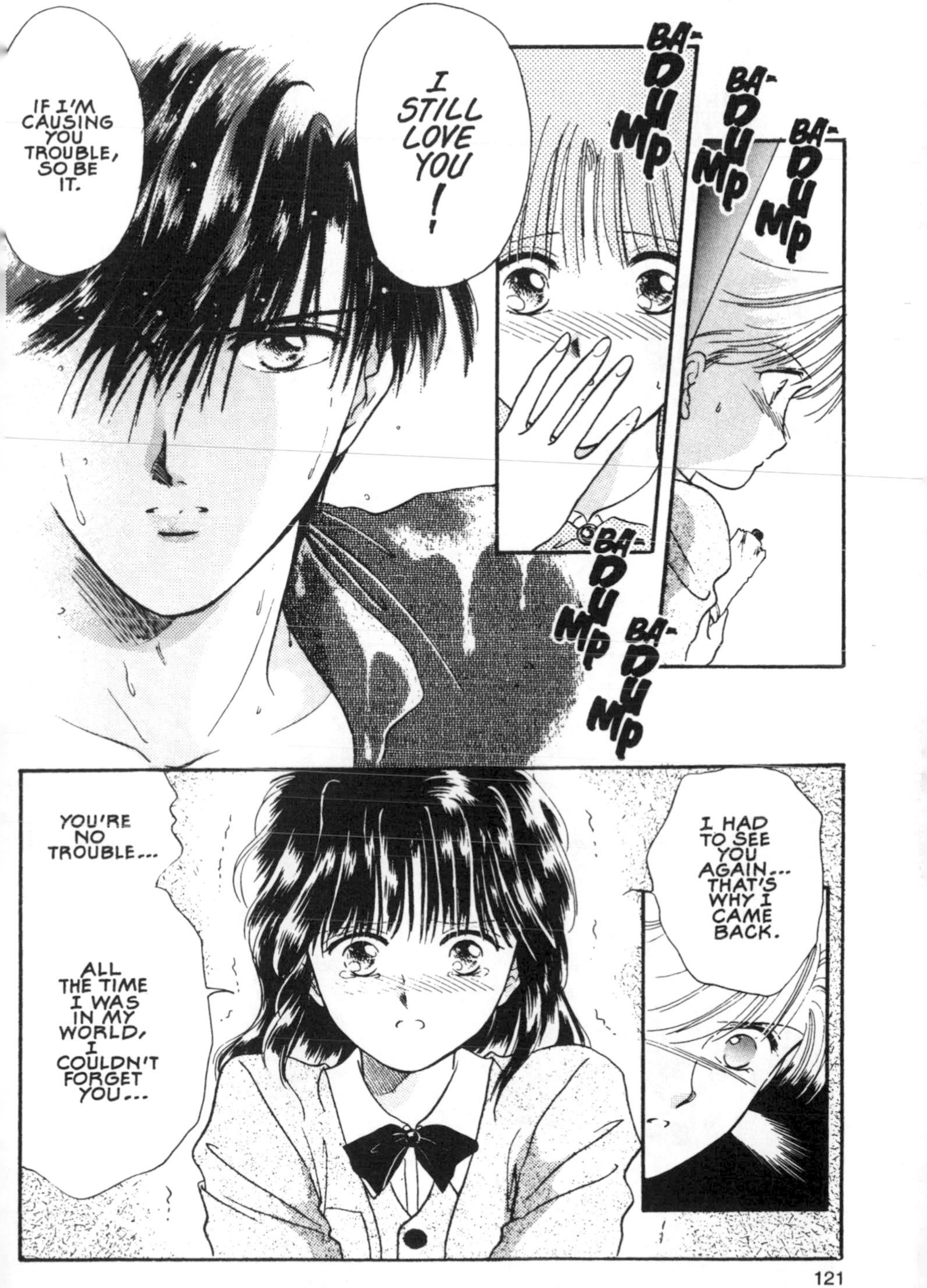
IF I'M CAUSING YOU TROUBLE, SO BE IT.
I STILL LOVE YOU!
BA-DUMP
BA-DUMP
BA-DUMP
BA-DUMP
BA-DUMP
YOU'RE NO TROUBLE...
ALL THE TIME I WAS IN MY WORLD, I COULDN'T FORGET YOU...
I HAD TO SEE YOU AGAIN... THAT'S WHY I CAME BACK.

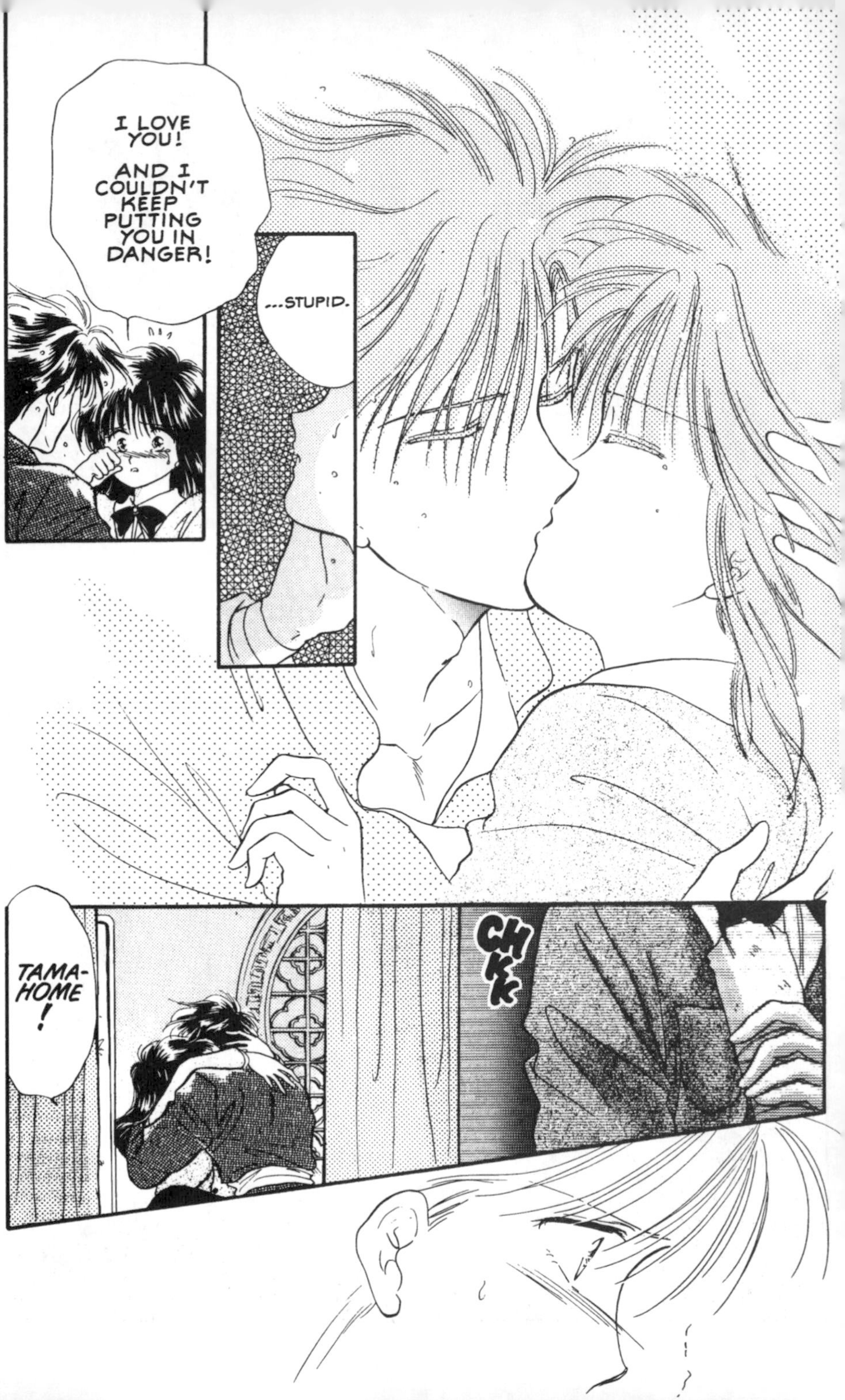

I LOVE YOU! AND I COULDN'T KEEP PUTTING YOU IN DANGER!
...STUPID.
TAMAHOME!
CHKK

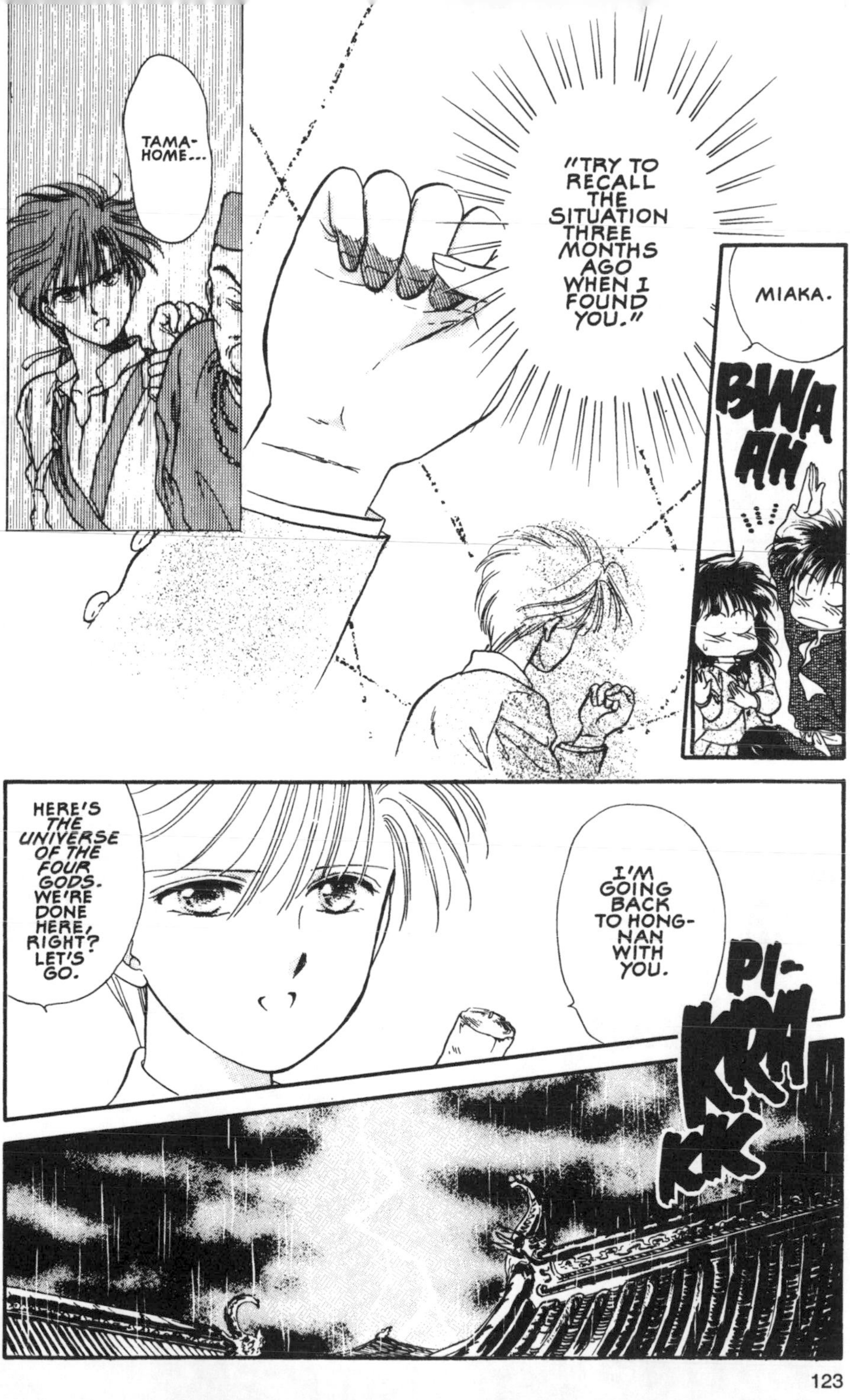

TAMA-HOME...
"TRY TO RECALL THE SITUATION THREE MONTHS AGO WHEN I FOUND YOU."
MIAKA.
BWAAAH
HERE'S THE UNIVERSE OF THE FOUR GODS. WE'RE DONE HERE, RIGHT? LET'S GO.
I'M GOING BACK TO HONG-NAN WITH YOU.
PI-KRAKK

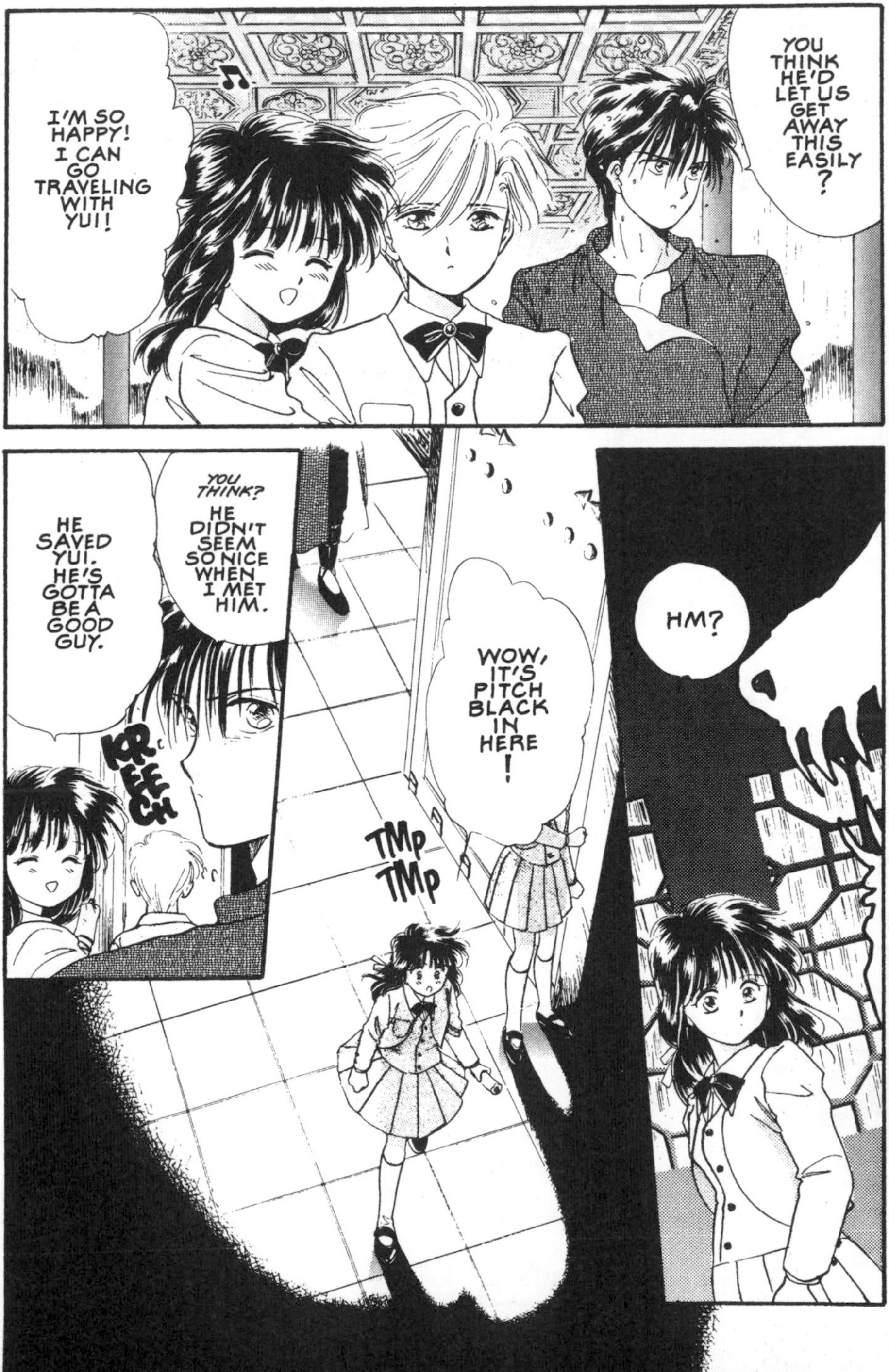
I'M SO HAPPY! I CAN GO TRAVELING WITH YUI!
YOU THINK HE'D LET US GET AWAY THIS EASILY?
HE SAVED YUI. HE'S GOTTA BE A GOOD GUY.
YOU THINK? HE DIDN'T SEEM SO NICE WHEN I MET HIM.
KREEECH
WOW, IT'S PITCH BLACK IN HERE!
TMP TMP
HM?

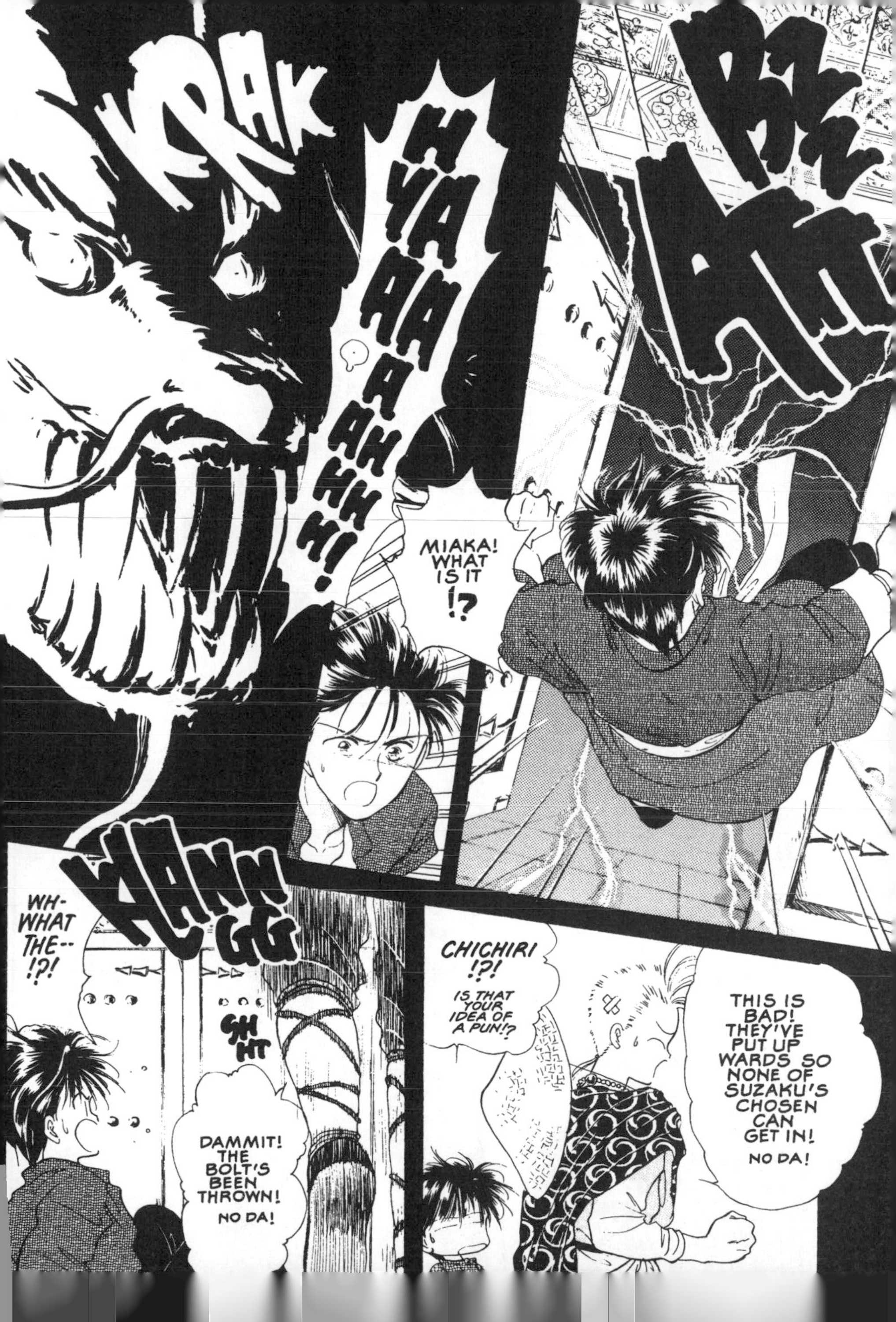
KRAK
HYAAAAAAAHHHH!
MIAKA! WHAT IS IT!?
HANNGG
WH-WHAT THE--!?!
SHHT
DAMMIT! THE BOLT'S BEEN THROWN! NO DA!
CHICHIRI!?!
IS THAT YOUR IDEA OF A PUN!?
THIS IS BAD! THEY'VE PUT UP WARDS SO NONE OF SUZAKU'S CHOSEN CAN GET IN! NO DA!

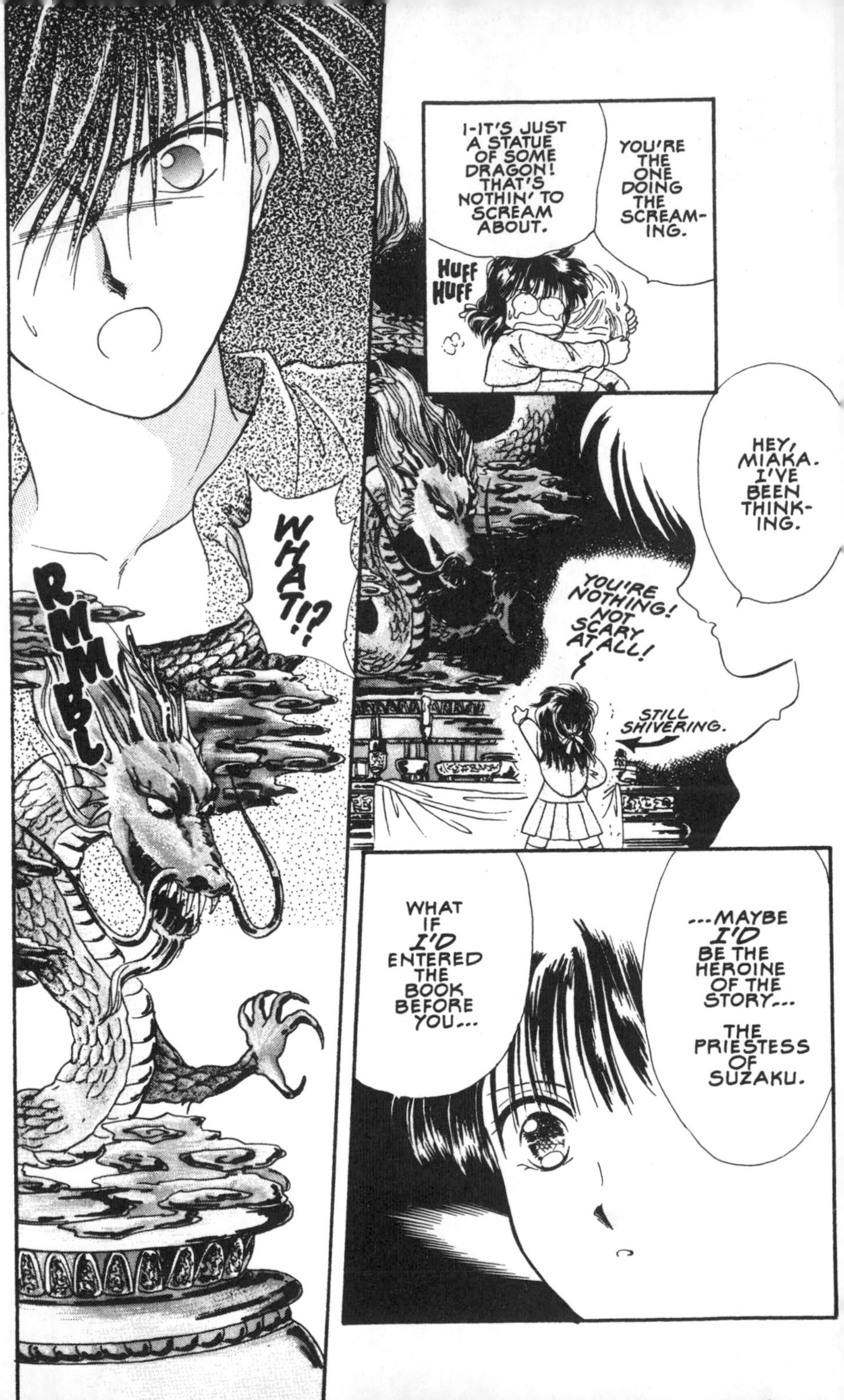
WHAT!?
RMMBL
I-IT'S JUST A STATUE OF SOME DRAGON! THAT'S NOTHIN' TO SCREAM ABOUT.
YOU'RE THE ONE DOING THE SCREAM-ING.
HUFF HUFF
YOU'RE NOTHING! NOT SCARY AT ALL!
STILL SHIVERING.
HEY, MIAKA. I'VE BEEN THINK-ING.
WHAT IF I'D ENTERED THE BOOK BEFORE YOU...
...MAYBE I'D BE THE HEROINE OF THE STORY...
THE PRIESTESS OF SUZAKU.

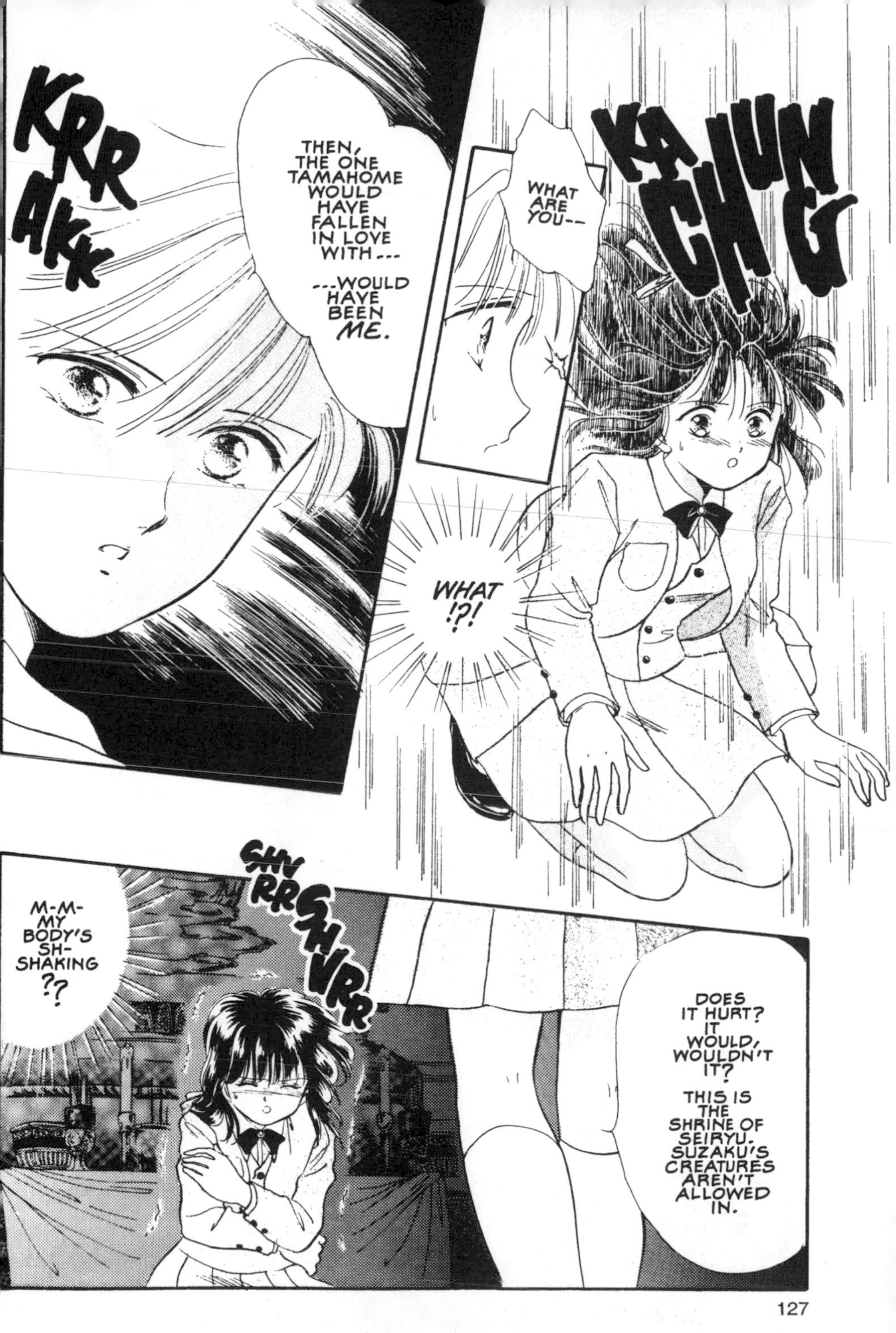
WHAT ARE YOU--
KACHUN CHG
WHAT !?!
KRRAKK
THEN, THE ONE TAMAHOME WOULD HAVE FALLEN IN LOVE WITH...
...WOULD HAVE BEEN *ME*.
DOES IT HURT? IT WOULD, WOULDN'T IT?
THIS IS THE SHRINE OF SEIRYU. SUZAKU'S CREATURES AREN'T ALLOWED IN.
SHVRR SHVRR
M-M-MY BODY'S SH-SHAKING ??

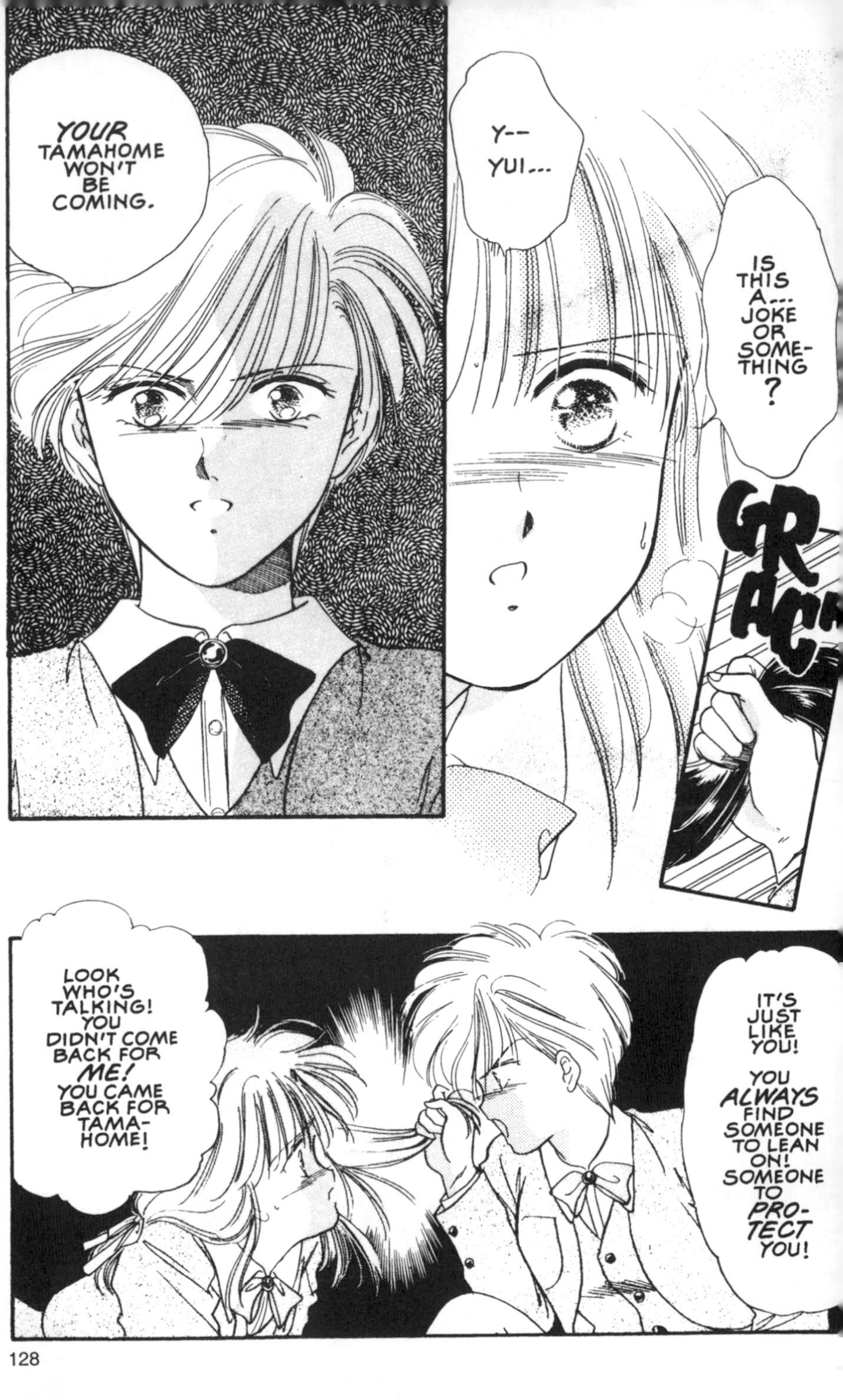
YOUR TAMAHOME WON'T BE COMING.
Y-- YUI...
IS THIS A... JOKE OR SOME-THING?
GR-ACK
LOOK WHO'S TALKING! YOU DIDN'T COME BACK FOR ME! YOU CAME BACK FOR TAMA-HOME!
IT'S JUST LIKE YOU!
YOU ALWAYS FIND SOMEONE TO LEAN ON! SOMEONE TO PRO-TECT YOU!

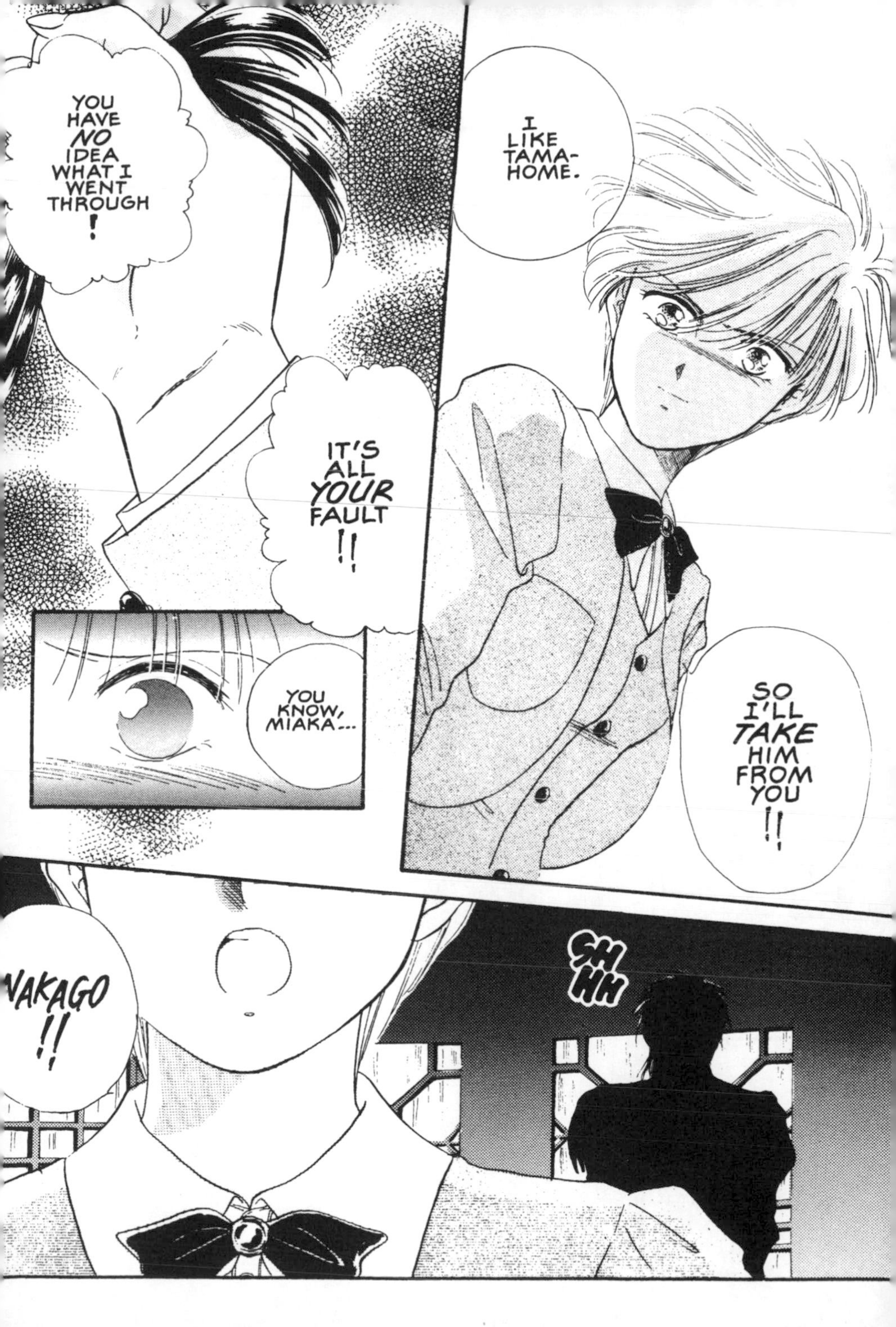
YOU HAVE NO IDEA WHAT I WENT THROUGH!
IT'S ALL YOUR FAULT!!
YOU KNOW, MIAKA...
I LIKE TAMA-HOME.
SO I'LL TAKE HIM FROM YOU!!
NAKAGO!!
SHHH

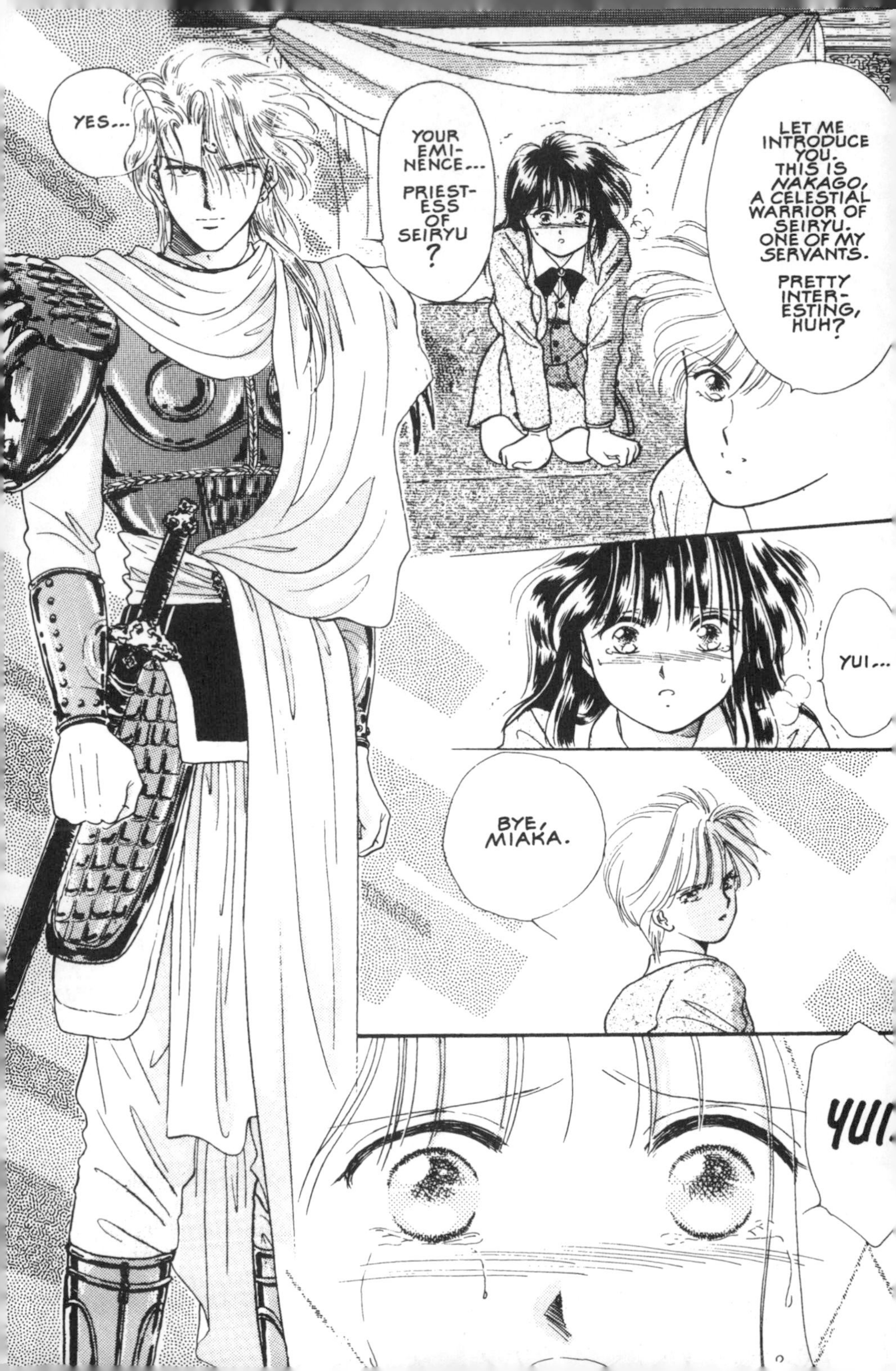
YES...
YOUR EMINENCE... PRIESTESS OF SEIRYU?
LET ME INTRODUCE YOU. THIS IS NAKAGO, A CELESTIAL WARRIOR OF SEIRYU. ONE OF MY SERVANTS.
PRETTY INTERESTING, HUH?
YUI...
BYE, MIAKA.
YUI!

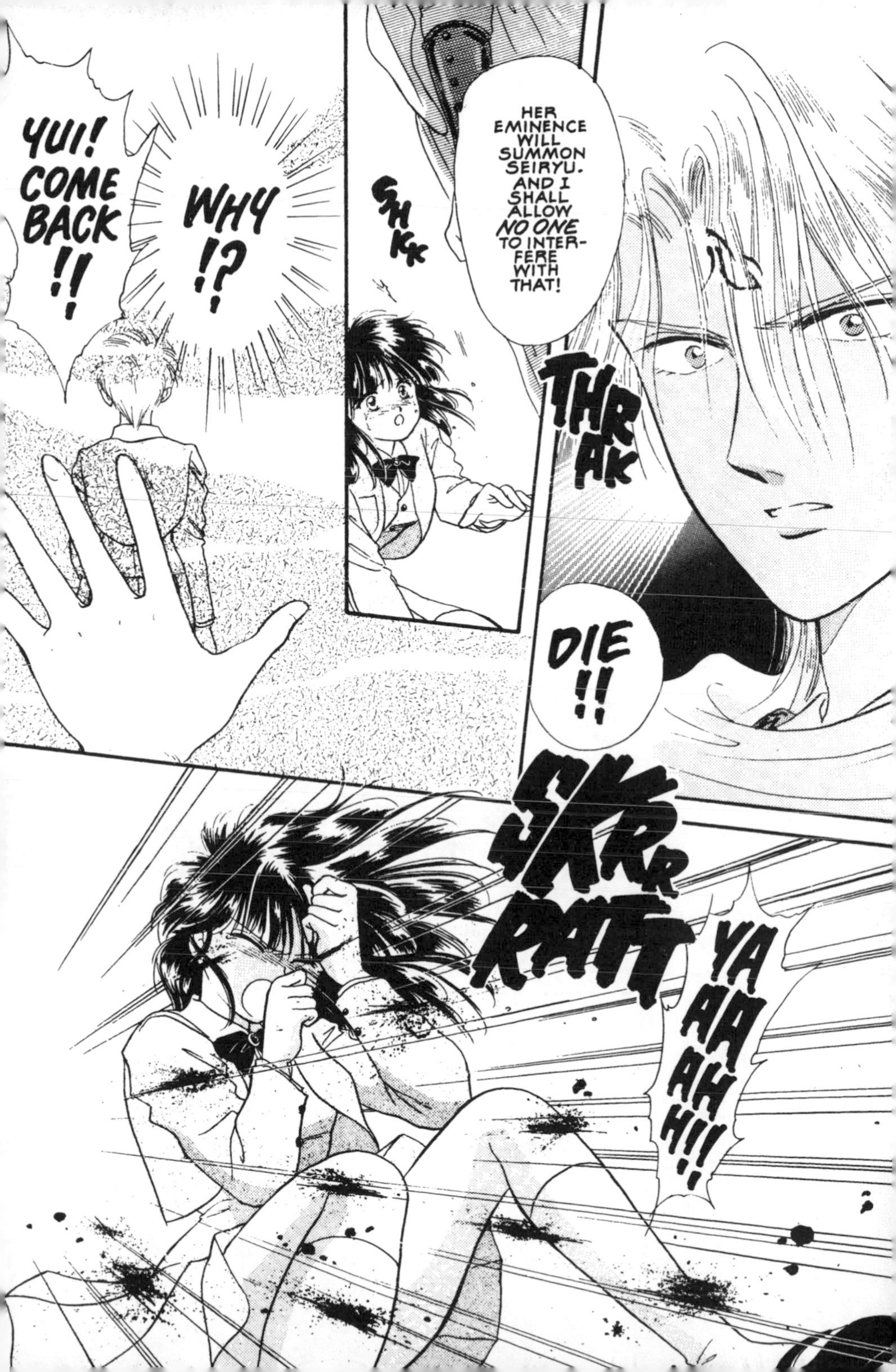
YUI! COME BACK!!
WHY!?
HER EMINENCE WILL SUMMON SEIRYU. AND I SHALL ALLOW *NO ONE* TO INTERFERE WITH THAT!
SHKK
THRAK
DIE!!
SKRRRATT
YAAAAAHH!!

BACK POPULAR DEMAND!
Pardon the Parody is newly retitled as:

ふしぎ悪戯 FUSHIGI AKUGI
THE MALICIOUS PLAY

ANOTHER IDEA BY MANGA ARTIST Y.M.

YOU HAVE NO IDEA WHAT I WENT THROUGH!
IT'S ALL YOUR FAULT!!
YOU KNOW, MIAKA...
I LIKE TAMA-HOME.
SO I'LL TAKE HIM FROM YOU!!
NAKAGO!!
SHHH

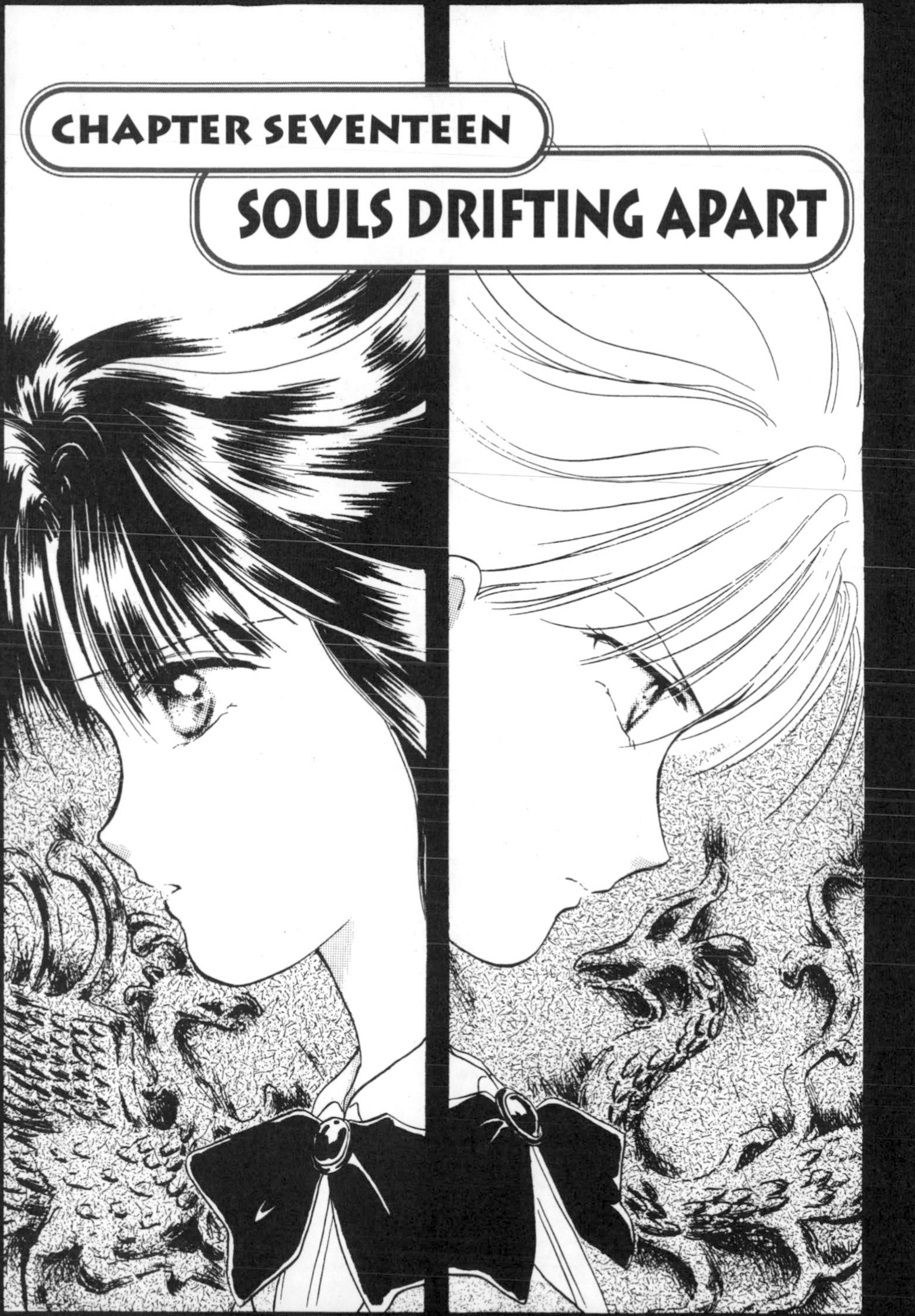
CHAPTER SEVENTEEN
SOULS DRIFTING APART

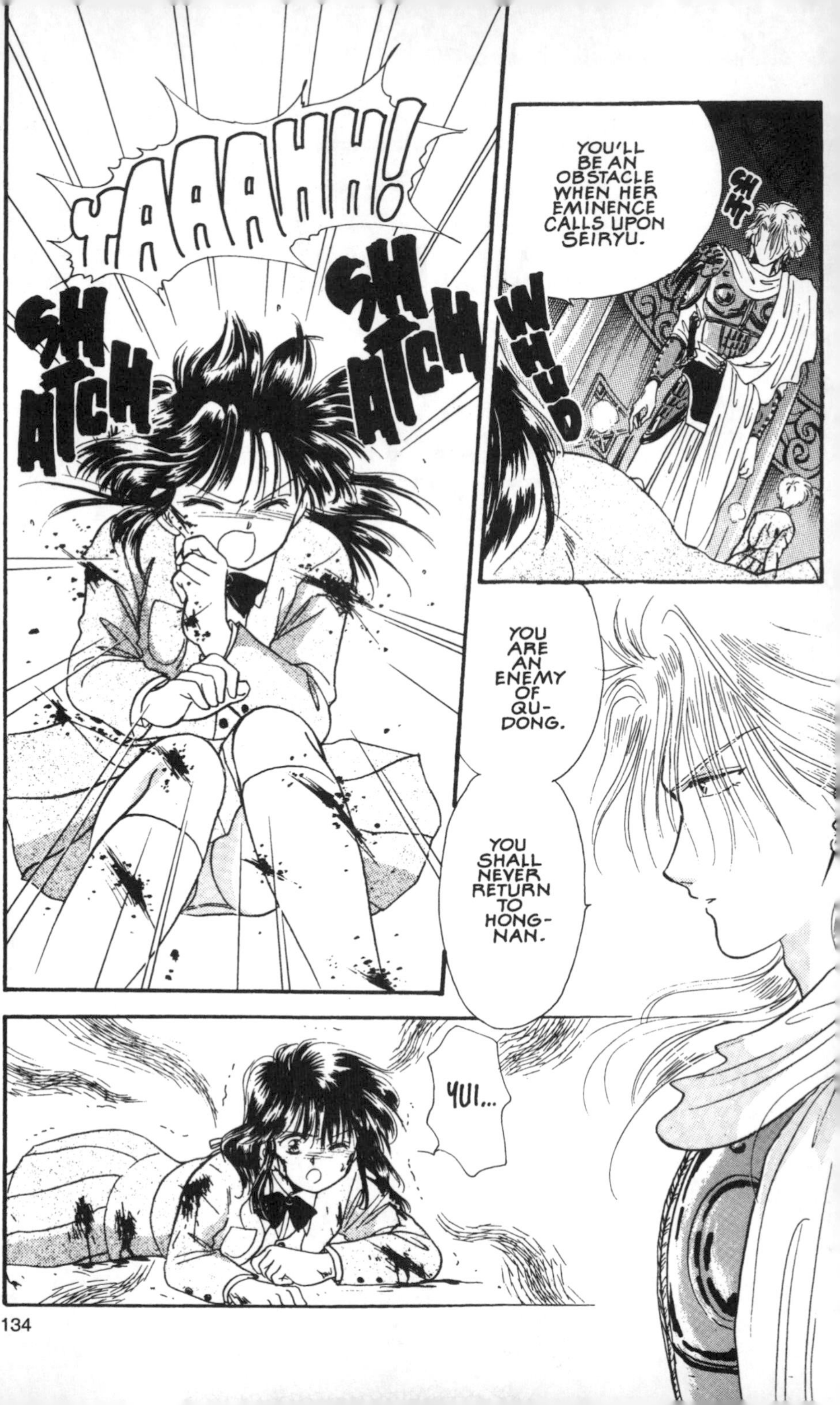
YAAAHH!
SHATCH
SHATCH
WHUD
YOU'LL BE AN OBSTACLE WHEN HER EMINENCE CALLS UPON SEIRYU.
SHHT
YOU ARE AN ENEMY OF QU-DONG.
YOU SHALL NEVER RETURN TO HONG-NAN.
YUI...

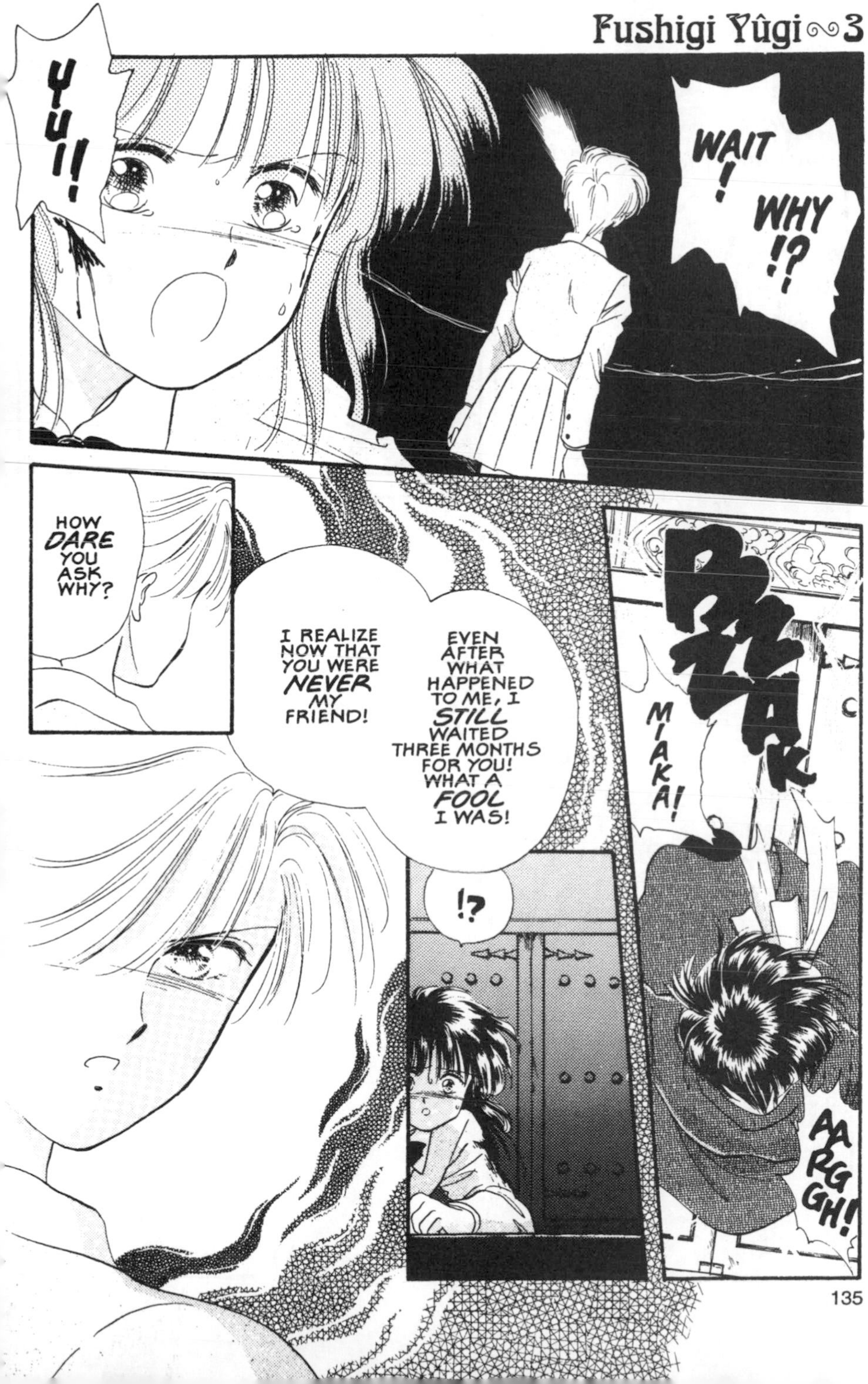
YUI!
WAIT! WHY!?
HOW DARE YOU ASK WHY?
I REALIZE NOW THAT YOU WERE NEVER MY FRIEND!
EVEN AFTER WHAT HAPPENED TO ME, I STILL WAITED THREE MONTHS FOR YOU! WHAT A FOOL I WAS!
!?
BZZAK
MIAKA!
AARGGH!

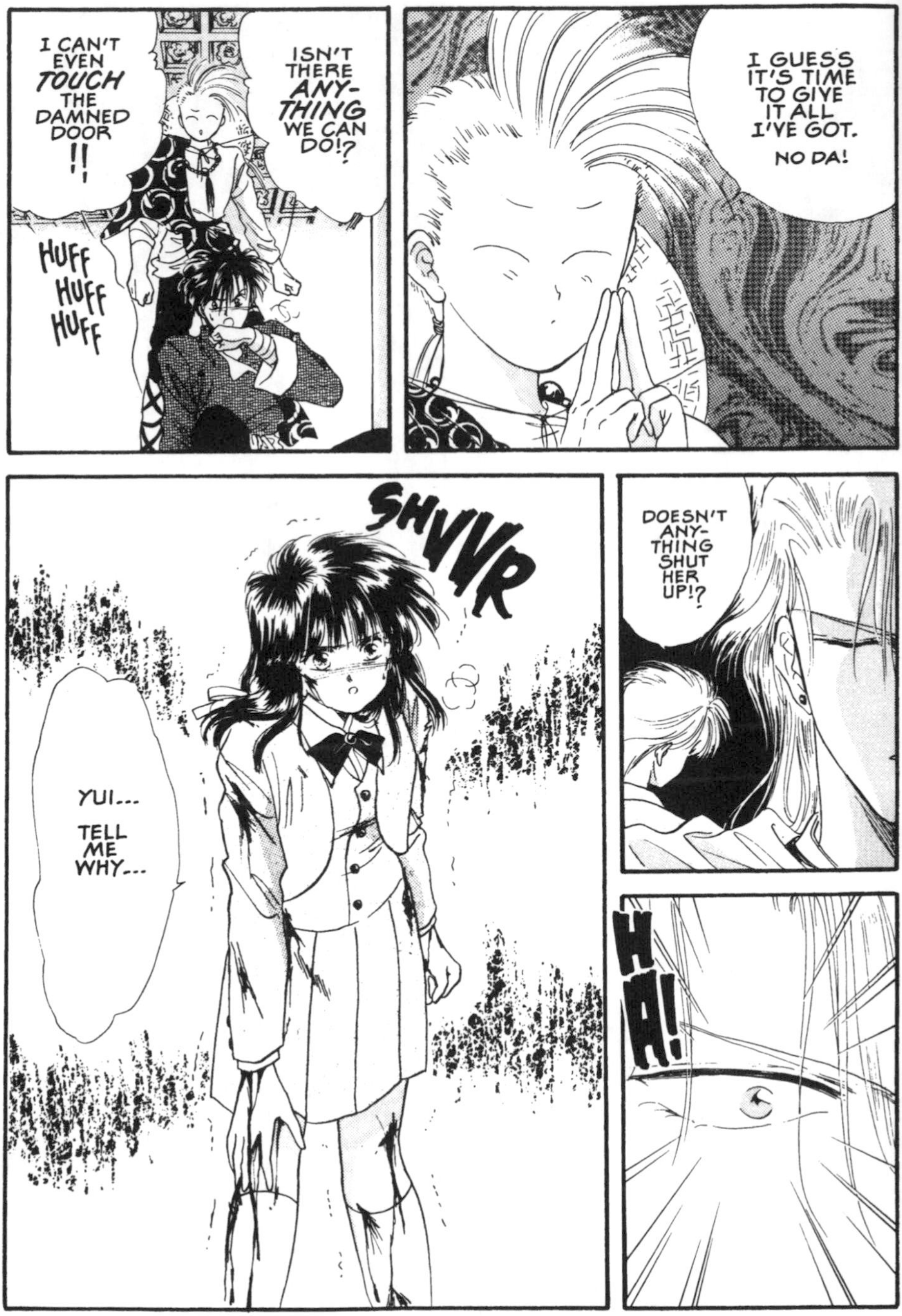
I CAN'T EVEN TOUCH THE DAMNED DOOR !!
ISN'T THERE ANYTHING WE CAN DO!?
HUFF HUFF HUFF
I GUESS IT'S TIME TO GIVE IT ALL I'VE GOT.
NO DA!
SHVVR
YUI...
TELL ME WHY...
DOESN'T ANYTHING SHUT HER UP!?
HA!

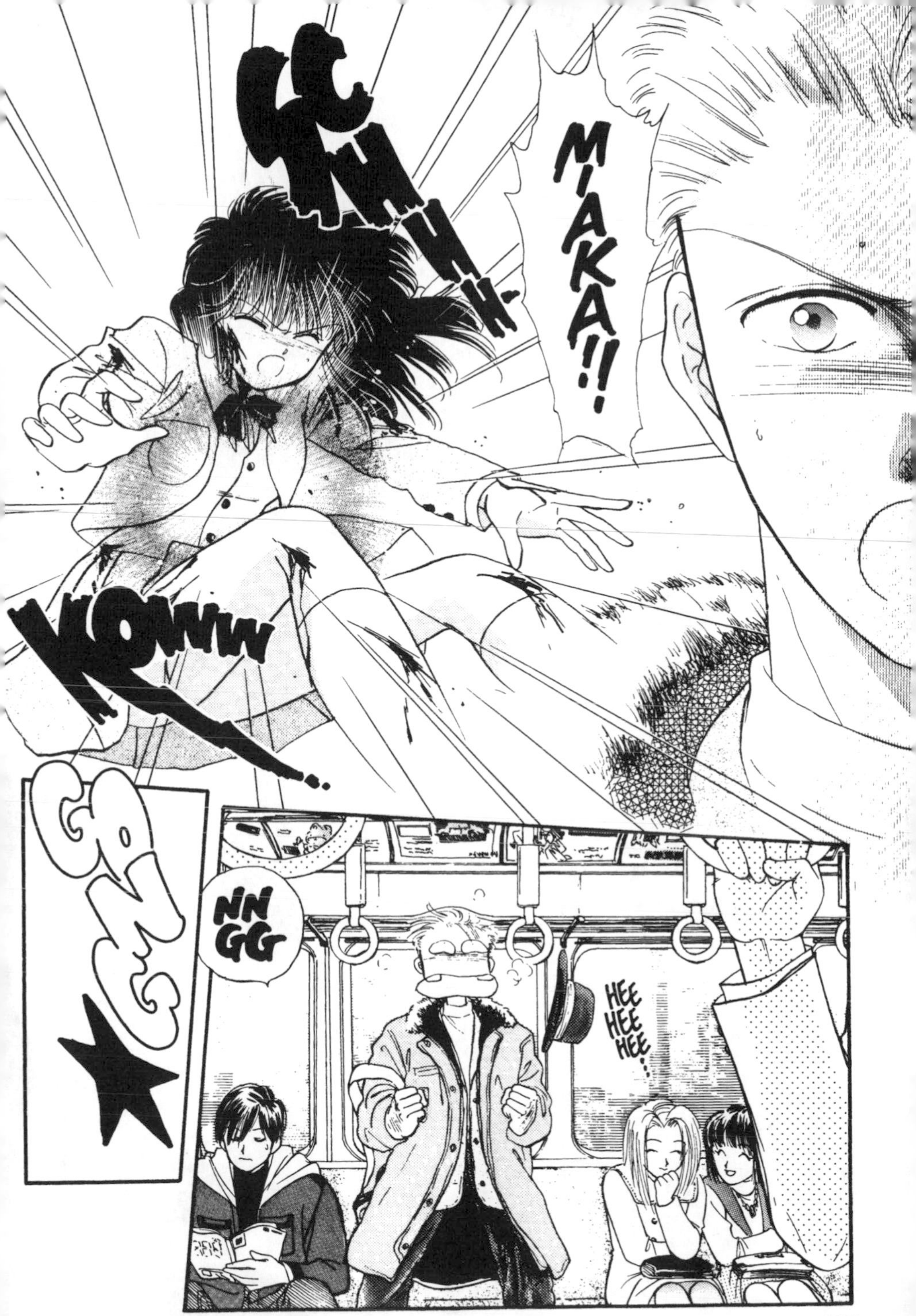
MIAKA!!
KONNN...
GONG★
NN GG
HEE HEE HEE...

KLAKETTA KLAKETTA

J-J-JUST A DREAM ??

HEE HEE HEE..

The Universe of the Four Gods

Japanese Translation by Einosuke Okuda

....

YOU DROPPED YOUR BOOK.

OH! THANKS.

SORRY!

"KEEP THIS AND DON'T EVER LOSE IT!"

"IT'S THE CONNECTION THAT WILL KEEP US IN CONTACT!"

FLLASSHH

"THE UNIVERSE OF THE FOUR GODS," HUH? I DIDN'T REALIZE THAT I'D TAKEN IT FROM THE LIBRARY.

BUT WHO'D EVER BELIEVE ME IF I SAID I WANTED TO BORROW IT BECAUSE MY LITTLE SISTER GOT SUCKED INTO IT?

RIBBON
⇩

I HAVE TO FIGURE OUT WHAT'S BEHIND THIS BOOK, AND I HAVE TO DO IT ON MY OWN.
TAKE CARE OF YOURSELF, MIAKA---
---BIG BROTHER IS ON THE JOB!
BEEE
EEEN
The Universe of the Four Gods
Japanese Translation by Einosuke Okuda
FU

Disciple

According to M, the best thing about computer games is the computer graphics. "I look forward to the sequences when you clear each stage." What's to look forward to? Your favorite character stripping! Okay, for women over age 20...If you stroked his ego, Hotohori might be willing to take it all off. But when we realized that most of the players would be guys, our ideas got really out of control. "Fushigi Yûgi Uncensored!" "What if Miaka and Yui were young boys and each of the constellations were different kinds of gorgeous girls!?" "The boys wouldn't be able to resist THAT!" "Okay, if you finish the entire game the regular way, the special 'For Boys' version will appear." Will someone make this game!? The other thing we thought of was a SD Chichiri doll. When you squeeze it, it says "No da!" I'm sorry for getting so carried away. But these ideas do seem like fun, huh?

I'm not serious, of course!

So, now that you've finished chapter 16, it must have been something of a shock. BWA HA HA HA! This was part of my plan all along! I only had the stories through chapter 16 planned at the start, though. Who'da thought this series would have ever gone 15 chapters in the first place!? Now the readers become divided between supporting Miaka or Yui. One thing that made me go "Eh!?" were the letters from readers who wrote in claiming that, "after reading Chapter 16, I don't like Miaka because she's a liar!" Please read from chapters 12 to 15 again, okay? Miaka lied to Tamahome in order to find Yui. Are you really reading this story closely? I don't mind it if you've always disliked Miaka. Sometimes, people change their minds, and that's interesting in itself. Anyway, I'm taking all your responses into consideration. By the way, I just remembered, speaking of games, (sorry I'm changing the subject all the time), my game system was disconnected when I moved recently, and I forgot to have it reinstalled!! AARGH! I can't play Final Fantasy! Actually, I don't have any time to play!! Game Boy is more popular at my place anyway. When I'm stuck or need a break, Parodius is good to play. I wish I had time to play more games!!

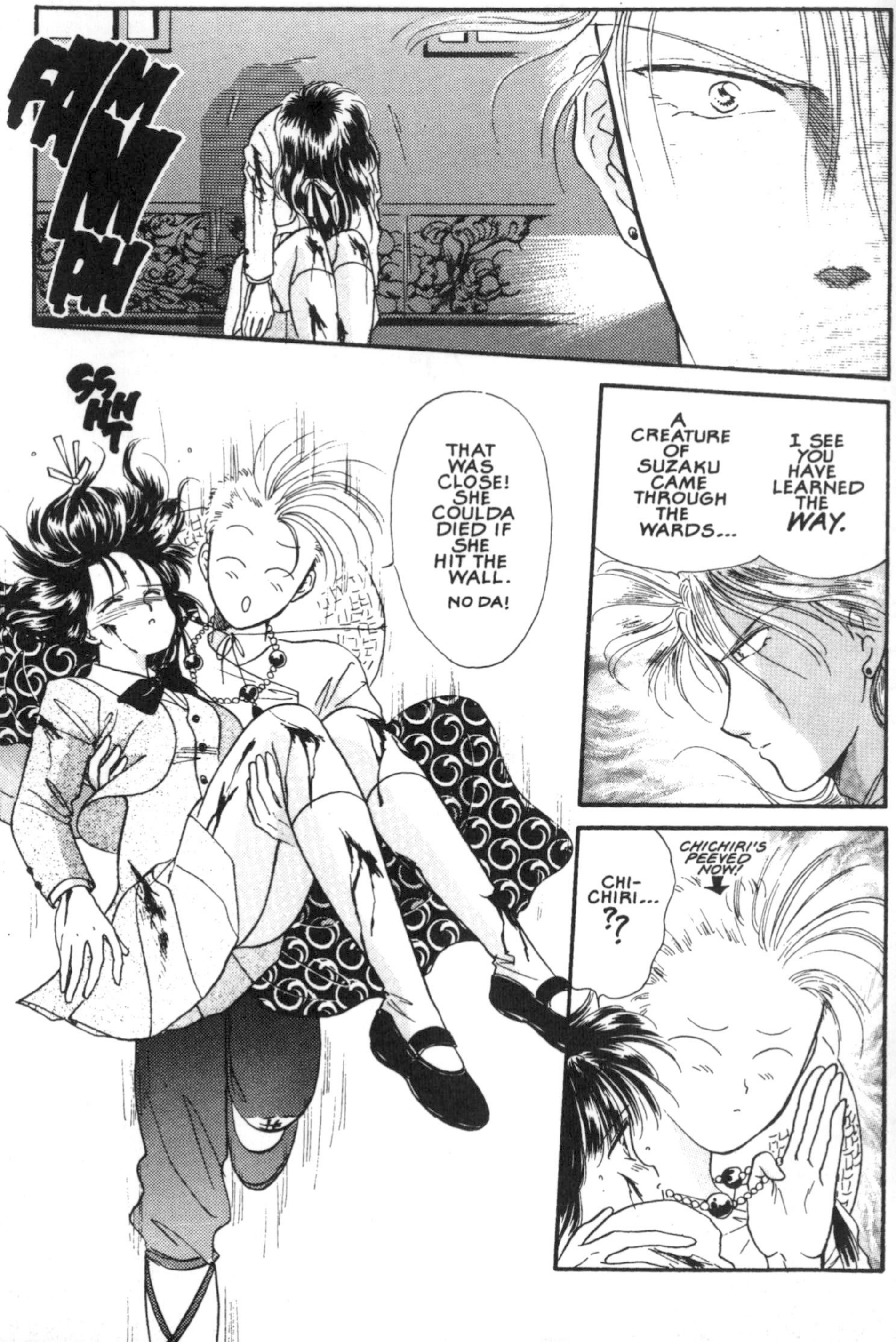
SSHHT
THAT WAS CLOSE! SHE COULDA DIED IF SHE HIT THE WALL.
NO DA!
A CREATURE OF SUZAKU CAME THROUGH THE WARDS...
I SEE YOU HAVE LEARNED THE *WAY*.
CHI-CHIRI... ??
CHICHIRI'S PEEVED NOW!

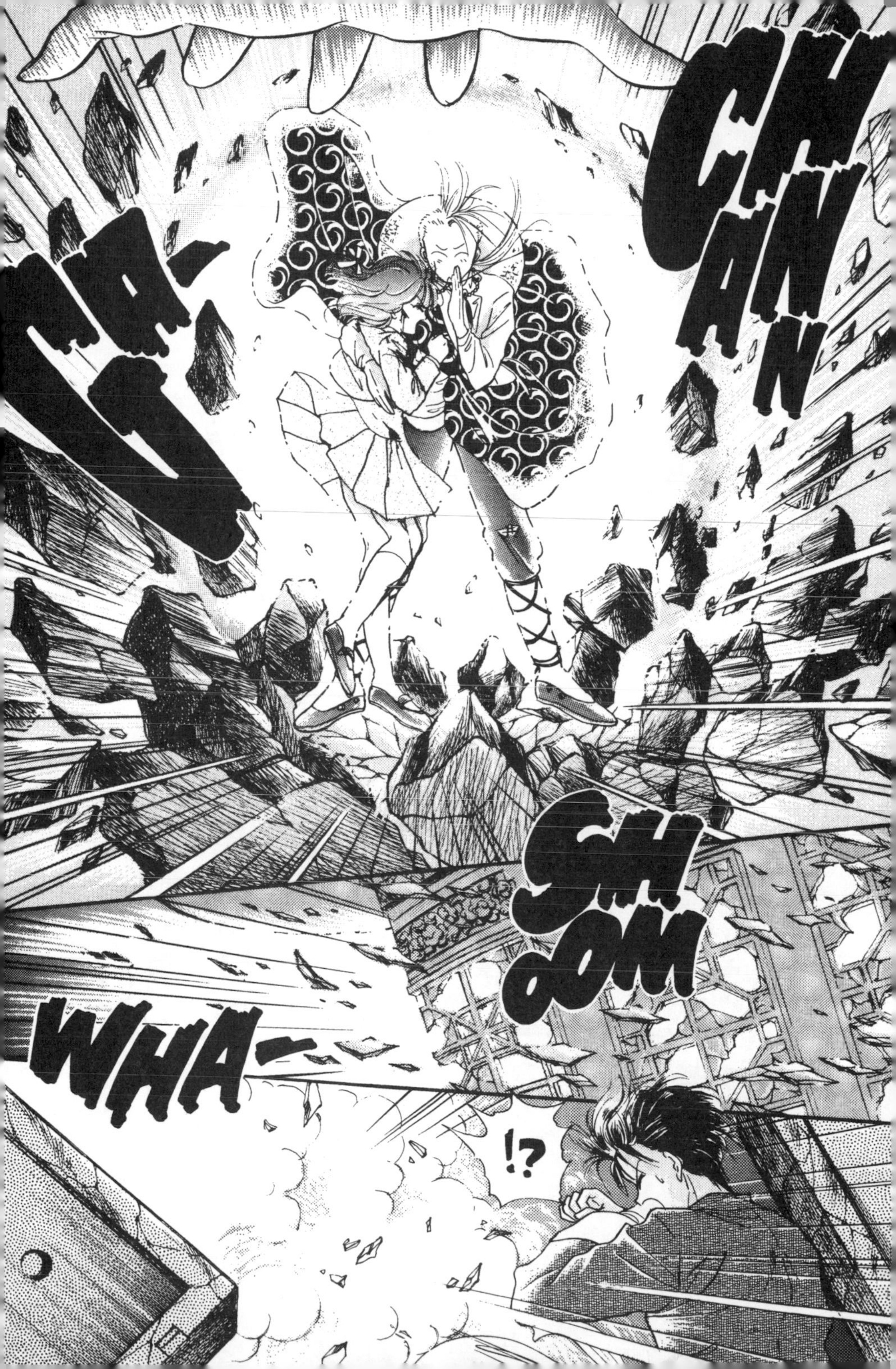
CHANANN
WHA–
SHOOM
!?

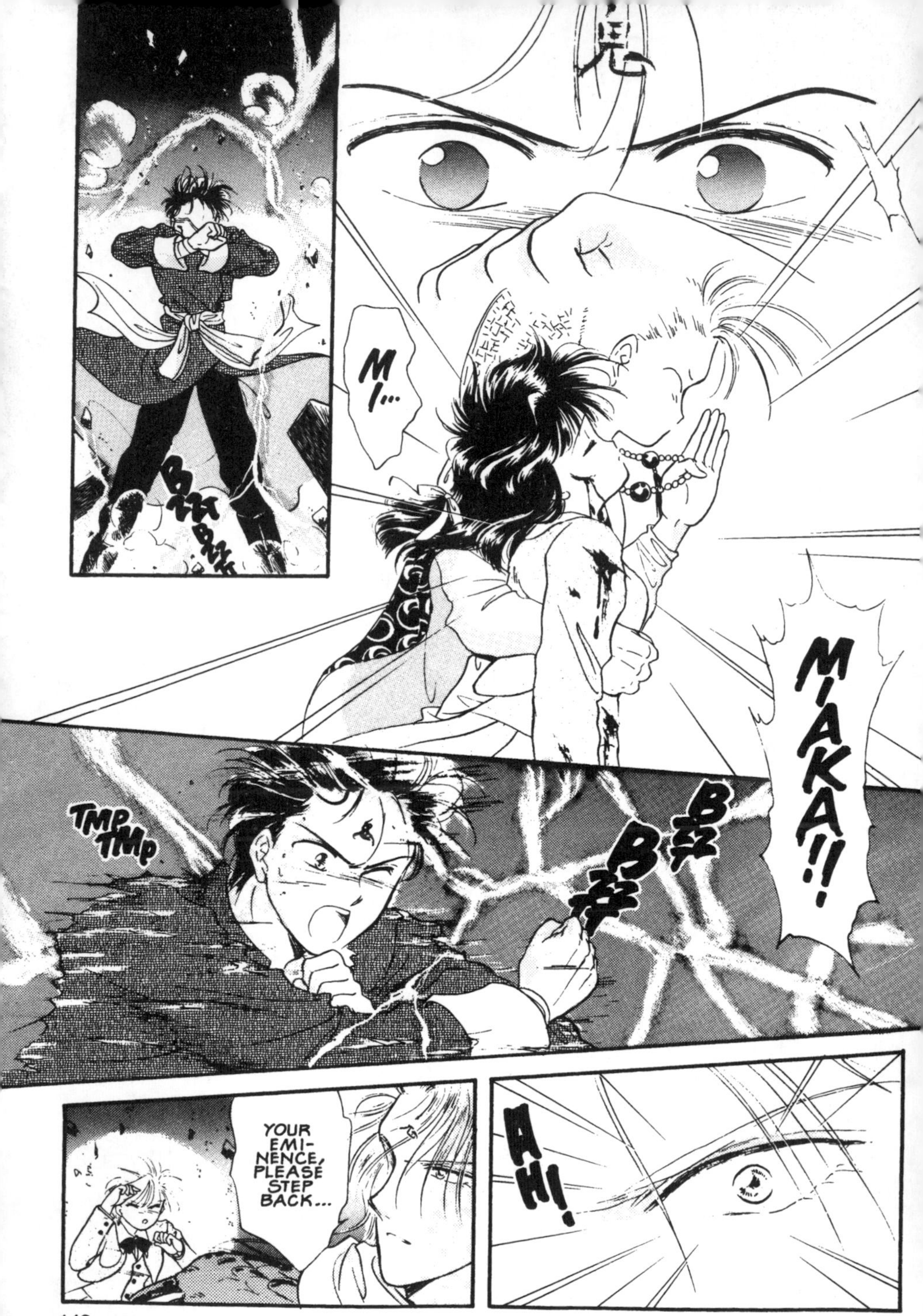
BZZT
BZZT
M-I...
MIAKA!!!
TMP
TMP
BZZT
BZZT
YOUR EMINENCE, PLEASE STEP BACK...
AH!

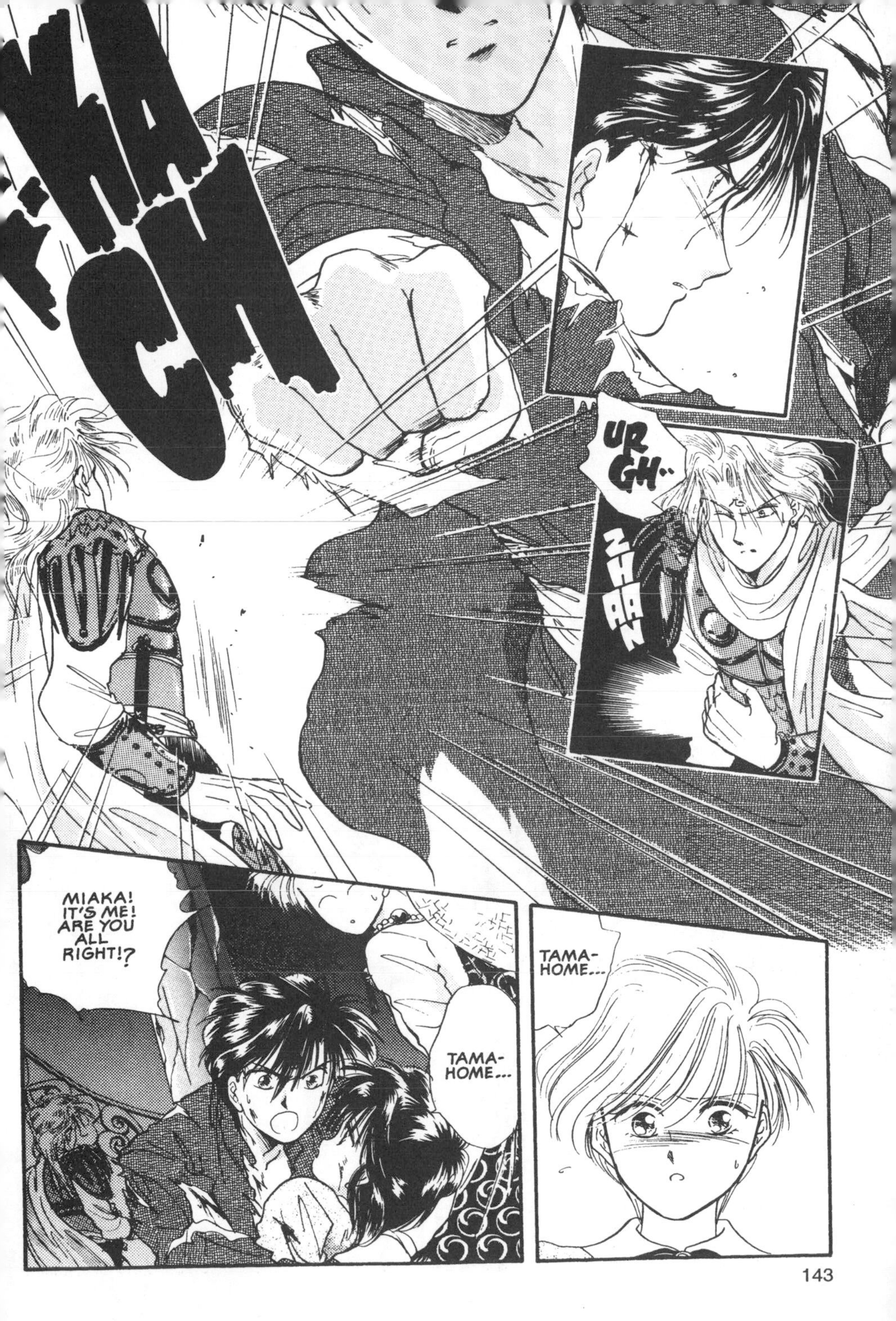
WACH
UR GH..
ZHAAN
MIAKA! IT'S ME! ARE YOU ALL RIGHT!?
TAMA-HOME...
TAMA-HOME...

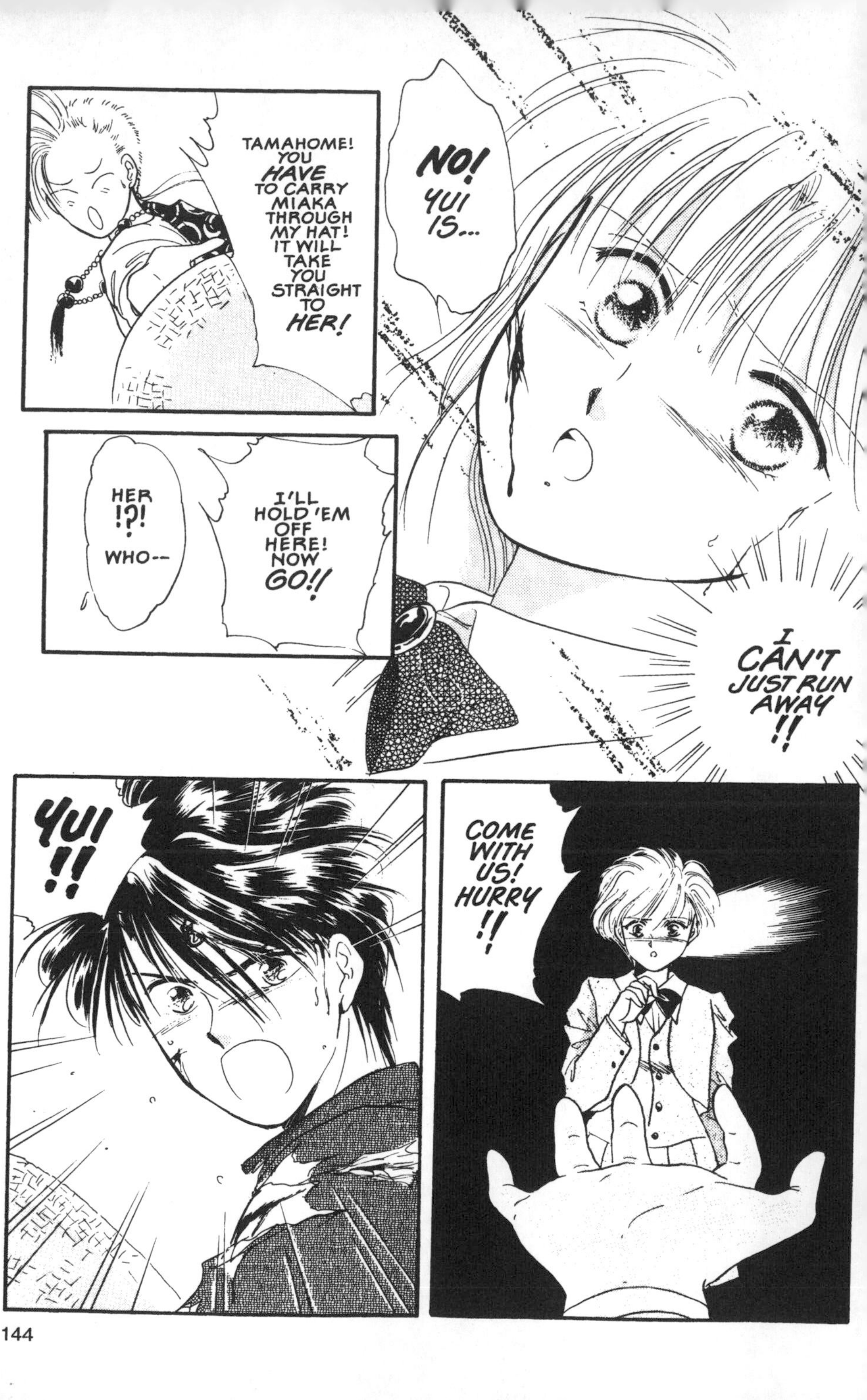
TAMAHOME! YOU HAVE TO CARRY MIAKA THROUGH MY HAT! IT WILL TAKE YOU STRAIGHT TO HER!
NO! YUI IS...
HER !?! WHO--
I'LL HOLD 'EM OFF HERE! NOW GO!!
I CAN'T JUST RUN AWAY!!
YUI!!
COME WITH US! HURRY!!

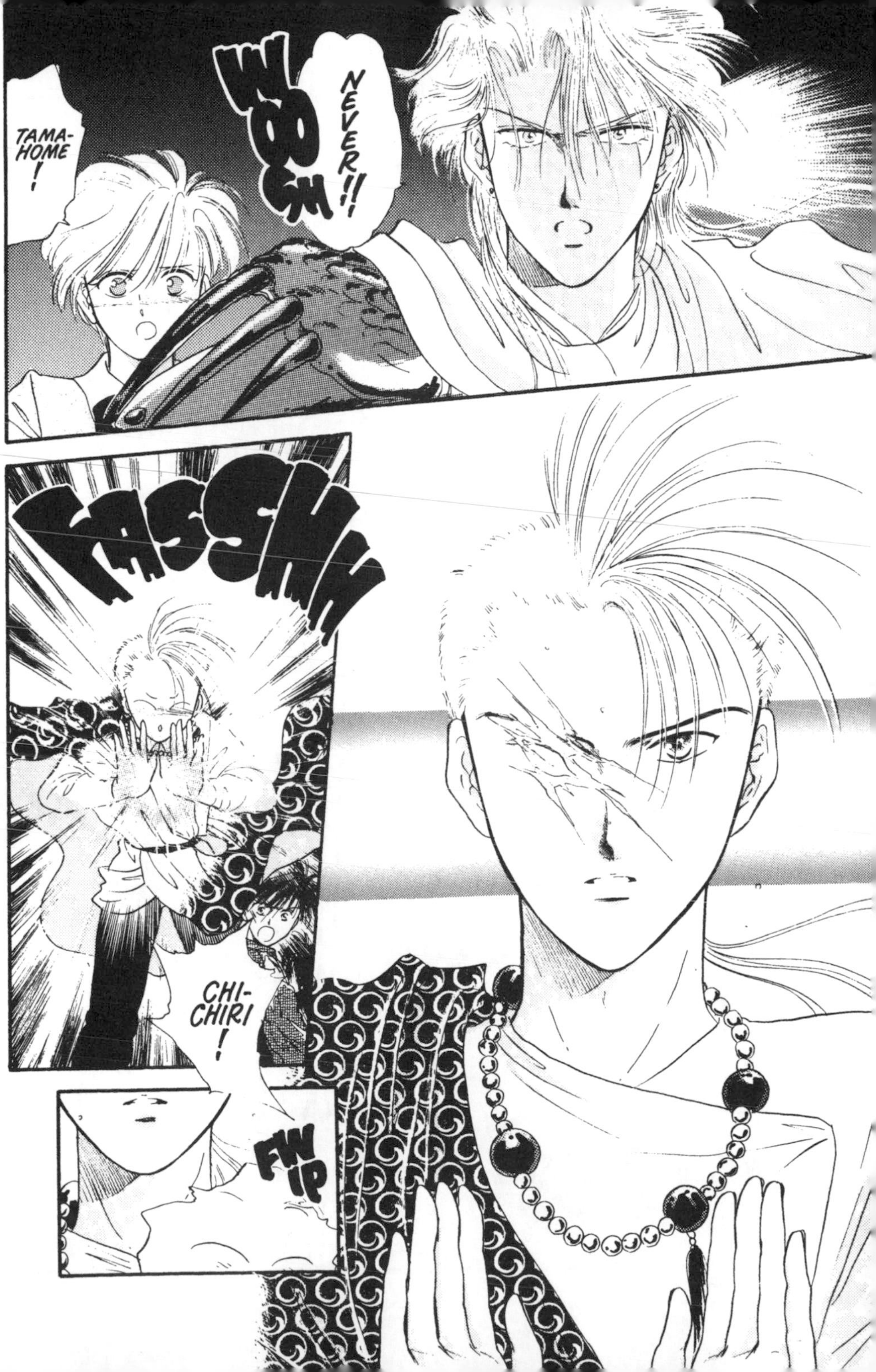
TAMA-HOME!
WHOOSH
NEVER!!
KASSHHH
CHI-CHIRI!
FWIP

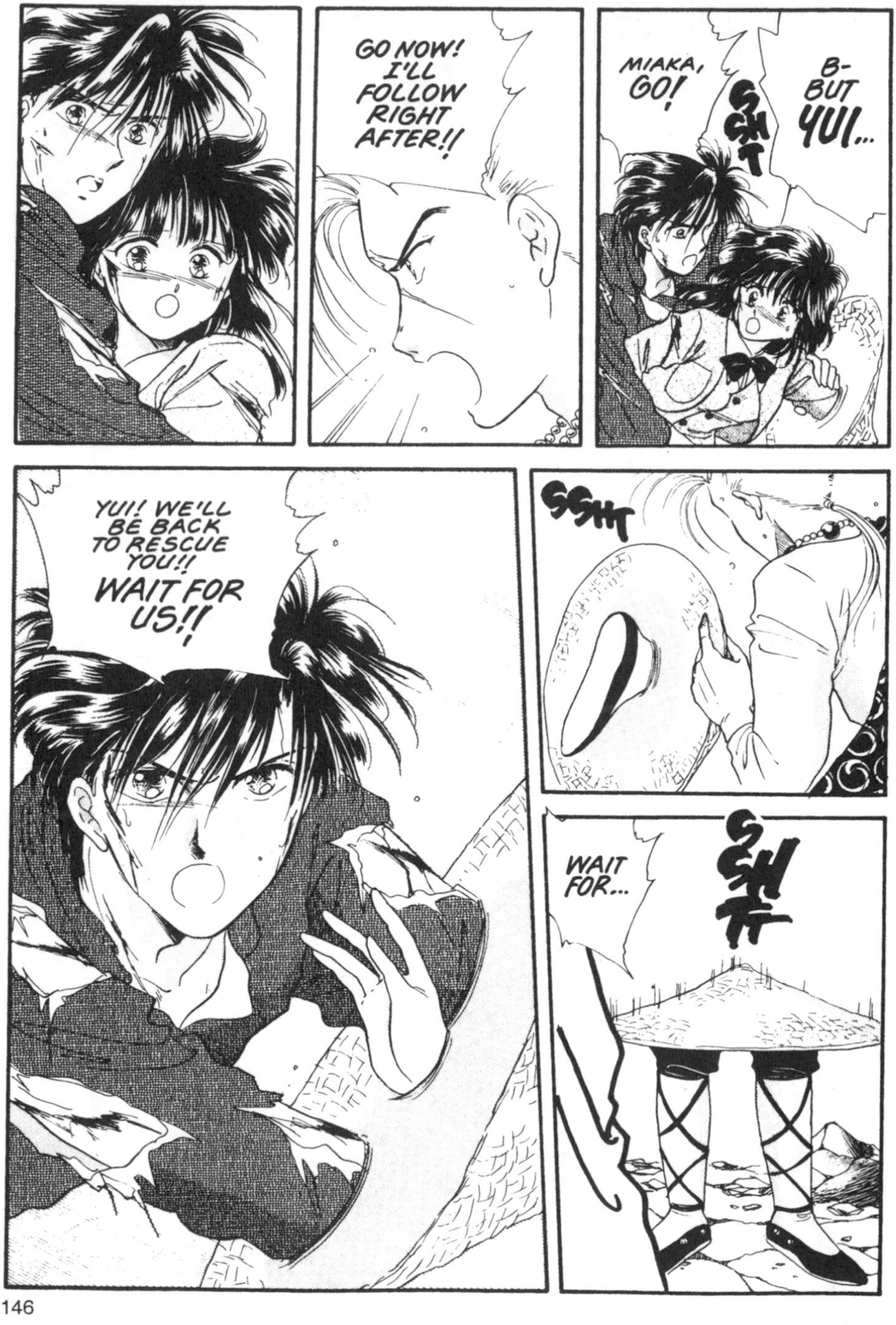
GO NOW! I'LL FOLLOW RIGHT AFTER!!
MIAKA, GO!
SSHT
B-BUT YUI...
YUI! WE'LL BE BACK TO RESCUE YOU!! WAIT FOR US!!
SSHT
WAIT FOR...
SSHTT

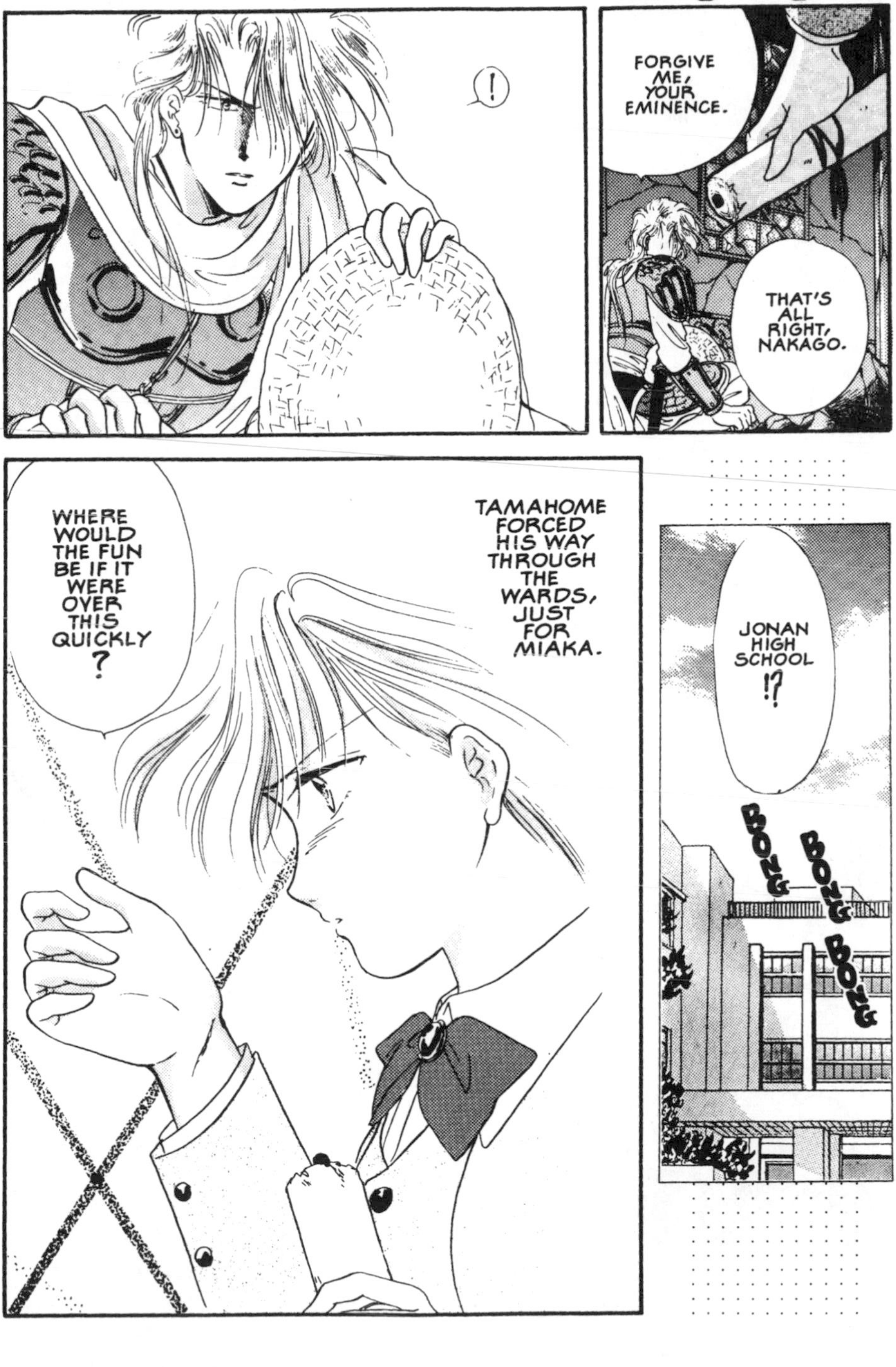
!
FORGIVE ME, YOUR EMINENCE.
THAT'S ALL RIGHT, NAKAGO.
WHERE WOULD THE FUN BE IF IT WERE OVER THIS QUICKLY?
TAMAHOME FORCED HIS WAY THROUGH THE WARDS, JUST FOR MIAKA.
JONAN HIGH SCHOOL!?
BONG
BONG BONG BONG

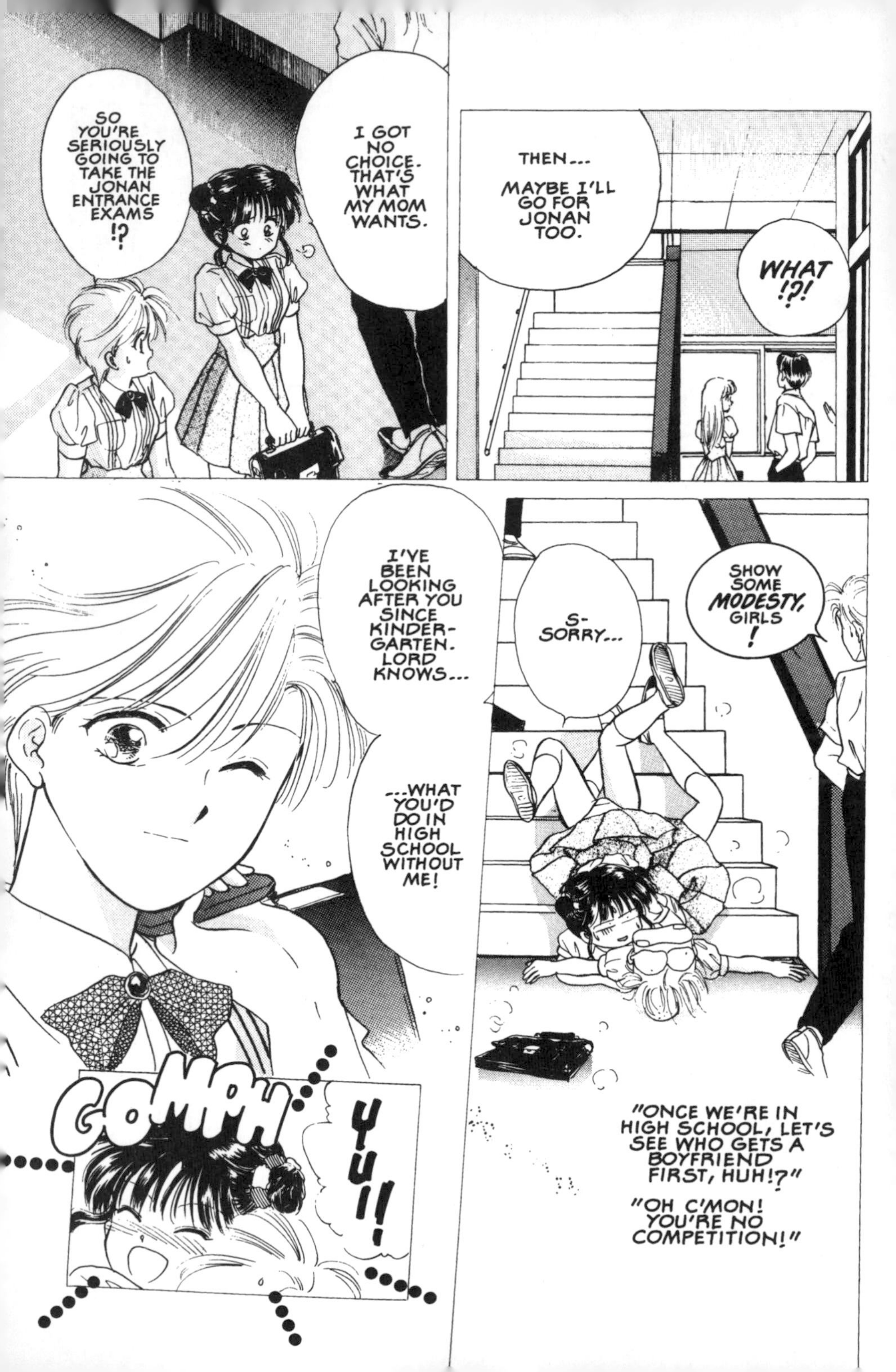
SO YOU'RE SERIOUSLY GOING TO TAKE THE JONAN ENTRANCE EXAMS !?
I GOT NO CHOICE. THAT'S WHAT MY MOM WANTS.
THEN... MAYBE I'LL GO FOR JONAN TOO.
WHAT !?!
I'VE BEEN LOOKING AFTER YOU SINCE KINDER-GARTEN. LORD KNOWS...
...WHAT YOU'D DO IN HIGH SCHOOL WITHOUT ME!
GOMPH
YUI!
S-SORRY...
SHOW SOME MODESTY, GIRLS !
"ONCE WE'RE IN HIGH SCHOOL, LET'S SEE WHO GETS A BOYFRIEND FIRST, HUH!?"
"OH C'MON! YOU'RE NO COMPETITION!"

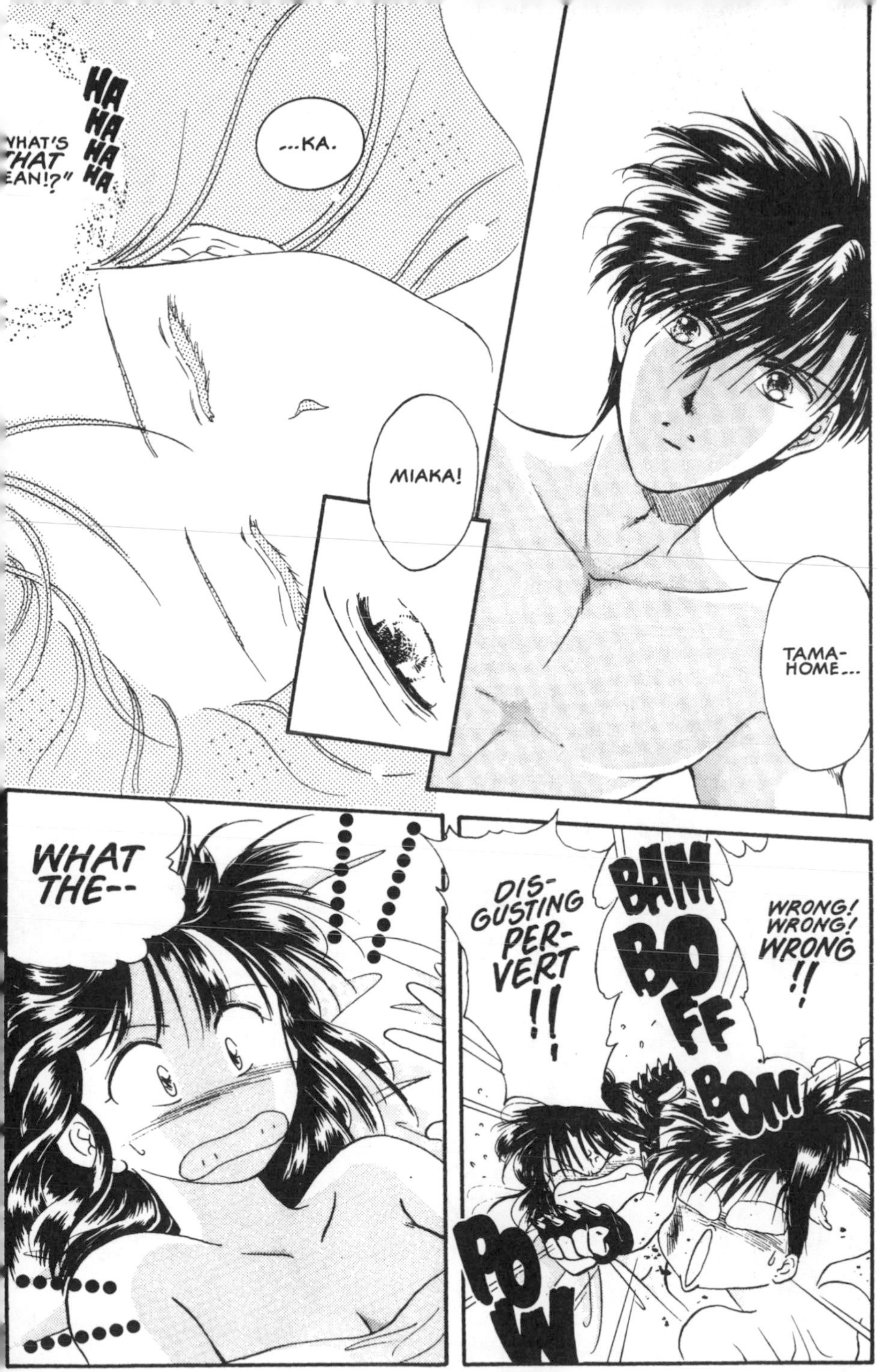

WHAT'S
THAT
EAN!?"
HA HA HA HA
...KA.
MIAKA!
TAMA-HOME...
WHAT THE--
......
DIS-GUSTING PER-VERT!!
BAM BOFF BOM
WRONG! WRONG! WRONG!!
POW

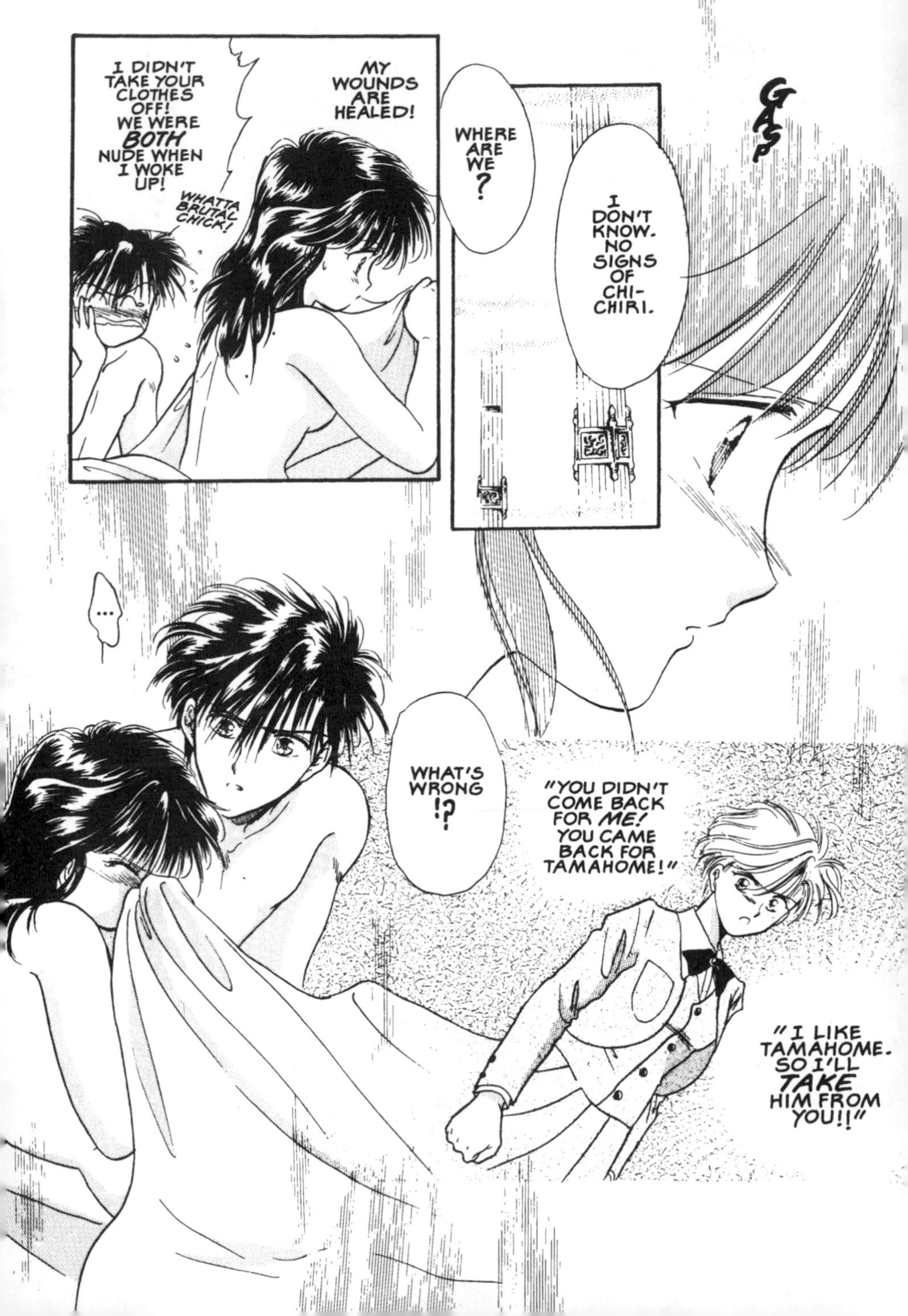
I DIDN'T TAKE YOUR CLOTHES OFF! WE WERE *BOTH* NUDE WHEN I WOKE UP!
MY WOUNDS ARE HEALED!
WHATTA BRUTAL CHICK!
WHERE ARE WE?
I DON'T KNOW. NO SIGNS OF CHI-CHIRI.
GASP
...
WHAT'S WRONG!?
"YOU DIDN'T COME BACK FOR *ME!* YOU CAME BACK FOR TAMAHOME!"
"I LIKE TAMAHOME. SO I'LL *TAKE* HIM FROM YOU!!"

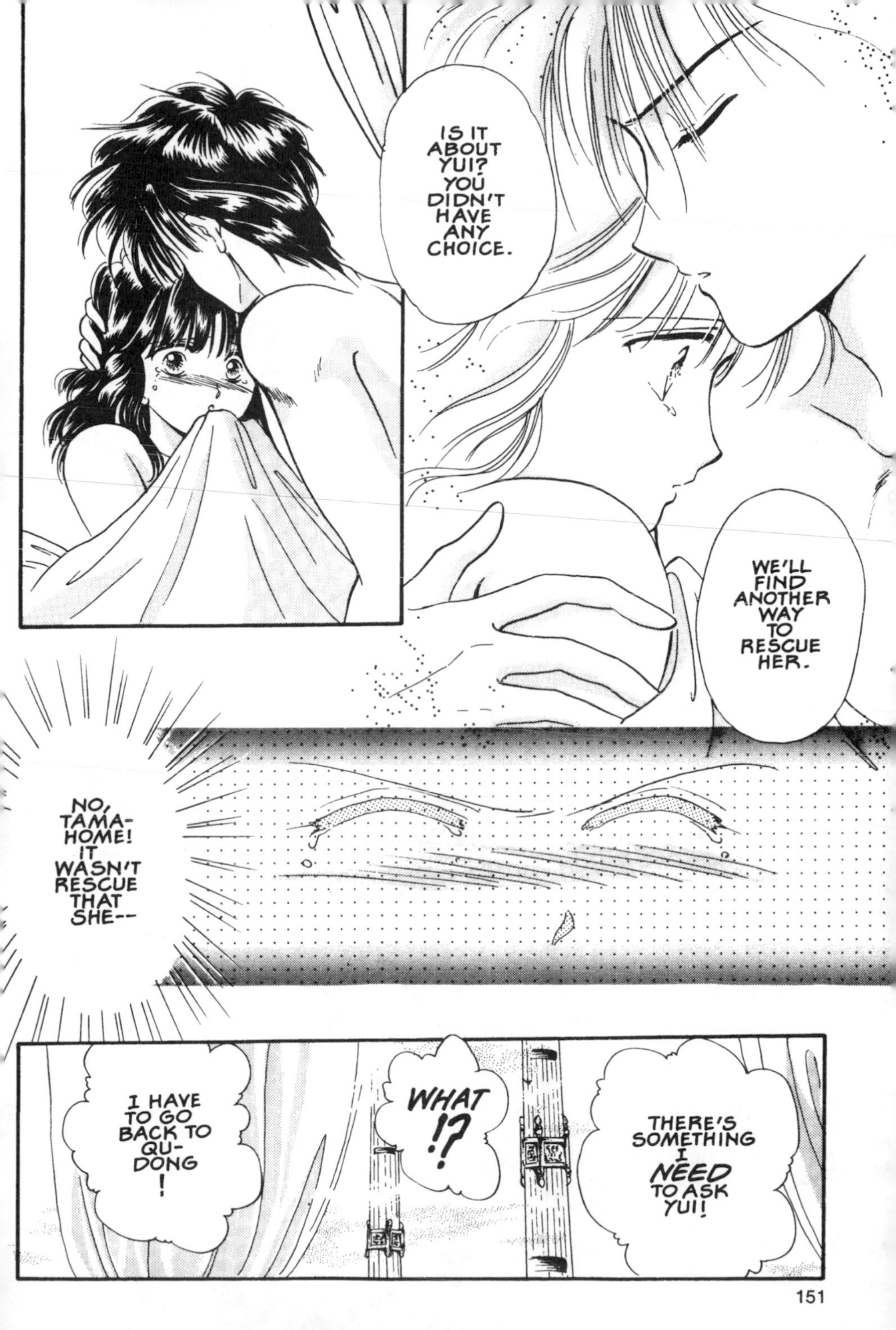
IS IT ABOUT YUI? YOU DIDN'T HAVE ANY CHOICE.
WE'LL FIND ANOTHER WAY TO RESCUE HER.
NO, TAMAHOME! IT WASN'T RESCUE THAT SHE--
I HAVE TO GO BACK TO QU-DONG!
WHAT!?
THERE'S SOMETHING I NEED TO ASK YUI!

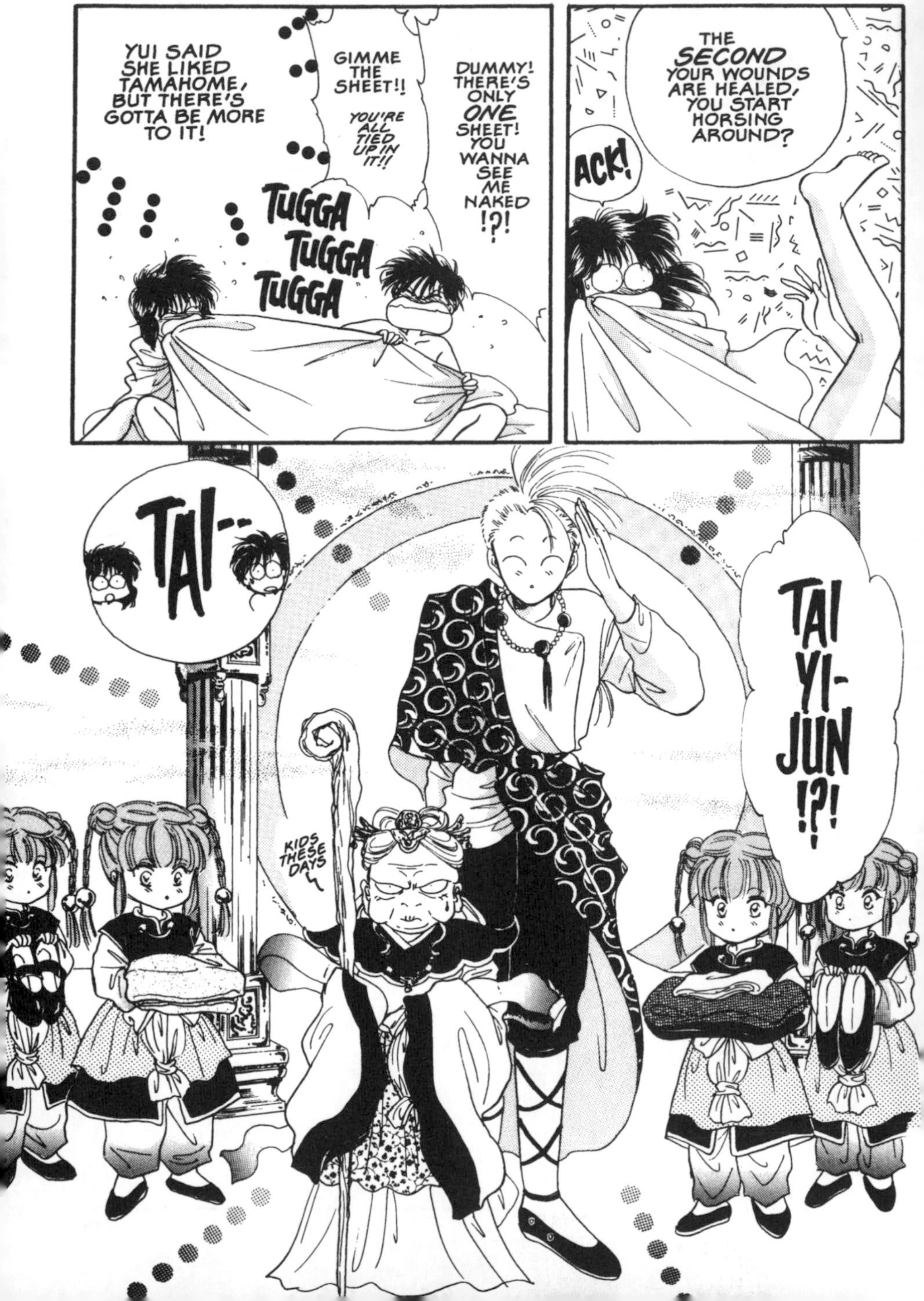
YUI SAID SHE LIKED TAMAHOME, BUT THERE'S GOTTA BE MORE TO IT!
GIMME THE SHEET!!
YOU'RE ALL TIED UP IN IT!!
DUMMY! THERE'S ONLY ONE SHEET! YOU WANNA SEE ME NAKED !?!
TUGGA TUGGA TUGGA
THE SECOND YOUR WOUNDS ARE HEALED, YOU START HORSING AROUND?
ACK!
TAI--
KIDS THESE DAYS
TAI YI-JUN !?!

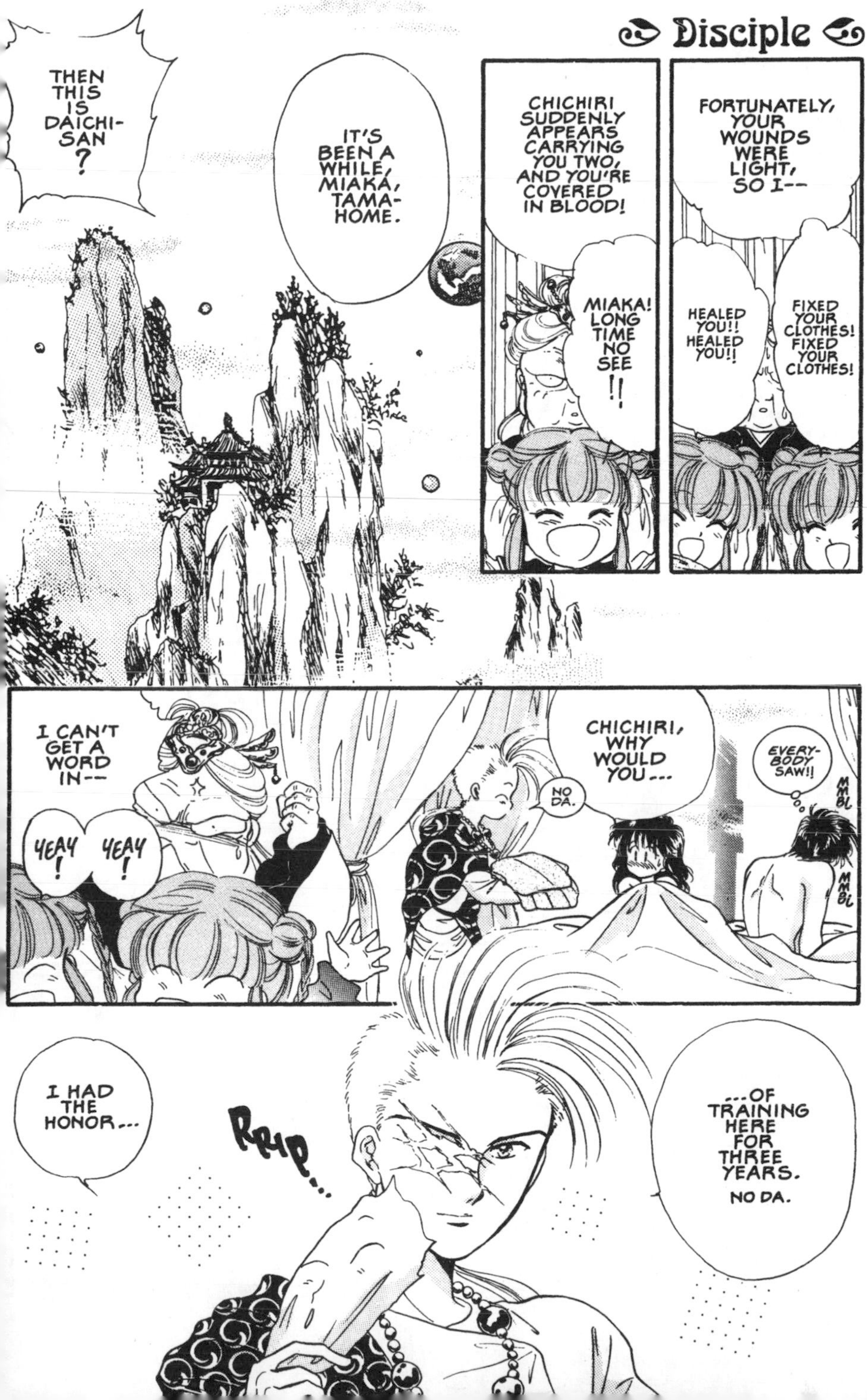
THEN THIS IS DAICHI-SAN?
IT'S BEEN A WHILE, MIAKA, TAMAHOME.
CHICHIRI SUDDENLY APPEARS CARRYING YOU TWO, AND YOU'RE COVERED IN BLOOD!
MIAKA! LONG TIME NO SEE!!
FORTUNATELY, YOUR WOUNDS WERE LIGHT, SO I--
HEALED YOU!! HEALED YOU!!
FIXED YOUR CLOTHES! FIXED YOUR CLOTHES!
I CAN'T GET A WORD IN--
YEAY!
YEAY!
NO DA.
CHICHIRI, WHY WOULD YOU...
EVERYBODY SAW!!
MMBL
MMBL
I HAD THE HONOR...
RRIP...
...OF TRAINING HERE FOR THREE YEARS.
NO DA.

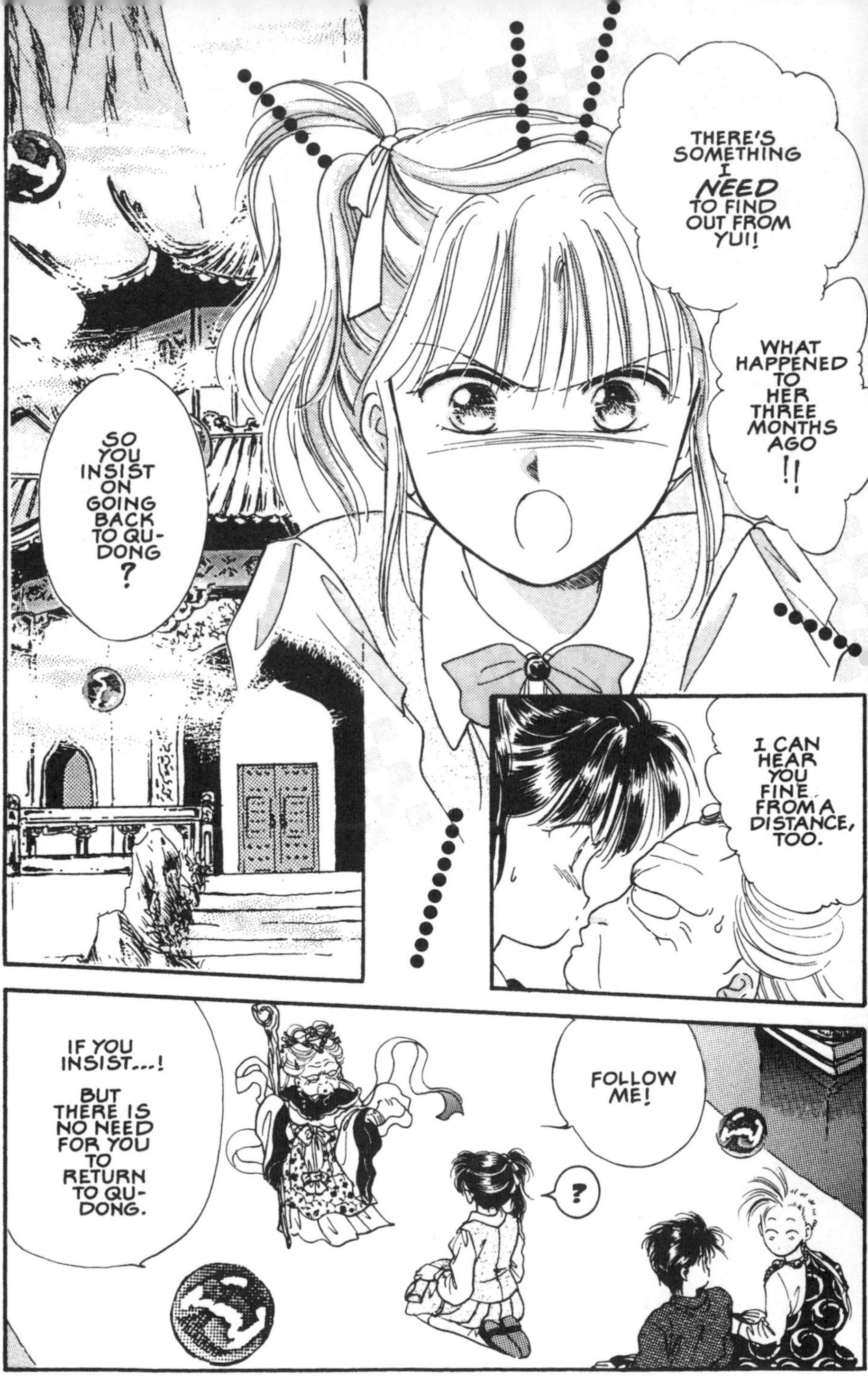
SO YOU INSIST ON GOING BACK TO QU-DONG?
THERE'S SOMETHING I NEED TO FIND OUT FROM YUI!
WHAT HAPPENED TO HER THREE MONTHS AGO!!
I CAN HEAR YOU FINE FROM A DISTANCE, TOO.
IF YOU INSIST...! BUT THERE IS NO NEED FOR YOU TO RETURN TO QU-DONG.
FOLLOW ME!
?

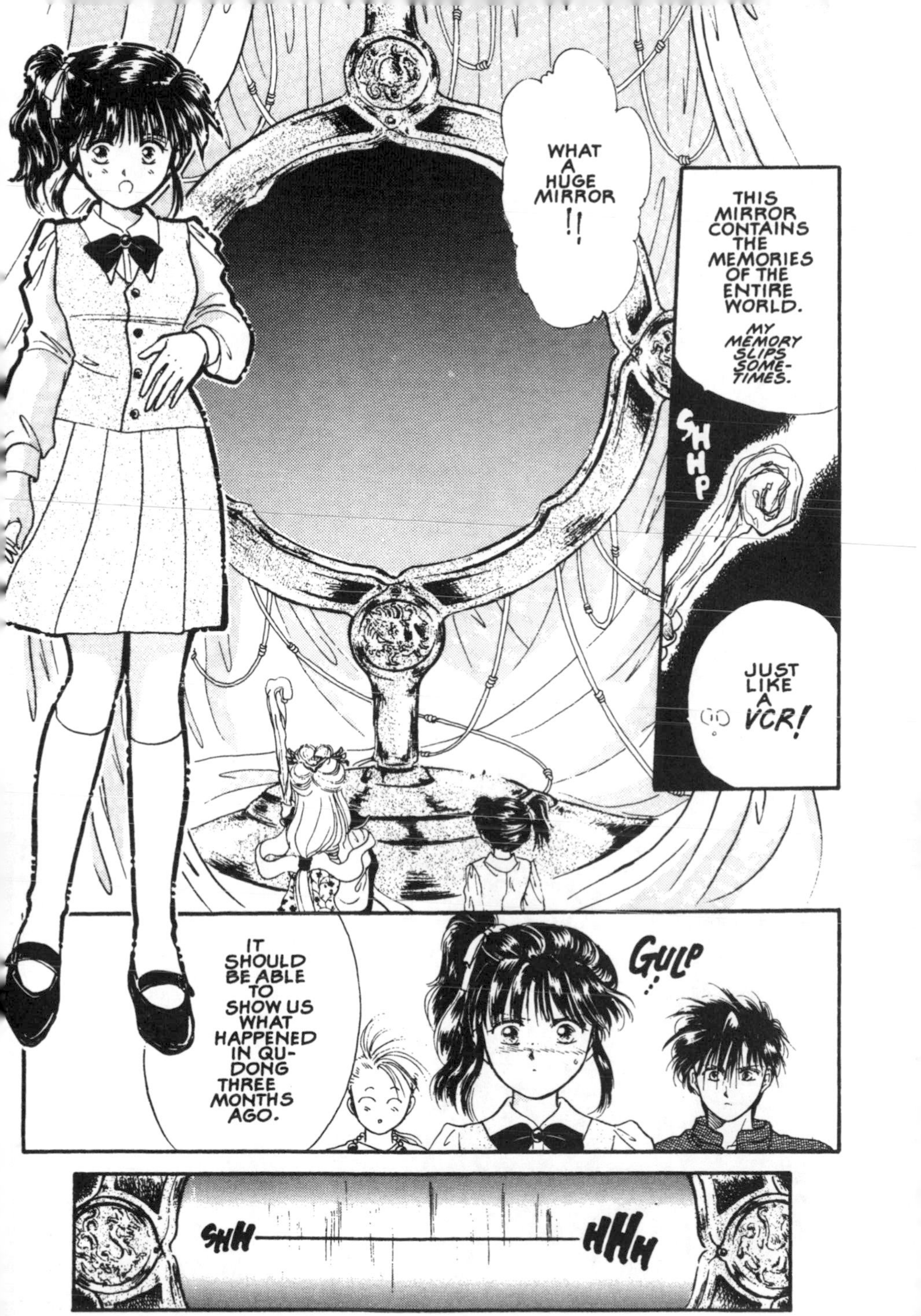
WHAT A HUGE MIRROR !!
THIS MIRROR CONTAINS THE MEMORIES OF THE ENTIRE WORLD.
MY MEMORY SLIPS SOME-TIMES.
SHHP
JUST LIKE A VCR!
IT SHOULD BE ABLE TO SHOW US WHAT HAPPENED IN QU-DONG THREE MONTHS AGO.
GULP
SHH——HHH

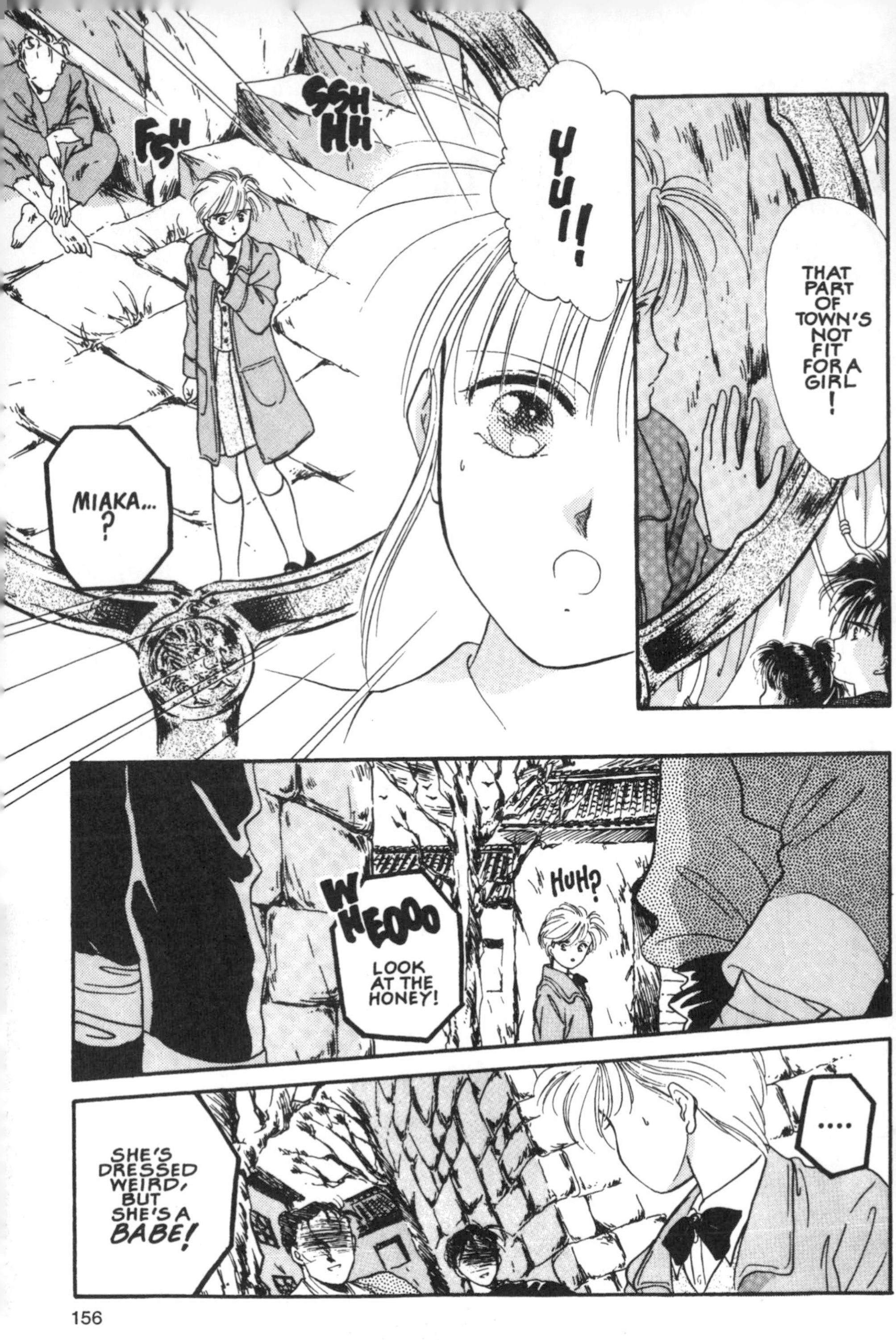
FSH
SSHHH
MIAKA...?
YUI!!
THAT PART OF TOWN'S NOT FIT FOR A GIRL!
WHEOOO
LOOK AT THE HONEY!
HUH?
SHE'S DRESSED WEIRD, BUT SHE'S A BABE!
....

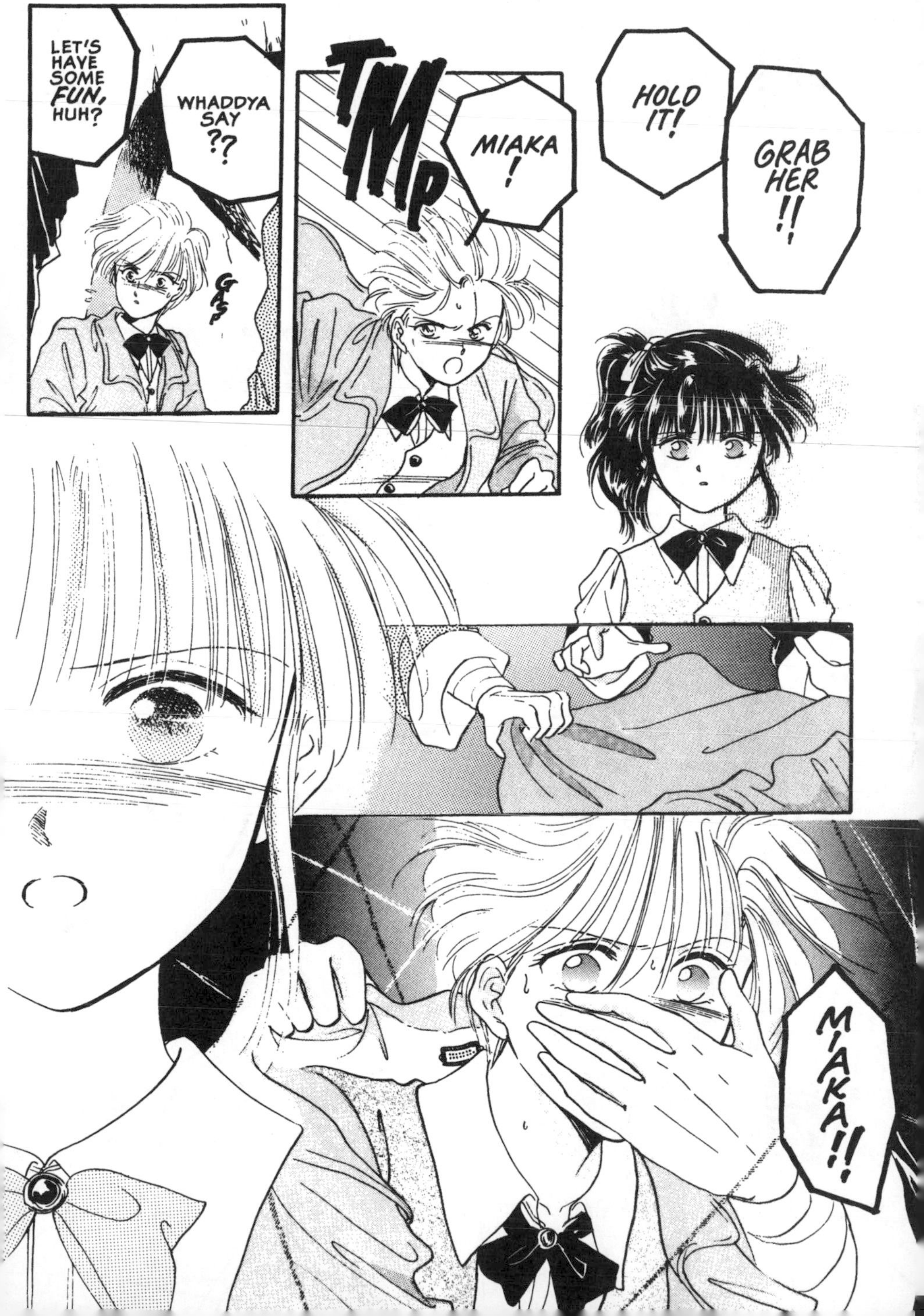
LET'S HAVE SOME FUN, HUH?
WHADDYA SAY ??
GASP
TMP
MIAKA!
HOLD IT!
GRAB HER!!
MIAKA!!

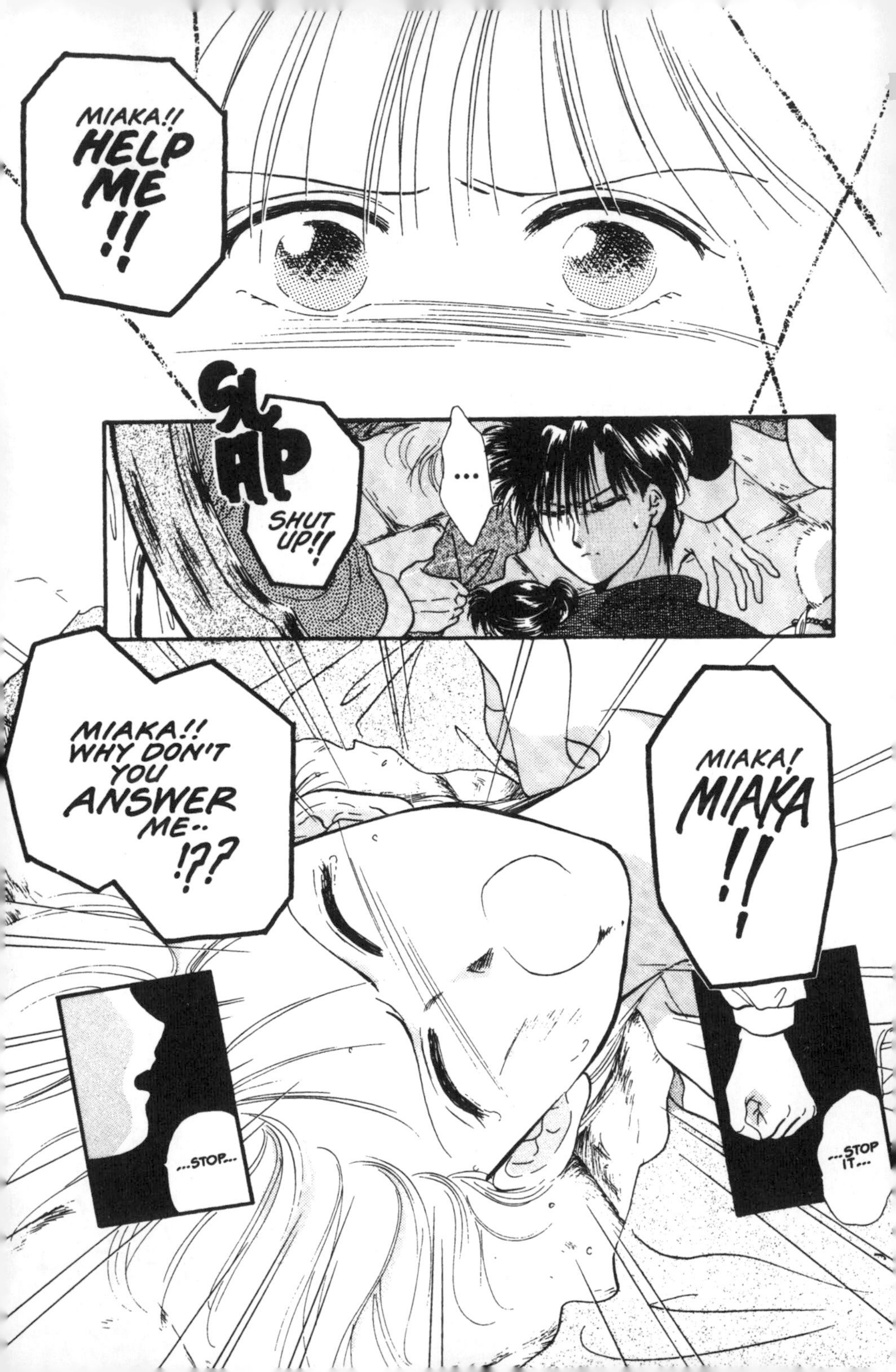
MIAKA!! HELP ME !!
SLAP
SHUT UP!!
...
MIAKA!! WHY DON'T YOU ANSWER ME.. !??
MIAKA! MIAKA !!
...STOP...
...STOP IT...

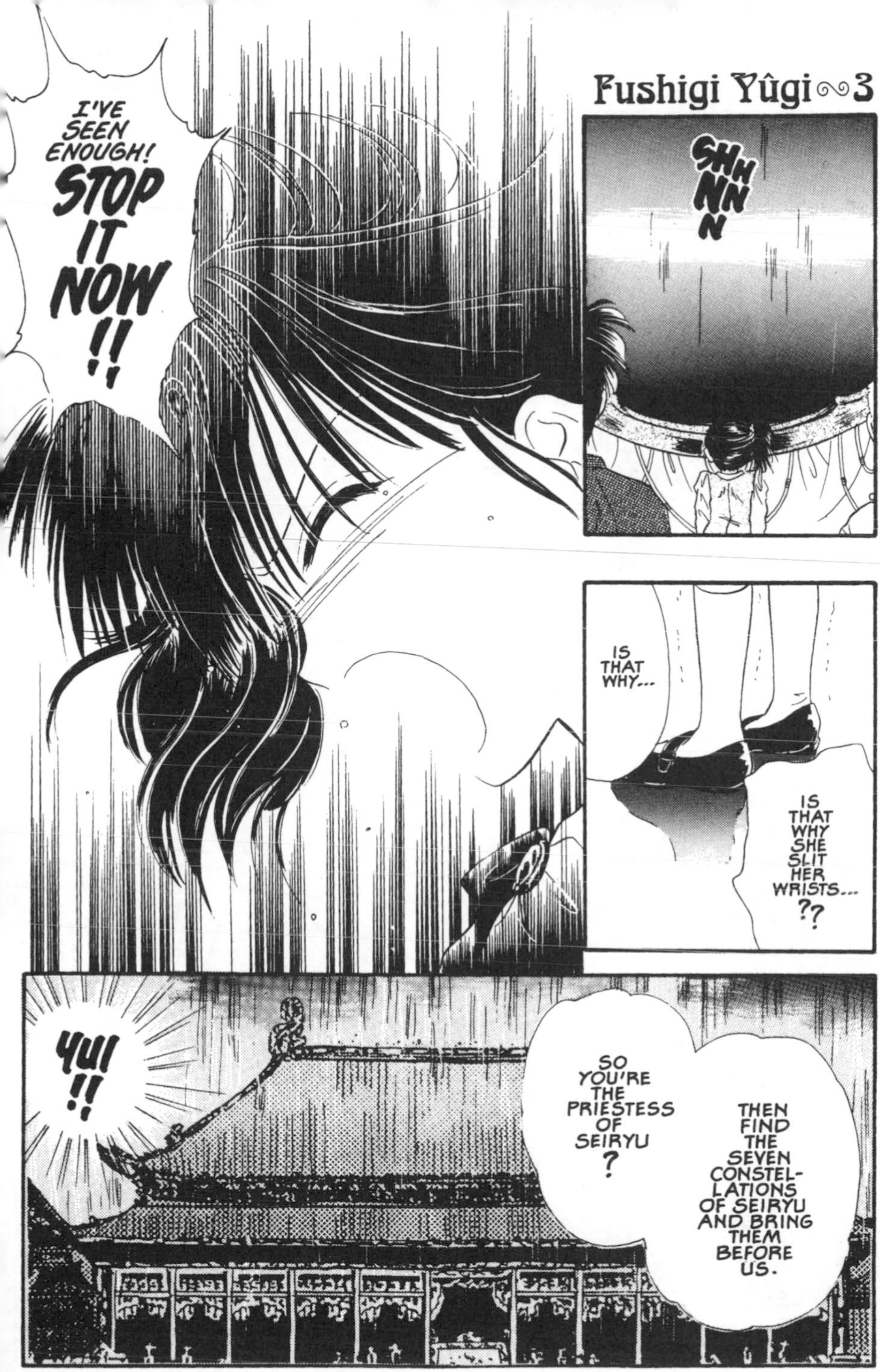
I'VE SEEN ENOUGH! STOP IT NOW!!
SHHNNN
IS THAT WHY...
IS THAT WHY SHE SLIT HER WRISTS...??
YUI!!
SO YOU'RE THE PRIESTESS OF SEIRYU?
THEN FIND THE SEVEN CONSTEL-LATIONS OF SEIRYU AND BRING THEM BEFORE US.

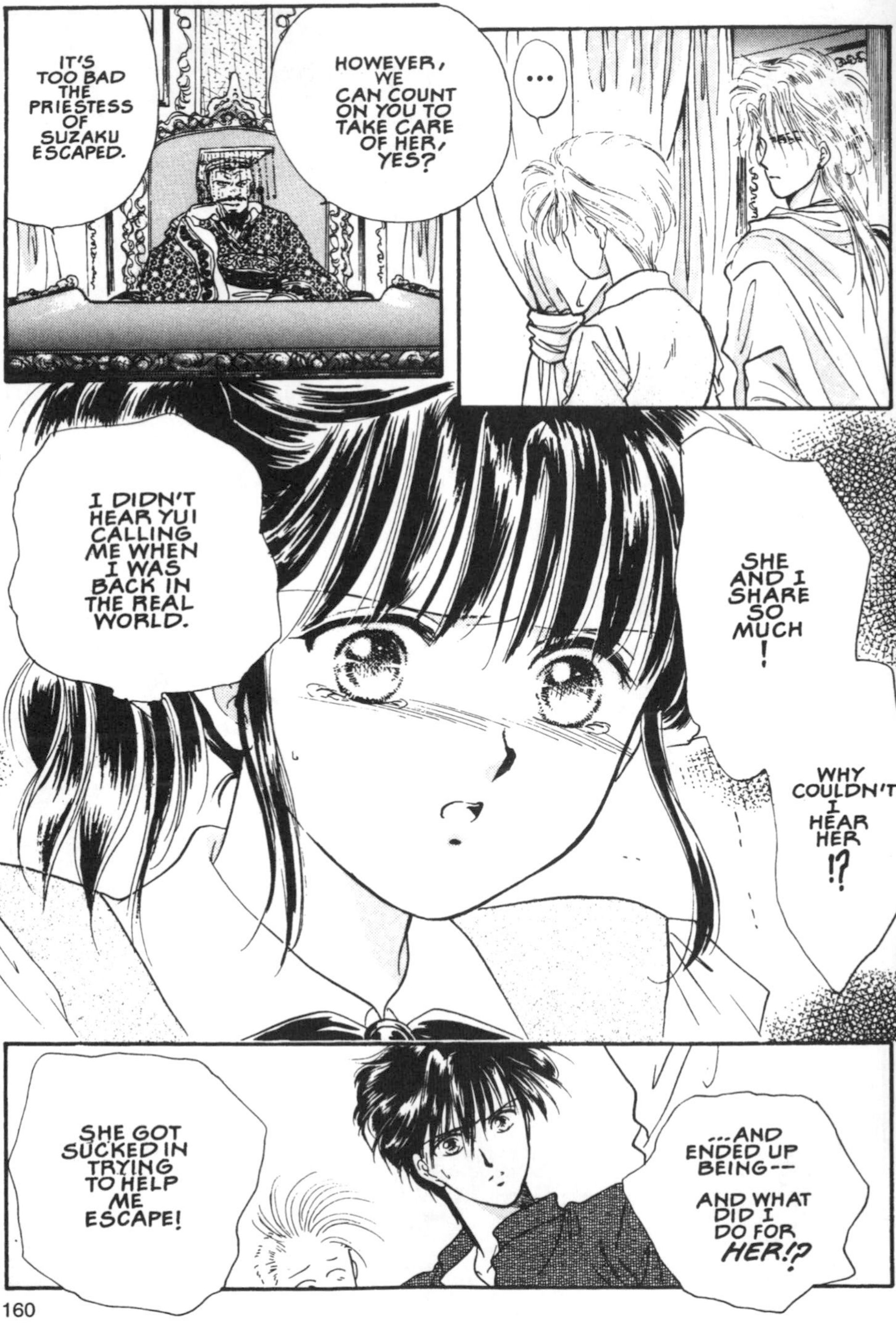
IT'S TOO BAD THE PRIESTESS OF SUZAKU ESCAPED.
HOWEVER, WE CAN COUNT ON YOU TO TAKE CARE OF HER, YES?
...
I DIDN'T HEAR YUI CALLING ME WHEN I WAS BACK IN THE REAL WORLD.
SHE AND I SHARE SO MUCH!
WHY COULDN'T I HEAR HER!?
SHE GOT SUCKED IN TRYING TO HELP ME ESCAPE!
...AND ENDED UP BEING--
AND WHAT DID I DO FOR HER!?

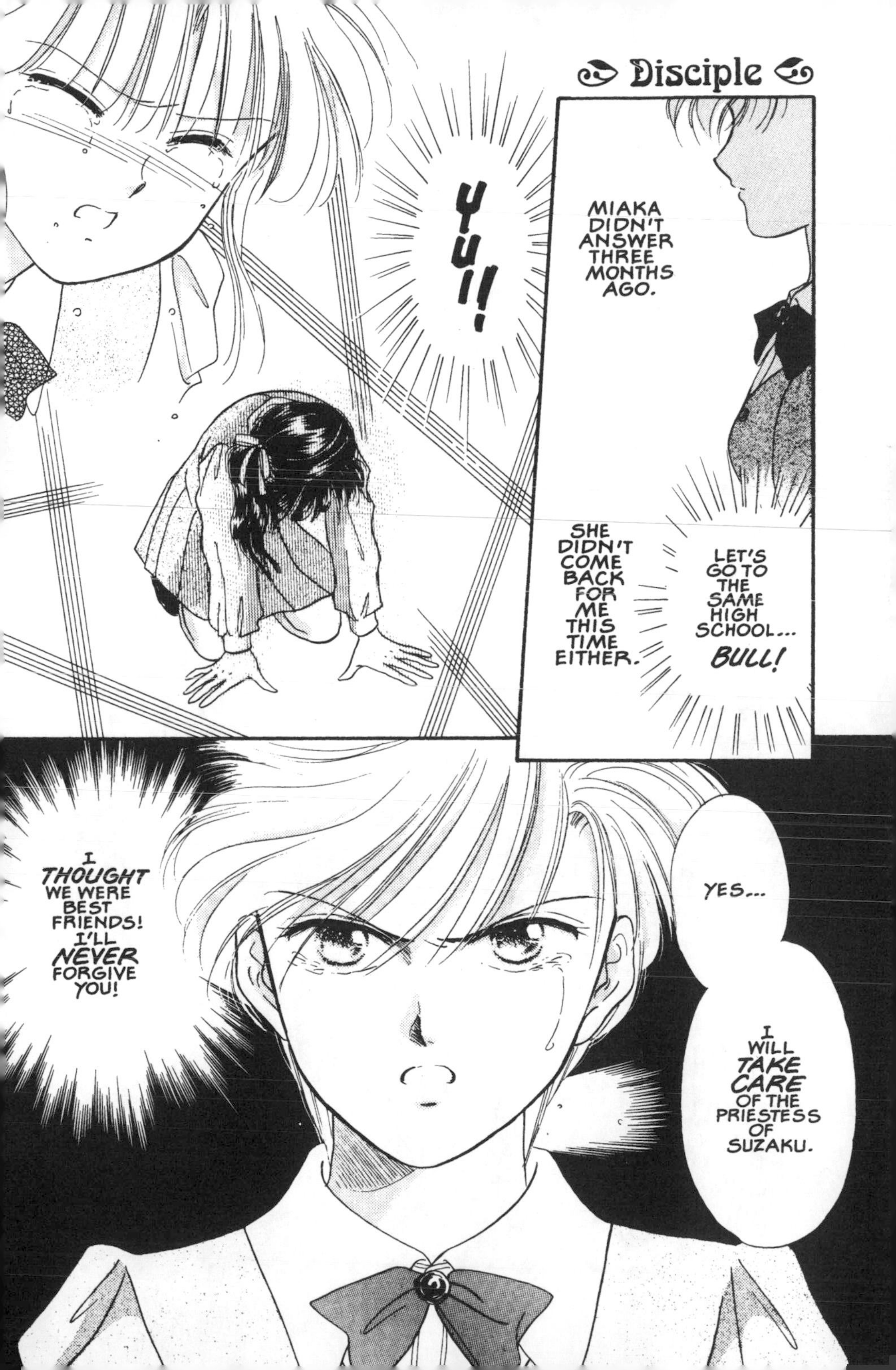
YUI!
MIAKA DIDN'T ANSWER THREE MONTHS AGO.
SHE DIDN'T COME BACK FOR ME THIS TIME EITHER.
LET'S GO TO THE SAME HIGH SCHOOL... *BULL!*
I *THOUGHT* WE WERE BEST FRIENDS! I'LL *NEVER* FORGIVE YOU!
YES...
I WILL *TAKE CARE* OF THE PRIESTESS OF SUZAKU.

BACK POPULAR DEMAND!
Pardon the Parody is newly retitled as:

ふしぎ悪戯 FUSHIGI AKUGI
THE MALICIOUS PLAY

With a slight change of wording you can make this into something you'll forever regret!

C'mon, kids! Try this at home! (Try WHAT!?)

F-KA CH
....
?
I COULDA SWORN SOMETHING JUST BRUSHED BY ME.
SKE CHA SKE CHA

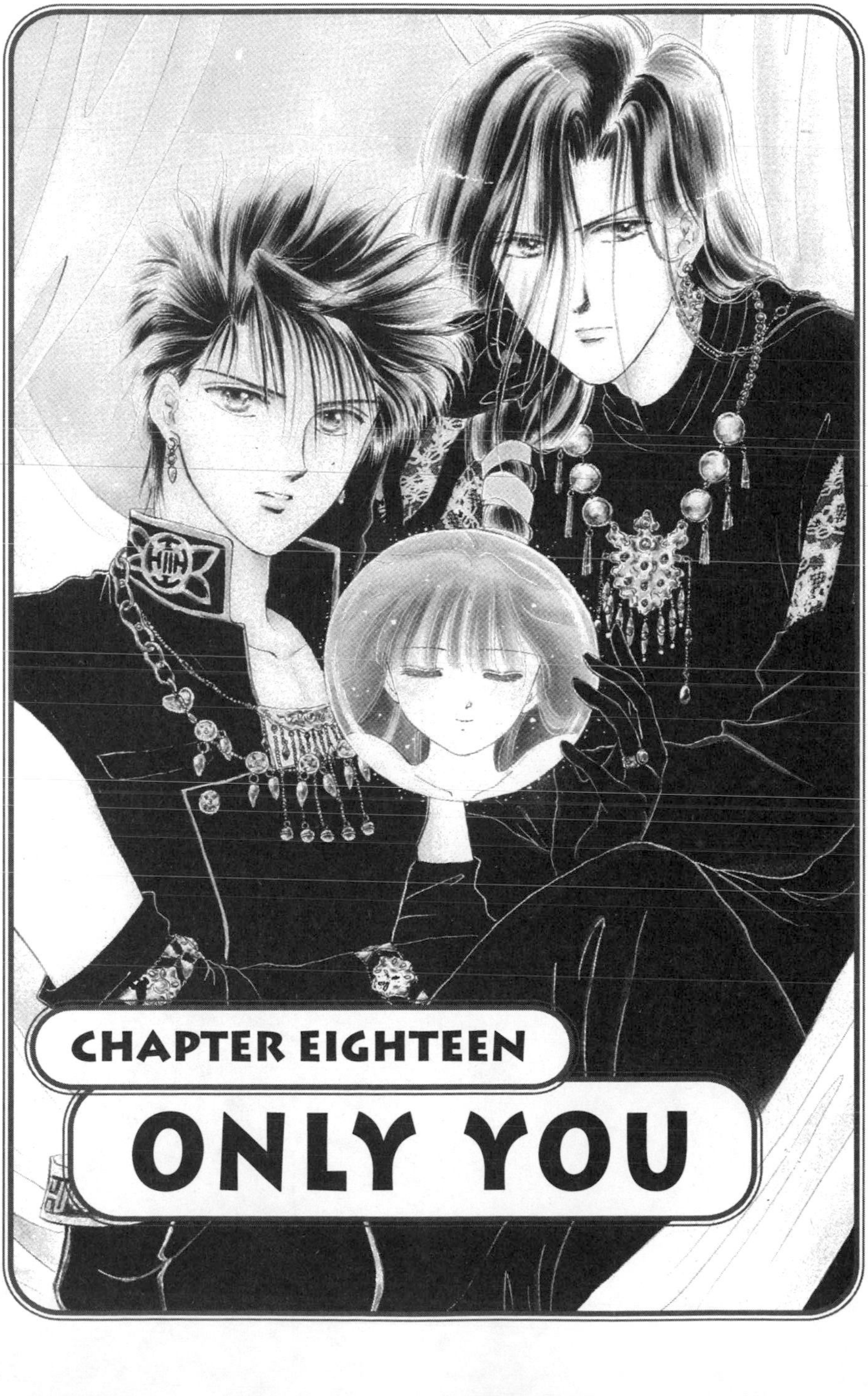

CHAPTER EIGHTEEN

ONLY YOU

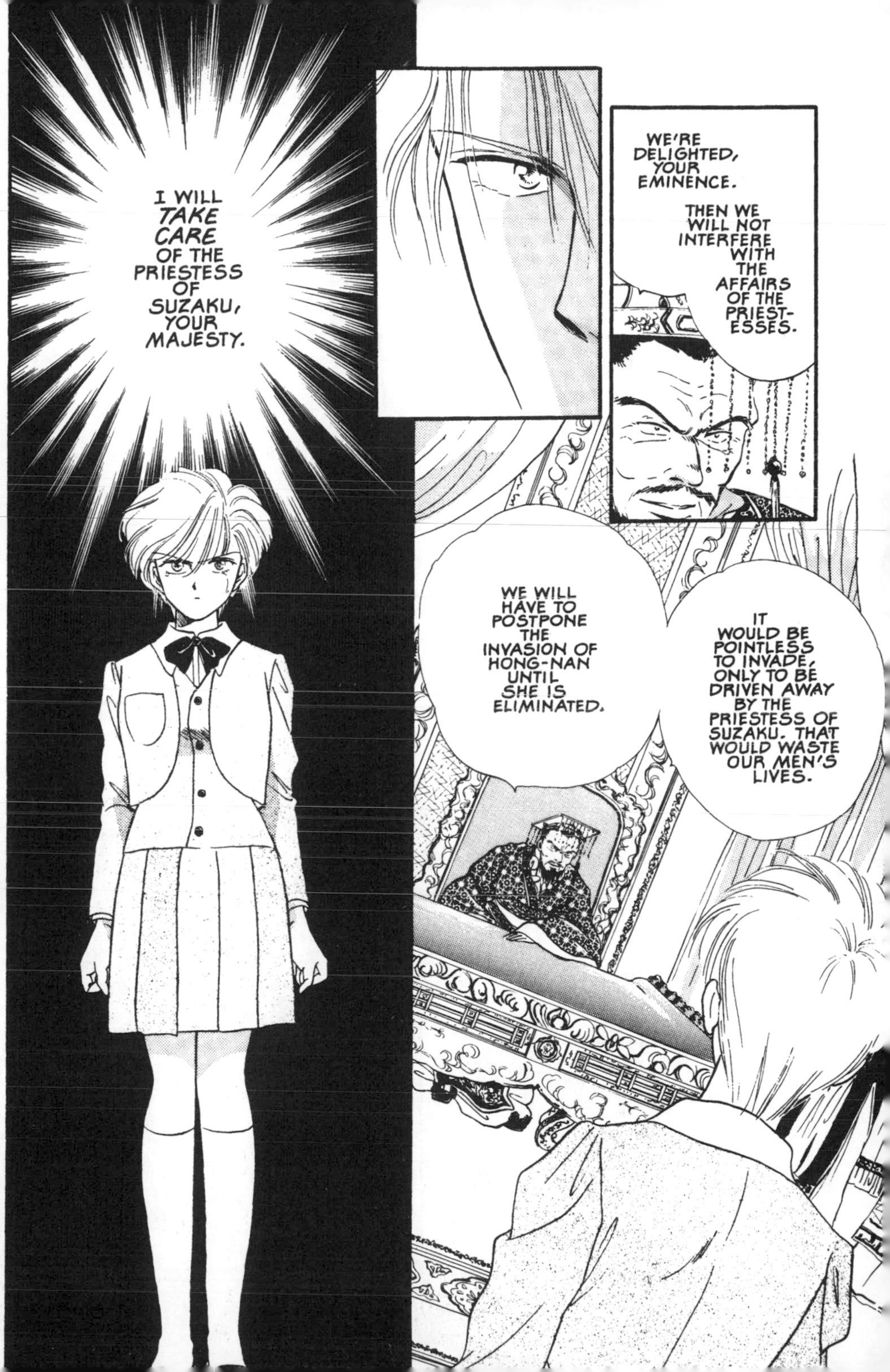
I WILL *TAKE CARE* OF THE PRIESTESS OF SUZAKU, YOUR MAJESTY.
WE'RE DELIGHTED, YOUR EMINENCE.
THEN WE WILL NOT INTERFERE WITH THE AFFAIRS OF THE PRIEST-ESSES.
WE WILL HAVE TO POSTPONE THE INVASION OF HONG-NAN UNTIL SHE IS ELIMINATED.
IT WOULD BE POINTLESS TO INVADE, ONLY TO BE DRIVEN AWAY BY THE PRIESTESS OF SUZAKU. THAT WOULD WASTE OUR MEN'S LIVES.

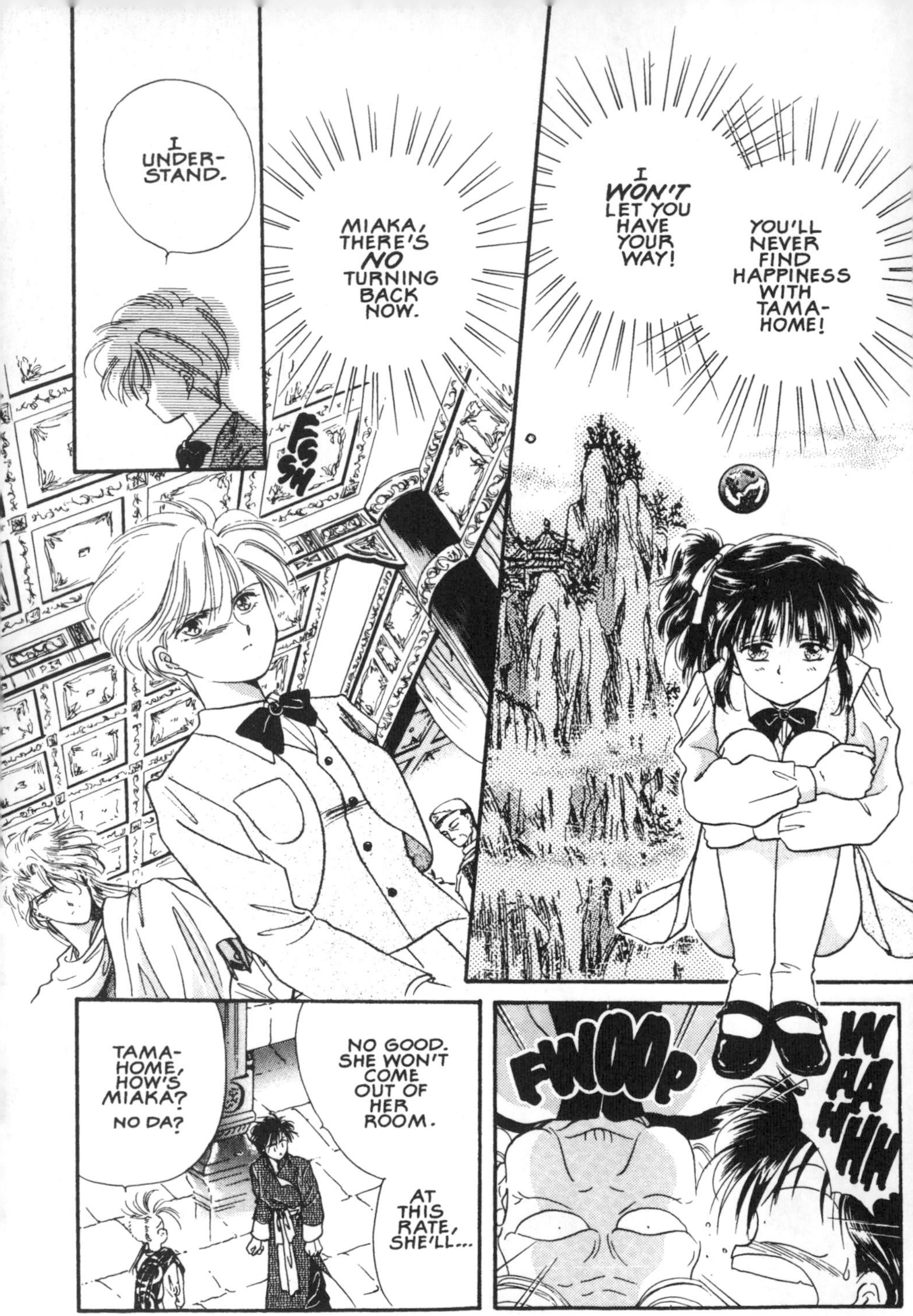
I UNDER-STAND.
MIAKA, THERE'S NO TURNING BACK NOW.
FSSH
I WON'T LET YOU HAVE YOUR WAY!
YOU'LL NEVER FIND HAPPINESS WITH TAMA-HOME!
TAMA-HOME, HOW'S MIAKA?
NO DA?
NO GOOD. SHE WON'T COME OUT OF HER ROOM.
AT THIS RATE, SHE'LL...
FWOOP
WAAHHH

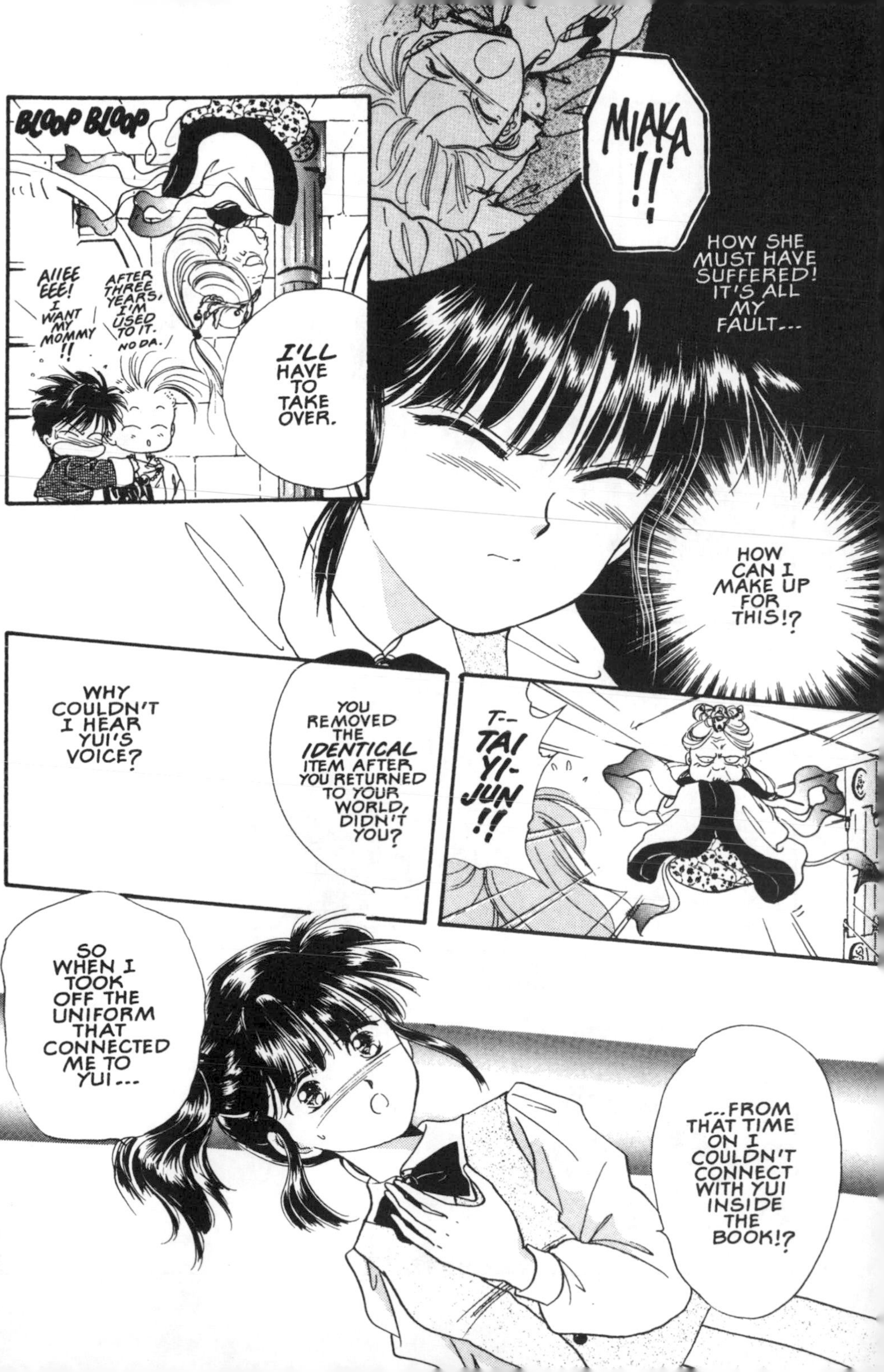
BLOOP BLOOP
AIIEE EEE! I WANT MY MOMMY !!
AFTER THREE YEARS, I'M USED TO IT. NO DA.
I'LL HAVE TO TAKE OVER.
MIAKA !!
HOW SHE MUST HAVE SUFFERED! IT'S ALL MY FAULT...
HOW CAN I MAKE UP FOR THIS!?
WHY COULDN'T I HEAR YUI'S VOICE?
YOU REMOVED THE IDENTICAL ITEM AFTER YOU RETURNED TO YOUR WORLD, DIDN'T YOU?
T-- TAI YI-JUN !!
SO WHEN I TOOK OFF THE UNIFORM THAT CONNECTED ME TO YUI...
...FROM THAT TIME ON I COULDN'T CONNECT WITH YUI INSIDE THE BOOK!?

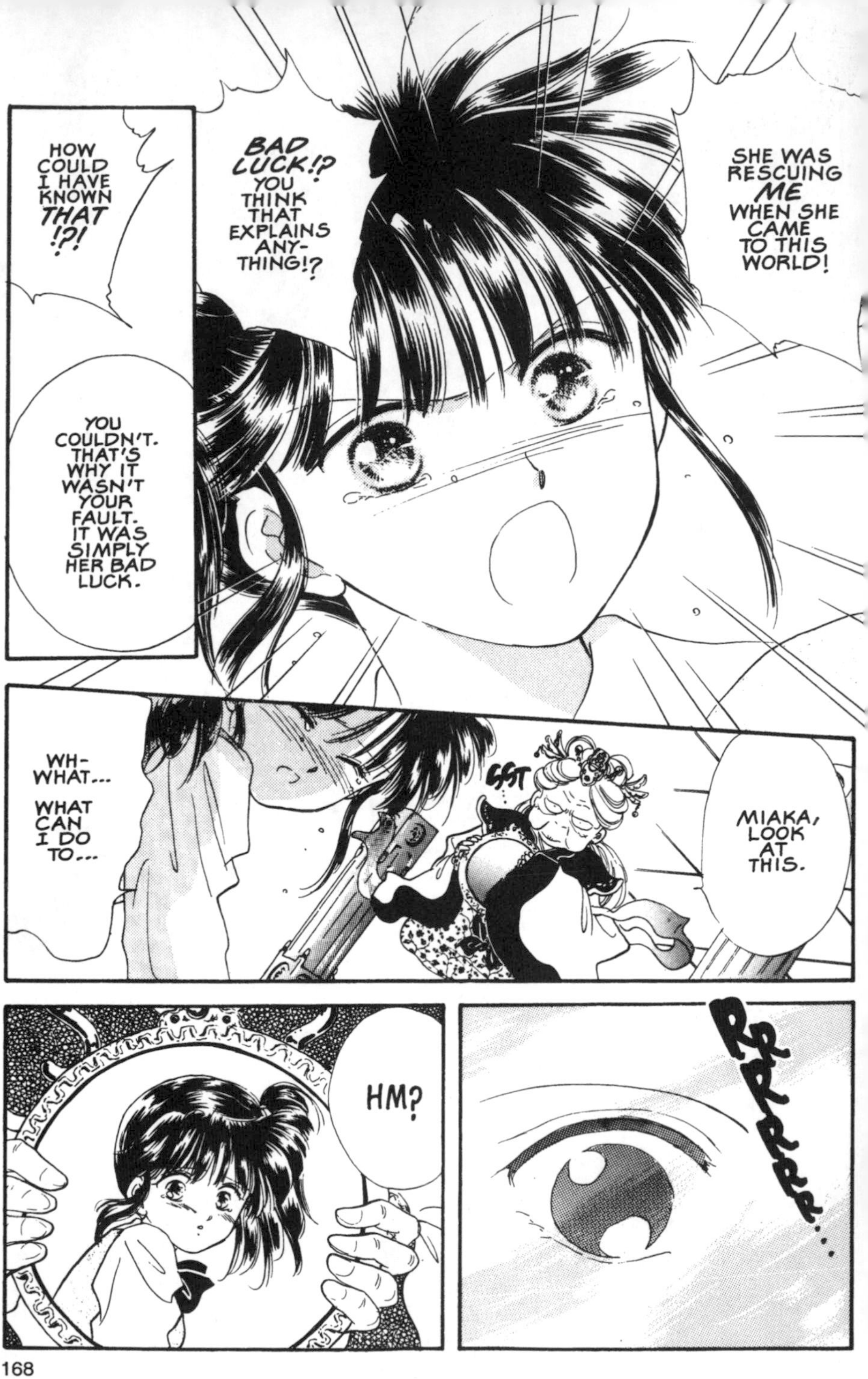
HOW COULD I HAVE KNOWN THAT!?!
YOU COULDN'T. THAT'S WHY IT WASN'T YOUR FAULT. IT WAS SIMPLY HER BAD LUCK.
BAD LUCK!? YOU THINK THAT EXPLAINS ANY-THING!?
SHE WAS RESCUING ME WHEN SHE CAME TO THIS WORLD!
WH-WHAT... WHAT CAN I DO TO...
GSST
MIAKA, LOOK AT THIS.
HM?
RRRRRRR...

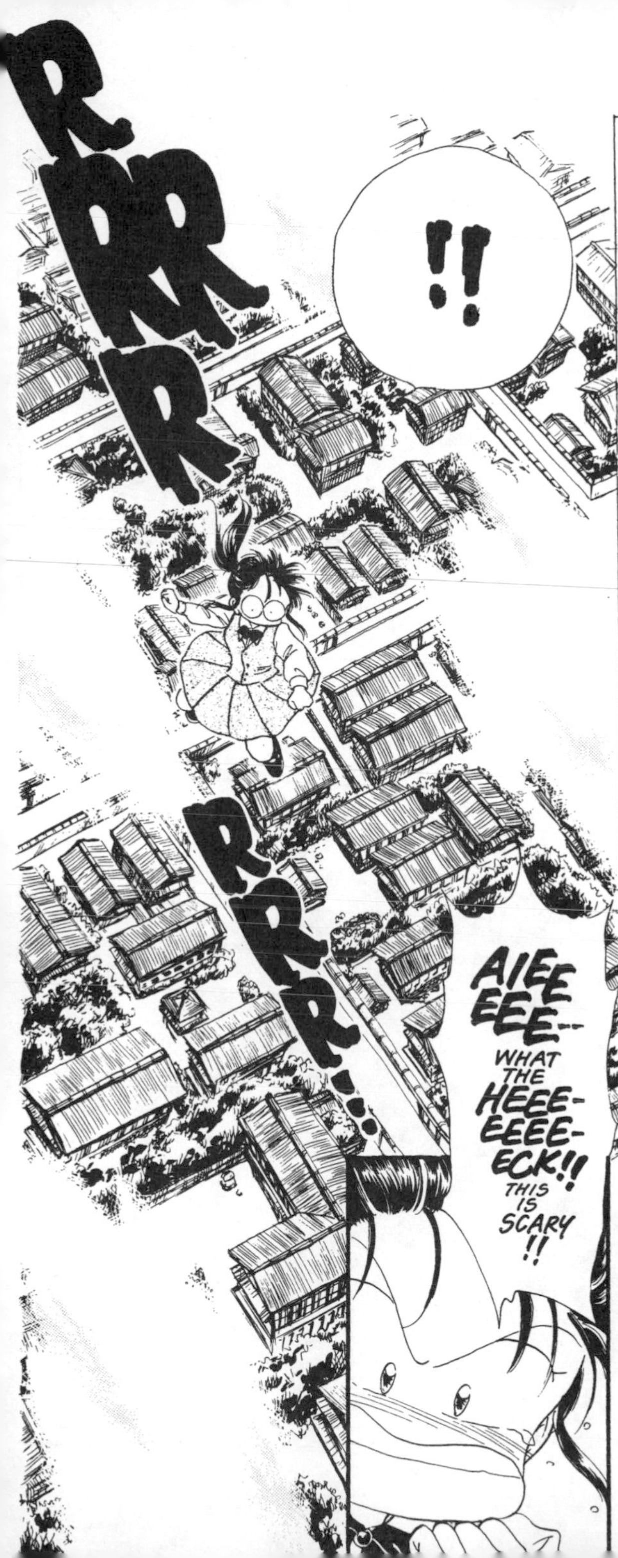
RRRR
!!
RRRR...
AIEEE EEE--
WHAT THE HEEEE-EEEE-ECK!!
THIS IS SCARY!!

Fushigi Yûgi ∾ 3

Well, I've been getting responses from you regarding this free chat section. One person wrote in to complain about how I wouldn't give official approval for a project. According to the letter, my failure to give official approval indicated that I was becoming more distant from my readers. But it was my editors' decision. I guess they had problems in the past. I'm not trying to distance myself from my readers! I'm glad to hear that you wouldn't want that, but there's no need to get hung up over getting "official" approval. So don't worry about it, okay? Just because there isn't an official approval doesn't mean that I don't like it.
I keep on receiving a lot of fanzines, and I take the time to look through all of them. So go right ahead and make fanzines or dojinshi and send them my way. *I thought I'd said that before already.* I think it's fine to draw parodies of my work (as long as they're not gross or boring).
Once my story gets published in a magazine, then it becomes part of each reader's imagination, fueled by the way he or she feels about the characters. That's how a work finally becomes complete. *I don't know what I'm saying!* All I want to say is this book in your hands is your own unique "Fushigi Yûgi." *If you see what I mean.* Manga is for the reader so... *Urgh, I'm getting confused.* Those readers who were fans of my work before it merited any "official seal of approval" became the ones that I respect the most. I'm not getting distant! AARGH, I'm getting all jumbled up!
--after a rest--
So fanzines are fine, okay? Oh yeah, I forgot during my rant, I have to apologize for the "Prepubescence Special Edition" not coming out on time. It's not my fault this time! The good news is that a book of illustrations is scheduled to come out next year (I hope). *If it doesn't sorry again!* It should be a book of colored illustrations for "Prepubescence" and "Fushigi Yûgi." You want a story, too? Yessir!! I'll do my best.
One last common question: "Do you do illustrations for novels?" I've never had any requests to do one. That's all. This time I answered a lot of questions. Lotta work for those who read through this section.

But who's working hardest here!?

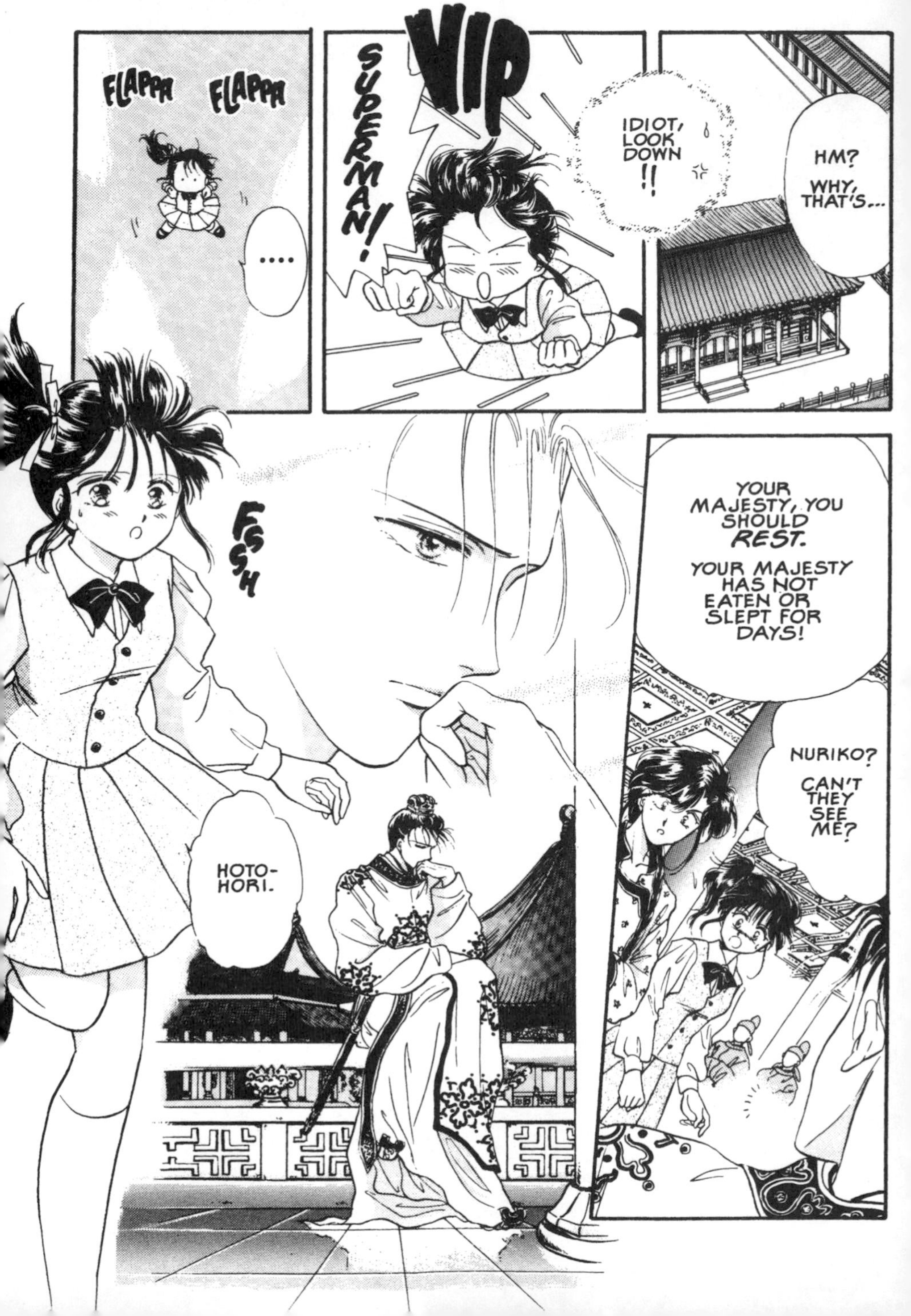
FLAPPA FLAPPA
.....
SUPERMAN!
VIP
IDIOT, LOOK DOWN!!
HM?
WHY, THAT'S...
FSSH
HOTO-HORI.
YOUR MAJESTY, YOU SHOULD REST.
YOUR MAJESTY HAS NOT EATEN OR SLEPT FOR DAYS!
NURIKO?
CAN'T THEY SEE ME?

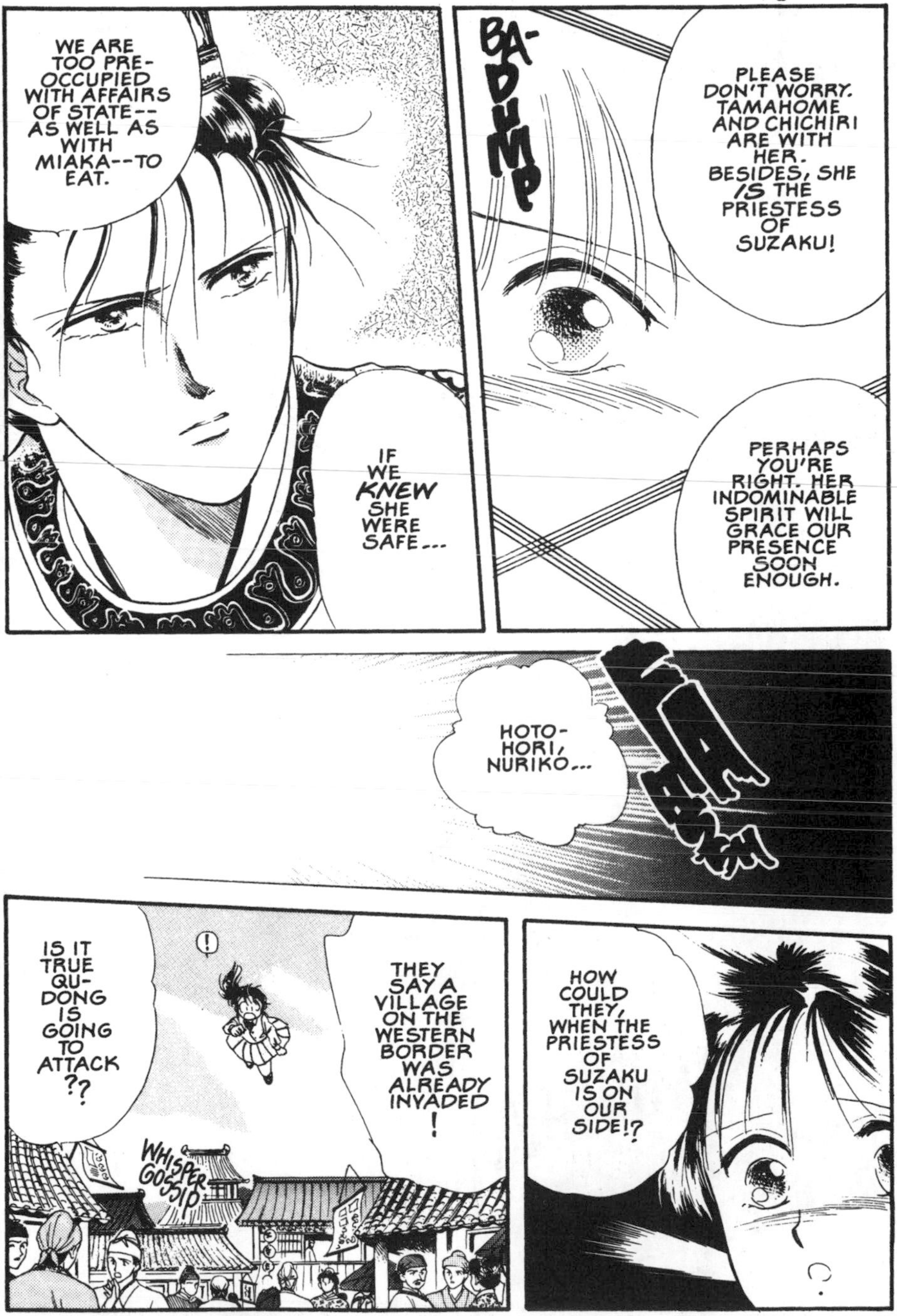
WE ARE TOO PRE-OCCUPIED WITH AFFAIRS OF STATE--AS WELL AS WITH MIAKA--TO EAT.
IF WE *KNEW* SHE WERE SAFE...
BA-DUMP
PLEASE DON'T WORRY. TAMAHOME AND CHICHIRI ARE WITH HER. BESIDES, SHE *IS* THE PRIESTESS OF SUZAKU!
PERHAPS YOU'RE RIGHT. HER INDOMINABLE SPIRIT WILL GRACE OUR PRESENCE SOON ENOUGH.
HOTO-HORI, NURIKO...
IS IT TRUE QU-DONG IS GOING TO ATTACK??
!
THEY SAY A VILLAGE ON THE WESTERN BORDER WAS ALREADY INVADED!
WHISPER GOSSIP
HOW COULD THEY, WHEN THE PRIESTESS OF SUZAKU IS ON OUR SIDE!?

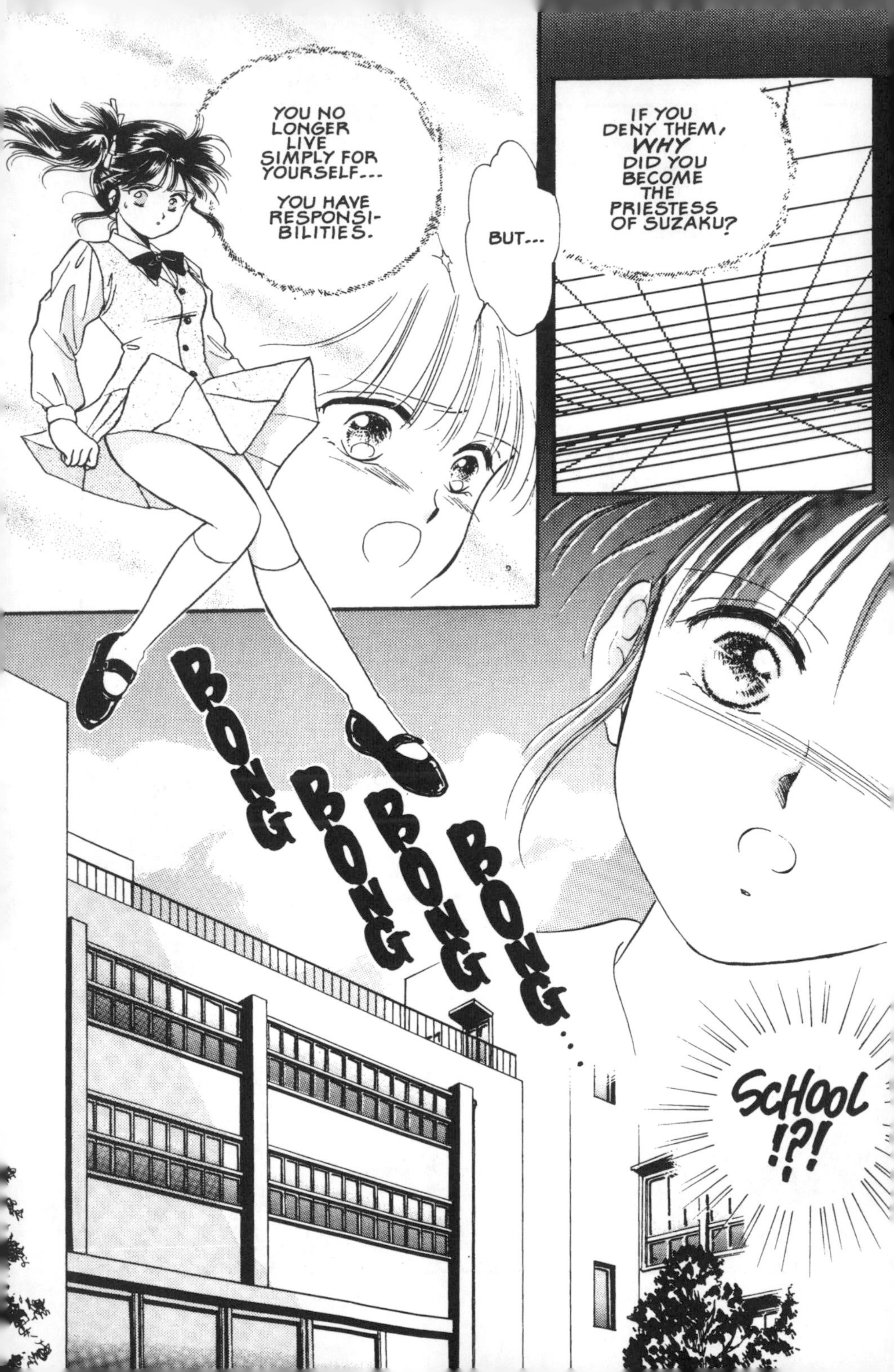
YOU NO LONGER LIVE SIMPLY FOR YOURSELF...
YOU HAVE RESPONSIBILITIES.
BUT...
IF YOU DENY THEM, WHY DID YOU BECOME THE PRIESTESS OF SUZAKU?
BONG BONG BONG BONG...
SCHOOL !?!

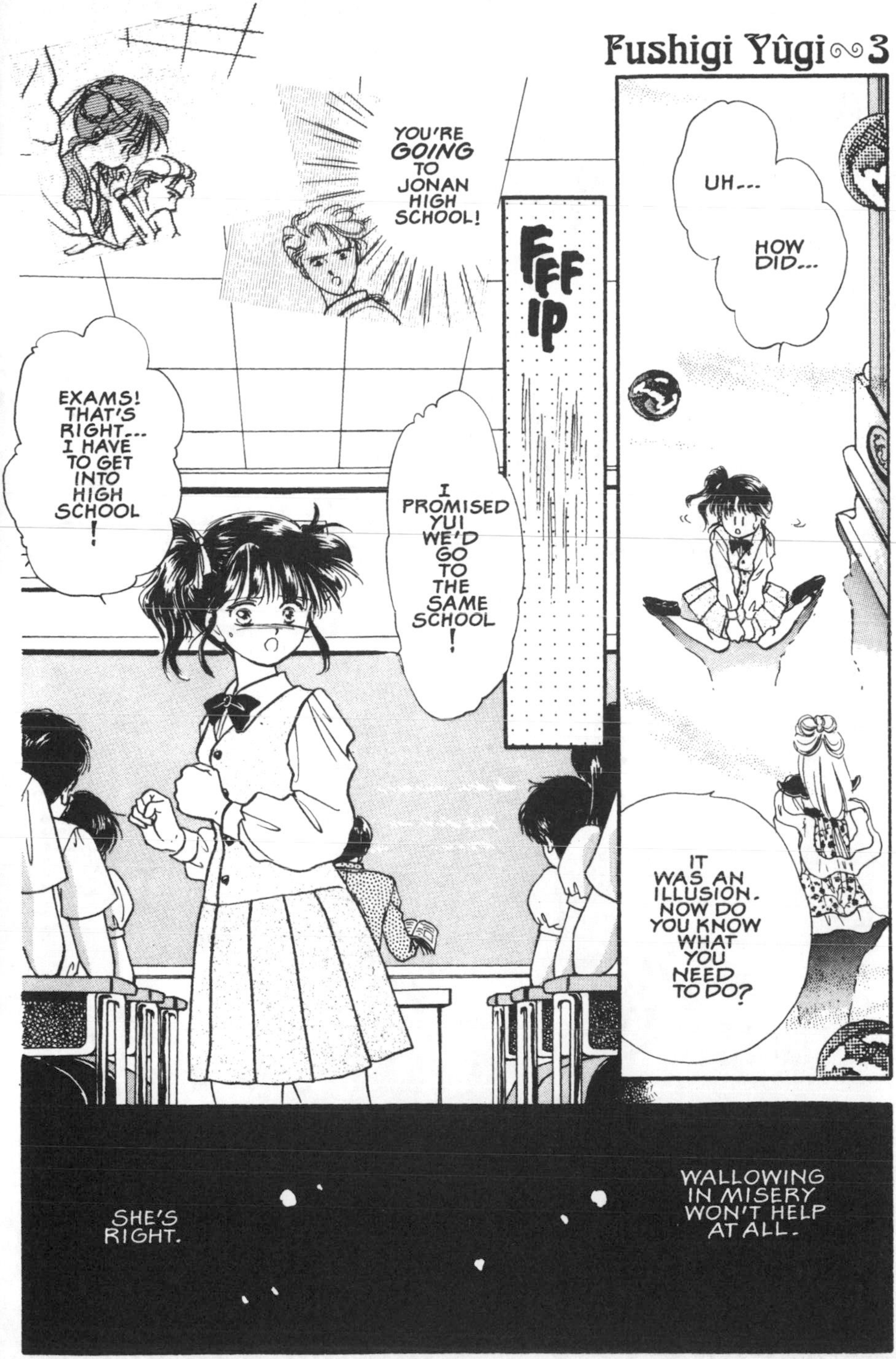
YOU'RE GOING TO JONAN HIGH SCHOOL!
EXAMS! THAT'S RIGHT... I HAVE TO GET INTO HIGH SCHOOL!
I PROMISED YUI WE'D GO TO THE SAME SCHOOL!
FFFIP
UH...
HOW DID...
IT WAS AN ILLUSION. NOW DO YOU KNOW WHAT YOU NEED TO DO?
SHE'S RIGHT.
WALLOWING IN MISERY WON'T HELP AT ALL.

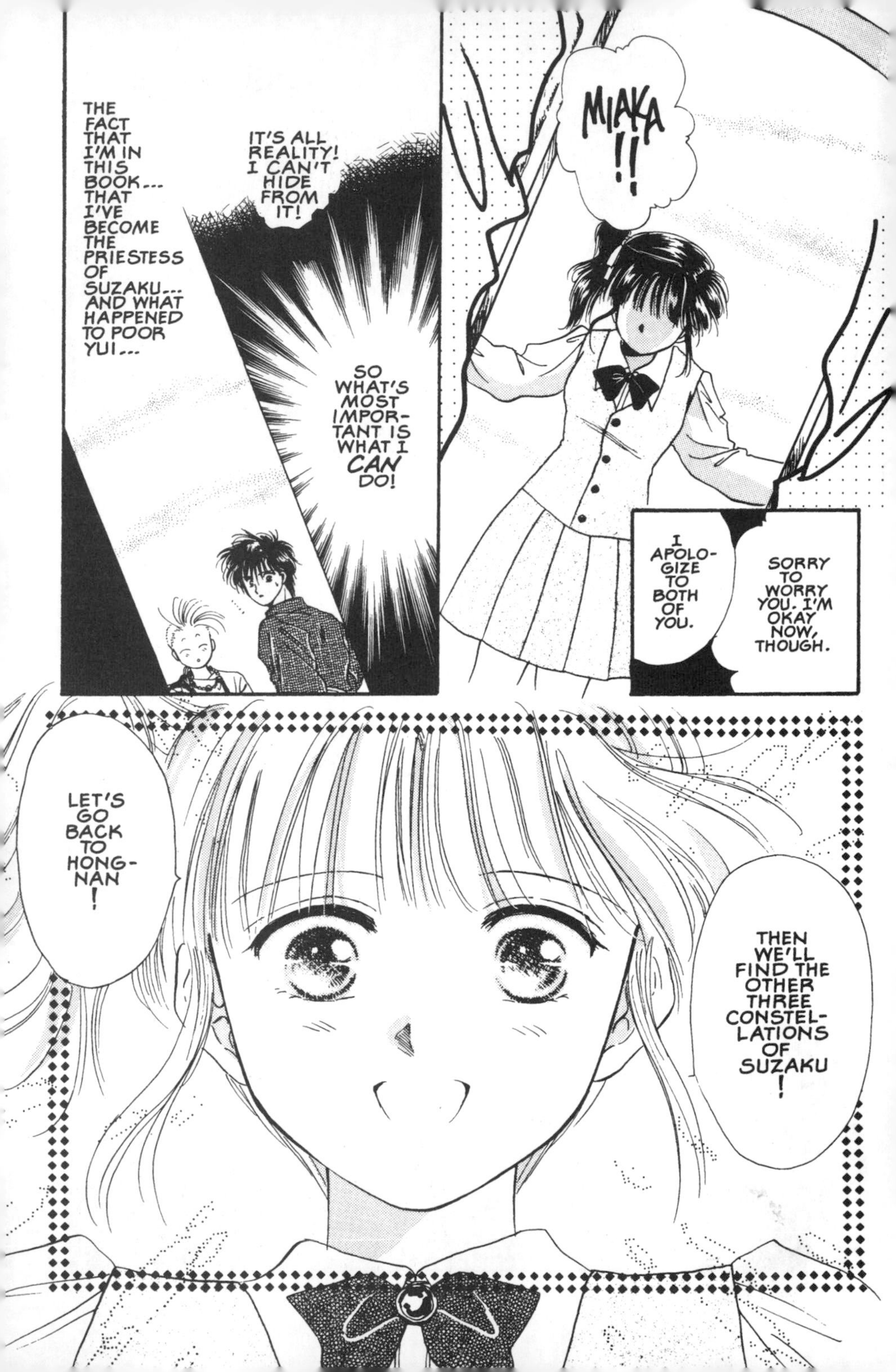

THE FACT THAT I'M IN THIS BOOK... THAT I'VE BECOME THE PRIESTESS OF SUZAKU... AND WHAT HAPPENED TO POOR YUI...
IT'S ALL REALITY! I CAN'T HIDE FROM IT!
SO WHAT'S MOST IMPOR-TANT IS WHAT I CAN DO!
MIAKA!!
I APOLO-GIZE TO BOTH OF YOU.
SORRY TO WORRY YOU. I'M OKAY NOW, THOUGH.
LET'S GO BACK TO HONG-NAN!
THEN WE'LL FIND THE OTHER THREE CONSTEL-LATIONS OF SUZAKU!

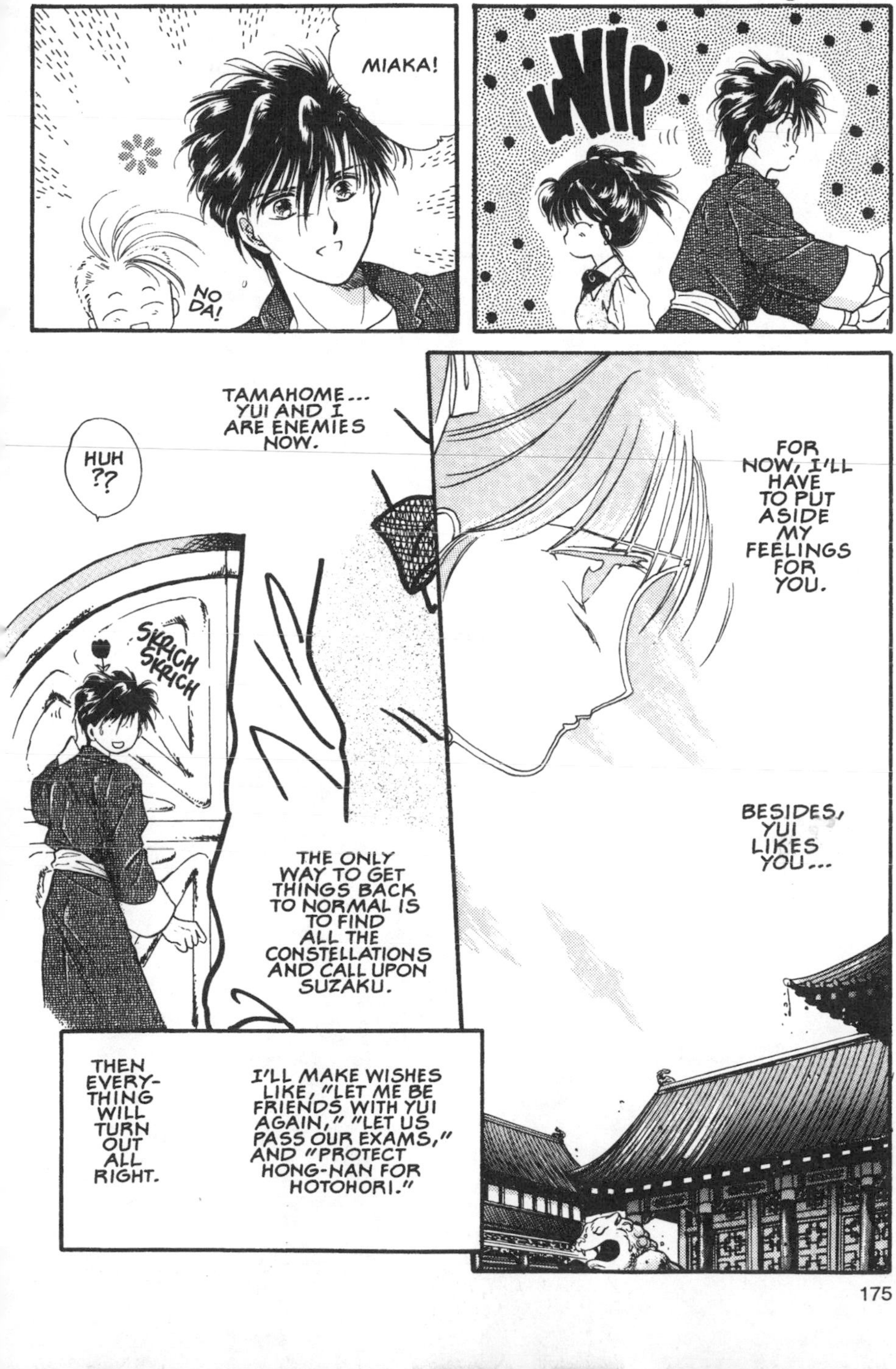
MIAKA!
NO DA!
WHIP
TAMAHOME... YUI AND I ARE ENEMIES NOW.
HUH ??
SKRICH SKRICH
THE ONLY WAY TO GET THINGS BACK TO NORMAL IS TO FIND ALL THE CONSTELLATIONS AND CALL UPON SUZAKU.
FOR NOW, I'LL HAVE TO PUT ASIDE MY FEELINGS FOR YOU.
BESIDES, YUI LIKES YOU...
THEN EVERYTHING WILL TURN OUT ALL RIGHT.
I'LL MAKE WISHES LIKE, "LET ME BE FRIENDS WITH YUI AGAIN," "LET US PASS OUR EXAMS," AND "PROTECT HONG-NAN FOR HOTOHORI."

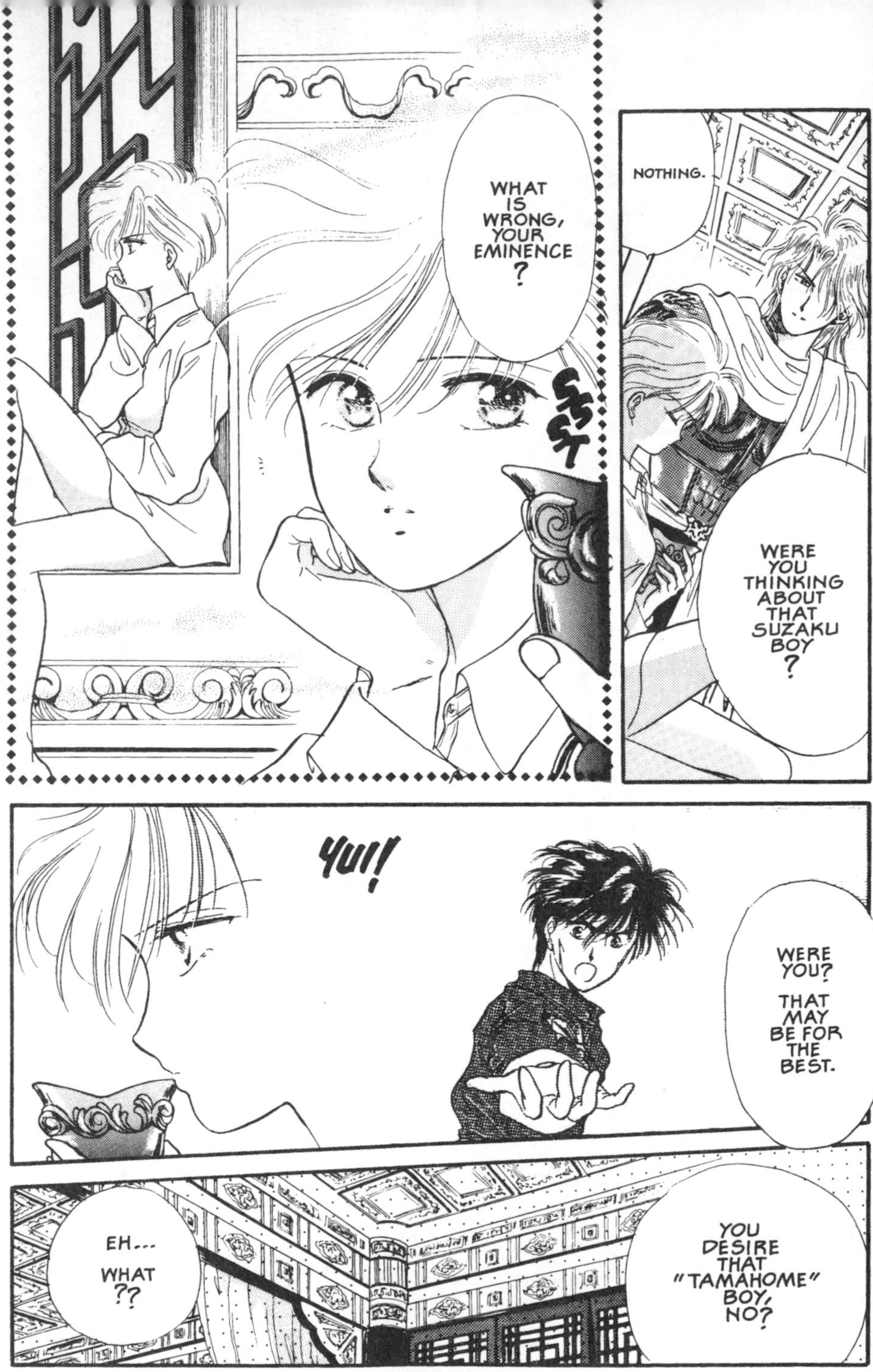
WHAT IS WRONG, YOUR EMINENCE?
NOTHING.
WERE YOU THINKING ABOUT THAT SUZAKU BOY?
YUI!
WERE YOU? THAT MAY BE FOR THE BEST.
EH... WHAT??
YOU DESIRE THAT "TAMAHOME" BOY, NO?

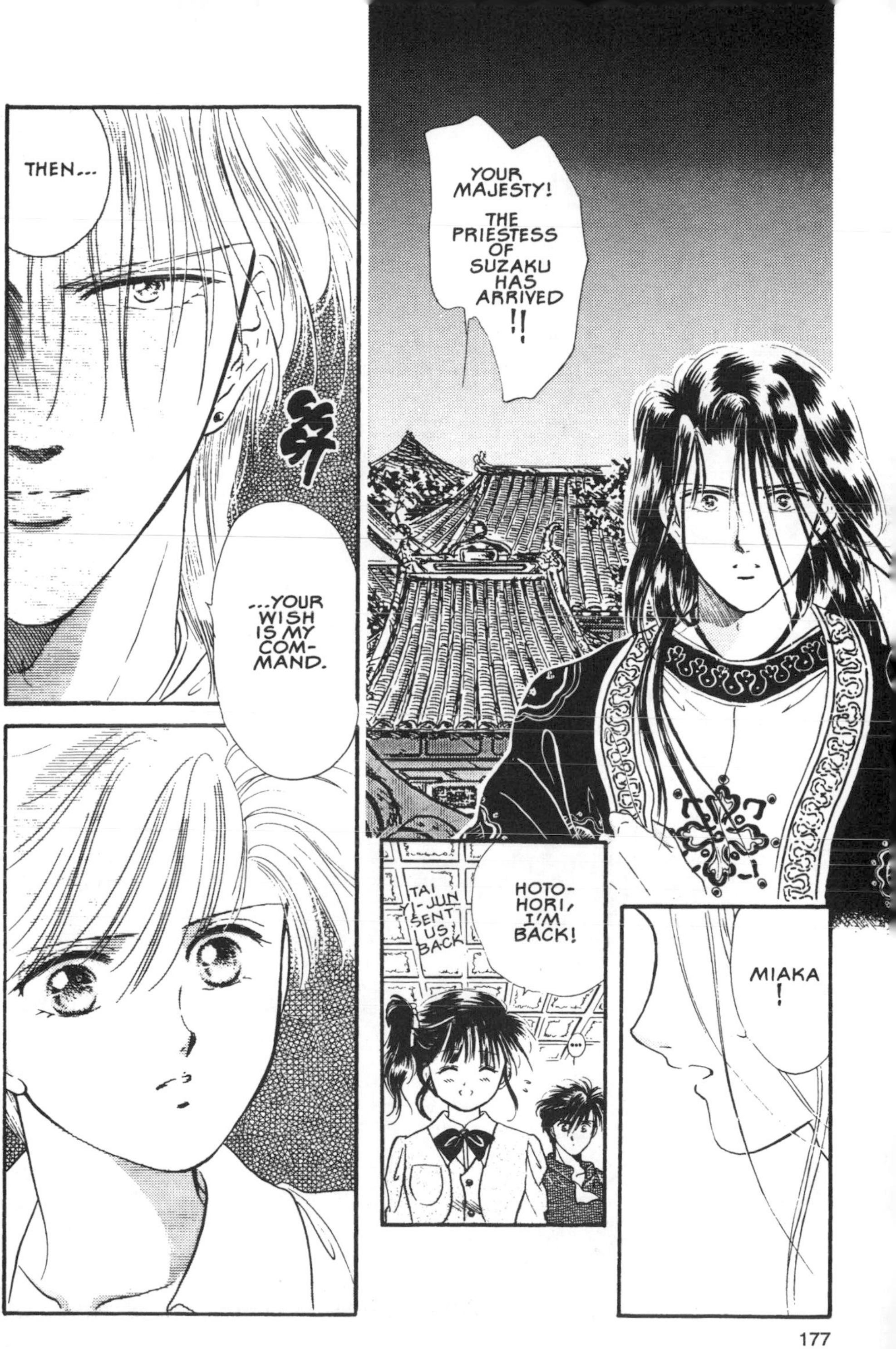
THEN...
...YOUR WISH IS MY COM-MAND.
YOUR MAJESTY! THE PRIESTESS OF SUZAKU HAS ARRIVED !!
HOTO-HORI, I'M BACK!
TAI YI-JUN SENT US BACK
...
MIAKA !

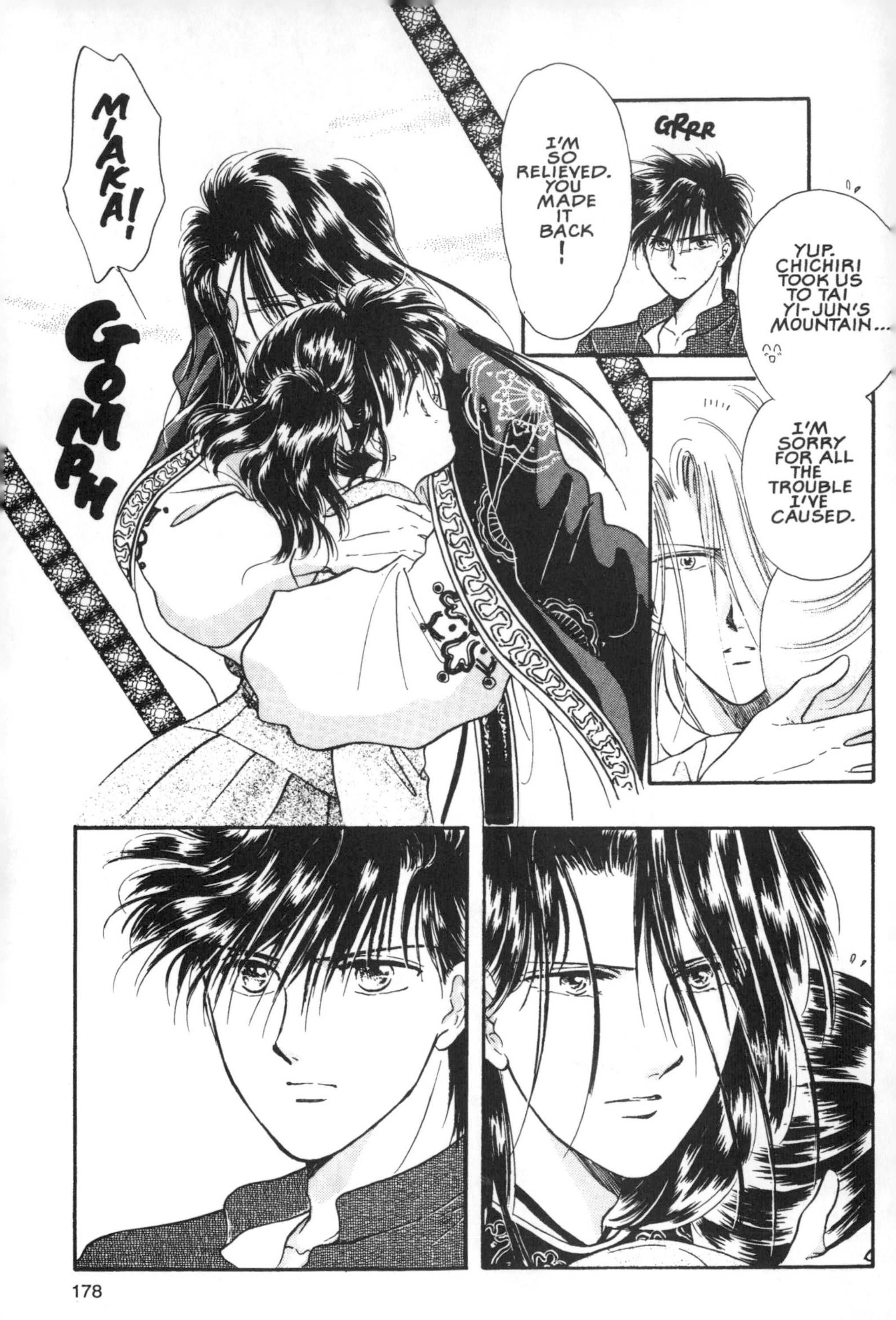
MIAKA!
GOMPH
I'M SO RELIEVED. YOU MADE IT BACK!
GRRR
YUP. CHICHIRI TOOK US TO TAI YI-JUN'S MOUNTAIN...
I'M SORRY FOR ALL THE TROUBLE I'VE CAUSED.

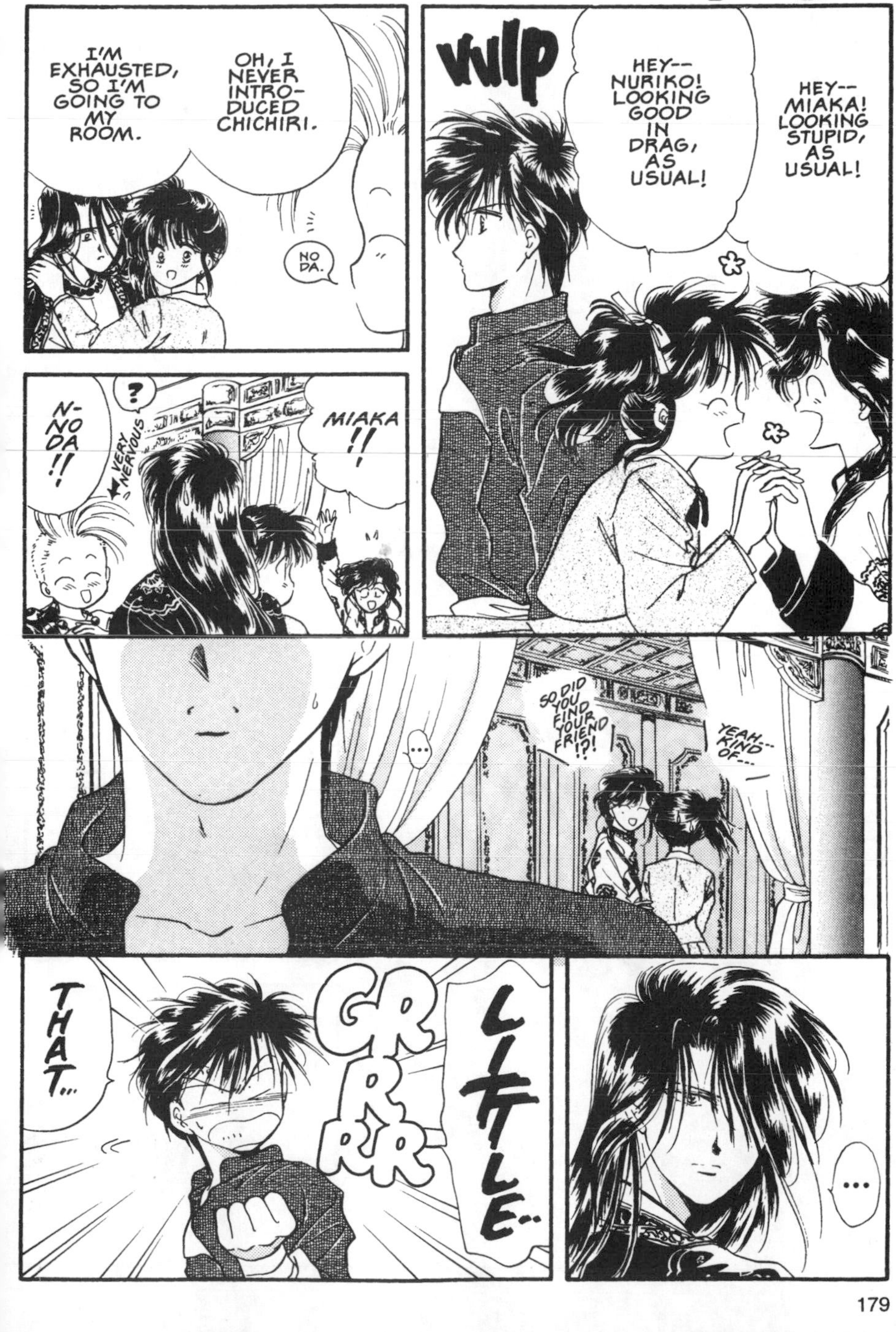
I'M EXHAUSTED, SO I'M GOING TO MY ROOM.
OH, I NEVER INTRODUCED CHICHIRI.
NO DA.
VVULP
HEY-- NURIKO! LOOKING GOOD IN DRAG, AS USUAL!
HEY-- MIAKA! LOOKING STUPID, AS USUAL!
?
N-NO DA!!
VERY NERVOUS
MIAKA!!
...
SO DID YOU FIND YOUR FRIEND!?!
YEAH... KIND OF...
THAT...
GRRR
LITTLE...
...

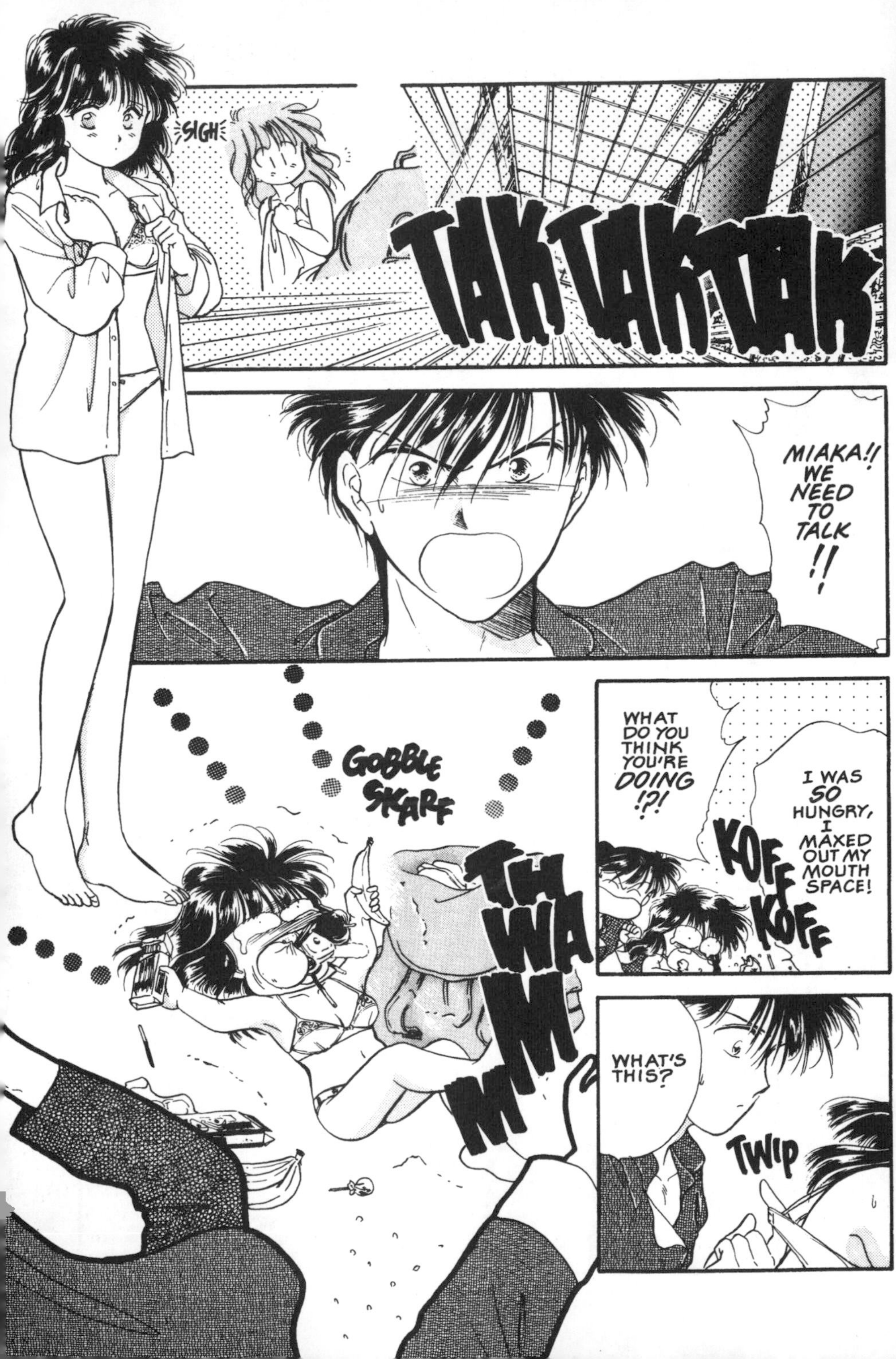
SIGH
TAK TAK TAK
MIAKA!! WE NEED TO TALK!!
GOBBLE SKARF
THWAMM
WHAT DO YOU THINK YOU'RE DOING!?!
I WAS SO HUNGRY, I MAXED OUT MY MOUTH SPACE!
KOFF KOFF
WHAT'S THIS?
TWIP

❧ Disciple ❧

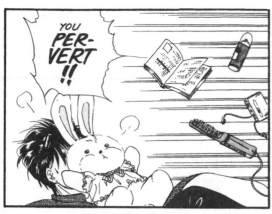

YOU PER-VERT!!

WHAT THE HECK IS THIS?

STUFF I BROUGHT FROM MY WORLD!

DON'T YOU KNOW ANY-THING!?

YOU WOULDN'T, WOULD YOU?

SHE'S WEARING A CAMISOLE

ZooooM

TAMA-HOME!!

OH, YEAH!

THAT'S NOT WHAT I CAME HERE FOR!

OLD HABITS TOOK OVER!

WHY ARE YOU AVOIDING ME!?

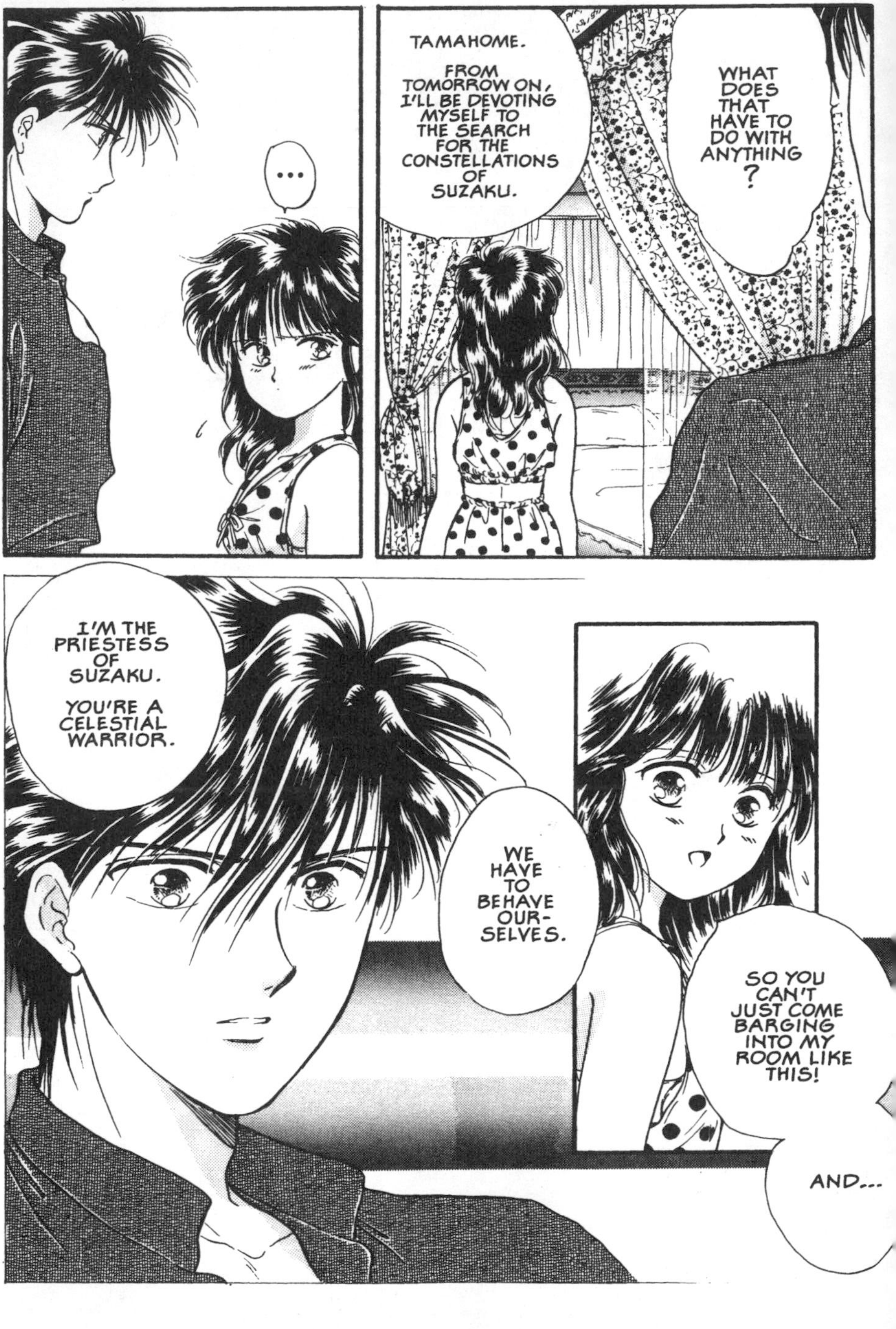
...
TAMAHOME.
FROM TOMORROW ON, I'LL BE DEVOTING MYSELF TO THE SEARCH FOR THE CONSTELLATIONS OF SUZAKU.
WHAT DOES THAT HAVE TO DO WITH ANYTHING?
I'M THE PRIESTESS OF SUZAKU.
YOU'RE A CELESTIAL WARRIOR.
WE HAVE TO BEHAVE OUR-SELVES.
SO YOU CAN'T JUST COME BARGING INTO MY ROOM LIKE THIS!
AND...

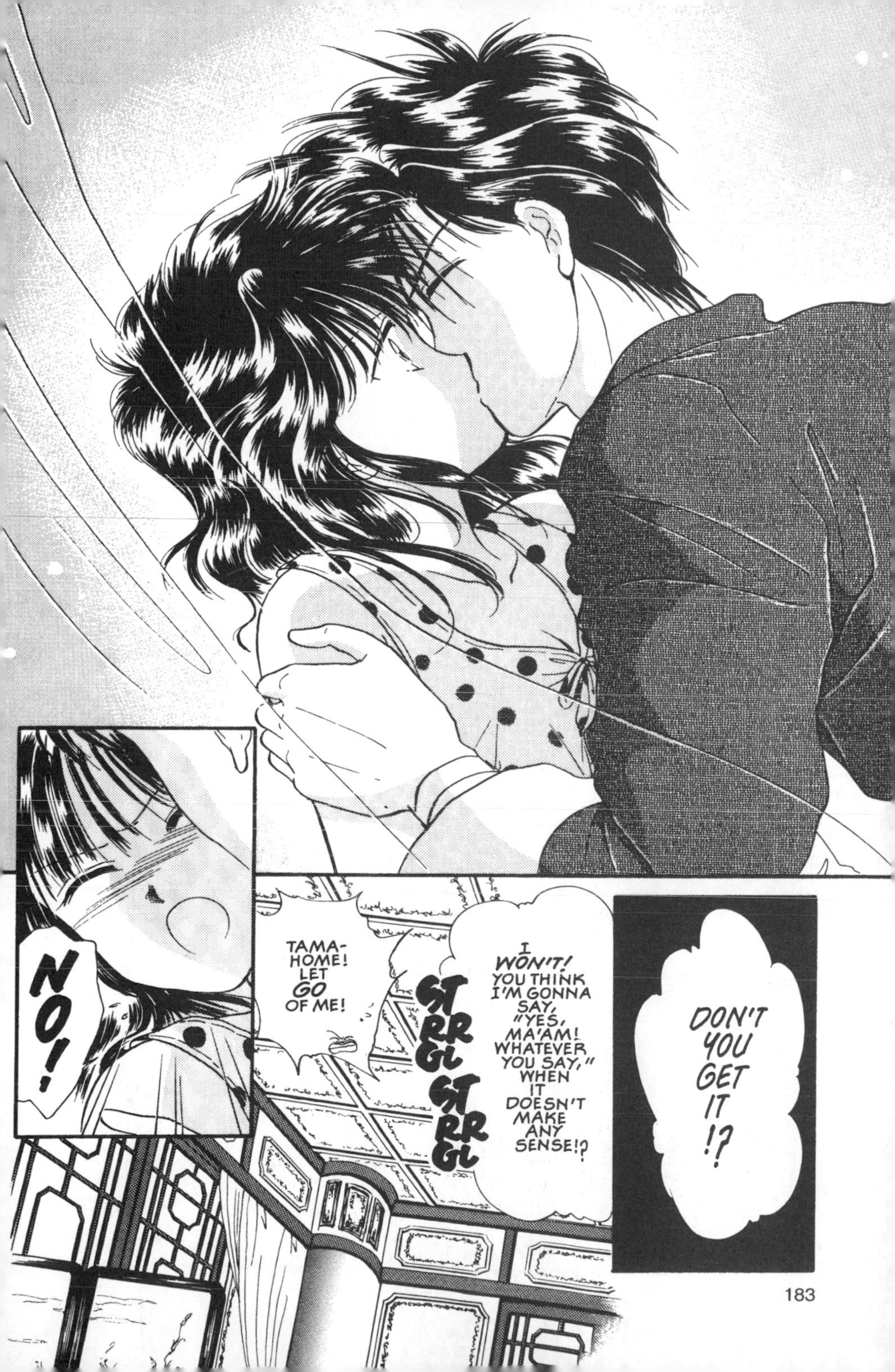

NO!!
TAMA-HOME! LET GO OF ME!
STRRGL STRRGL
I WON'T! YOU THINK I'M GONNA SAY, "YES, MA'AM! WHATEVER YOU SAY," WHEN IT DOESN'T MAKE ANY SENSE!?
DON'T YOU GET IT!?

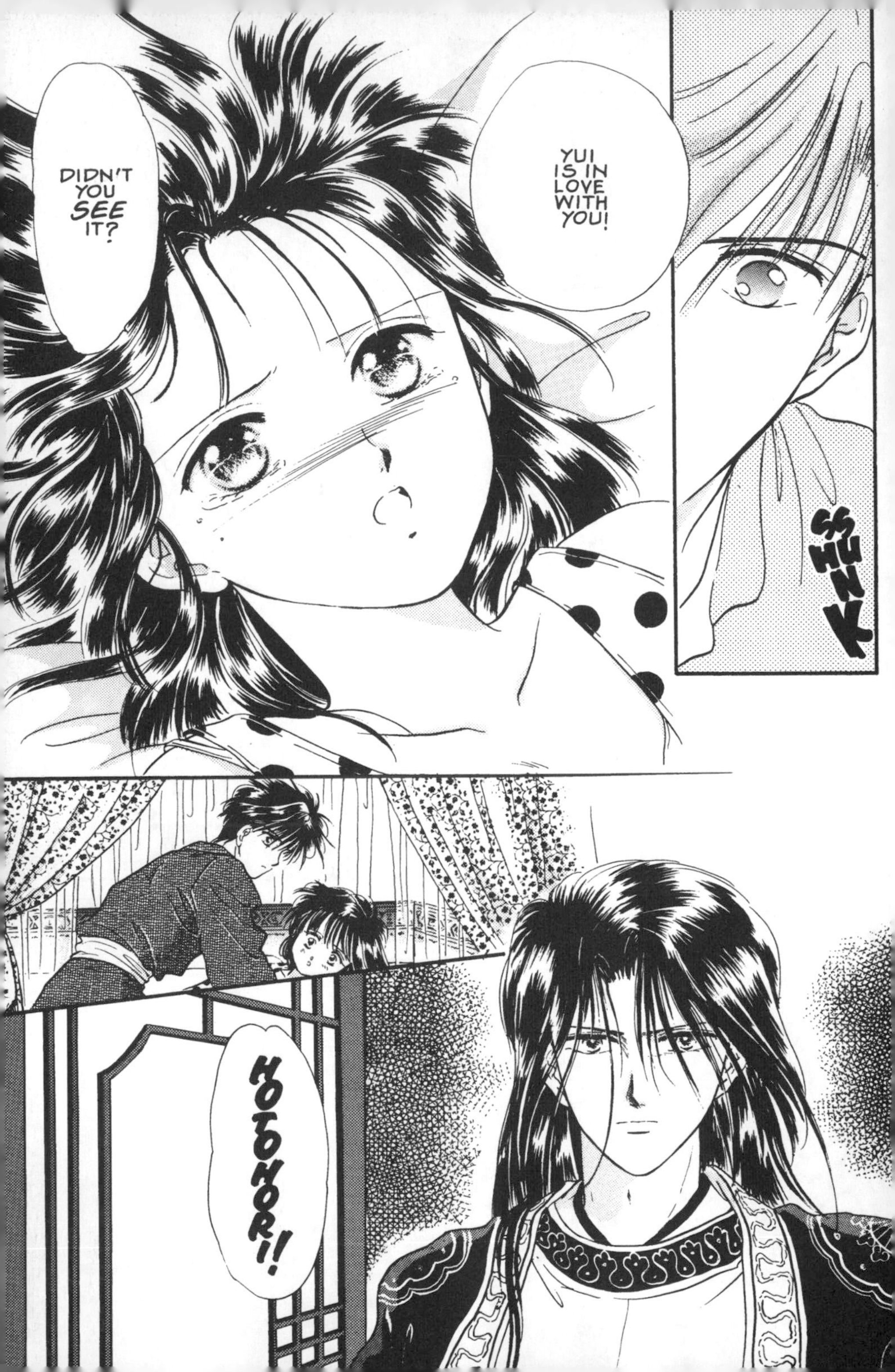
DIDN'T YOU SEE IT?
YUI IS IN LOVE WITH YOU!
SSHUNK
HOTOHORI!

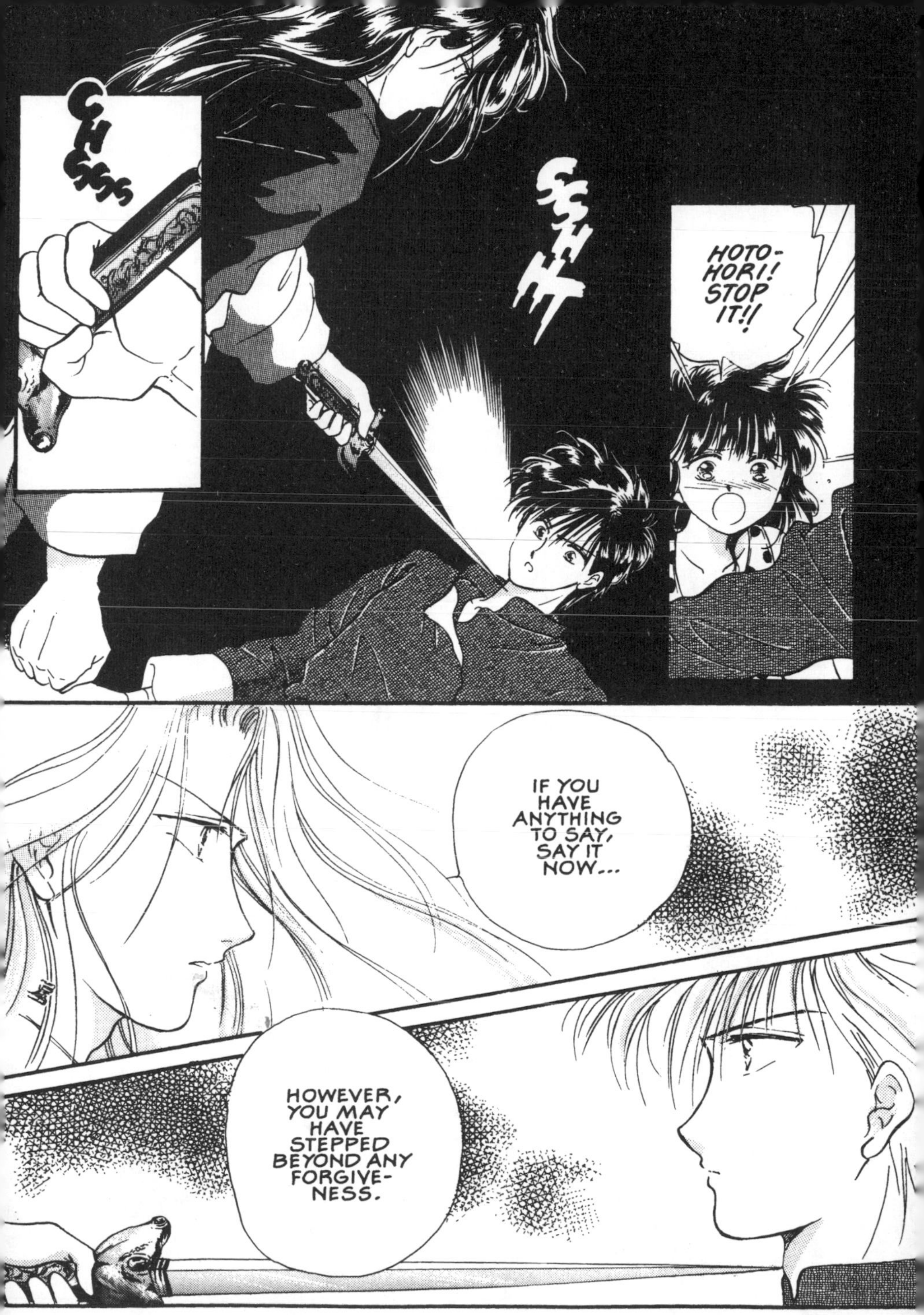
CHSSSS
SCHHH
HOTO-HORI! STOP IT!!
IF YOU HAVE ANYTHING TO SAY, SAY IT NOW...
HOWEVER, YOU MAY HAVE STEPPED BEYOND ANY FORGIVE-NESS.

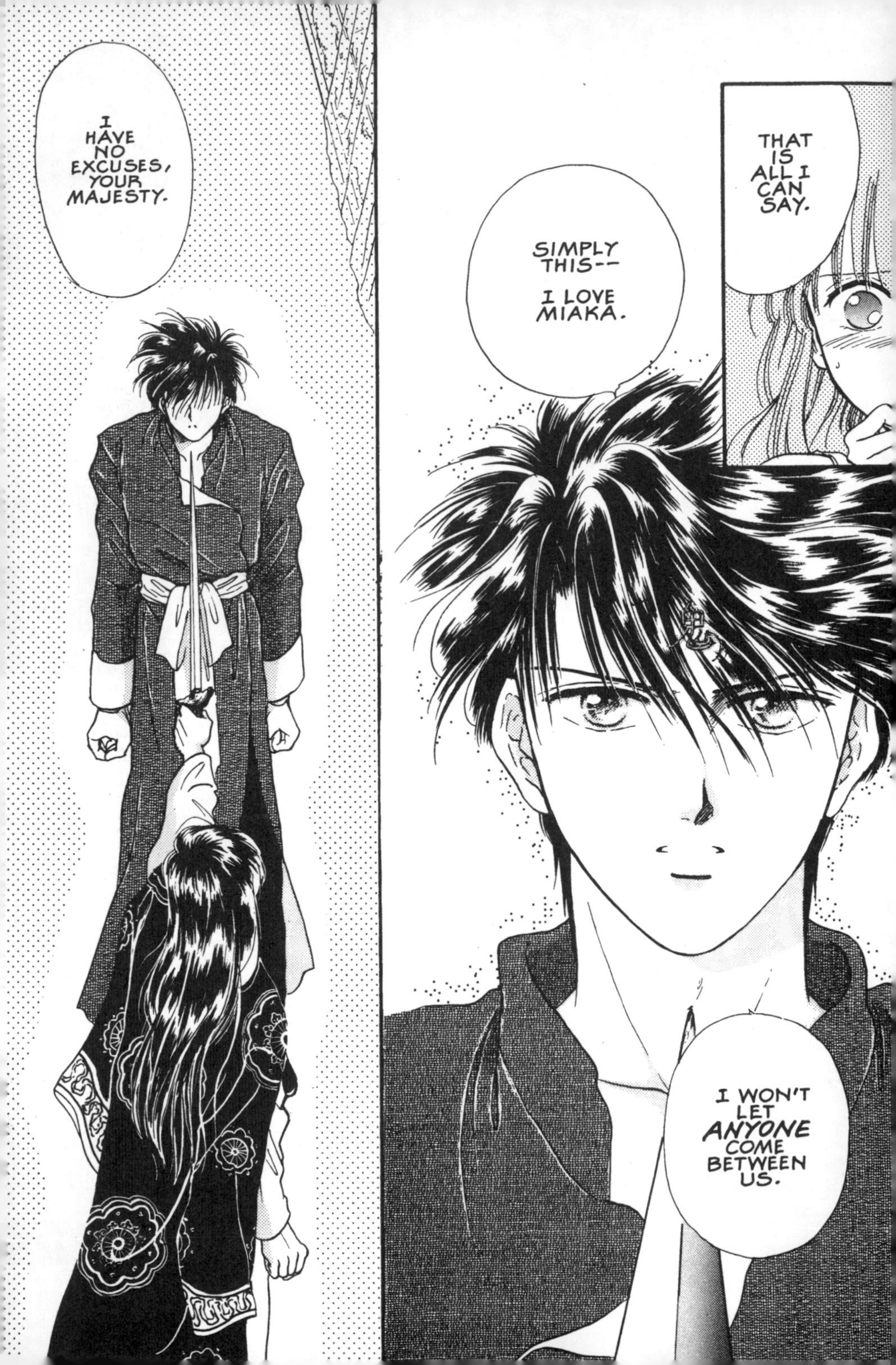
I HAVE NO EXCUSES, YOUR MAJESTY.
SIMPLY THIS-- I LOVE MIAKA.
THAT IS ALL I CAN SAY.
I WON'T LET ANYONE COME BETWEEN US.

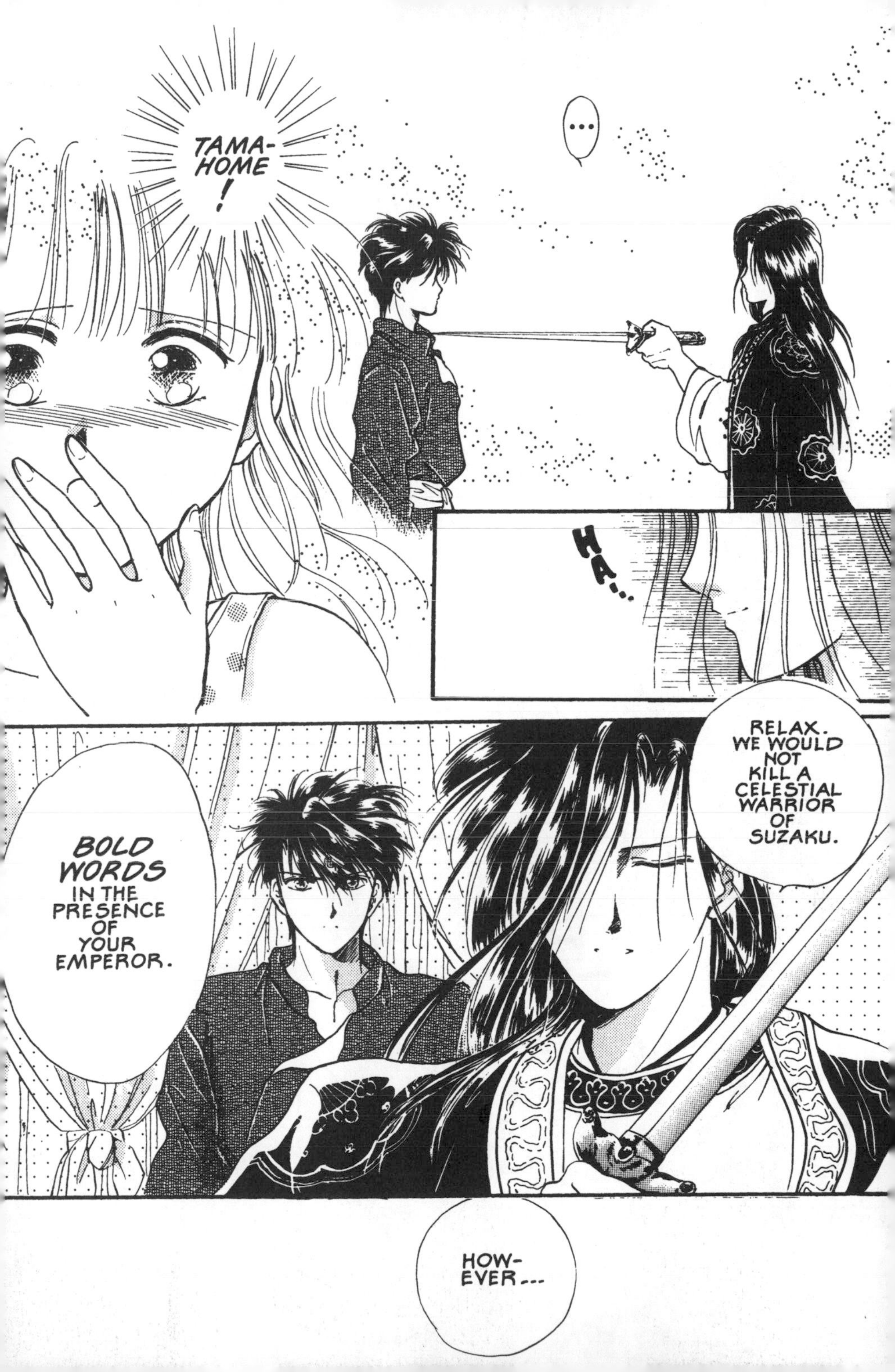
TAMA-HOME!
...
HA...
BOLD WORDS IN THE PRESENCE OF YOUR EMPEROR.
RELAX. WE WOULD NOT KILL A CELESTIAL WARRIOR OF SUZAKU.
HOW-EVER...

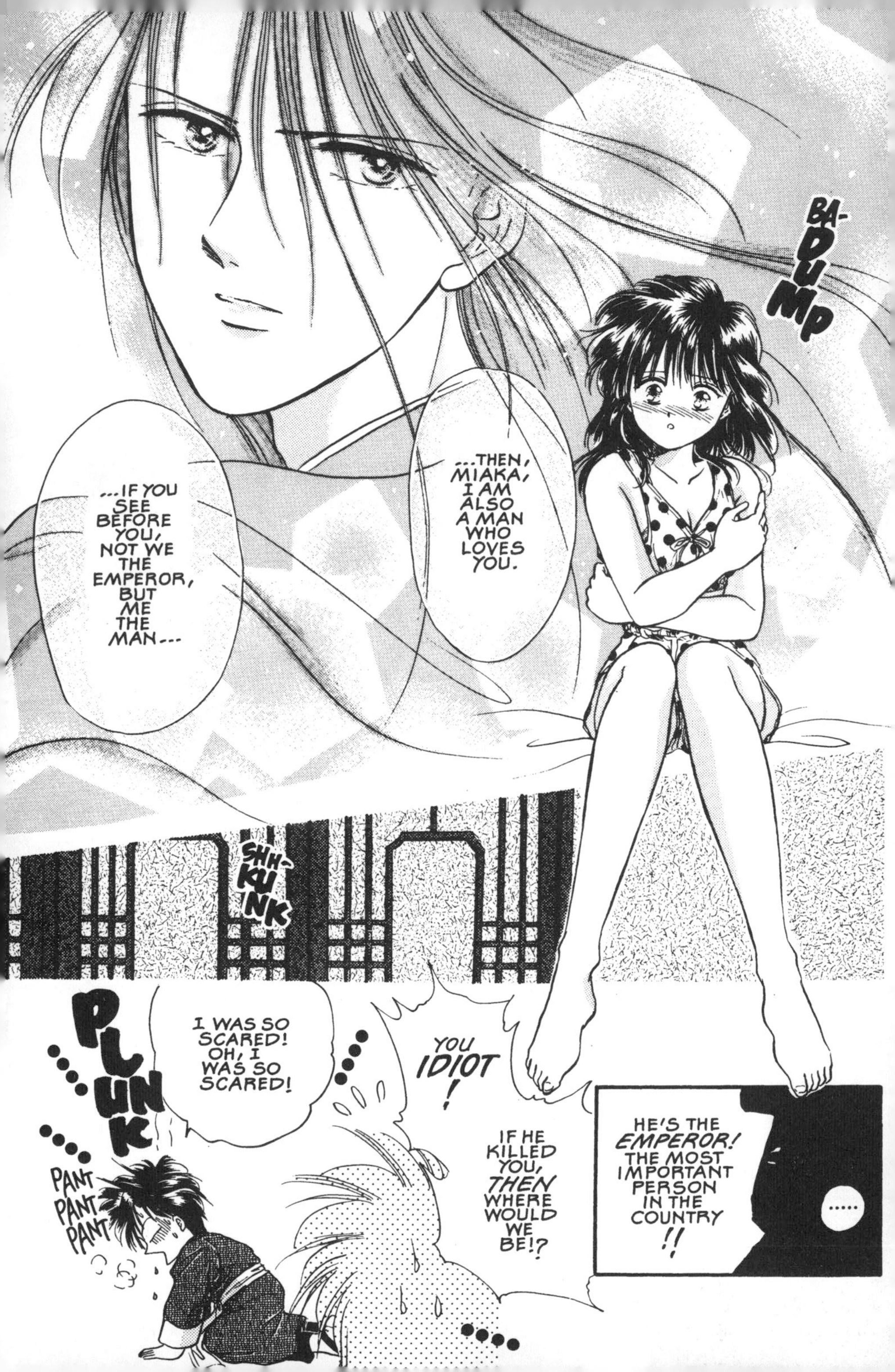

...IF YOU SEE BEFORE YOU, NOT WE THE EMPEROR, BUT ME THE MAN...
...THEN, MIAKA, I AM ALSO A MAN WHO LOVES YOU.
BA-DUMP
SHH-KUNK
PLUNK
....
PANT PANT PANT
I WAS SO SCARED! OH, I WAS SO SCARED!
....
YOU IDIOT!
IF HE KILLED YOU, THEN WHERE WOULD WE BE!?
HE'S THE EMPEROR! THE MOST IMPORTANT PERSON IN THE COUNTRY!!
......
....

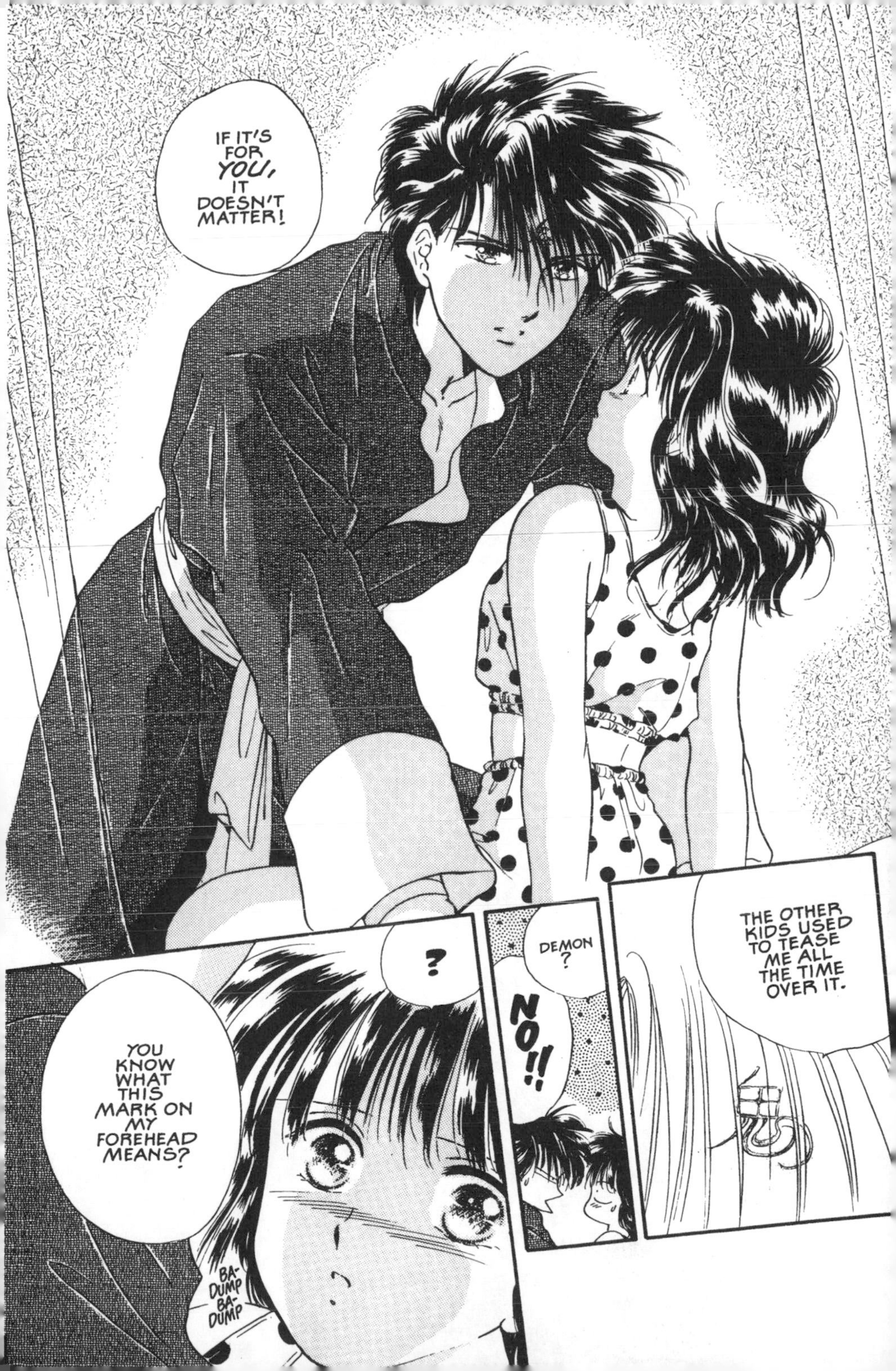

IF IT'S FOR YOU, IT DOESN'T MATTER!
?
YOU KNOW WHAT THIS MARK ON MY FOREHEAD MEANS?
BA-DUMP BA-DUMP
DEMON?
NO!!
THE OTHER KIDS USED TO TEASE ME ALL THE TIME OVER IT.

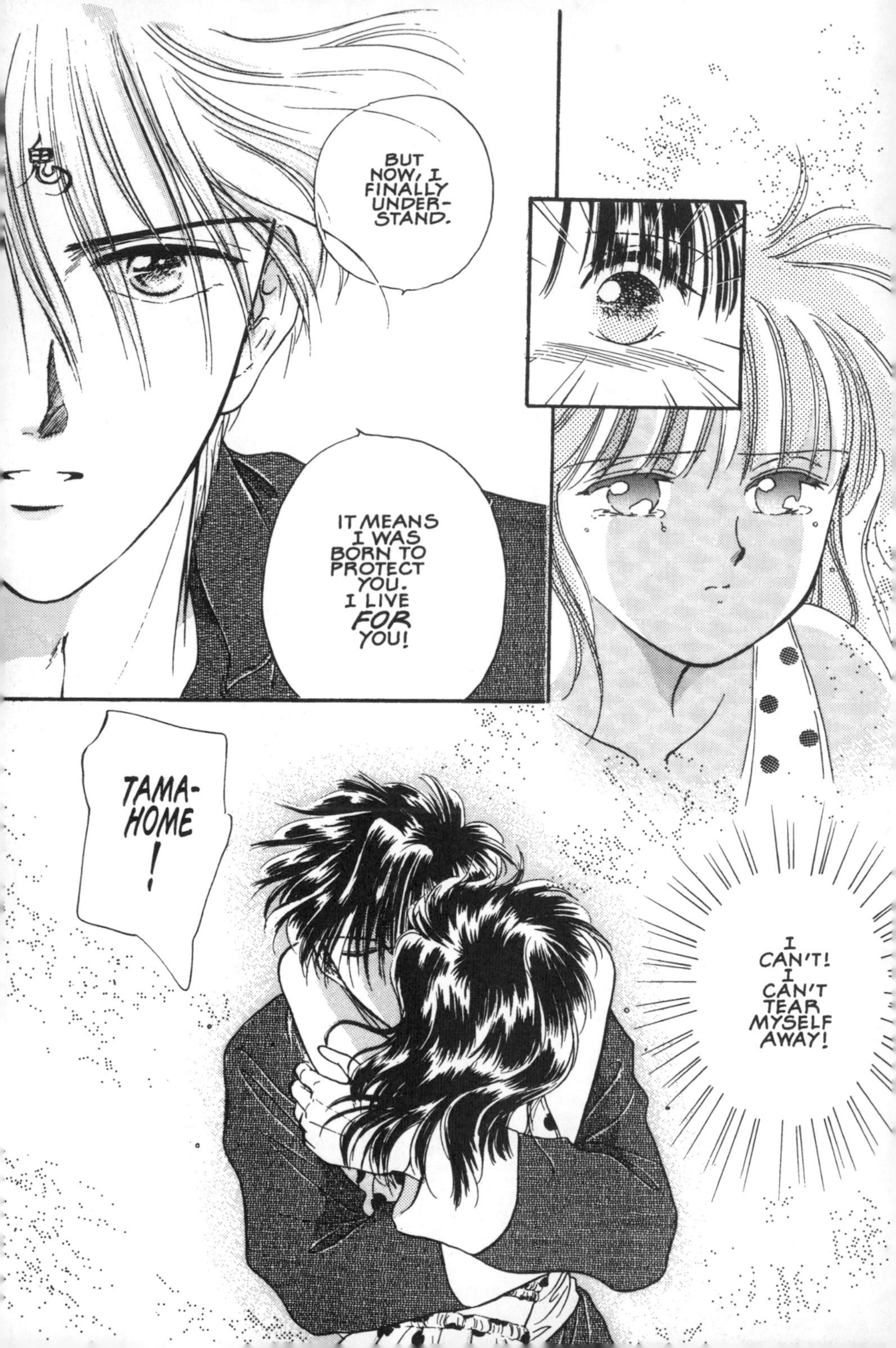

BUT NOW, I FINALLY UNDER-STAND.
IT MEANS I WAS BORN TO PROTECT YOU. I LIVE *FOR* YOU!
TAMA-HOME!
I CAN'T! I CAN'T TEAR MYSELF AWAY!

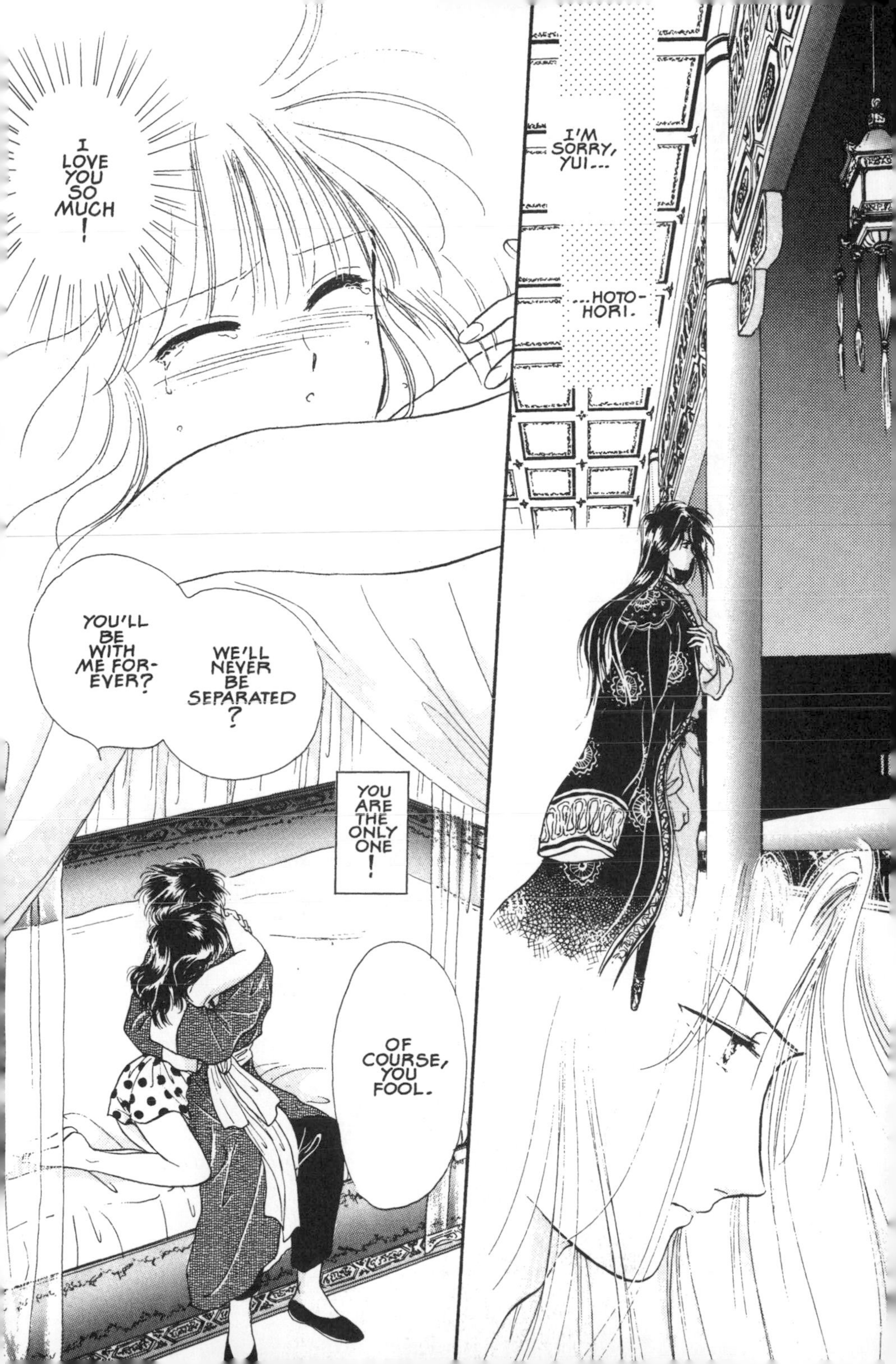

I LOVE YOU SO MUCH!
YOU'LL BE WITH ME FOREVER?
WE'LL NEVER BE SEPARATED?
YOU ARE THE ONLY ONE!
OF COURSE, YOU FOOL.
I'M SORRY, YUI...
...HOTOHORI.

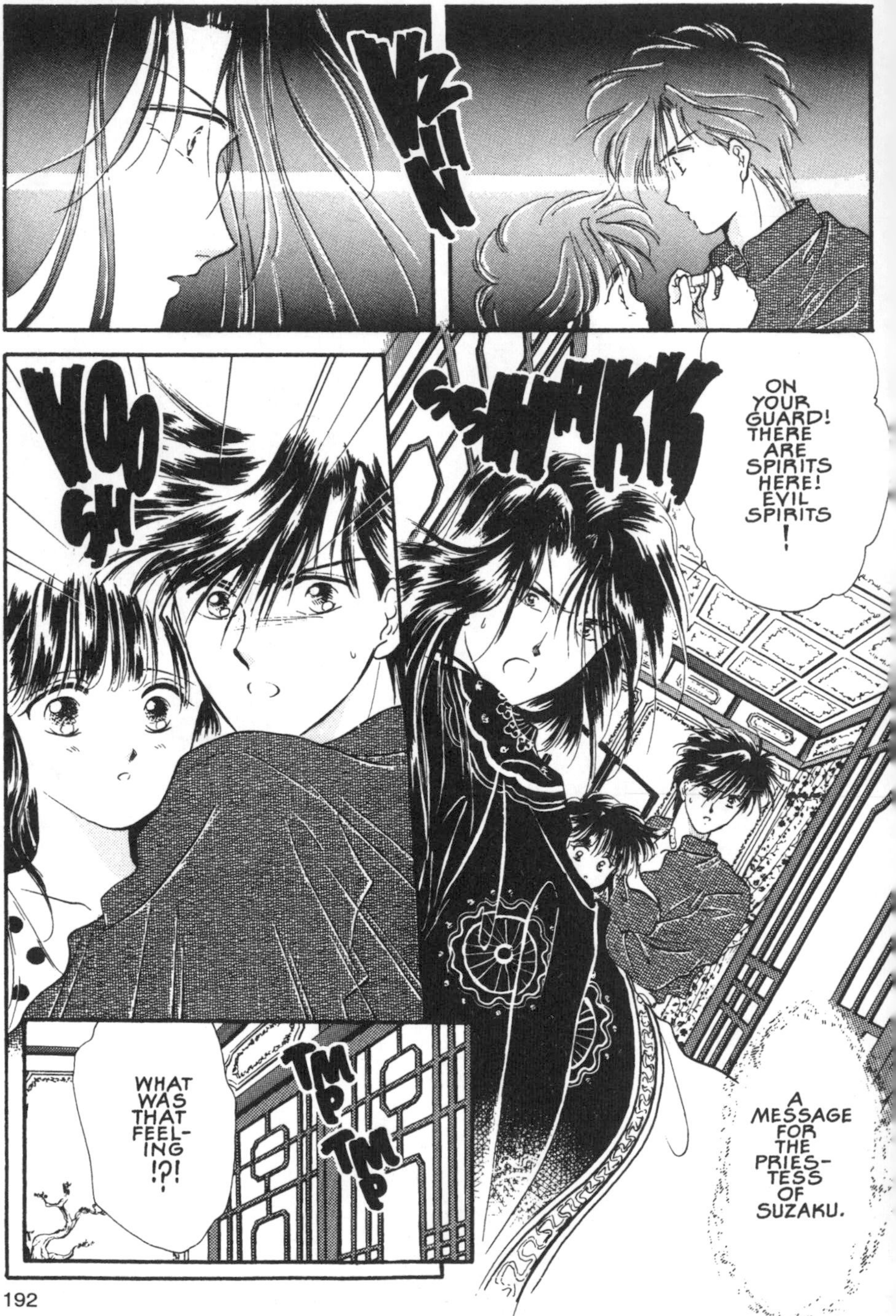
VZHIIN
VOOSH
SHAKK
ON YOUR GUARD! THERE ARE SPIRITS HERE! EVIL SPIRITS!
WHAT WAS THAT FEEL-ING !?!
TMP TMP TMP
A MESSAGE FOR THE PRIES-TESS OF SUZAKU.

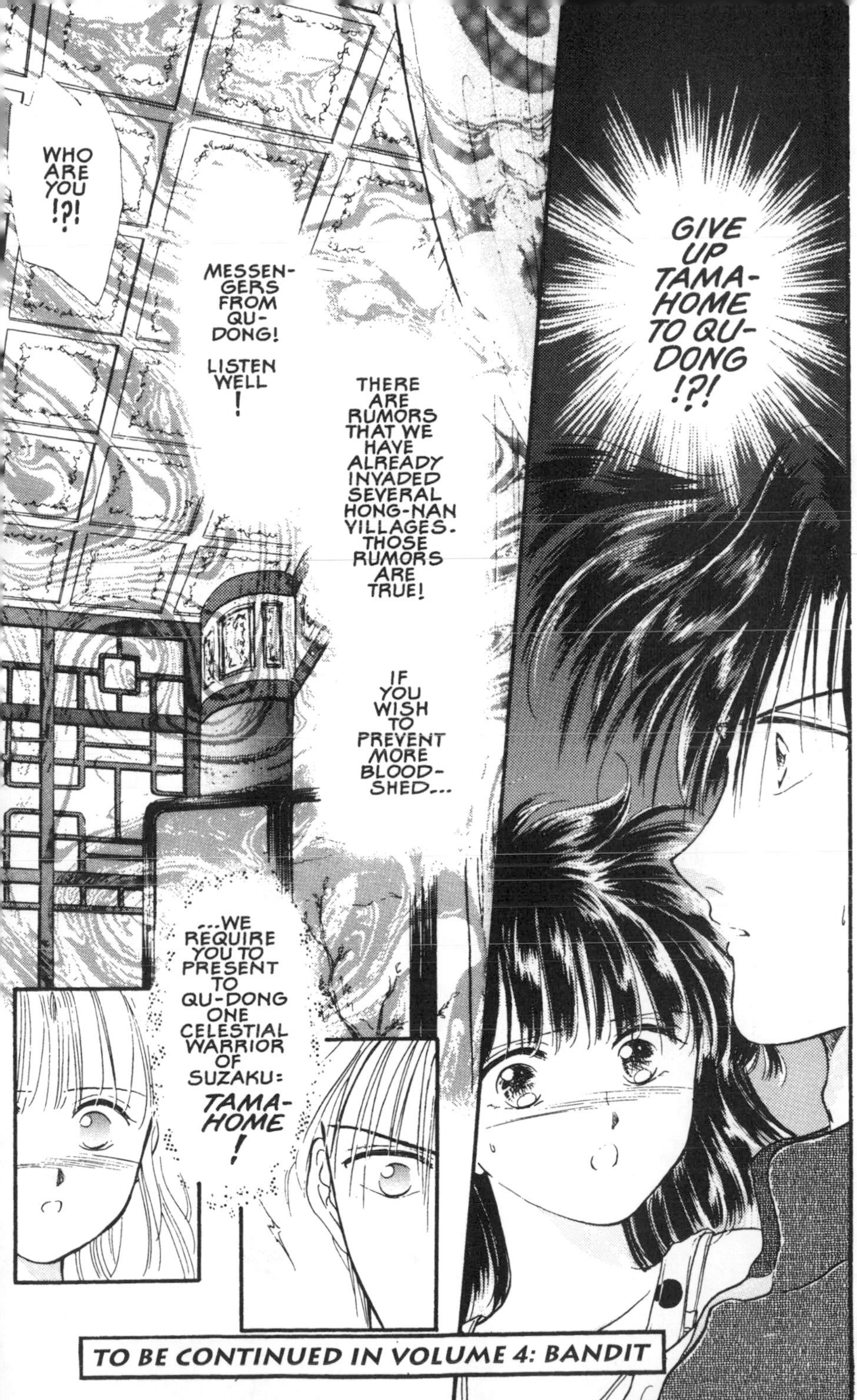
WHO ARE YOU !?!
MESSENGERS FROM QU-DONG!
LISTEN WELL !
THERE ARE RUMORS THAT WE HAVE ALREADY INVADED SEVERAL HONG-NAN VILLAGES. THOSE RUMORS ARE TRUE!
IF YOU WISH TO PREVENT MORE BLOODSHED...
...WE REQUIRE YOU TO PRESENT TO QU-DONG ONE CELESTIAL WARRIOR OF SUZAKU: TAMAHOME !
GIVE UP TAMAHOME TO QU-DONG !?!
TO BE CONTINUED IN VOLUME 4: BANDIT

YÛ WATASE

Yû Watase was born on March 5 in a town near Osaka and was raised there before moving to Tokyo to follow her dream of creating manga. In the decade since her debut short story, *PAJAMA DE OJAMA* ("An Intrusion in Pajamas"), she has produced more than 50 compiled volumes of short stories and continuing series. Her latest series, *AYASHI NO CERES* ("Ominous Ceres"), is currently running in the anthology magazine *SHÔJO COMIC*. She loves science fiction, fantasy and comedy.

A CELESTIAL LEGEND GIVEN FORM!

CERES
Celestial Legend

By Yû Watase

From the acclaimed author of "Fushigi Yûgi" Yû Watase, one of the most anticipated anime series of the year! The supernatural thriller begins on the day of Aya and her twin brother Aki's 16th birthday, when their grandfather decides it's time to share a long guarded secret. The twins are summoned to the massive, mysterious Mikage House where they find thier extended family assembled and waiting. They are given a curious gift and in that instant their destiny begins to unfold… Both the video and the monthly comic unveil the secret of Aya and Ceres, the Celestial Legend

AVAILABLE MONTHLY IN COMICS, VIDEOS, AND DVDS!

Become Part of The Revolution!

Revolutionary Girl UTENA

Volume 1: To Till

Chiho Saito has drawn *shôjo* (girls') comics for two decades, but when she teamed up with anime director Kunihiko Ikuhara (Sailor Moon) and a group of talented creators for Ikuhara's new project, it ignited a firestorm of creative and imaginative storytelling from which anime and manga has yet to recover. Now see the story that started the ball rolling!

One day, a little girl learns that her parents have died. The grade-school-age girl wanders the rain-soaked streets of her hometown with no distinct purpose. Drenched in rainwater and tears, she finds herself by a river and throws herself in. Suddenly a man appears—her prince—and he rescues her, banishes her tears, and tells her to grow up strong and noble. From then on she strives to grow up to be a prince just like him!

ANIMERICA EXTRA GRAPHIC NOVEL

Revolutionary Girl
UTENA
VOL. 1: To Till

MANGA BY
Chiho Saito

STORY BY
Be-Papas

Revolutionary Girl Utena Volume 1: To Till
By Chiho Saito & Be-Papas
Graphic Novel
B&W, 200 pages
$15.95 USA $25.95 CAN

Viz Comics
P.O. Box 77010
San Francisco, CA 94107

Phone: (800) 394-3042
Fax: (415) 348-8936

www.viz.com
www.j-pop.com
www.animerica-mag.com

VIZ COMICS

AGAINST A MACHINE THAT EATS PLANETS, DOES THE THREE-NINE STAND A CHANCE?

VIZ GRAPHIC NOVEL

galaxy express 999

vol. 5

232 pages
$18.95 U.S.
$30.95 Canada

松本零士

STORY and ART by
L.MATSUMOTO

Ranma ½

The next hilarious season of the classic martial arts/romantic comedy series in DVD format *Ranma 1/2: Anything-Goes Martial Arts Box Set DVD.*

RUMIKO TAKAHASHI's

Ranma ½

All 22 episodes of the second TV series!!

RECOMMENDED
AGES
13
AND
UP

ANYTHING-GOES MARTIAL ARTS
TV ANIME SEASON 2 DVD BOX SET

Pioneer

DVD VIDEO

SRP: $119.98

This 5 DVD set features 572 minutes of artist and author Rumiko Takahashi's most enduring work. Established favorite characters such as The Saotome family, the Tendo family, the eternally lost Ryoga and the comical Kuno return, while new characters are introduced including the devious matron Cologne, lovelorn Mousse, panty-stealing martial arts master Happosai, and many more!

This color DVD set also features English subtitles, Japanese and English audio tracks and stereo sound.

VIZ VIDEO